"[A] SPLENDID NEW NOVEL ...
SUPERB STORYTELLING."
—*The New York Times Book Review*

"Compelling ... Readers who loved Amy Tan's best-selling novels about the complex ties between mothers and daughters, *The Joy Luck Club* and *The Kitchen God's Wife*, will also be captivated by *The Bonesetter's Daughter*."
—*The Orlando Sentinel*

"A woman's struggle to find her voice has long been a favorite theme of Amy Tan. Nowhere has she explored it with more compassion or charm than in this touching new novel."
—*The Richmond Times-Dispatch*

"An enchanting story of a mother and daughter, the secrets they have kept from one another, and the common ground they finally come to occupy. ... A powerful, luminously written saga in which past and present are bound together into the tangled skein of a human life."
—*The Anniston Star*

"Poignant and bittersweet ... A story of secrets and revelation, estrangement and reconciliation."
—*Rocky Mountain News*

"A riveting, multi-layered tale ... Tan's storytelling skills are strong, and her plot line appeals to the rebellious daughter in all of us."
—*Toronto Globe and Mail*

Please turn the page
for more reviews. ...

"A BOOK TO READ, TO CHERISH, TO REMEMBER."
—*The Providence Sunday Journal*

"AMY TAN STRIKES GOLD ONCE AGAIN.

In her first novel in six years, Tan returns to the theme of mothers and daughters simultaneously estranged and bonded, a subject she treated so memorably in *The Joy Luck Club* and *The Kitchen God's Wife*. A beautifully modulated amalgam of grief, pride, resentment, and resignation."

—*Kirkus Reviews* (starred review)

"Any Tan enthusiasts will rejoice in her latest novel, *The Bonesetter's Daughter*. . . . Newcomers to Tan's work will be taken for the first time into the complex and often heartbreaking world of the Chinese–American family. . . . Through often beautiful prose and a born storyteller's talent for narration, Tan passes many a wise observation on to her readers."

—*Vogue*

"A suspenseful family saga set in contemporary San Francisco and in a quaint Chinese village a few decades earlier . . . In agile, lyrical prose, Tan effortlessly combines the mundane and the mythical to create another dynamic multigenerational odyssey."

—*US Weekly*

"Luminous and gripping . . . The novel exhibits a poignant clarity as it investigates the dilemma of adult children who must become caretakers of their elderly parents, a situation Tan articulates with integrity and exemplary empathy for both generations."

—*Publishers Weekly* (starred review)

THE
BONESETTER'S
DAUGHTER

AMY TAN

BALLANTINE BOOKS • NEW YORK

A Ballantine Book
Published by The Ballantine Publishing Group
Copyright © 2001 by Amy Tan
Reader's Guide copyright © 2003 by Amy Tan and The Ballantine Publishing Group, a division of Random House, Inc.

All rights reserved under International and Pan-American Copyright Conventions. Published in the United States by The Ballantine Publishing Group, a division of Random House, Inc., New York, and simultaneously in Canada by Random House of Canada Limited, Toronto.

Ballantine and colophon are registered trademarks of Random House, Inc. Ballantine Reader's Circle and colophon are trademarks of Random House, Inc.

www.ballantinebooks.com/BRC/

Library of Congress Control Number: 2002095642

ISBN 0-345-45737-4

This edition published by arrangement with G. P. Putnam's Sons, a division of the Putnam Berkeley Publishing Group, Inc.

Cover photograph of Gu Jingmei © Amy Tan

Manufactured in the United States of America

First Ballantine Books International Edition: August 2001
First Ballantine Books Domestic Edition: February 2002
First Ballantine Books Trade Edition: February 2003

10 9 8 7 6 5 4 3 2

I give endless thanks to my dear friend and editor, the late, great Faith Sale. To my astonishment, she could always sense the difference between what I was trying to write and what I wanted to write. She promised she would see me through this book, and though she died before I finished, I believe she kept her promise.

My writing teacher and longtime mentor, Molly Giles, took over as editor and resurrected this book during those days when I was scared to turn the pages. Thank you, Molly, for your keen eye and ear, as well as for suggestions that were always true to my intentions. I also much appreciated the heavy doses of optimism during times we can now acknowledge as dire.

I am blessed to have had the help, kindness, and protection of Lou and Greg, the guidance of Sandra Dijkstra, Anna Jardine, and Aimee Taub, and the spiritual sustenance of the late-night posters on AOL's Caregivers' Support for the Elderly.

As luck and fate would have it, two ghostwriters came to my assistance during the last draft. The heart of this story belongs to my grandmother, its voice to my mother. I give them credit for anything good, and have already promised them I will try harder the next time.

On the last day that my mother spent on earth,
I learned her real name, as well as that of my grandmother.
This book is dedicated to them.

THE

BONESETTER'S
DAUGHTER

TRUTH

These are the things I know are true:

My name is LuLing Liu Young. The names of my husbands were Pan Kai Jing and Edwin Young, both of them dead and our secrets gone with them. My daughter is Ruth Luyi Young. She was born in a Water Dragon Year and I in a Fire Dragon Year. So we are the same but for opposite reasons.

I know all this, yet there is one name I cannot remember. It is there in the oldest layer of my memory, and I cannot dig it out. A hundred times I have gone over that morning when Precious Auntie wrote it down. I was only six then, but very smart. I could count. I could read. I had a memory for everything, and here is my memory of that winter morning.

I was sleepy, still lying on the brick *k'ang* bed I shared with Precious Auntie. The flue to our little room was furthest from the stove in the common room, and the bricks beneath me had long turned cold. I felt my shoulder being shaken. When I opened my eyes, Precious Auntie began to write on a scrap of paper, then showed me what she had written. "I can't see," I complained. "It's too dark."

She huffed, set the paper on the low cupboard, and motioned that I should get up. She lighted the teapot brazier, and tied a scarf over her nose and mouth when it started to smoke. She poured face-washing

water into the teapot's chamber, and when it was cooked, she started
our day. She scrubbed my face and ears. She parted my hair and
combed my bangs. She wet down any strands that stuck out like
spider legs. Then she gathered the long part of my hair into two
bundles and braided them. She banded the top with red ribbon, the
bottom with green. I wagged my head so that my braids swung like
the happy ears of palace dogs. And Precious Auntie sniffed the air
as if she, too, were a dog wondering, What's that good smell? That
sniff was how she said my nickname, Doggie. That was how she
talked.

She had no voice, just gasps and wheezes, the snorts of a ragged
wind. She told me things with grimaces and groans, dancing eyebrows and darting eyes. She wrote about the world on my carry-
around chalkboard. She also made pictures with her blackened
hands. Hand-talk, face-talk, and chalk-talk were the languages I
grew up with, soundless and strong.

As she wound her hair tight against her skull, I played with her
box of treasures. I took out a pretty comb, ivory with a rooster
carved at each end. Precious Auntie was born a Rooster. "You wear
this," I demanded, holding it up. "Pretty." I was still young enough
to believe that beauty came from things, and I wanted Mother to favor her more. But Precious Auntie shook her head. She pulled off
her scarf and pointed to her face and bunched her brows. *What use
do I have for prettiness?* she was saying.

Her bangs fell to her eyebrows like mine. The rest of her hair was
bound into a knot and stabbed together with a silver prong. She had
a sweet-peach forehead, wide-set eyes, full cheeks tapering to a small
plump nose. That was the top of her face. Then there was the
bottom.

She wiggled her blackened fingertips like hungry flames. *See what
the fire did.*

I didn't think she was ugly, not in the way others in our family did. "Ai-ya, seeing her, even a demon would leap out of his skin," I once heard Mother remark. When I was small, I liked to trace my fingers around Precious Auntie's mouth. It was a puzzle. Half was bumpy, half was smooth and melted closed. The inside of her right cheek was stiff as leather, the left was moist and soft. Where the gums had burned, the teeth had fallen out. And her tongue was like a parched root. She could not taste the pleasures of life: salty and bitter, sour and sharp, spicy, sweet, and fat.

No one else understood Precious Auntie's kind of talk, so I had to say aloud what she meant. Not everything, though, not our secret stories. She often told me about her father, the Famous Bonesetter from the Mouth of the Mountain, about the cave where they found the dragon bones, how the bones were divine and could cure any pain, except a grieving heart. "Tell me again," I said that morning, wishing for a story about how she burned her face and became my nursemaid.

I was a fire-eater, she said with her hands and eyes. *Hundreds of people came to see me in the market square. Into the burning pot of my mouth I dropped raw pork, added chilis and bean paste, stirred this up, then offered the morsels to people to taste. If they said, "Delicious!" I opened my mouth as a purse to catch their copper coins. One day, however, I ate the fire, and the fire came back, and it ate me. After that, I decided not to be a cook-pot anymore, so I became your nursemaid instead.*

I laughed and clapped my hands, liking this made-up story best. The day before, she told me she had stared at an unlucky star falling out of the sky and then it dropped into her open mouth and burned her face. The day before that, she said she had eaten what she thought was a spicy Hunan dish only to find that it was the coals used for cooking.

No more stories, Precious Auntie now told me, her hands talking fast. *It's almost time for breakfast, and we must pray while we're still hungry.* She retrieved the scrap of paper from the cupboard, folded it in half, and tucked it into the lining of her shoe. We put on our padded winter clothes and walked into the cold corridor. The air smelled of coal fires in other wings of the compound. I saw Old Cook pumping his arm to turn the crank over the well. I heard a tenant yelling at her lazy daughter-in-law. I passed the room that my sister, GaoLing, shared with Mother, the two of them still asleep. We hurried to the south-facing small room, to our ancestral hall. At the threshold, Precious Auntie gave me a warning look. *Act humble. Take off your shoes.* In my stockings, I stepped onto cold gray tiles. Instantly, my feet were stabbed with an iciness that ran up my legs, through my body, and dripped out my nose. I began to shake.

The wall facing me was lined with overlapping scrolls of couplets, gifts to our family from scholars who had used our ink over the last two hundred years. I had learned to read one, a poem-painting: "Fish shadows dart downstream," meaning our ink was dark, beautiful, and smooth-flowing. On the long altar table were two statues, the God of Longevity with his white-waterfall beard, and the Goddess of Mercy, her face smooth, free of worry. Her black eyes looked into mine. Only she listened to the woes and wishes of women, Precious Auntie said. Perched around the statues were spirit tablets of the Liu ancestors, their wooden faces carved with their names. Not all my ancestors were there, Precious Auntie told me, just the ones my family considered most important. The in-between ones and those belonging to women were stuck in trunks or forgotten.

Precious Auntie lighted several joss sticks. She blew on them until they began to smolder. Soon more smoke rose—a jumble of our breath, our offerings, and hazy clouds that I thought were ghosts who would try to yank me down to wander with them in the World of Yin. Precious Auntie once told me that a body grows cold when it is dead. And since I was chilled to the bone that morning, I was afraid.

"I'm cold," I whimpered, and tears leaked out.

Precious Auntie sat on a stool and drew me to her lap. *Stop that, Doggie,* she gently scolded, *or the tears will freeze into icicles and poke out your eyes.* She kneaded my feet fast, as if they were dumpling dough. *Better? How about now, better?*

After I stopped crying, Precious Auntie lighted more joss sticks. She went back to the threshold and picked up one of her shoes. I can still see it—the dusty blue cloth, the black piping, the tiny embroidery of an extra leaf where she had repaired the hole. I thought she was going to burn her shoe as a send-away gift to the dead. Instead, from the shoe's lining, she took out the scrap of paper with the writing she had showed me earlier. She nodded toward me and said with her hands: *My family name, the name of all the bonesetters.* She put the paper name in front of my face again and said, *Never forget this name,* then placed it carefully on the altar. We bowed and rose, bowed and rose. Each time my head bobbed up, I looked at that name. And the name was—

Why can't I see it now? I've pushed a hundred family names through my mouth, and none comes back with the belch of memory. Was the name uncommon? Did I lose it because I kept it a secret too long? Maybe I lost it the same way I lost all my favorite things—the jacket GaoLing gave me when I left for the orphan school, the dress my second husband said made me look like a movie star, the first baby dress that Luyi outgrew. Each time I loved something with a special ache, I put it in my trunk of best things. I hid those things for so long I almost forgot I had them.

This morning I remembered the trunk. I went to put away the birthday present that Luyi gave me. Gray pearls from Hawaii, beautiful beyond belief. When I opened the lid, out rose a cloud of moths, a stream of silverfish. Inside I found a web of knitted holes, one after the other. The embroidered flowers, the bright colors, now gone. Almost all that mattered in my life has disappeared, and the worst is losing Precious Auntie's name.

Precious Auntie, what is our name? I always meant to claim it as my own. Come help me remember. I'm not a little girl anymore. I'm not afraid of ghosts. Are you still mad at me? Don't you recognize me? I am LuLing, your daughter.

PART ONE

ONE

For the past eight years, always starting on August twelfth, Ruth Young lost her voice.

The first time it happened was when she moved into Art's flat in San Francisco. For several days, Ruth could only hiss like an untended teakettle. She figured it was a virus, or perhaps allergies to a particular mold in the building.

When she lost her voice again, it was on their first anniversary of living together, and Art joked that her laryngitis must be psychosomatic. Ruth wondered whether it was. When she was a child, she lost her voice after breaking her arm. Why was that? On their second anniversary, she and Art were stargazing in the Grand Tetons. According to a park pamphlet, "During the peak of the Perseids, around August 12th, hundreds of 'shooting' or 'falling' stars streak the sky every hour. They are actually fragments of meteors penetrating the earth's atmosphere, burning up in their descent." Against the velvet blackness, Ruth silently admired the light show with Art. She did not actually believe that her laryngitis was star-crossed, or that the meteor shower had anything to do with her inability to speak. Her mother, though, had often told Ruth throughout her childhood that shooting stars were really "melting ghost bodies" and it was bad luck to see them. If you did, that meant a ghost was trying to talk to you.

To her mother, just about anything was a sign of ghosts: broken bowls, barking dogs, phone calls with only silence or heavy breathing at the other end.

The following August, rather than just wait for muteness to strike, Ruth explained to her clients and friends that she was taking a planned weeklong retreat into verbal silence. "It's a yearly ritual," she said, "to sharpen my consciousness about words and their necessity." One of her book clients, a New Age psychotherapist, saw voluntary silence as a "wonderful process," and decided he would engage in the same so they could include their findings in a chapter on either dysfunctional family dynamics or stillness as therapy.

From then on, Ruth's malady was elevated to an annual sanctioned event. She stopped talking two days before her voice faded of its own accord. She politely declined Art's offer that they both try speaking in sign language. She made her voiceless state a decision, a matter of will, and not a disease or a mystery. In fact, she came to enjoy her respite from talk; for a whole week she did not need to console clients, remind Art about social schedules, warn his daughters to be careful, or feel guilty for not calling her mother.

This was the ninth year. Ruth, Art, and the girls had driven the two hundred miles to Lake Tahoe for the Days of No Talk, as they called them. Ruth had envisioned the four of them holding hands and walking down to the Truckee River to watch the nightly meteor showers in quiet awe. But the mosquitoes were working overtime, and Dory whimpered that she saw a bat, to which Fia teased, "Who cares about rabies when the forest is full of ax murderers?" After they fled back to the cabin, the girls said they were bored. "There's no cable television?" they complained. So Art drove them to Tahoe City and rented videos, mainly horror flicks. He and the girls slept through most of them, and though Ruth hated the movies, she could not stop watching. She dreamed of deranged baby-sitters and oozing aliens.

On Sunday, when they returned home to San Francisco, cranky and sweaty, they discovered they had no hot water. The tank had leaked, and the heating element apparently had fried to death. They were forced to make do with kettle-warmed baths; Art didn't want to be gouged by emergency plumbing rates. Without a voice, Ruth couldn't argue, and she was glad. To argue would mean she was offering to foot the bill, something she had done so often over their years of living together that it had become expected of her. But because she did not offer, she felt petty, then irked that Art said nothing further about the matter. At bedtime he nuzzled her neck and bumped gently into her backside. When she tensed, he said, "Suit yourself," and rolled over, and this left her feeling rebuffed. She wanted to explain what was wrong—but she realized she did not know. There was nothing specific beyond her bad mood. Soon Art's sonorous breathing rumbled out of sync with her frustration, and she lay wide-eyed in the dark.

It was now nearly midnight, and in another few hours, Ruth would be able to talk. She stood in the Cubbyhole, a former pantry that served as her home office. She stepped onto a footstool and pushed open a tiny window. There it was, a sliver of a million-dollar view: the red towers of the Golden Gate Bridge that bifurcated the waters, marking bay from ocean. The air was moist and antiseptically cold against her face. She scanned the sky, but it was too light and misty to see any "ghost bodies" burning up. Foghorns started to blare. And after another minute, Ruth saw the billows, like an ethereal down comforter covering the ocean and edging toward the bridge. Her mother used to tell her that the fog was really the steam from fighting dragons, one water, the other fire. "Water and fire, come together make steam," LuLing would say in the strangely British-accented English she had acquired in Hong Kong. "You know this. Just like teapot. You touch, burn you finger off."

The fog was sweeping over the ramparts of the bridge, devouring the headlamps of cars. Nine out of ten drivers were drunk at this hour—Ruth had read that somewhere. Or maybe she had written that for a client. She stepped down, but left the window open.

The foghorns continued to wail. They sounded like tubas in a Shostakovich opera, comedically tragic. But was tragedy ever funny? Or was it only the audience who laughed knowingly as the victims walked into trapdoors and trick mirrors?

Still wide awake, Ruth turned to her desk. Just then she felt a tug of worry, something she was not supposed to forget. Did it have to do with money, a client, or a promise she had made to the girls? She set to straightening her desk, aligning her research books, sorting faxes and drafts, color-coding them according to client and book. Tomorrow she had to return to routine and deadlines, and a clean desk gave her the sense of a fresh start, an uncluttered mind. Everything had its place. If an item was of questionable priority or value, she dumped it in the bottom right-hand drawer of her desk. But now the drawer was full with unanswered letters, abandoned drafts, sheets of jotted-down ideas that might be usable in the future. She pulled out a clipped stack of paper from the bottom of the drawer, guessing she could toss out whatever had lain there the longest by neglect.

They were pages written in Chinese, her mother's writing. LuLing had given them to her five or six years before. "Just some old things about my family," she had said, with the kind of awkward nonchalance that meant the pages were important. "My story, begin little-girl time. I write for myself, but maybe you read, then you see how I grow up, come to this country." Ruth had heard bits of her mother's life over the years, but she was touched by her shyness in asking Ruth to read what she had obviously labored over. The pages contained precise vertical rows, without crossouts, leaving Ruth to surmise that her mother had copied over her earlier attempts.

Ruth had tried to decipher the pages. Her mother had once drilled Chinese calligraphy into her reluctant brain, and she still recognized some of the characters: "thing," "I," "truth." But unraveling the rest required her to match LuLing's squiggly radicals to uniform ones in a Chinese-English dictionary. "These are the things I know are true," the first sentence read. That had taken Ruth an hour to translate. She set a goal to decipher a sentence a day. And in keeping with her plan, she translated another sentence the next evening: "My name is LuLing Liu Young." That was easy, a mere five minutes. Then came the names of LuLing's husbands, one of whom was Ruth's father. Husbands? Ruth was startled to read that there had been another. And what did her mother mean by "our secrets gone with them"? Ruth wanted to know right away, but she could not ask her mother. She knew from experience what happened whenever she asked her mother to render Chinese characters into English. First LuLing scolded her for not studying Chinese hard enough when she was little. And then, to untangle each character, her mother took side routes to her past, going into excruciating detail over the infinite meanings of Chinese words: "Secret not just mean cannot say. Can be hurt-you kinda secret, or curse-you kind, maybe do you damage forever, never can change after that. . . ." And then came rambling about who told the secret, without saying what the secret itself was, followed by more rambling about how the person had died horribly, why this had happened, how it could have been avoided, if only such and such had not occurred a thousand years before. If Ruth showed impatience in listening to any of this, LuLing became outraged, before sputtering an oath that none of this mattered because soon she too would die anyway, by accident, because of bad-luck wishes, or on purpose. And then the silent treatment began, a punishment that lasted for days or weeks, until Ruth broke down first and said she was sorry.

So Ruth did not ask her mother. She decided instead to set aside several days when she could concentrate on the translation. She told her mother this, and LuLing warned, "Don't wait too long." After that, whenever her mother asked whether she had finished her story, Ruth answered, "I was just about to, but something came up with a client." Other crises also intervened, having to do with Art, the girls, or the house, as did vacation.

"Too busy for mother," LuLing complained. "Never too busy go see movie, go away, go see friend."

The past year, her mother had stopped asking, and Ruth wondered, Did she give up? Couldn't be. She must have forgotten. By then the pages had settled to the bottom of the desk drawer.

Now that they had resurfaced, Ruth felt pangs of guilt. Perhaps she should hire someone fluent in Chinese. Art might know of someone— a linguistics student, a retired professor old enough to be versed in the traditional characters and not just the simplified ones. As soon as she had time, she would ask. She placed the pages at the top of the heap, then closed the drawer, feeling less guilty already.

When she woke in the morning, Art was up, doing his yoga stretches in the next room. "Hello," she said to herself. "Is anyone there?" Her voice was back, though squeaky from disuse.

As she brushed her teeth in the bathroom, she could hear Dory screeching: "I want to watch that. Put it back! It's my TV too." Fia hooted: "That show's for babies, and that's what you are, wnnh-wnnh-wnnh."

Since Art's divorce, the girls had been dividing their time between their mom and stepdad's home in Sausalito and Art's Edwardian flat on Vallejo Street. Every other week, the four of them—Art, Ruth, Sofia, and Dory—found themselves crammed into five miniature rooms, one of them barely big enough to squeeze in a bunk bed.

There was only one bathroom, which Ruth hated for its antiquated inconvenience. The claw-footed iron tub was as soothing as a sarcophagus, and the pedestal sink with its separate spigots dispensed water that was either scalding hot or icy cold. As Ruth reached for the dental floss, she knocked over other items on the windowsill: potions for wrinkles, remedies for pimples, nose-hair clippers, and a plastic mug jammed with nine toothbrushes whose ownership and vintage were always in question. While she was picking up the mess, desperate pounding rattled the door.

"You'll have to wait," she called in a husky voice. The pounding continued. She looked at the bathroom schedule for August, which was posted on both sides of the door. There it said, clear as could be, whose turn it was at each quarter-hour. She had assigned herself to be last, and because everyone else ran late, she suffered the cumulative consequences. Below the schedule, the girls had added rules and amendments, and a list of violations and fines for infractions concerning the use of the sink, toilet, and shower, as well as a proclamation on what constituted the right to privacy versus a TRUE EMERGENCY (underlined three times).

The pounding came again. "Ru-uuth! I said it's the phone!" Dory opened the door a crack and shoved in a cordless handset. Who was calling at seven-twenty in the morning? Her mother, no doubt. LuLing seemed to have a crisis whenever Ruth had not called in several days.

"Ruthie, is your voice back? Can you talk?" It was Wendy, her best friend. They spoke nearly every day. She heard Wendy blow her nose. Was she actually crying?

"What happened?" Ruth whispered. Don't tell me, don't tell me, she mouthed in rhythm to her racing heart. Wendy was about to tell her she had cancer, Ruth was sure of it. Last night's uneasy feeling started to trickle through her veins.

"I'm still in shock," Wendy went on. "I'm about to . . . Hold on. I just got another call."

It must not be cancer, Ruth thought. Maybe she was mugged, or thieves had broken into the house, and now the police were calling to take a report. Whatever it was, it must have been serious, otherwise Wendy would not be crying. What should she say to her? Ruth crooked the phone in her neck and dragged her fingers through her close-cropped hair. She noticed that some of the mirror's silver had flaked off. Or were those white roots in her hair? She would soon turn forty-six. When had the baby fat in her face started to recede? To think she used to resent having the face and skin of a perpetual teenager. Now she had creases pulling down the corners of her mouth. They made her look displeased, like her mother. Ruth brightened her mouth with lipstick. Of course, she wasn't like her mother in other respects, thank God. Her mother was permanently unhappy with everything and everybody. LuLing had immersed her in a climate of unsolvable despair throughout Ruth's childhood. That was why Ruth hated it whenever she and Art argued. She tried hard not to get angry. But sometimes she reached a breaking point and erupted, only to wonder later how she had lost control.

Wendy came back on the line. "You still there? Sorry. We're casting victims for that earthquake movie, and a million people are calling all at once." Wendy ran her own agency that hunted extras as San Francisco local color—cops with handlebar mustaches, six-foot-six drag queens, socialites who were unknowing caricatures of themselves. "On top of everything, I feel like shit," Wendy said, and stopped to sneeze and blow her nose. So she wasn't crying, Ruth realized, before the phone clicked twice. "Damn," Wendy said. "Hang on. Let me get rid of this call."

Ruth disliked being put on hold. What was so dire that Wendy had to tell her first thing in the morning? Had Wendy's husband had an affair? Joe? Not good old Joe. What, then?

Art ducked his head through the doorway and tapped his watch. Seven twenty-five, he mouthed. Ruth was about to tell him it was Wendy with an emergency, but he was already striding down the narrow hallway. "Dory! Fia! Let's hustle! Ruth is taking you to the ice rink in five minutes. Get a move on." The girls squealed, and Ruth felt like a horse at the starting gate.

"I'll be there in a sec!" she called out. "And girls, if you didn't eat breakfast, I want you to drink milk, a full glass, so you won't fall over dead from hypoglycemic shock."

"Don't say 'dead.' " Dory griped. "I hate it when you say that."

"My God. What's going on there?" Wendy was back on the line.

"The usual start of the week," Ruth said. "Chaos is the penance for leisure."

"Yeah, who said that?"

"I did. So anyway, you were saying . . . ?"

"Promise me first you won't tell anyone." Wendy sneezed again. "Of course."

"Not even Art, and especially not Miss Giddy."

"Gideon? Gee, I don't know if I can promise about *him*."

"So last night," Wendy began, "my mother called in a state of euphoria." As Wendy went on, Ruth dashed to the bedroom to finish getting dressed. When she was not in a hurry, she enjoyed listening to her friend's ramblings. Wendy was a divining rod for strange disturbances in the earth's atmosphere. She was witness to bizarre sights: three homeless albinos living in Golden Gate Park, a BMW suddenly swallowed up by an ancient septic tank in Woodside, a loose buffalo strolling down Taraval Street. She was the maven of parties that led people to make scenes, start affairs, and commit other self-renewing scandals. Ruth believed Wendy made her life more sparkly, but today was not a good time for sparkles.

"Ruth!" Art said in a warning tone. "The girls are going to be late."

"I'm really sorry, Wendy. I have to take the girls to ice-skating school—"

Wendy interrupted. "Mommy married her personal trainer! That's what she called to tell me. He's thirty-eight, she's sixty-four. Can you believe it?"

"Oh . . . Wow." Ruth was stunned. She pictured Mrs. Scott with a groom in a bow tie and gym shorts, the two of them reciting vows on a treadmill. Was Wendy upset? She wanted to say the right thing. What, though? About five years before, her own mother had had a boyfriend of sorts, but he had been eighty. Ruth had hoped T.C. would marry LuLing and keep her occupied. Instead T.C. had died of a heart attack.

"Listen, Wendy, I know this is important, so can I call you back after I drop off the girls?"

Once she had hung up, Ruth reminded herself of the tasks she needed to do today. Ten things, and she tapped first her thumb. One, take the girls to skating school. Two, pick up Art's suits at the dry cleaner's. Three, buy groceries for dinner. Four, pick up the girls from the rink and drop them off at their friend's house on Jackson Street. Five and Six, phone calls to that arrogant client, Ted, then Agapi Agnos, whom she actually liked. Seven, finish the outline for a chapter of Agapi Agnos's book. Eight, call her agent, Gideon, whom Wendy disliked. And Nine—what the hell was Nine? She knew what Ten was, the last task of the day. She had to call Miriam, Art's ex-wife, to ask if she would let them have the girls the weekend of the Full Moon Festival dinner, the annual reunion of the Youngs, which she was hosting this year.

So what was Nine? She always organized her day by the number of digits on her hands. Each day was either a five or a ten. She wasn't rigid about it: add-ons were accommodated on the toes of her feet, room for ten unexpected tasks. Nine, Nine . . . She could make call-

ing Wendy number One and bump everything back. But she knew
that call should be a toe, an extra, an Eleven. What was Nine? Nine
was usually something important, a significant number, what her
mother termed the number of fullness, a number that also stood for
Do not forget, or risk losing all. Did Nine have something to do with
her mother? There was always *something* to worry about with her
mother. That was not anything she had to remember in particular. It
was a state of mind.

LuLing was the one who had taught her to count fingers as a
memory device. With this method, LuLing never forgot a thing, especially lies, betrayals, and all the bad deeds Ruth had done since she
was born. Ruth could still picture her mother counting in the Chinese style, pointing first to her baby finger and bending each finger
down toward her palm, a motion that Ruth took to mean that all
other possibilities and escape routes were closed. Ruth kept her own
fingers open and splayed, American style. What was Nine? She put
on a pair of sturdy sandals.

Art appeared at the doorway. "Sweetie? Don't forget to call the
plumber about the hot-water tank."

The plumber was *not* going to be number Nine, Ruth told herself,
absolutely not. "Sorry, honey, but could you call? I've got a pretty
full day."

"I have meetings, and three appeals coming up." Art worked as a
linguistics consultant, this year on cases involving deaf prisoners
who had been arrested and tried without access to interpreters.

It's your house, Ruth was tempted to say. But she forced herself
to sound reasonable, unassailable, like Art. "Can't you call from
your office in between meetings?"

"Then I have to phone you and figure out when you'll be here for
the plumber."

"I don't know *exactly* when I'll be home. And you know those guys. They say they're coming at one, they show up at five. Just because I work at home doesn't mean I don't have a real job. I've got a really crazy day. For one thing, I have to . . ." And she started to list her tasks.

Art slumped his shoulders and sighed. "Why do you have to make everything so *difficult?* I just thought *if* it were possible, *if* you had time—Aw, forget it." He turned away.

"Okay, okay, I'll take care of it. But if you get out of your meetings early, can you come home?"

"Sure thing." Art gave her a kiss on the forehead. "Hey, thanks. I wouldn't have asked if I weren't completely swamped." He kissed her again. "Love you."

She didn't answer, and after he left, she grabbed her coat and keys, then saw the girls standing at the end of the hallway, staring critically at her. She wiggled her big toe. Twelve, hot water.

Ruth started the car and pumped the brakes to make sure they worked. As she drove Fia and Dory to the skating rink, she was still mulling over what Nine might be. She ran through the alphabet, in case any of those letters might trigger a memory. Nothing. What had she dreamed the night before, when she finally fell asleep? A bedroom window, a dark shape in the bay. The curtains, she now recalled, had turned out to be sheer and she was naked. She had looked up and saw the neighbors in nearby apartments grinning. They had been watching her most private moments, her most private *parts.* Then a radio began to blare. *Whonk! Whonk! Whonk!* "This has been a test of the American Broadcasting System's early-warning signal for disaster preparedness." And another voice came on, her mother's: "No, no, this is not test! This real!" And the dark shape in the bay rose and became a tidal wave.

Maybe number Nine was related to the plumber after all: tidal wave, broken water heater. The puzzle was solved. But what about the sheer curtains? What did that mean? The worry billowed up again.

"You know that new girl Darien likes?" she heard Fia say to her sister. "She has the best hair. I could just kill her."

"Don't say 'kill'!" Dory intoned. "Remember what they told us in assembly last year? Use that word, go to jail."

Both girls were in the backseat. Ruth had suggested that one of them sit up front with her, so she wouldn't feel like a chauffeur. But Dory had replied, "It's easier to open just one door." Ruth had said nothing in response. She often suspected the girls were testing her, to see if they could get a rise out of her. When they were younger, they had loved her, Ruth was sure of it. She had felt that with a ticklish pleasure in her heart. They used to argue over who could hold her hand or sit next to her. They had cuddled against her when scared, as they had often pretended to be, squeaking like helpless kittens. Now they seemed to be in a contest over who could irritate her more, and she sometimes had to remind herself that teenagers had souls.

Dory was thirteen and chunky, larger than her fifteen-year-old sister. They wore their long chestnut hair alike, pulled into ponytails high on their heads so that they cascaded like fountain spray. All their friends wore their hair in an identical style, Ruth had noticed. When she was their age, she had wanted to grow her hair long the way the other girls did, but her mother made her cut it short. "Long hair look like suicide maiden," LuLing had said. And Ruth knew she was referring to the nursemaid who had killed herself when her mother was a girl. Ruth had had nightmares about that, the ghost with long hair, dripping blood, crying for revenge.

Ruth pulled up to the unloading zone at the rink. The girls scrambled out of the car and swung their satchels onto their backs. "See ya!" they shouted.

Suddenly Ruth noticed what Fia was wearing—low-slung jeans and a cropped shirt that bared a good six inches of belly. She must have had her jacket zipped up when they had left home. Ruth lowered the car window and called out: "Fia, sweetie, come here a second. . . . Am I wrong, or did your shirt shrink drastically in the last ten minutes?"

Fia turned around slowly and rolled her eyes upward.

Dory grinned. "I told you she would."

Ruth stared at Fia's navel. "Does your mother *know* you're wearing that?"

Fia dropped her mouth in mock shock, her reaction to most things. "Uh, she *bought* it for me, okay?"

"Well, I don't think your dad would approve. I want you to keep your jacket on, even when you're skating. And Dory, you tell me if she doesn't."

"I'm not telling on nobody!"

Fia turned and walked away.

"Fia? Fia! Come back here. You promise me now, or I'm going to take you home to change clothes."

Fia stopped but didn't turn around. "All right," she grumbled. As she yanked up the jacket zipper, she said to Dory, loud enough for Ruth to hear: "Dad's right. She loves to make everything *sooo difficult.*"

The remark both humiliated and rankled her. Why had Art said that, and especially in front of the girls? He knew how much that would hurt her. A former boyfriend had once told her she made life more complicated than it was, and after they broke up, she was so horrified that his accusations might be true that she made it a point to be reasonable, to present facts, not complaints. Art knew that and had even assured her the boyfriend was a jerk. Yet he still sometimes teased that she was like a dog that circles and bites its own tail, not recognizing she was only making herself miserable.

Ruth thought of a book she had helped write a few years before, *The Physics of Human Nature.* The author had recast the principles of physics into basic homilies to remind people of self-defeating behavioral patterns. "The Law of Relative Gravity": Lighten up. A problem is only as heavy as you let it be. "The Doppler Effect of Communication": There is always distortion between what a speaker says and what a listener wants it to mean. "The Centrifugal Force of Arguments": The farther you move from the core of the problem, the faster the situation spins out of control.

At the time, Ruth thought the analogies and advice were simplistic. You couldn't reduce real life into one-liners. People were more complex than that. She certainly was, wasn't she? Or was she too *complicated*? Complex, complicated, what was the difference? Art, on the other hand, was the soul of understanding. Her friends often said as much: "You are *so* lucky." She had been proud when she first heard that, believing she had chosen well in love. Lately she had considered whether they might have meant he was to be admired for putting up with *her*. But then Wendy reminded her, "You were the one who called Art a fucking saint." Ruth wouldn't have put it that way, but she knew the sentiment must have been true. She remembered that before she ever loved Art, she had admired him—his calm, the stability of his emotions. Did she still? Had he changed, or was it she? She drove toward the dry cleaner's, mulling over these questions.

She had met Art nearly ten years before, at an evening yoga class she had attended with Wendy. The class was her first attempt in years to exercise. Ruth was naturally thin and didn't have an incentive at first to join a health club. "A thousand bucks a year," she had marveled, "to jump on a machine that makes you run like a hamster in a wheel?" Her preferred form of exercise, she told Wendy, was stress.

"Clench muscles, hold for twelve hours, release for a count of five, then clench again." Wendy, on the other hand, had put on thirty-five pounds since her days as a high school gymnast and was eager to get back into shape. "Let's at least take the free fitness test," she said. "No obligation to join."

Ruth secretly gloated when she scored better than Wendy in sit-ups. Wendy cheered aloud at besting Ruth in push-ups. Ruth's body-fat ratio was a healthy twenty-four percent. Wendy's was thirty-seven. "It's the enduring genetics of my Chinese peasant stock," Ruth kindly offered. But then Ruth scored in the "very poor" range for flexibility. "Wow," Wendy remarked. "According to this chart, that's about one point above rigor mortis."

"Look here, they have yoga," Wendy later said as they perused the schedule of classes at the club. "I hear yoga can change your life. Plus they have night classes." She nudged Ruth. "It might help you get over Paul."

In the locker room that first night, they overheard two women talking. "The guy next to me asked if I'd like to go with him to that midnight class, Togaless Yoga. You know, he says, the *nude* one."

"*Nude?* What a scumbag! . . . Was he at least good-looking?"

"Not bad. But can you imagine facing the naked butts of twenty people doing Downward-Facing Dog?" The two women walked out of the locker room. Ruth turned to Wendy. "Who the hell would do nude yoga?"

"Me," Wendy said. "And don't look at me like that, Miss Shock-and-Dismay. At least it wouldn't be boring."

"Nude, with total strangers?"

"No, with my CPA, my dentist, my boss. Who do you think?"

In the crowded workout room, thirty disciples, most of them women, were staking out their turf, then adjusting mats as stragglers came in. When a man rolled out his mat next to Ruth's, she avoided

looking at him, in case he was the scumbag. She glanced around.
Most of the women had pedicured nails, precision-applied nail polish. Ruth's feet were broad, and her naked toes looked like the pig-
gies from the children's rhyme. Even the man next to her had
better-looking feet, smooth skin, perfectly tapered toes. And then
she caught herself—she shouldn't have nice thoughts about the feet
of a potential pervert.

The class started with what sounded like a cult incantation, followed by poses that seemed to be saluting a heathen god. *"Urdhva
Muka Svanasana! Adho Muka Svanasana!"* Everyone except Ruth
and Wendy knew the routines. Ruth followed along as if she were
playing Simon Says. Every now and then the yoga teacher, a ropy-
muscled woman, walked by and casually bent, tilted, or lifted a part
of Ruth's body. I probably look like a torture victim, Ruth thought,
or one of those freaks my mother saw in China, boneless beggar
boys who twisted themselves up for the amusement of others. By
this time she was perspiring heavily and had observed enough about
the man next to her to be able to describe him to the police, if necessary. "The nude yoga rapist was five-eleven, maybe a hundred and
sixty pounds. He had dark hair, large brown eyes and thick eyebrows, a neatly cropped beard and mustache. His fingernails were
clean, perfectly trimmed."

He was also incredibly limber. He could wrap his ankles around
his neck, balance like Baryshnikov. She, in comparison, looked like a
woman getting a gynecological exam. A *poor* woman. She was wearing an old T-shirt and faded leggings with a hole in one knee. At
least it was obvious she wasn't on the prowl, not like those who were
wearing designer sports outfits and full makeup.

And then she noticed the man's ring, a thick band of hammered
gold on his right hand, no ring on his left. Not all married men wore
rings, of course, but a wedding band on the right hand was a dead

giveaway, at least in San Francisco, that he was gay. Now that she thought about it, the signs were obvious: the neat beard, the trim torso, the graceful way he moved. She could relax. She watched the bearded man bend forward, grab the bottoms of his feet, and press his forehead to his knees. No straight man could do that. Ruth flopped over and dangled her hands to midcalf.

Toward the end of the class came the headstands. The novices moved to the wall, the competitive types rose immediately like sunflowers toward the noon sun. There was no more room at the wall, so Ruth simply sat on her mat. A moment later, she heard the bearded man speak: "Need some help? I can hold on to your ankles until you get balanced."

"Thanks, but I'll pass. I'm afraid I'd get a cerebral hemorrhage."

He smiled. "Do you always live in such a dangerous world?"

"Always. Life's more exciting that way."

"Well, the headstand is one of the most important postures you can do. Being upside down can turn your life around. It can make you happy."

"Really?"

"See? You're already laughing."

"You win," she said, placing the crown of her head on a folded blanket. "Hoist away."

Within the first week, Wendy was off yoga and onto a home gizmo that looked like a rickshaw with oars. Ruth continued with yoga three times a week. She had found a form of exercise that relaxed her. She especially liked the practice of staying focused, of eliminating everything from her mind except breath. And she liked Art, the bearded man. He was friendly and funny. They started going to a coffee shop around the corner after class.

Over decaf cappuccinos one evening, she learned that Art had grown up in New York, and had a doctorate in linguistics from UC Berkeley. "So what languages do you speak?" she asked.

"I'm not a true polyglot," he said. "Most linguists I know aren't. My actual language specialty at Berkeley was American Sign Language, ASL. I now work at the Center on Deafness at UCSF."

"You became an expert on silence?" she joked.

"I'm not an expert on anything. But I love language in all forms— sounds and words, facial expressions, hand gestures, body posture and its rhythms, what people mean but don't necessarily say with words. I've always loved words, the power of them."

"So what's your favorite word?"

"Hm, that's an *excellent* question." He fell quiet, stroking his beard in thought.

Ruth was thrilled. He was probably groping for a word that was arcane and multisyllabic, one of those crossword items that could be confirmed only in the *Oxford English Dictionary*.

"Vapors," he said at last.

"Vapors?" Ruth thought of chills and cold, mists and suicide ghosts. That was not a word she would have chosen.

"It appeals to all the senses," he explained. "It can be opaque but never solid. You can feel it, but it has no permanent shape. It might be hot or cold. Some vapors smell terrible, others quite wonderful. Some are dangerous, others are harmless. Some are brighter than others when burned, mercury versus sodium, for instance. Vapors can go up your nose with a sniff and permeate your lungs. And the sound of the word, how it forms on your lips, teeth, and tongue— *vaporzzzzz*—it lilts up, then lingers and fades. It's perfectly matched to its meanings."

"It is," Ruth agreed. "Vaporzzz," she echoed, savoring the buzz on her tongue.

"And then there's vapor pressure," Art continued, "and reaching that balance point between two states, one hundred degrees Celsius." Ruth nodded and gave him what she hoped was a look of intelligent concentration. She felt dull and badly educated. "One moment you have water," Art said, his hands forming undulating motions. "But under pressure from heat, it turns into steam." His fingers flittered upward.

Ruth nodded vigorously. Water to steam, that she understood, sort of. Her mother used to talk about fire and water combining to make steam, and steam looked harmless but could peel your skin right off. "Like yin and yang?" she ventured.

"Duality of nature. Exactly."

Ruth shrugged. She felt like a fraud.

"What about you?" he said. "What's your favorite word?"

She put on her idiot face. "Gosh oh golly, there are so many! Let's see. 'Vacation.' 'Jackpot.' Then there's 'free.' 'Sale.' 'Bargain.' You know, the usual."

He had laughed throughout, and she felt pleased. "Seriously," he said. "What?"

Seriously? She plucked at what surfaced in her mind, but they sounded trite: *peace, love, happiness.* And what would those words say about her? That she lacked those qualities? That she had no imagination? She considered saying *onomatopoeia,* a word that had enabled her to win a spelling bee in the fifth grade. But *onomatopoeia* was a jumble of syllables, not at all like the simple sounds it was supposed to represent. Crash, boom, bang.

"I don't have a favorite yet," she finally answered. "I guess I've been living off words for so long it's hard to think about them beyond what's utilitarian."

"What do you do?"

"I used to be in corporate communications. Then I started free-lance editing, and a few years ago I took on more full-scale book collaboration, mostly inspirational and self-improvement books, better health, better sex, better soul, that kind of thing."

"You're a book doctor."

Ruth liked that he said that. Book doctor. She had never called herself that, nor had anyone else. Most people called her a ghostwriter—she hated the term. Her mother thought it meant that she could actually write to ghosts. "Yes," she told Art. "I suppose you could say that, book doctor. But I tend to think of myself as more of a translator, helping people transfer what's in their brain onto the blank page. Some books need more help than others."

"Have you ever wanted to write your own book?"

She hesitated. Of course she had. She wanted to write a novel in the style of Jane Austen, a book of manners about the upper class, a book that had nothing to do with her own life. Years before, she had dreamed of writing stories as a way to escape. She could revise her life and become someone else. She could be somewhere else. In her imagination she could change everything, herself, her mother, her past. But the idea of revising her life also frightened her, as if by imagination alone she were condemning what she did not like about herself or others. Writing what you wished was the most dangerous form of wishful thinking.

"I suppose most people want to write their own book," she answered. "But I think I'm better at translating what others want to say."

"And you enjoy that? It's satisfying?"

"Yes. Absolutely. There's still a lot of freedom to do what I want."

"You're lucky."

"I am," she conceded. "I certainly am."

It pleased her to discuss such matters with him. With Wendy she tended to talk about peeves more than passions. They commiserated on rampant misogyny, bad manners, and depressed mothers, whereas Art and she talked to discover new things about themselves and each other. He wanted to know what inspired her, what the difference was between her hopes and her goals, her beliefs and her motivations.

"Difference?" she asked.

"Some things you do for yourself," he answered. "Some things you do for others. Maybe they're the same."

Through such conversations, she realized for instance that she was lucky to be a freelance editor, a book doctor. The discoveries were refreshing.

One evening, about three weeks after she met him, their conversation became more personal. "Frankly, I like living alone," she heard herself saying. She had convinced herself this was true.

"And what if you met the ideal partner?"

"He can stay ideal in his place, and I'll stay ideal in mine. Then we won't get into all that shit about whose pubic hair is clogging up the drain."

Art chuckled. "God! Did you actually live with someone who complained about *that?*"

Ruth forced a laugh, staring into her coffee cup. She was the one who had complained. "We were opposites about cleanliness," she answered. "Thank God we didn't marry." As she said this, she sensed the words were at last true and not a cover-up for pain.

"So you were going to marry."

She had never been able to confide fully to anyone, not even Wendy, about what had happened with her and Paul Shinn. She had told Wendy of the many ways Paul irked her, that she was tempted to break up with him. When she announced to Wendy that they had split up, Wendy exclaimed, "*Finally* you did it. Good for you." With Art, the past seemed easier to talk about, because he had not been part of it. He was her yoga buddy, on the periphery of her life. He did not know what her earlier hopes and fears had been. With him, she could dissect the past with emotional detachment and frank intelligence.

"We thought about marriage," she said. "How can you not when you live together for four years? But you know what? Over time, passion wanes, differences don't. One day he told me he'd put in for a transfer to New York and it had come through." Ruth recalled to herself how surprised she had been, and how she complained to Paul about his not telling her sooner. "Of course, I can work almost anywhere," she had told him, annoyed yet excited at the prospect of moving to Manhattan, "but it's a jolt to uproot, not to mention leave my mother behind, and relocate in a city where I don't have any contacts. Why'd you tell me at the last minute?" She had meant that rhetorically. Then came Paul's awkward silence.

"I didn't ask to go, he didn't ask me to come," she told Art simply. She avoided eye contact. "It was a civil way to break up. We both agreed it was time to move on, only separately. He was decent enough to try to put the blame on himself. Said he was immature, whereas I was more *responsible*." She gave Art a goofy grin, as if this were the most ironic thing anyone could have said about her. "The worst part was, he was so *nice* about it—like he was embarrassed to have to do this to me. And naturally, I spent the last year trying to analyze what it was about us, about *me*, that didn't work. I went over just about every argument that we'd had. I had said he was careless, he said I made simple problems have difficult solutions. I said he never planned, he said I obsessed to the point of killing all spontaneity. I thought he was selfish, he said I worried over him to the point of suffocation, then pitied myself when he didn't fall all over himself saying thank you. And maybe we were both right and that was why we were wrong for each other."

Art touched her hand. "Well, I think he lost a terrific woman."

She was flooded with self-consciousness and gratitude.

"You are. You're terrific. You're honest and funny. Smart, interested."

"Don't forget responsible."

"What's wrong with being responsible? I wish more people were. And you know what else? You're willing to be vulnerable. I think that's endearing."

"Aw, shucks."

"Seriously."

"Well, that's sweet of you to say. I'll buy you coffee next time." She laughed and put her hand over his. "How about you? Tell me about your love life and all your past disasters. Who's your current partner?"

"I don't have one right now. Half the time I live alone, the other half I'm picking up toys and making jelly sandwiches for my two daughters."

This was a surprise. "You adopted them?"

He looked puzzled. "They're mine. And my ex-wife's, of course."

Ex-wife? That made three gay men she knew who had once been married. "So how long were you married before you came out?"

"Came out?" He made a screwy face. "Wait a minute. Do you think I'm *gay*?"

In an instant, she knew her mistake. "Of course not!" she scrambled to say. "I meant when you came out from New York."

He was laughing convulsively. "This whole time you thought I was *gay*?"

Ruth flushed. What had she said! "It was the ring," she admitted, and pointed to his gold band. "Most of the gay couples I know wear rings on that hand."

He slipped off the ring and rotated it in the light. "My best friend made it for my wedding," Art said solemnly. "Ernesto, a rare spirit. He was a poet and a goldsmith by avocation, made his living as a limo driver. See these indentations? He told me they were to remind me that there are a lot of bumps in life and that I should remember what lies between them. Love, friendship, hope. I stopped wearing it when Miriam and I split up. Then Ernesto died, brain cancer. I decided to wear the ring to remind me of him, what he said. He was a good friend—but *not* a lover."

He slid the ring over to Ruth so she could see the details. She picked it up. It was heavier than she had thought. She held it to her eye and looked through its center at Art. He was so gentle. He was not judgmental. She felt a squeezing in her heart that both hurt her and made her want to giggle and shout. How could she not love him?

As she gathered up Art's clothes at the dry cleaner's, Ruth flexed her big toe and remembered she was supposed to call Wendy. Mrs. Scott and a boy toy, what a shock. She decided to wait until she was in the parking lot by the grocery store, rather than risk a head-on collision during a juicy cell-phone conversation.

She and Wendy were the same age. They had known each other since the sixth grade, but had gone through periods when they did not see each other for years. Their friendship had grown via accidental reunions and persistence on Wendy's part. While Wendy was not the person Ruth would have chosen for her closest friend, Ruth was glad it had turned out to be so. She needed Wendy's boisterousness as balance to her own caution, Wendy's bluntness as antidote to her reserve. "Stop being such a worrywort," Wendy often ordered. Or "You don't always have to act so fucking polite," she might say. "You're making me look like shit."

Wendy answered on the first ring. "Can you believe it?" she said, as though she had not stopped repeating this since their last conversation. "And I thought she was over the top when she had the facelift. Last night she told me that she and Patrick were getting it on twice a night. She's telling me this—*me,* the daughter she once sent to confession for asking how babies were made."

Ruth imagined Mrs. Scott taking off her Chanel suit, her tri-focals, her diamond-encrusted designer crucifix, then embracing her beach boy.

"She's getting more sex than I am," Wendy exclaimed. "I can't remember the last time I even wanted to do anything in bed with Joe except sleep."

Wendy had often joked about her dwindling sex drive. But Ruth didn't think she meant it was absent. Would this happen to her as well? She and Art were not exactly the red-hot lovers they'd been in earlier years. They prepared less for romance and accepted more readily excuses of fatigue. She wiggled a toe: Get estrogen levels checked. That might be the reason she felt a sense of unease, fluctua-ting hormones. She had no other reason to feel anxious. Not that her life was perfect, but whatever problems she had, they were small. And she should keep them that way. She vowed to be more affection-ate with Art.

"I can see why you're upset," Ruth consoled her.

"Actually, I'm more worried than upset," Wendy said. "It's just weird. It's like the older she gets, the younger she acts. And part of me says, Good for her, you go, girl. And the other part is like, Whoa. Is she crazy or what? Do I have to watch over her now, act like her mother and make sure she doesn't get herself in trouble? You know what I mean?"

"I've been that way with my mother all my life," Ruth said. Sud-denly she remembered what had been eluding her. Her mother was supposed to see the doctor at four this afternoon. Over the past year, Ruth had been vaguely worried about her mother's health. Nothing was terribly wrong; it was just that LuLing seemed slightly off, hazy. For a while, Ruth had reasoned that her mother was tired, that her hearing might be going, or that her English was getting worse. As a precaution, Ruth had also gnawed over the worst possibilities—brain tumor, Alzheimer's, stroke—believing this would ensure that it was not these things. History had always proven that she worried for nothing. But a few weeks before, when her mother mentioned she had an appointment for a checkup, Ruth said she would drive her.

After she and Wendy finished their conversation, Ruth stepped out of the car and walked toward the grocery store, still thinking. Nine, Mom's doctor. And she started to count on her fingers the questions she should ask the doctor. Thank God she could, speak once again.

TWO

In the vegetable aisle, Ruth headed toward a bin of beautifully shaped turnips. They were each the size of apples, symmetrical and scrubbed, with striations of purple. Most people did not appreciate the aesthetics of turnips, Ruth thought as she chose five good ones, whereas she loved them, their crunchiness, the way they absorbed the flavor of whatever they were immersed in, gravy or pickling juice. She loved cooperative vegetables. And she loved turnips best when they were sliced into wedges and preserved in vinegar and chilies, sugar and salt.

Every year, before their family reunion dinner in September, her mother started two new fermenting jars of spicy turnips, one of which she gave to Ruth. When Ruth was a little girl, she called them *la-la*, hot-hot. She would suck and munch on them until her tongue and lips felt inflamed and swollen. She still gorged on them from time to time. Was it a craving for salt, or for pain? When the supply grew low, Ruth would toss in more chopped-up turnips and a pinch of salt, and let them pickle for a few days. Art thought the taste was okay in small doses. But the girls said they smelled like "something farted in the fridge." At times Ruth secretly ate the spicy turnips in the morning, her way of seizing the day. Even her mother considered that strange.

Her mother—and Ruth tapped her ring finger to remind herself again of the doctor's appointment. Four o'clock. She had to squeeze a lot of work into the shortened day. She hurried, grabbing Fuji apples for Fia, Granny Smiths for Dory, Braeburns for Art.

At the meat counter, she evaluated the options. Dory would not eat anything with eyes, and ever since seeing that pig movie *Babe*, Fia had been trying to be a vegetarian. Both girls made an exception for fish, because seafood was "not cute." When they announced that, Ruth said to them, "Just because something isn't cute, is its life worth less? If a girl wins a beauty contest, is she better than a girl who doesn't?" And Fia scrunched up her face and replied: "What are you talking about? Fish don't enter beauty contests."

Ruth now pushed her cart toward the fish counter. She longed for prawns in the shell, always her first choice. Art wouldn't eat them, however. He claimed that the predominant taste of any crustacean or mollusk was that of its alimentary tract. She settled on Chilean sea bass. "That one," she told the man at the counter. Then she reconsidered: "Actually, give me the bigger one." She might as well ask her mother to dinner, since they were already going to the doctor's together. LuLing was always complaining she didn't like to cook for just herself.

At the checkout counter, Ruth saw a woman in front of her scoop up bunches of ivory- and peach-colored tulips, at least fifty dollars' worth. Ruth was amazed at how some people casually bought flowers as household staples, as if they were as necessary as toilet paper. And tulips, of all choices! They wilted and dropped their petals after a few days. Was the woman having an important dinner party on a weeknight? When Ruth bought flowers, she had to assess their value in several ways to justify what she bought. Daisies were cheerful and cheap, but they had an unpleasant smell. Baby's breath was even cheaper, but as Gideon pointed out, it was *the* lowest of floral low taste, what old queens used, along with lace doilies they inherited from their grandmothers. Tuberoses smelled wonderful and gave an architectural touch, but they were expensive at this store, nearly four dollars a stalk. At the flower mart, they were only a dollar. She liked hydrangeas in a pot. They were making a comeback, and while they cost a lot, they lasted a month or two, *if* you remembered to water them. The trick was to cut them before they died, then let them dry in a pottery pitcher, so you could keep them as a permanent floral arrangement, that is, until someone like Art threw them out, citing that they were already dead.

Ruth had not grown up with flowers in the house. She could not remember LuLing ever buying them. She had not thought this a deprivation until the day she went grocery shopping with Auntie Gal and her cousins. At the supermarket in Saratoga, ten-year-old Ruth had watched as they dumped into the cart whatever struck their fancy at the moment, all kinds of good things Ruth was never allowed to eat: chocolate milk, doughnuts, TV dinners, ice-cream sandwiches, Hostess Twinkies. Later they stopped at a little stand where Auntie Gal bought cut flowers, pink baby roses, even though nobody had died or was having a birthday.

Remembering this, Ruth decided to splurge and buy a small orchid plant with ivory blooms. Orchids looked delicate but thrived on neglect. You didn't have to water them but once every ten days. And while they were somewhat pricey, they bloomed for six months or more, then went dormant before surprising you with new blooms all over again. They never died—you could count on them to reincarnate themselves forever. A lasting value.

Back at the flat, Ruth put the groceries away, set the orchid on the dining room table, and went into the Cubbyhole. She liked to think that limited space inspired limitless imagination. The walls were painted red with flecks of metallic gold, Wendy's idea. The overhead light was softened by a desk lamp with an amber mica shade. On the lacquer-black shelves were reference books instead of jars of jam. A pull-out cutting board held her laptop, a flour bin had been removed for knee space.

She turned on her computer and felt drained before she even started. What was she doing ten years ago? The same thing. What would she be doing ten years from now? The same thing. Even the subjects of the books she helped write were not that different, only the buzzwords had changed. She took a deep breath and phoned the new client, Ted. His book, *Internet Spirituality*, was about the ethics created by cosmic computer connections, a topic he felt sure was hot right now but would lose its cachet if the publisher didn't get it to market as soon as possible. He had said so in several urgent phone messages he had left over the weekend when Ruth was in Tahoe.

"I have nothing to do with arranging publishing dates," Ruth now tried to explain.

"Stop thinking in terms of constraints," he told her. "If you write this book with me, you have to believe in its principles. Anything is possible, as long as it's for the good of the world. Make the exception. Live exceptionally. And if you can't do that, maybe we should consider whether you're right for this project. Think about it, then let's talk tomorrow."

Ruth hung up. She thought about it. The good of the world, she muttered to herself, was her agent's job. She would warn Gideon that the client was pushy and might try to change the publication date. She would stand firm this time. To do what the client wanted while meeting her other commitments would require her to work 'round the clock. Fifteen years earlier she could have done that—in the days when she also smoked cigarettes and equated busyness with feeling wanted. Not now. Untense the muscles, she reminded herself. She took another deep breath and exhaled as she stared at the shelves of books she had helped edit and write.

The Cult of Personal Freedom. The Cult of Compassion. The Cult of Envy.

The Biology of Sexual Attraction. The Physics of Human Nature. The Geography of the Soul.

The Yin and Yang of Being Single. The Yin and Yang of Being Married. The Yin and Yang of Being Divorced.

The most popular books were *Defeat Depression with Dogs, Procrastinate to Your Advantage,* and *To Hell with Guilt.* The last book had become a controversial bestseller. It had even been translated into German *and* Hebrew.

In the coauthoring trade, "Ruth Young" was the small-type name that followed "with," that is, if it appeared at all. After fifteen years, she had nearly thirty-five books to her credit. Most of her early work had come from corporate communications clients. Her expertise had woven its way into communication in general, then communication problems, behavioral patterns, emotional problems, mind-body connections, and spiritual awakening. She had been in the business long enough to see the terms evolve from "chakras" to "ch'i," "prana," "vital energy," "life force," "biomagnetic force," "bioenergy fields," and finally back to "chakras." In bookstores, most of her clients' words of wisdom were placed in the light or popular sections—Self-Help, Wellness, Inspirational, New Age. She wished she were working on books that would be categorized as Philosophy, Science, Medicine.

By and large, the books she helped write were interesting, she often reminded herself, and if not, it was her job to *make* them interesting. And though she might pooh-pooh her own work just to be modest, it irked her when others did not take her seriously. Even Art did not seem to recognize how difficult her job was. But that was partly her fault. She preferred to make it look easy. She would rather that others discern for themselves what an incredible job she did in spinning gold out of dross. They never did, of course. They didn't know how hard it was to be diplomatic, to excavate lively prose from

incoherent musings. She had to assure clients that her straight-
forward recasting of their words still made them sound articulate,
intelligent, and important. She had to be sensitive to the fact the authors saw their books as symbolic forms of immortality, believing
that their words on the printed page would last far longer than their
physical bodies. And when the books were published, Ruth had to sit
back quietly at parties while the clients took the credit for being brilliant. She often claimed she did not need to be acknowledged to feel
satisfied, but that was not exactly true. She wanted *some* recognition,
and not like the kind she had received two weeks before, at the party
for her mother's seventy-seventh birthday.

Auntie Gal and Uncle Edmund had brought along a friend from
Portland, an older woman with thick glasses, who asked Ruth what
she did for a living. "I'm a book collaborator," she answered.

"Why you say that?" LuLing scolded. "Sound bad, like you traitor and spy."

Auntie Gal then said with great authority, "She's a ghostwriter,
one of the best there is. You know those books that say 'as told to' on
the cover? That's what Ruth does—people tell her stories and she
writes them down, word for word, exactly as told." Ruth had no time
to correct her.

"Like court stenographers," the woman said. "I hear they have to
be very fast and accurate. Did you go through special training?"

Before Ruth could answer, Auntie Gal chirped: "Ruthie, you
should tell my story! Very exciting, plus all true. But I don't know if
you can keep up. I'm a pretty fast talker!"

Now LuLing jumped in: "Not just type, *lots* work!" And Ruth
was grateful for this unexpected defense, until her mother added,
"She correct spelling too!"

Ruth looked up from her notes on her phone conference with the
Internet Spirituality author and reminded herself of all the ways she
was lucky. She worked at home, was paid decent money, and at least

the publishers appreciated her, as did the publicists, who called her for talking points when booking radio interviews for the authors. She was always busy, unlike some freelance writers who fretted over the trickle of jobs in the pipeline.

"So busy, so success," her mother had said recently when Ruth told her she didn't have any free time to see her. "Not free," LuLing added, "because every minute must charge money. What I should pay you, five dollar, ten dollar, then you come see me?" The truth was, Ruth did not have much free time, not in her opinion. Free time was the most precious time, when you should be doing what you loved, or at least slowing down enough to remember what made your life worthwhile and happy. Her free time was usually usurped by what seemed at the time urgent and later unnecessary. Wendy said the same thing: "Free time doesn't exist anymore. It has to be scheduled with a dollar amount attached to it. You're under this constant pressure to get your money's worth out of rest, relaxation, and restaurants that are hard to get into." After hearing that, Ruth didn't agonize as much over time constraints. It wasn't her fault she didn't have enough time to do what was necessary. The problem was universal. But try explaining that to her mother.

She pulled out her notes for chapter seven of Agapi Agnos's latest book, *Righting the Wronged Child,* and punched Agapi's number. Ruth was one of the few people who knew that Agapi's real name was Doris DeMatteo, that she had chosen her pseudonym because *agapi* meant "love" and *agnos* referred to ignorance, which she redefined as a form of innocence. That was how she signed her books, "Love & Innocence, Agapi Agnos." Ruth enjoyed working with her. Though Agapi was a psychiatrist, she didn't come across as intimidating. She knew that much of her appeal was her Zsa Zsa Gabor shtick, her accent, the flirtatious yet intelligent personality she exuded when she answered questions in TV and radio interviews.

During their phone meeting, Ruth reviewed the chapter that presented the Five Don'ts and Ten Do's of becoming a more engaged parent.

"Darling," Agapi said, "why does it always have to be a list of five and ten? I can't always limit myself to such regular numbers."

"It's just easier for people to remember in series of fives and tens," Ruth answered. "I read a study somewhere about that." Hadn't she? "It probably has to do with counting on our fingers."

"That makes perfect sense, my dear! I knew there was a reason."

After they hung up, Ruth began work on a chapter titled "No Child Is an Island." She replayed a tape of Agapi and herself talking:

". . . A parent, intentionally or not, imposes a cosmology on the little child——" Agapi paused. "You want to say something?" What cue had she given that let Agapi know she wanted to add a thought? Ruth seldom interrupted people.

"We should define 'cosmology' here," she heard herself say, "perhaps in a sidebar. We don't want people to think we're talking about cosmetics or astrology."

"Yes, yes, excellent point, my dear. Cosmology, let's see . . . what we *believe*, subconsciously, implicitly, or both, how the universe works—you want to add something?"

"Readers will think we mean planets or the Big Bang theory."

"You are such a cynic! All right, you write the definition, but just include something about how each of us fits into our families, society, the communities we come into contact with. Talk about those various roles, as well as how we believe we got them—whether it's destiny, fate, luck, chance, self-determination, et cetera, et cetera. Oh, and Ruth, darling, make it sound sexy and easy to grasp."

"No problem."

"All right, so we assume everyone understands cosmology. We go on to say that parents pass along this cosmology to children through their behaviors, their reactions to daily events, often mundane— You look puzzled."

"Examples of mundane."

"Mealtime, for instance. Perhaps dinner always happens at six and Mom is an elaborate planner, dinner is a ritual, but nothing happens, no talk, unless it's argument. Or meals are eaten catch-as-catch-can. With just these contrasts, the child might grow up thinking either that day and night are predictable, though not always pleasant, or that the world is chaotic, frantic, or freely evolving. Some children do beautifully, no matter what the early influences. Whereas others grow up into great big adults who require a lifetime of very, *very* expensive psychotherapy."

Ruth listened to their laughter on the tape. She had never gone into therapy, as Wendy had. She worked with too many therapists, saw that they were human, full of foibles, in need of help themselves. And while Wendy thought it worthwhile to know that a professional was dedicated to her and her alone for two one-hour sessions a week, Ruth could not justify spending a hundred fifty dollars an hour to listen to herself talk. Wendy often said Ruth should see a shrink about her compulsion with number counting. To Ruth, however, the counting was practical, not compulsive; it had to do with remembering things, not warding off some superstitious nonsense.

"Ruth, darling," Agapi's taped voice continued, "can you look at the folder marked 'Fascinating Case Studies' and pick out suitable ones for this chapter?"

"Okay. And I was thinking, how about including a section on the cosmology imparted by television as artificial caregiver? Just a suggestion, since it would probably also work as an angle for television shows and radio interviews."

"Yes, yes, wonderful! What shows do you think we should do?"

"Well, starting with the fifties, you know, *Howdy Doody, The Mickey Mouse Club,* all the way to *The Simpsons* and *South Park*—"

"No, dear, I mean what shows *I* might be on. *Sixty Minutes,*

Today, Charlie Rose—oh, I would love to be on *that* show, that man is *so* sexy. . . ."

Ruth took notes and started an outline. No doubt Agapi would call her that night to discuss what she had written. Ruth suspected she was the only writer in the business who believed a deadline was an actual date.

Her watch sounded at eleven. She tapped her finger, Eight, call Gideon. When she reached him, she began with the demands of the *Internet Spirituality* author. "Ted wants me to push everything else aside and make his project top priority under rush deadlines. I was very firm about saying I couldn't do that, and he hinted pretty strongly that he might replace me with another writer. Frankly, I'd be relieved if he fired me," Ruth said. She was preparing herself for rejection.

"He never will," Gideon replied. "You'll cave in, you always do. You'll probably be calling HarperSanFrancisco by the end of the week, persuading them to change the schedule."

"What makes you say that?"

"Face it, sweetheart, you're accommodating. Willing to bend over backward. And you have this knack for making even the dickheads believe they're the best at what they do."

"Watch it," Ruth said. "That's a hooker you're describing."

"It's true. You're a dream when it comes to collaboration," Gideon went on. "You listen as the clients blather on, egos unchecked. They walk all over you, and you just take it. You're easy."

Why wasn't Art hearing this? Ruth wanted to gloat: See, *others* don't think I'm difficult. Then she realized Gideon was saying she was a pushover. She wasn't really, she reasoned. She knew her limits, but she wasn't the type to get into a conflict over things that were ultimately not that important. She didn't understand people who thrived on argument and being right all the time. Her mother was

that way, and what did that get her? Nothing but unhappiness, dis-
satisfaction, and anger. According to her mother's cosmology, the
world was against her and no one could change this, because this was
a curse.

But the way Ruth saw it, LuLing got into fights mainly because
of her poor English. She didn't understand others, or they didn't
understand her. Ruth used to feel she was the one who suffered because of that. The irony was, her mother was actually *proud* she had
taught herself English, the choppy talk she had acquired in China
and Hong Kong. And since immigrating to the United States fifty
years before, she had not improved either her pronunciation or her
vocabulary. Yet her sister, GaoLing, had come to the States around
the same time, and her English was nearly perfect. She could talk
about the difference between crinoline and organza, name the specific trees she liked: oak, maple, gingko, pine. To LuLing, cloth was
classified as "cost too much," "too slippery," "scratchy skin," and
"last long time." And there were only two kinds of trees: "shady"
and "drop leaf all the time." Her mother couldn't even say Ruth's
name right. It used to mortify Ruth when she shouted for her up and
down the block. "Lootie! Lootie!" Why had her mother chosen a
name with sounds she couldn't pronounce?

But this was the worst part: Being the only child of a widow,
Ruth had always been forced to serve as LuLing's mouthpiece. By
the time she was ten, Ruth was the English-speaking "Mrs. LuLing
Young" on the telephone, the one who made appointments for the
doctor, who wrote letters to the bank. Once she even had to compose
a humiliating letter to the minister.

"Lootie give me so much trouble," LuLing dictated, as if Ruth
were invisible, "maybe I send her go Taiwan, school for bad children. What you think?"

Ruth revised that to: "Perhaps Ruth might attend a finishing school in Taiwan where she can learn the manners and customs of a young lady. What is your opinion?"

In an odd way, she now thought, her mother was the one who had taught her to become a book doctor. Ruth had to make life better by revising it.

At three-ten, Ruth finished paying the plumber. Art had never come home, nor had he called. A whole new water heater was needed, not just a replacement part. And because of the leak, the plumber had had to shut off the electricity to the entire flat until he had suctioned out the standing water and removed the old tank. Ruth had been unable to work.

She was running late. She faxed the outline to Agapi, then raced around the house, gathering notes, her cell phone, her address book. Once in the car, she drove to the Presidio Gate and then through the eucalyptus forest to California Street. Her mother lived fifty blocks west, in a part of San Francisco known as the Sunset district, close to Land's End.

The doctor's appointment was ostensibly a routine visit. Her mother had overlooked having an annual checkup for the last few years, though it was included free in her HMO plan. LuLing was never sick. Ruth could not remember the last time she had had the flu or even a cold. At seventy-seven, her mother had none of the common geriatric problems, arthritis, high cholesterol, or osteoporosis. Her worst ailment—the one she frequently complained about to Ruth, in excruciating detail—was constipation.

Recently, though, Ruth had some concerns that her mother was becoming not forgetful, exactly, but careless. She would say "ribbon" when she meant "wrapping paper," "envelope" when she meant "stamp." Ruth had made a mental list of examples to tell the doctor.

The accident last March, she should mention that as well. LuLing had bashed her car into the back of a truck. Luckily, she had only bumped her head on the steering wheel, and no one else was hurt. Her car was totaled.

"Scare me to pieces," LuLing had reported. "My skin almost fall off." She blamed a pigeon that had flown up in front of her windshield. Maybe, Ruth now considered, it was not a flutter of wings, but one in her brain, a stroke, and the bump on her head was more serious, a concussion, a skull fracture. Whatever was wrong, the police report and insurance company said it was LuLing's fault, not the pigeon's. LuLing was so outraged that she canceled her car insurance, then complained when the company refused to reinstate her policy.

Ruth had related the incident to Agapi Agnos, who said inattention and anger could be related to depression in the elderly.

"My mother's been depressed and angry all her life," Ruth told Agapi. She did not bring up the threats of suicide, which she had heard so often she tried not to react to them.

"I know of some excellent therapists who've worked with Chinese patients," Agapi said. "Quite good with cultural differences— magical thinking, old societal pressures, the flow of ch'i."

"Believe me, Agapi, my mother is *not* like other Chinese people." Ruth used to wish her mother were more like Auntie Gal. She didn't talk about ghosts or bad luck or ways she might die.

"In any case, my dear, you should have a doctor give her a thorough, thorough checkup. And you put your arms around her and give that mother of yours a great big healing hug from me." It was a nice thought, but Ruth rarely exchanged embraces with LuLing. When she tried, her mother's shoulders turned rigid, as if she were being attacked.

Driving toward LuLing's building, Ruth entered the typical fog of summer. Then came block after block of bungalows built in the twenties, cottages that sprang up in the thirties, and characterless apartments from the sixties. The ocean view skyline was marred by electrical wires strewn from pole to house and house to pole. Many of the picture windows had sea-misty smears. The drainpipes and gutters were rusted, as were the bumpers of old cars. She turned up a street lined with more upscale homes, architectural attempts at Bauhaus sleekness, their small lawns decorated with shrubs cut in odd shapes, like the cotton-candy legs of show poodles.

She pulled up to LuLing's place, a two-unit Mediterranean-style with an apricot-colored curved front and a fake bay window balcony with wrought-iron grating. LuLing had once proudly tended her yard. She used to water and cut the hedge herself, neaten the border of white stones that flanked the short walkway. When Ruth lived at home, she had had to mow the seven-by-seven foot squares of lawn. LuLing always criticized any edges that touched the sidewalk. She also complained about the yellow urine spots, made by the dog from across the street. "Lootie, you tell that man don't let dog do that." Ruth reluctantly went across the street, knocked on the door, asked the neighbor if he had seen a black-and-white cat, then walked back and told her mother that the man said he would try. When she went away to college and came home to visit, her mother still asked her to complain to the man across the street almost as soon as she walked in the door. The missing-cat routine was getting old, and it was hard to think of new excuses for knocking on the man's door. Ruth usually procrastinated, and LuLing nagged about more and more yellow spots, as well as Ruth's laziness, her forgetfulness, her lack of concern for family, on and on. Ruth tried to ignore her by reading or watching TV.

One day Ruth worked up the courage to tell LuLing she should hire a lawyer to sue the man or a gardener to fix the lawn. Her college roommate had suggested she say this, telling Ruth she was crazy to let her mother push her around as if she were still six years old.

"Is she *paying* you to be a punching bag?" her roommate had said, building the case.

"Well, she does give me money for college expenses," Ruth admitted.

"Yeah, but every parent does that. They're supposed to. But that doesn't give them the right to make you their slave."

Thus bolstered, Ruth confronted her mother: "If it bothers you so much, you take care of it."

LuLing stared at her, silent for five full minutes. Then she burst like a geyser: "You wish I dead? You wish no mother tell you what to do? Okay, maybe I die soon!" And just like that, Ruth had been up-ended, flung about, was unable to keep her balance. LuLing's threats to die were like earthquakes. Ruth knew that the potential was there, that beneath the surface, the temblors could occur at any time. And despite this knowledge, when they erupted she panicked and wanted to run away before the world fell down.

Strangely, after that incident, LuLing never mentioned anything about the dog peeing on the lawn. Instead, whenever Ruth came home, LuLing made it a point to take out a spade, get on her hands and knees, and painfully dig out the yellow spots and reseed them, two square inches at a time. Ruth knew it was her mother's version of emotional torture, but still it made her stomach hurt as she pretended not to be affected. LuLing finally did hire someone to take care of the yellow spots, a cement contractor, who constructed a frame and a mold, then poured a patio of red and white concrete diamonds. The walkway was red as well. Over the years, the red diamonds faded. The white ones turned grimy. Some areas looked as though they had experienced the upheavals of Lilliputian volcanos. Spiny weeds and strawlike tufts grew in the cracks. I should call someone to spruce up the place, Ruth thought as she approached the house. She was sad that her mother no longer cared as much about appearances. She also felt guilty that she had not helped out more around the house. Perhaps she could call her own handyman to do cleanup and repairs.

As Ruth neared the steps to the upper unit, the downstairs tenant stepped out of her doorway, signaling that she wanted to speak to her. Francine was an anorexically thin woman in her thirties, who seemed to be wearing a size-eight skin over a size-two body. She often griped to Ruth about repairs needed for the building: The electricity kept shorting out. The smoke detectors were old and should be replaced. The back steps were uneven and could cause an accident—and a lawsuit.

"Never satisfy!" LuLing told Ruth.

Ruth knew not to take sides with the tenant. But she worried that there might really be a problem like a fire one day, and she dreaded the headlines "Slum Landlady Jailed, Ignored Deadly Hazards." So Ruth surreptitiously handled some of the more resolvable problems. When she bought Francine a new smoke detector, LuLing found out and became apoplectic. "You think she right, I wrong?" As had happened throughout Ruth's childhood, LuLing's fury escalated until she could barely speak, except to sputter the old threat: "Maybe I die soon!"

"You need to talk to your mom," Francine was now saying in a whiny voice. "She's been accusing me of not paying the rent. I *always* pay on time, the first of the month. I don't know what she's talking about, but she goes on and on, like a broken record."

Ruth had a sinking feeling. She did not want to hear this.

"I even showed her the canceled check. And she said, 'See, you still have the check!' It was weird, like she wasn't making any sense."

"I'll take care of it," Ruth said quietly.

"It's just that she's harassing me like a hundred times a day. It's making me nuts."

"I'll get it straightened out."

"I hope so, because I was just about to call the police to get a restraining order!"

Restraining order? Who's the nut here? "I'm sorry this happened," Ruth said, and remembered a book she helped write on mirroring a child's feelings. "You must be frustrated when it's clear you've done nothing wrong."

It worked. "Okay, then," Francine said, and backed into her doorway like a cuckoo in a Swiss clock.

Ruth used her own key to let herself into her mother's apartment. She heard LuLing call to her: "Why so late?"

Seated in her brown vinyl easy chair, LuLing looked like a petulant child on a throne. Ruth gave her a once-over to see if she could detect anything wrong, a twitch in her eye, a slight paralysis, perhaps, on one side of her face. Nothing, the same old mom. LuLing was wearing a purple cardigan with gold-tone buttons, her favorite, black slacks, and size-four black pumps with low heels. Her hair was smoothed back and gathered like Fia's and Dory's, only she had the ponytail wound into a netted bun, thickened with a hairpiece. Her hair was jet-black, except for the roots at the back, where she could not see that she had failed to apply enough dye. From a distance, she looked like a much younger woman, sixty instead of seventy-seven. Her skin was even-toned and smooth, no need for foundation or powder. You had to stand a foot away before you could see the fine etching of wrinkles on her cheeks. The deepest lines were at the corners of her mouth, which were often turned down, as they were now.

LuLing groused. "You say doctor visit one o'clock."

"I said the appointment was at four."

"No! One o'clock! You say be ready. So I get ready, you don't come!"

Ruth could feel the blood draining out of her head. She tried another tack. "Well, let me call the doctor and see if we can still get in at four." She went to the back, where her mother did her calligraphy and painting, to the room that had been her own long before. On her mother's drawing table lay a large sheet of watercolor paper. Her mother had started a poem-painting, then stopped in mid-character. The brush lay on the paper, its tip dried and stiff. LuLing was not careless. She treated her brushes with fanatical routine, washing them in spring water, not tap, so that chlorine would not damage them. Perhaps she had been in the middle of painting and heard the teakettle crying and bolted. Maybe the phone rang after that, one thing after another. But then Ruth looked closer. Her mother had tried to write the same character over and over again, each time stopping at the same stroke. What character? And why had she stopped in mid-flight?

When Ruth was growing up, her mother supplemented her income as a teacher's aide with side businesses, one of which was bilingual calligraphy, Chinese and English. She produced price signs for supermarkets and jewelry stores in Oakland and San Francisco, good-luck couplets for restaurant openings, banners for funeral wreaths, and announcements for births and weddings. Over the years, people had told Ruth that her mother's calligraphy was at an artist's level, first-rate classical. This was the piecework that earned her a reliable reputation, and Ruth had had a role in that success: she checked the spelling of the English words.

"It's 'grapefruit,' " eight-year-old Ruth once said, exasperated, "not 'grapefoot.' It's a fruit not a foot."

That night, LuLing started teaching her the mechanics of writing Chinese. Ruth knew this was punishment for what she had said earlier.

"Watch," LuLing ordered her in Chinese. She ground an inkstick onto an inkstone and used a medicine dropper to add salt water in

doses the size of tears. "Watch," she said, and selected a brush from
the dozens hanging with their tips down. Ruth's sleepy eyes tried to
follow her mother's hand as she swabbed the brush with ink, then
held it nearly perpendicular to the page, her wrist and elbow in mid-
air. Finally she began, flicking her wrist slightly so that her hand
waved and dipped like a moth over the gleam of white paper. Soon
the spidery images formed: "Half Off!" "Amazing Discounts!"
"Going Out of Business!"

"Writing Chinese characters," her mother told her, "is entirely different from writing English words. You think differently. You feel differently." And it was true: LuLing was different when she was writing
and painting. She was calm, organized, and decisive.

"Bao Bomu taught me how to write," LuLing said one evening.
"She taught me how to think. When you write, she said, you must
gather the free-flowing of your heart." To demonstrate, LuLing wrote
the character for "heart." "See? Each stroke has its own rhythm, its
balance, its proper place. Bao Bomu said everything in life should be
the same way."

"Who's Bao Bomu again?" Ruth asked.

"She took care of me when I was a girl. She loved me very much,
just like a mother. *Bao,* well, this means 'precious,' and together with
bomu, this means 'Precious Auntie.' " Oh, *that* Bao Bomu, the crazy
ghost. LuLing started to write a simple horizontal line. But the movements were not simple. She rested the tip of the brush on the paper, so
it was like a dancer *sur les pointes.* The tip bent slightly downward,
curtsied, and then, as if blown by capricious winds, swept to the
right, paused, turned a half-step to the left and rose. Ruth blew out a
sigh. Why even try? Her mother would just get upset that she could
not do it right.

Some nights LuLing found ways to help Ruth remember the
characters. "Each radical comes from an old picture from a long time
ago." She made a horizontal stroke and asked Ruth if she could see

what the picture was. Ruth squinted and shook her head. LuLing made the identical stroke. Then again and again, asking each time if Ruth knew what it was. Finally, her mother let out a snort, the compressed form of her disappointment and disgust.

"This line is like a beam of light. Look, can you see it or not?"

To Ruth, the line looked like a sparerib picked clean of meat.

LuLing went on: "Each character is a thought, a feeling, meanings, history, all mixed into one." She drew more lines—dots and dashes, downstrokes and upstrokes, bends and hooks. "Do you see this?" she said over and over, *tink-tink-tink*. "This line, and this and this—the shape of a heavenly temple." And when Ruth shrugged in response, LuLing added, "In the *old* style of temples," as if this word *old* would bump the Chinese gears of her daughter's mind into action. *Ping-ping!* Oh, I see.

Later LuLing had Ruth try her hand at the same character, the whole time stuffing Chinese logic into her resistant brain. "Hold your wrist this way, firm but still loose, like a young willow branch—ai-ya, not collapsed like a beggar lying on the road. . . . Draw the stroke with grace, like a bird landing on a branch, not an executioner chopping off a devil's head. The way you drew it—well, look, the whole thing is falling down. Do it like this . . . light first, then temple. See? Together, it means 'news from the gods.' See how this knowledge always comes from above? See how Chinese words make sense?"

With Chinese words, her mother did make sense, Ruth now reasoned to herself. Or did she?

She called the doctor and got the nurse. "This is Ruth Young, LuLing Young's daughter. We're coming to see Dr. Huey for a checkup at four, but I just wanted to mention a few things. . . ." She felt like a collaborator, a traitor and a spy.

When Ruth returned to the living room, she found her mother searching for her purse.

"We don't need any money," Ruth said. "And if we do, I can pay."

"No, no pay! Nobody pay!" LuLing cried. "Inside purse put my health card. I don't show card, doctor charge me extra. Everything suppose be free."

"I'm sure they have your records there. They won't need to see the card."

LuLing kept searching. Abruptly she straightened herself and said, "I know. Leave my purse at GaoLing house. Must be she forget tell me."

"What day did you go?"

"Three days go. Monday."

"Today's Monday."

"How can be Monday? I go three days go, not today!"

"You took BART?" Since the car accident, LuLing had been taking public transportation when Ruth wasn't able to act as chauffeur.

"Yes, and GaoLing late pick me up! I wait two hour. Fin'y she come. And then she accuse me, say, Why you come early, you suppose come here eleven. I tell her, No, I never say come eleven. Why I say coming eleven when I already know I coming nine o'clock? She pretend I crazy, make me so mad."

"Do you think you might have left it on the BART train?"

"Left what?"

"Your purse."

"Why you always take her side?"

"I'm not taking sides. . . ."

"Maybe she keep my purse, don't tell me. She always want my things. Jealous of me. Little-girl time, she want my *chipao* dress, want my melon fruit, want everybody attention."

The dramas her mother and Auntie had gone through over the

years resembled those off-Broadway plays in which two characters perform all the roles: best friends and worst enemies, archrivals and gleeful conspirators. They were only a year apart, seventy-seven and seventy-six, and that closeness seemed to have made them competitive with each other.

The two sisters came to America separately, and married a pair of brothers, sons of a grocer and his wife. LuLing's husband, Edwin Young, was in medical school, and as the elder, he was "destined" as LuLing put it, to be smarter and more successful. Most of the family's attention and privileges had been showered on him. Gao-Ling's husband, Edmund, the little brother, was in dental school. He was known as the lazy one, the careless boy who would always need a big brother to watch over him. But then big brother Edwin was killed in a hit-and-run car accident while leaving the UCSF library one night. Ruth had been two years old at the time. Her uncle Edmund went on to become the leader of the family, a well-respected dentist, and an even more savvy real estate investor in low-income rental units.

When the grocer and then his wife died, in the 1960s, most of the inheritance—money, the house, the store, gold and jade, family photos—went to Edmund, with only a small cash gift given to LuLing in consideration of her brief marriage to Edwin. "Only give me *this much*," LuLing often described, pinching her fingers as if holding a flea. "Just because you not a boy."

With the death money, along with her years of savings, LuLing bought a two-unit building on Cabrillo and Forty-seventh, where she and Ruth lived in the top flat. GaoLing and Edmund moved to Saratoga, a town of vast-lawned ranch-style homes and kidney-shaped pools. Occasionally they would offer LuLing furniture they were going to replace with something better. "Why I should take?" she would fume. "So they can pity for me? Feel so good for themself, give me things they don't want?"

Throughout the years, LuLing lamented in Chinese, "Ai-ya, if only your father had lived, he would be even more successful than your uncle. And still we wouldn't spend so carelessly like them!" She also noted what *should* have been Ruth's rightful property: Grandmother Young's jade ring, money for a college fund. It shouldn't have mattered that Ruth was a girl or that Edwin had died. That was old Chinese thinking! LuLing said this so often Ruth could not help fantasizing what her life might have been like had her father lived. She could have bought patent-leather shoes, rhinestone-covered barrettes, and baby roses. Sometimes she stared at a photo of her father and felt angry he was dead. Then she felt guilty and scared. She tried to convince herself that she deeply loved this father she could not even remember. She picked the flowerlike weeds that grew in the cracks of sidewalks and put them in front of his framed picture.

Ruth now watched as LuLing searched in the closet for her purse. She was still pointing out GaoLing's transgressions. "Later grown-up time, want my things too. Want your daddy marry her. Yes, you don't know this. Edwin not Edmund, because he oldest, more success. Every day smile for him, show off her teeth, like monkey." LuLing turned around and demonstrated. "But he not interest in her, only me. She so mad. Later she marry Edmund, and when you daddy die, she say, Ooooh, so lucky I not marry Edwin! So stupid she saying that. To my face! Don't consider me, only concerning herself. I say nothing. I never complaining. Do I ever complaining?"

Ruth joined in the search, sticking her hands under seat cushions.

LuLing straightened herself to all four feet, eleven inches of indignity. "And now you see! Why GaoLing *still* want my money? She crazy, you know. She always think I got more, hiding somewhere. That's why I think she take my purse."

The dining room table, which LuLing never used, was a raft of junk mail. Ruth pushed aside the Chinese-language newspapers and magazines. Her mother had always been sanitary, but never neat. She hated grease but didn't mind chaos. She kept junk mail and coupons, as if they were personal greeting cards.

"Here it is!" Ruth cried. What a relief. She pulled out a green pocketbook from underneath a mound of magazines. As LuLing checked that her money and credit cards were still inside, Ruth noticed what had obscured the purse in the first place: new issues of *Woodworking Today*, *Seventeen*, *Home Audio and Video*, *Runner's World*, *Cosmopolitan*, *Dog Fancy*, *Ski*, *Country Living*—magazines her mother would never read in a million years.

"Why do you have all these?"

LuLing smiled shyly. "First I thinking, Get money, then tell you. Now you ask, so now I show you." She went to the kitchen drawer where she kept years of expired coupons and pulled out an oversized envelope.

"News from the gods," LuLing murmured. "I won ten million dollar! Open and see."

Sure enough, inside were a sweepstakes promotion coupon that resembled a check, and a sheet of peel-off miniature magazine covers. Half the covers were missing. LuLing must have ordered three dozen magazines. Ruth could picture the mail carrier dragging over a sackful of them every day, spilling them onto the driveway, her mother's hopes and logic jumbled into the same pile.

"You surprise?" LuLing wore a look of absolute joy.

"You should tell the doctor your good news."

LuLing beamed, then added, "I win all for you."

Ruth felt a twinge in her chest. It quickly grew into an ache. She wanted to embrace her mother, shield her, and at the same time wanted her mother to cradle her, to assure her that she was okay, that she had not had a stroke or worse. That was how her mother had always been, difficult, oppressive, and odd. And in exactly that way, LuLing had loved her. Ruth knew that, felt it. No one could have loved her more. Better perhaps, but not more.

"Thanks, Ma. It's wonderful. We'll talk about it later, what to do with the money. But now we have to go. The doctor said we could still come at four, and we shouldn't be late."

LuLing turned crabby again. "You fault we late."

Ruth had to remind her to take her newly found purse, then her coat, finally her keys. She felt ten years old again, translating for her mother how the world worked, explaining the rules, the restrictions, the time limits on money-back guarantees. Back then she had been resentful. Now she was terrified.

THREE

In the hospital waiting room, Ruth saw that all the patients, except one pale balding man, were Asian. She read the blackboard listing of doctors' names: Fong, Wong, Wang, Tang, Chin, Pon, Kwak, Koo. The receptionist looked Chinese; so did the nurses.

In the sixties, mused Ruth, people railed against race-differentiated services as ghettoization. Now they demanded them as culturally sensitive. Then again, San Francisco was about a third Asian, so Chinese-targeted medicine could also be a marketing strategy. The balding man was glancing about, as if seeking an escape route. Did he have a last name like Young that had been mistakenly identified as Chinese by a race-blind computer? Did he also get calls from Chinese-speaking telemarketers trying to sign him up for long-distance calling plans for Hong Kong and Taiwan? Ruth knew what it meant to feel like an outsider, because she had often been one as a child. Moving to a new home eight times made her aware of how she didn't fit in.

"Fia start six grade?" LuLing was now asking.

"You're thinking of Dory," Ruth answered. Dory had been held back a year because of attention deficit disorder. She now received special tutoring.

"How can be Dory?"

"Fia's the older one, she's going into tenth. Dory's thirteen. She'll be in seventh."

"I know who who!" LuLing grumbled. She counted, flipping her fingers down as she listed: "Dory, Fia, oldest one Fu-Fu, seventeen." Ruth used to joke that Fu-Fu, her feral cat, born with a nasty disposition, was the grandchild LuLing never had. "How Fu-Fu do?" LuLing asked.

Hadn't she told her mother Fu-Fu had died? She must have. Or Art had. Everyone knew that Ruth had been depressed for weeks after it happened.

"Fu-Fu's dead," she reminded her mother.

"Ai-ya!" LuLing's face twisted with agony. "How this can be! What happen?"

"I told you—"

"No, you never!"

"Oh . . . Well, a few months ago, she went over the fence. A dog chased her. She couldn't climb back up fast enough."

"Why you have dog?"

"It was a neighbor's dog."

"Then why you let neighbor's dog come your backyard? Now see what happen! Ai-ya, die no reason!"

Her mother was speaking far too loudly. People were looking up from their knitting and reading, even the balding man. Ruth was pained. That cat had been her baby. She had held her the day she was born, a tiny wild ball of fur, found in Wendy's garage on a rainy day. Ruth had also held her as the vet gave the lethal shot to end her misery. Thinking about this nearly put Ruth over the edge, and she did not want to burst into tears in a waiting room full of strangers.

At that moment, luckily, the receptionist called out, "LuLing Young!" As Ruth helped her mother gather her purse and coat, she saw the balding man leap up and walk quickly toward an elderly

Chinese woman. "Hey, Mom," Ruth heard him say. "How'd everything check out? Ready to go home?" The woman gruffly handed him a prescription note. He must be her son-in-law, Ruth surmised. Would Art ever take her mother to the doctor's? She doubted it. How about in the case of an emergency, a heart attack, a stroke?

The nurse spoke to LuLing in Cantonese and she answered in Mandarin. They settled on accented English as their common ground. LuLing quietly submitted to the preliminaries. Step on the scale. Eighty-five pounds. Blood pressure. One hundred over seventy. Roll up your sleeve and make a fist. LuLing did not flinch. She had taught Ruth to do the same, to look straight at the needle and not cry out. In the examination room, Ruth turned away as her mother slipped out of her cotton camisole and stood in her waist-high flowered panties.

LuLing put on a paper gown, climbed onto the examining table, and dangled her feet. She looked childlike and breakable. Ruth sank into a nearby chair. When the doctor arrived, they both sat up straight. LuLing had always had great respect for doctors.

"Mrs. Young!" the doctor greeted her jovially. "I'm Dr. Huey." He glanced at Ruth.

"I'm her daughter. I called your office earlier."

He nodded knowingly. Dr. Huey was a pleasant-looking man, younger than Ruth. He started asking LuLing questions in Cantonese, and her mother pretended to understand, until Ruth explained, "She speaks Mandarin, not Cantonese."

The doctor looked at her mother. *"Guoyu?"*

LuLing nodded, and Dr. Huey shrugged apologetically. "My Mandarin is pretty terrible. How's your English?"

"Good. No problem."

At the end of the examination, Dr. Huey smiled and announced, "Well, you are one very strong lady. Heart and lungs are great.

Blood pressure excellent. Especially for someone your age. Let's see, what year were you born?" He scanned the chart, then looked up at LuLing. "Can you tell me?"

"Year?" LuLing's eyes darted upward as if the answer were on the ceiling. "This not so easy say."

"I want the truth, now," the doctor joked. "Not what you tell your friends."

"Truth is 1916," LuLing said.

Ruth interrupted. "What she means is—" and she was about to say 1921, but the doctor put up his hand to stop her from speaking. He glanced at the medical chart again, then said to LuLing, "So that makes you . . . how old?"

"Eighty-two this month!" she said.

Ruth bit her lip and looked at the doctor.

"Eighty-two." He wrote this down. "So tell me, were you born in China? Yes? What city?"

"Ah, this also not so easy say," LuLing began shyly. "Not really city, more like little place we call so many different name. Forty-six kilometer from bridge to Peking."

"Ah, Beijing," the doctor said. "I went there on a tour a couple of years ago. My wife and I saw the Forbidden City."

LuLing warmed up. "In those day, so many thing forbidden, can't see. Now everyone pay money see forbidden thing. You say this forbidden that forbidden, charge extra."

Ruth was about to burst. Her mother must sound garbled to Dr. Huey. She had had concerns about her, but she didn't want her concerns to be fully justified. Her worries were supposed to preclude any real problem. They always had.

"Did you go to school there as well?" Dr. Huey asked.

LuLing nodded. "Also my nursemaid teach me many things. Painting, reading, writing—"

"Very good. I was wondering if you could do a little math for me. I want you to count down from a hundred, subtracting seven each time."

LuLing went blank.

"Start at a hundred."

"Hundred!" LuLing said confidently, then nothing more.

Dr. Huey waited, and finally said, "Now count down by seven."

LuLing hesitated. "Ninety-two, ah, ninety-three. Ninety-three!"

This is not fair, Ruth wanted to shout. She has to convert the numbers into Chinese to do the calculations, then remember that, and put the answer back into English. Ruth's mind raced ahead. She wished she could lay out the answers for her mother telephatically. Eighty-six! Seventy-nine!

"Eighty . . . Eighty . . ." LuLing was stuck.

"Take your time, Mrs. Young."

"Eighty," she said at last. "After that, eighty-seven."

"Fine," Dr. Huey declared, with no change of expression. "Now I want you to name the last five presidents in reverse order."

Ruth wanted to protest: Even I can't do that!

LuLing's eyebrows bunched in thought. "Clinton," she said after a pause. "Last five year still Clinton." Her mother had not even understood the question! Of course she hadn't. She had always depended on Ruth to tell her what people meant, to give her what they said from another angle. "Reverse order" means "go backward," she would have told LuLing. If Dr. Huey could ask that same question in fluent Mandarin, it would be no problem for LuLing to give the right answer. "This president, that president," her mother would have said without hesitation, "no difference, all liar. No tax before election, more tax after. No crime before, more crime after. And always don't cut welfare. I come this country, I don't get welfare. What so fair? No fair. Only make people lazy to work!"

More ridiculous questions followed.

"Do you know today's date?"

"Monday." Date and day always sound the same to her.

"What was the date five months ago?"

"Still Monday." When you stop to think about it, she's right.

"How many grandchildren do you have?"

"Don't now. She not married yet." He doesn't see that she's joking!

LuLing was like the losing contestant on *Jeopardy!* Total for LuLing Young: minus five hundred points. And now for our final *Jeopardy!* round . . .

"How old is your daughter?"

LuLing hesitated. "Forty, maybe forty-one." To her mother, she was always younger than she really was.

"What year was she born?"

"Same as me. Dragon year." She looked at Ruth for confirmation. Her mother was a Rooster.

"What month?" Dr. Huey asked.

"What month?" LuLing asked Ruth. Ruth shrugged helplessly. "She don't know."

"What year is it now?"

"Nineteen ninety-eight!" She looked at the doctor as if he were an idiot not to know that. Ruth was relieved that her mother had answered one question right.

"Mrs. Young, could you wait here while your daughter and I go outside to schedule another appointment?"

"Sure-sure. I not go anywhere."

As Dr. Huey turned for the door, he stopped. "And thank you for answering all the questions. I'm sure you must have felt like you were on the witness stand."

"Like O.J."

Dr. Huey laughed. "I guess everyone watched that trial on TV."

LuLing shook her head. "Oh no, not just watch TV, I there when it happen. He kill wife and that friend, bring her glasses. Everything I see."

Ruth's heart started to thump. "You saw a documentary," she said for Dr. Huey's benefit, "a reenactment of what might have happened, and it was *like* watching the real thing. Is that what you're saying?"

LuLing waved to dismiss this simple answer. "Maybe *you* see document. *I* see real thing." She demonstrated with motions. "He grab her like this, cut neck here—very deep, so much blood. Awful."

"So you were in Los Angeles that day?" Dr. Huey asked.

LuLing nodded.

Ruth was flailing for logic. "I don't remember you *ever* going to L.A."

"How I go, don't know. But I there. This true! I follow that man, oh he sneaky. O.J. hide in bush. Later, I go his house too. Watch him take glove, stick in garden, go back inside change clothes—" LuLing caught herself, embarrassed. "Well, he change clothes, course I don't look, turn my eyes. Later he run to airport, almost late, jump on plane. I see whole thing."

"You saw this and didn't tell anyone?"

"I scared!"

"The murder must have been an awful thing for you to see," Dr. Huey said.

LuLing nodded bravely.

"Thank you for sharing that. Now, if you'll just wait here a few minutes, your daughter and I are going to step into another room and schedule your next appointment."

"No hurry."

Ruth followed the doctor into another room. "How long have you noticed this kind of confusion?" Dr. Huey asked right away.

Ruth sighed. "It's been a little worse in the last six months, maybe

longer than that. But today she seems worse than usual. Except for
the last thing she said, she hasn't been that weird or forgetful. It's
more like mix-ups, and most of it is due to her not speaking English
that well, as you may have noticed. The story about O.J. Simpson—
you know, that may be another language problem. She's never been
good at expressing herself—"

"It sounded pretty clear to me that she thought she was there,"
Dr. Huey said gently.

Ruth looked away.

"You mentioned to the nurse that she had a car accident. Was
there a head injury?"

"She did bump her head on the steering wheel." Ruth was suddenly hopeful that this was the missing piece to the puzzle.

"Does her personality seem to be changing? Is she depressed,
more argumentative?"

Ruth tried to guess what an affirmative response might indicate.
"My mother's always gotten into arguments, all her life. She has a
terrible temper. And as long as I've known her, she's been depressed.
Her husband, my father, was killed forty-four years ago. Hit-and-
run. She never got over it. Maybe the depression is becoming worse,
but I'm so used to it I'd be the last one to notice. As for her confusion, I was wondering if it was a concussion from the car accident or
if she might have had a mini-stroke." Ruth tried to remember the
correct medical term. "You know, a TIA."

"So far I don't see any evidence of that. Her motor movements
are good, reflexes are fine. Blood pressure is excellent. But we'll
want to run a few more tests, also make sure she's not diabetic or
anemic, for instance."

"Those could cause problems like this?"

"They could, as could Alzheimer's and other forms of dementia."

Ruth felt her stomach had been punched. Her mother wasn't *that* bad off. He was talking about a horrible terminal illness. Thank God she had not told the doctor about the other things she had tabulated: the argument her mother had had with Francine over the rent; the ten-million-dollar check from the magazine sweepstakes; her forgetting that Fu-Fu had died. "So it could be depression," Ruth said.

"We haven't ruled out anything yet."

"Well, if it is, you'll have to tell her the antidepressants are ginseng or *po chai* pills."

Dr. Huey laughed. "Resistance to Western medication is common among our elderly patients here. And as soon as they feel better, they stop taking it to save money." He handed her a form. "Give this to Lorraine at the computer station around the corner. Let's schedule your mother to see the folks in Psychiatry and Neurology, then have her come back to see me again in a month."

"Around the Full Moon Festival."

Dr. Huey looked up. "Is that when it is? I can never keep track."

"I only know because I'm hosting this year's family reunion dinner."

That evening, as Ruth steamed the sea bass, she told Art in an offhanded way, "I took my mom to see the doctor. She may have depression."

And Art said, "So what else is new?"

At dinner, LuLing sat next to Ruth. "Too salty," she remarked in Chinese, poking at her portion of fish. And then she added: "Tell those girls to finish their fish. Don't let them waste food."

"Fia, Dory, why aren't you eating?" Ruth said.

"I'm full," Dory answered. "We stopped at Burger King in the Presidio and ate a bunch of fries before we came home."

"You shouldn't let them eat those things!" LuLing scolded, continuing in Mandarin. "Tell them you don't allow this anymore."

"Girls, I wish you wouldn't ruin your appetites with junk food."

·· "And I wish you two would stop talking like spies in Chinese," Fia said. "It's like really rude." ·

LuLing glared at Ruth, and Ruth glanced at Art, but he was looking down at his plate. "Waipo speaks Chinese," Ruth said, "because that's the language she's used to." Ruth had told them to call LuLing "Waipo," the Chinese honorific for "Grandmother," and at least they did that, but then again, they thought it was just a nickname.

"She can speak English too," Dory said.

"Tst!" LuLing grumbled to Ruth. "Why doesn't their father scold them? He should tell them to listen to you. Why doesn't he have more concern for you? No wonder he never married you. No respect for you. Say something to him. Why don't you tell him to be nicer to you? . . ."

Ruth wished she could go back to being mute. She wanted to shout for her mother to stop complaining about things she could not change. Yet she also wanted to defend her to the girls, especially now that something was wrong with her. LuLing acted eternally strong, but she was also fragile. Why couldn't Fia and Dory understand that and act a little kinder?

Ruth remembered how she felt when she was their age. She too had resented LuLing's speaking Chinese in front of others, knowing they couldn't understand her covert remarks. "Look how fat that lady is," LuLing might say. Or, "Luyi, go ask that man to give us a better price." If Ruth obeyed, she was mortified. And if she didn't, as she now recalled, even more dire consequences followed.

By using Chinese words, LuLing could put all kinds of wisdom in Ruth's mind. She could warn her away from danger, disease, and death.

"Don't play with her, too many germs," LuLing told six-year-old

Ruth one day, nodding toward the girl from across the street. The girl's name was Teresa, and she had two front teeth missing, a scab on one knee, and a dress smeared with handprints. "I saw her pick up old candy off the sidewalk and eat it. And look at her nose, sickness pouring out all over the place."

Ruth liked Teresa. She laughed a lot and always kept in her pockets things she had found: balls of foil, broken marbles, flower heads. Ruth had just started at another new school, and Teresa was the only girl who played with her. Neither of them was very popular.

"Did you hear me?" LuLing said.

"Yes," Ruth answered.

The next day, Ruth was playing in the schoolyard. Her mother was on the other side of the yard, monitoring other kids. Ruth climbed up the slide, eager to tumble down the silver curl into cool, dark sand. She had done this with Teresa a dozen times without her mother's seeing.

But then a familiar voice, loud and shrill, rang across the playground: "No! Luyi, stop! What are you doing? You want to break your body in half?"

Ruth stood at the top of the slide, frozen with shame. Her mother was the busybody watcher of kindergartners, whereas Ruth was in the first grade! Some of the other first-graders were laughing down below. "Is that your mother?" they shouted. "What's that gobbledy-gook-gook she's saying?"

"She's not my mother!" Ruth shouted back. "I don't know who she is!" Her mother's eyes locked on hers. Although she was clear across the playground, she heard everything, saw everything. She had magic eyes on the back of her head.

You can't stop me, Ruth thought fiercely. She threw herself down the slide, head first, arms straight out—the position that only the bravest and wildest boys would take—fast, fast, fast into the sand.

And then she crashed face first, with such force that she bit her lip, bumped her nose, bent her glasses, and broke her arm. She lay still. The world was burning, shot full of red lightning.

"Ruthie's dead!" a boy yelled. Girls began screaming.

I'm not dead, Ruth tried to cry out, but it was like speaking in a dream. Nothing came from her lips the way she wanted. Or was she truly dead? Was that how it felt, this oozing from her nose, the pain in her head and arm, the way she moved, as slowly and heavily as an elephant in water? Soon she felt familiar hands brushing over her head and neck. Her mother was lifting her, murmuring tenderly, "Ai-ya, how could you be so foolish? Look at you."

Blood ran from Ruth's nose and dripped onto the front of her white blouse, staining the broad lace-trimmed collar. She lay limply in her mother's lap, looking up at Teresa and the faces of the other children. She saw their fright, but also their awe. If she could have moved, she would have smiled. At last they were paying attention to her, the new girl at school. She then saw her mother's face, the tears streaming down her cheeks, falling on her own face like wet kisses. Her mother wasn't angry, she was worried, full of love. And in her amazement, Ruth forgot her pain.

Later she lay on a cot in the nurse's office. Her nosebleed was stanched with gauze, her punctured lip was cleansed. A cold washcloth covered her forehead, and her arm was elevated on a bag of ice.

"She may have fractured her arm," the nurse told LuLing. "And her nerves might be torn. There's a great deal of swelling, but she's not complaining of too much pain."

"She good, never complain."

"You need to take her to the doctor. Do you understand? Go see a doctor."

"Okay, okay, go see doctor."

As LuLing led her out, a teacher said, "Look how brave she is! She's not even crying." Two popular girls gave Ruth big smiles of admiration. They waved. Teresa was also there, and Ruth gave her a quick, secret smile.

In the car on the way to the doctor's office, Ruth noticed that her mother was strangely quiet. She kept looking at Ruth, who expected harsh words to start any moment: I told you that big slide was dangerous. Why didn't you listen to me? You could have cracked open your brain like a watermelon! Now I have to work overtime to pay for this. Ruth waited, but her mother only asked every now and then if she was hurting. Each time Ruth shook her head.

As the doctor examined Ruth's arm, LuLing sucked air between her teeth in agony and moaned: "*Ai-ya!* Careful, careful, careful. She hurt real bad." When the cast was put on, LuLing said proudly, "Teacher, children, all very impress. Lootie no cry, no complain, nothing, just quiet."

By the time they arrived home, the excitement had worn off, and Ruth felt a throbbing pain in her arm and head. She tried not to cry. LuLing put her in her vinyl La-Z-Boy and made her as comfortable as possible. "You want me to cook you rice porridge? Eat. That will help you get well. How about spicy turnips? You want some now, while I cook dinner?"

The less Ruth said, the more her mother tried to guess what she might want. As she lay in the recliner, she heard LuLing talking to Auntie Gal on the phone.

"She was almost killed! Scared me to death. Really! I'm not exaggerating. She was nearly yanked from this life and on her way to the yellow springs. . . . I just about cracked my own teeth to see how much pain she was in. . . . No, no tears, she must have inherited the strength of her grandmother. Well, she's eating a little bit now. She can't talk, and I thought at first she bit off her tongue, but I think it's only the fright. Come over to visit? Fine, fine, but tell your kids to be careful. I don't want her arm to fall off."

They came bearing gifts. Auntie Gal brought a bottle of *eau de toilette*. Uncle Edmund gave Ruth a new toothbrush and matching plastic cup. Her cousins handed her coloring books, crayons, and a stuffed dog. LuLing had pushed the television set close to the La-Z-Boy, since Ruth had a hard time seeing without her glasses.

"Does it hurt?" her younger cousin, Sally, asked.

Ruth shrugged, though her arm was now aching.

"Man oh man, I wish I had a cast," Billy said. He was the same age as Ruth. "Daddy, can I have one too?"

"Don't say such bad-luck things!" Auntie Gal warned.

When Billy tried to change the television channel, Uncle Edmund sternly ordered him to put it back to the program Ruth had been watching. She had never heard her uncle be strict with her cousins. Billy was a spoiled brat.

"Why aren't you talking?" Sally asked. "Did you break your mouth too?"

"Yeah," Billy said. "Did the fall make you stupid or something?"

"Billy, stop teasing," Auntie Gal said. "She's resting. She has too much pain to talk."

Ruth wondered whether this was true. She thought about making a little sound so small no one would even hear. But if she did, then all the good things that were happening might disappear. They would decide she was fine, and everything would go back to normal. Her mother would start scolding her for being careless and disobedient.

For two days after the fall, Ruth was helpless; her mother had to feed, dress, and bathe her. LuLing would tell her what to do: "Open your mouth. Eat a little more. Put your arm in here. Try to keep your head still while I brush your hair." It was comforting to be a baby again, well loved, blameless.

When she returned to school, Ruth found a big streamer of

butcher paper hanging at the front of the classroom. "Welcome Back, Ruth!" it said. Miss Sondegard, the teacher, announced that every single boy and girl had helped make it. She led the classroom in clapping for Ruth's bravery. Ruth smiled shyly. Her heart was about to burst. She had never been as proud and happy. She wished she had broken her arm a long time before.

During lunch, girls vied with one another to present her with imaginary trinkets and serve as her maiden-in-waiting. She was invited to step into the "secret castle," a rock-bordered area near a tree at the edge of the sandbox. Only the most popular girls could be princesses. The princesses now took turns drawing on Ruth's cast. One of them gingerly asked, "Is it still broken?" Ruth nodded, and another girl whispered loudly: "Let's bring her magic potions." The princesses scampered off in search of bottle caps, broken glass, and fairy-sized clover.

At the end of the day, Ruth's mother went to her classroom to pick her up. Miss Sondegard took LuLing aside, and Ruth had to act as though she were not listening.

"I think she's a bit tired, which is natural for the first day back. But I'm a little concerned that she's so quiet. She didn't say a word all day, not even ouch."

"She never complain," LuLing agreed.

"It may not be a problem, but we'll need to watch if this continues."

"No problem," LuLing assured her. "She no problem."

"You must encourage her to talk, Mrs. Young. I don't want this to turn into a problem."

"No problem!" her mother reiterated.

"Make her say 'hamburger' before letting her eat a hamburger. Make her say 'cookie' before she gets a cookie."

That night LuLing took the teacher's advice literally: she served hamburger, which she had never done. LuLing did not cook or eat beef of any kind. It disgusted her, reminded her of scarred flesh. Yet

now, for her daughter's sake, she put an unadorned patty in front of
Ruth, who was thrilled to see her mother had actually made American food for once.

"Hambugga? You say 'hambugga,' then eat."

Ruth was tempted to speak, but she was afraid to break the spell.
One word and all the good things in her life would vanish. She shook
her head. LuLing encouraged her until the hamburger's rivulets of
fat had congealed into ugly white pools. She put the patty in the
fridge, then served Ruth a bowl of steaming rice porridge, which she
said was better for her health anyway.

After dinner, LuLing cleared the dining table and started to work.
She laid out ink, brushes, and a roll of paper. With quick and perfect
strokes, she wrote large Chinese characters: "Going Out of Business. Last few days! No offer refused!" She set the banner aside to
dry, then cut a new length of paper.

Ruth, who was watching television, noticed after a while that her
mother was staring at her. "Why you not do study?" LuLing asked.
She had made Ruth practice reading and writing since kindergarten,
to help her be "one jump ahead."

Ruth held up her broken right arm in its cast.

"Come sit here," her mother said in Chinese.

Ruth slowly stood up. Uh-oh. Her mother was back to her old ways.

"Now hold this." LuLing placed a brush in Ruth's left hand.
"Write your name." Her first attempts were clumsy, the R almost un-
recognizable, the hump of the h veering off the paper like an out-of-
control bicycle. She giggled.

"Hold the brush straight up," her mother instructed, "not at a
slant. Use a light touch, like this."

The next results were better, but they had taken up a whole
length of paper.

"Now try to write smaller." But the letters looked like blotches
made by an ink-soaked fly twirling on its back. When it was finally

time for bed, the practice session had consumed nearly twenty sheets of paper, both front and back. This was a sign of success as well as extravagance. LuLing never wasted anything. She gathered the used sheets, stacked them, and set them in a corner of the room. Ruth knew she would use them later, as practice sheets for her own calligraphy, as blotters for spills, as bundled-up hot pads for pans.

The following evening, after dinner, LuLing presented Ruth with a large tea tray filled with smooth wet sand gathered from the playground at school. "Here," she said, "you practice, use this." She held a chopstick in her left hand, then scratched the word "study" on the miniature beach. When she finished, she swept the sand clean and smooth with the long end of the chopstick. Ruth followed suit and found that it was easier to write this way, also fun. The sand-and-chopstick method did not require the delicate, light-handed technique of the brush. She could apply a force that steadied her. She wrote her name. Neat! It was like playing with the Etch-A-Sketch that her cousin Billy received last Christmas.

LuLing went to the refrigerator and brought out the cold beef patty. "Tomorrow what you want eat?"

And Ruth scratched back: B-U-R-G-R.

LuLing laughed. "Hah! So now you can talk back this way!"

The next day, LuLing brought the tea tray to school and filled it with sand from the same part of the schoolyard where Ruth had broken her arm. Miss Sondegard agreed to let Ruth answer questions this way. And when Ruth raised her hand during an arithmetic drill and scrawled "7," all the other kids jumped out of their chairs to look. Soon they were clamoring that they too wanted to do sand-writing. At recess, Ruth was very popular. She heard them fussing over her. "Let me try!" "Me, me! She said I could!" "You gotta use your left hand, or it's cheating!" "Ruth, you show Tommy how to do it. He's so dumb."

They returned the chopstick to Ruth. And Ruth wrote quickly

and easily the answers to their questions: Does your arm hurt? *A little.* Can I touch your cast? *Yes.* Does Ricky love Betsy? *Yes.* Will I
get a new bike for my birthday? *Yes.*

They treated her as though she were Helen Keller, a genius who
didn't let injury keep her from showing how smart she was. Like
Helen Keller, she simply had to work harder, and perhaps this was
what made her smarter, the effort and others' admiring that. Even at
home, her mother would ask her, "What you think?" as if Ruth
would know, just because she had to write the answers to her questions in sand.

"How does the bean curd dish taste?" LuLing asked one night.

And Ruth etched: *Salty.* She had never said anything bad about
her mother's cooking before, but that was what her mother always
said to criticize her own food.

"I thought so too," her mother answered.

This was amazing! Soon her mother was asking her opinion on all
kinds of matters.

"We go shop dinner now or go later?" *Later.*

"What about stock market? I invest, you think I get lucky?"
Lucky.

"You like this dress?" *No, ugly.* Ruth had never experienced such
power with words.

Her mother frowned, then murmured in Mandarin. "Your father
loved this old dress, and now I can never throw it away." She became
misty-eyed. She sighed, then said in English: "You think you daddy
miss me?"

Ruth wrote *Yes* right away. Her mother beamed. And then Ruth
had an idea. She had always wanted a little dog. Now was the time to
ask for one. She scratched in the sand: *Doggie.*

Her mother gasped. She stared at the words and shook her head
in disbelief. Oh well, Ruth thought, that was one wish she was not
going to get. But then her mother began to whimper, "Doggie, dog-

gie," in Chinese. She jumped up and her chest heaved. "Precious Auntie," LuLing cried, "you've come back. This is your Doggie. Do you forgive me?"

Ruth put down the chopstick.

LuLing was now sobbing. "Precious Auntie, oh Precious Auntie! I wish you never died! It was all my fault. If I could change fate, I would rather kill myself than suffer without you. . . ."

Oh, no. Ruth knew what this was. Her mother sometimes talked about this Precious Auntie ghost who lived in the air, a lady who had not behaved and who wound up living at the End of the World. That was where all bad people went: a bottomless pit where no one would ever find them, and there they would be stuck, wandering with their hair hanging to their toes, wet and bloody.

"Please let me know you are not mad at me," her mother went on. "Give me a sign. I have tried to tell you how sorry I am, but I don't know if you've heard. Can you hear me? When did you come to America?"

Ruth sat still, unable to move. She wanted to go back to talking about food and clothes.

Her mother put the chopstick in Ruth's hand. "Here, do this. Close your eyes, turn your face to heaven, and speak to her. Wait for her answer, then write it down. Hurry, close your eyes."

Ruth squeezed her eyes shut. She saw the lady with hair to her toes.

She heard her mother speak again in polite Chinese: "Precious Auntie, I did not mean what I said before you died. And after you died, I tried to find your body."

Ruth's eyes flew open. In her imagination, the long-haired ghost was walking in circles.

"I went down into the ravine. I looked and looked. Oh, I was crazy with grief. If only I had found you, I would have taken your bones to the cave and given you a proper burial."

Ruth felt something touch her shoulder, and she jumped. "Ask

her if she understood everything I just said," LuLing ordered. "Ask
her if my luck has changed. Is the curse over? Are we safe? Write
down her answer."

What curse? Ruth now stared at the sand, half believing the dead
woman's face would appear in a pool of blood. What answer did her
mother want? Did *Yes* mean the curse was gone? Or that it was still
there? She put the chopstick in the sand, and not knowing what to
write, she drew a line and another below that. She drew two more
lines and made a square.

"Mouth!" her mother cried, tracing over the square. "That's the
character for 'mouth'!" She stared at Ruth. "You wrote that and you
don't even know how to write Chinese! Did you feel Precious Auntie guiding your hand? What did it feel like? Tell me."

Ruth shook her head. What was happening? She wanted to cry
but didn't dare. She wasn't supposed to be able to make a sound.

"Precious Auntie, thank you for helping my daughter. Forgive
me that she speaks only English. It must be hard for you to communicate through her this way. But now I know that you can hear me.
And you know what I'm saying, that I wish I could take your bones
to the Mouth of the Mountain, to the Monkey's Jaw. I've never forgotten. As soon as I can go to China, I will finish my duty. Thank
you for reminding me."

Ruth wondered what she had written. How could a square mean
all that? Was there really a ghost in the room? What was in her hand
and the chopstick? Why was her hand shaking?

"Since I may not be able to go back to China for a long time,"
LuLing continued, "I hope you will still forgive me. Please know
that my life has been miserable ever since you left me. That is why I
ask you to take my life, but to spare my daughter if the curse cannot
be changed. I know her recent accident was a warning."

Ruth dropped the chopstick. The lady with bloody hair was try-

ing to kill her! So it was true, that day at the playground, she almost
died. She had thought so, and it was true.

LuLing retrieved the chopstick and tried to put it in Ruth's hand.
But Ruth balled her fist. She pushed the sand tray away. Her mother
pushed it back and kept babbling nonsense: "I'm so happy you've finally found me. I've been waiting for so many years. Now we can
talk to each other. Every day you can guide me. Every day you can
tell me how to conduct my life in the way I should."

LuLing turned to Ruth. "Ask her to come every day." Ruth
shook her head. She tried to slide off her chair. "Ask," LuLing insisted, and tapped the table in front of the tray. And then Ruth finally
found her voice.

"No," she said out loud. "I can't."

"Wah! Now you can talk again." Her mother had switched to English. "Precious Auntie cure you?"

Ruth nodded.

"That mean curse gone?"

"Yes, but she says she has to go back now. And she said I need
to rest."

"She forgive me? She——"

"She said everything will be all right. *Everything.* All right?
You're not supposed to worry anymore."

Her mother sobbed with relief.

As Ruth drove her mother home after dinner, she marveled at the
worries she had had at such an early age. But that was nothing com-
pared with what most children had to go through these days. An unhappy mother? That was a piece of cake next to guns and gangs and
sexually transmitted diseases, not to mention the things parents had
to be concerned about: pedophiles on the Web, designer drugs like

ecstasy, school shootings, anorexia, bulimia, self-mutilation, the ozone
layer, superbacteria. Ruth counted these automatically on her hand,
and this reminded her she had one more task to do before the end
of the day: call Miriam about letting the girls come to the reunion
dinner.

She glanced at her watch. It was almost nine, an iffy time to telephone people who were not close friends. True, she and Miriam were
bound by the closest of reasons, the girls and their father. But they
treated each other with the politeness of strangers. She often ran into
Miriam at drop-off and pick-up points for the girls, at school athletic
events, and once she'd seen her in the emergency room, where Ruth
had taken Dory when she broke her ankle. She and Miriam made
small talk about recent illnesses, bad weather, and traffic jams. If it
weren't for the circumstances, they might have enjoyed each other's
company. Miriam was clever, funny, and opinionated, and Ruth liked
these qualities. But it bothered Ruth when Miriam made passing remarks about intimacies she had shared with Art when they were
married: the funny time they had on a trip to Italy, a mole on his back
that had to be checked for melanoma, his love of massage. For Art's
birthday the year before, Miriam had given him a certificate for two
sessions with her favorite massage therapist, a gift Ruth thought in-
appropriately personal. "Do you still get that mole checked every
year?" Miriam asked Art on another occasion, and Ruth pretended
not to hear, all the while imagining what they had been like together
when they were younger and in love, and she still cared deeply
enough to notice the slightest change in the size of a mole. She pictured them lazing about in a Tuscan villa with a bedroom window
that overlooked rolling hills of orchards, giggling and naming moles
on each other's naked backs as if they were constellations. She could
see it: the two of them massaging olive oil into their thighs with
long-reaching strokes. Art once tried that on her, and Ruth figured

he must have learned the maneuver from *someone*. Whenever he tried to massage her thighs, though, it made her tense. With massage, she just couldn't relax. She felt she was being tickled, pushed out of control, then felt claustrophobic, panicky enough to want to leap up and run.

She never told Art about the panic; she said only that with her, massage was a waste of time and money. And although she was curious about Art's sex life with Miriam and other women, she never asked what he had done in bed with his former lovers. And he did not ask about hers. It shocked her that Wendy badgered Joe to give her explicit details about his past escapades in beds and on beaches, as well as tell her his precise feelings when he first slept with her. "And he tells you whatever you ask?" Ruth said.

"He states his name, birthdate, and Social Security number. And then I beat him up until he tells me."

"Then you're happy?"

"I'm pissed!"

"So why do you ask?"

"It's like part of me thinks everything about him is mine, his feelings, his fantasies. I know that's not right, but emotionally that's how I feel. His past is my past, it belongs to me. Shit, if I could find his childhood toy box I'd want to look inside that and say, 'Mine.' I'd want to see what girlie magazines he hid under the mattress and pulled out to masturbate to."

Ruth laughed out loud when Wendy said that, but inside she was uncomfortable. Did most women ask men those kinds of questions? Had Miriam asked Art things like these? Did more of Art's past belong to Miriam than it did to her?

Her mother's voice startled her. "So how Fu-Fu do?"

Not again. Ruth took a deep breath. "Fu-Fu's fine," she said this time.

"Really?" LuLing said. "That cat old. You lucky she not dead yet."

Ruth was so surprised she snorted in laughter. This was like the torment of being tickled. She couldn't stand it, but she could not stop her reflex to laugh out loud. Tears stung her eyes and she was glad for the darkness of the car.

"Why you laugh?" LuLing scolded. "I not kidding. And don't let dog in backyard. I know someone do this. Now cat dead!"

"You're right," Ruth answered, trying to keep her mind on the road ahead. "I'll be more careful."

.FOUR

On the night of the Full Moon Festival, the Fountain Court restaurant was jammed with a line flowing out the door like a dragon's tail. Art and Ruth squeezed through the crowd. "Excuse us. We have reservations."

Inside, the dining room roared with the conversations of a hundred happy people. Children used chopsticks to play percussion on teacups and water glasses. The waiter who led Ruth and Art to their tables had to shout above the clatter of plates being delivered and taken away. As Ruth followed, she inhaled the mingled fragrances of dozens of entrées. At least the food would be good tonight.

Ruth had picked Fountain Court because it was one of the few restaurants where her mother had *not* questioned the preparation of the dishes, the attitude of the waiters, or the cleanliness of the bowls. Originally Ruth had made reservations for two tables, seating for her side of the family and friends, as well as the two girls and Art's parents, who were visiting from New Jersey. Those she had not counted on were Art's ex-wife Miriam, her husband Stephen, and their two little boys, Andy and Beauregard. Miriam had called Art the week before with a request.

When Ruth learned what the request was, she balked.

"There isn't room for four more people."

"You know Miriam," Art said. "She doesn't accept no as an answer to anything. Besides, it's the only chance my folks will have to see her before they leave for Carmel."

"So where are they going to sit? At another table?"

"We can always squeeze in more chairs," Art countered. "It's just a dinner."

To Ruth, this particular gathering was not "just a dinner." It was their Chinese thanksgiving, the reunion that she was hosting for the first time. She had given much thought to setting it up, what it should mean, what family meant, not just blood relatives but also those who were united by the past and would remain together over the years, people she was grateful to have in her life. She wanted to thank all the celebrants for their contribution to her feeling of family. Miriam would be a reminder that the past was not always good and the future was uncertain. But to say all this would sound petty to Art, and Fia and Dory would think she was being mean.

Without more disagreement, Ruth made the last-minute changes: Called the restaurant to change the head count. Revised the seating plan. Ordered more dishes for two adults and two children who didn't like Chinese food all that much. She suspected that Fia's and Dory's fussiness over unfamiliar food came from their mother.

Art's parents were the first to arrive at the restaurant. "Arlene, Marty," Ruth greeted them. They exchanged polite two-cheek kisses. Arlene hugged her son, and Marty gave a light two-punch to his shoulder and then his jaw. "You knock me out," Art said, supplying their traditional father-son refrain.

The Kamens were impeccable in their classy outfits and stood out amid the crowd of casually attired customers. Ruth wore an Indonesian batik-print top and crinkled skirt. It occurred to her that Miriam dressed like the Kamens, in designer-style clothing that had to be professionally pressed and dry-cleaned. Miriam loved Art's parents, and they adored her, whereas, Ruth felt, the Kamens had never warmed to her. Even though she had met Art after the divorce was nearly final, Marty and Arlene probably saw her as the interloper, the reason Miriam and Art did not reconcile. Ruth had sensed that the Kamens hoped she was only a brief interlude in Art's life. They never knew how to introduce her. "This is Art's, uh, Ruth," they'd say. They were nice to her, certainly. They had given her lovely birthday presents, a silk velvet scarf, Chanel No. 5, a lacquered tea tray, but nothing she might share with Art or pass on to his girls—or any future children, for that matter, since she was beyond the possibility of giving the Kamens additional grandchildren. Miriam, on the other hand, was now and forever the mother of the Kamens' granddaughters, the keeper of heirlooms for Fia and Dory. Marty and Arlene already had given her the family sterling, china, and the mezuzah kissed by five generations of Kamens since the days they lived in the Ukraine.

"Miriam! Stephen!" Ruth exclaimed with enthusiastic effort. She shook hands, and Miriam gave her a quick hug and waved to Art across the table. "Glad you could join us," Ruth said awkwardly, then turned to the boys. "Andy, Beauregard, how you doing?"

The younger one, who was four, piped up: "I'm called Boomer now."

"It's awfully nice of you to include us," Miriam gushed to Ruth. "I hope it wasn't any trouble."

"Not at all."

Miriam opened wide her arms toward Marty and Arlene, and rushed to give them effusive hugs. She was wearing a maroon-and-olive outfit with a huge circular pleated collar. Her copper-colored hair was cut in a severe page boy. Ruth was reminded why the hairstyle was called that. Miriam looked like one of those pages in Renaissance paintings.

Ruth's cousin Billy—now called Bill by others—showed up, trailed by his second wife, Dawn, and their combined four children, ages nine through seventeen. Ruth and Billy rocked in embrace. He thumped her back, as guys did with their buddies. He had been a skinny brat and a bully to Ruth in childhood, but those qualities had turned out to be leadership skills. Today he ran a biotech company and had grown chubby with success. "God, it's good to see you," he said. Ruth immediately felt better about the dinner.

Sally, always the social one, made a loud entrance, shouting names and squealing as her husband and two boys followed. She was an aeronautical engineer, who traveled widely as an expert witness for law firms, plaintiff attorneys only. She inspected records and sites of airplane disasters, mostly small craft. Always a talker, she was perky and outgoing, not intimidated by anyone or any new adventure. Her husband, George, was a violinist with the San Francisco Symphony, quiet but happy to take the lead whenever Sally fed him a line. "George, tell them about the dog that ran onstage at Stern Grove and peed on the microphone and shorted out the entire sound system." Then George would repeat exactly what Sally had just said.

Ruth looked up and saw Wendy and Joe, gazing about the crowd. Behind them was Gideon, nattily dressed and perfectly groomed as usual, holding an expensive bouquet of tropical flowers. When Wendy turned and saw him, she smiled in mock delight, and he pretended to be just as enthusiastic. She had once called him "a starfucker who practically gives himself neck strain looking past your shoulder for more important people to talk to." Gideon, in turn, had said that Wendy was "a vulgarian, who lacks the nuance to know why it's not good manners to grace everybody with lurid details of one's menstrual problems at the dinner table." Ruth had thought about inviting one and not the other, but in a stupid moment of resolve, she decided they would just have to work it out between them, even if it gave her heartburn to watch.

Wendy waved both hands when she spotted Ruth, and then she and Joe eased their way through the restaurant. Gideon trailed a comfortable distance behind. "We found a parking space right in front!" Wendy boasted. She held up her lucky charm, a plastic angel with the face of a parking meter. "I tell you, works every time!" She had given one to Ruth, who had placed it on the dashboard but only received parking tickets. "Hi, sweetie," Gideon said in his usual low-key manner. "You're looking radiant. Or is that sweat and nervousness?" Ruth, who had told him on the phone about Miriam's crashing the party, kissed him on both cheeks and whispered where Art's ex was. He had already suggested he act as spy and report everything appalling that she said.

Art came up to Ruth. "How's it going?"

"Where are Fia and Dory?"

"They went to check out a CD at Green Apple Annex."

"You let them go by themselves?"

"It's just up the street, and they said they'd be back in ten minutes."

"So where are they?"

"Probably abducted."

"That's *not* funny." Her mother used to say it was bad luck even to speak words like that. On cue, LuLing entered, her petite frame contrasting with GaoLing's sturdier one. A few seconds later, Uncle Edmund came in. Ruth sometimes wondered whether this was how her father would have looked—tall, stoop-shouldered, with a crown of thick white hair and a large, relaxed swing to his arms and legs. Uncle Edmund was given to telling jokes badly, consoling scared children, and dispensing stock market tips. LuLing often said the two brothers weren't similar at all, that Ruth's father had been much more handsome, smarter, and very honest. His only fault was that he was too trusting, also maybe absentminded when he was concentrating too hard, just like Ruth. LuLing often recounted the circumstances in which he died as a warning to Ruth when she was not paying attention to her mother. "You daddy see green light, he trust that car stop. Poom! Run over, drag him one block, two block, never stop." She said he died because of a curse, the same one that made Ruth break her arm. And because the subject of the curse often came up when LuLing was displeased with Ruth, as a child Ruth thought the curse and her father's death were related to her. She had recurrent nightmares of mutilating people in a brakeless car. She always tested and retested her brakes before heading out in the car.

Even from across the big room, Ruth could see that LuLing was beaming at her with motherly adoration. This gave Ruth heart pangs, made her both happy and sad to see her mother on this special day. Why wasn't their relationship always like this? How many more gatherings like this would they have?

"Happy Full Moon," Ruth said when her mother reached the table. She motioned for LuLing to sit next to her. Auntie Gal took the other chair next to Ruth, and then the rest of the family sat down. Ruth saw that Art was with Miriam at the other table, what was fast becoming the non-Chinese section.

"Hey, are we in the white ghetto or what?" Wendy called out. She was sitting with her back to Ruth.

When Fia and Dory finally showed up, Ruth did not feel she could chastise them in front of their mother or Arlene and Marty. They did a mass wave, "Hi, everybody," then gurgled, "Hi, Bubbie and Poppy," and threw their arms around their grandparents' necks. The girls never voluntarily hugged LuLing.

The dinner began with a flurry of appetizers set on the lazy Susan, what LuLing called the "go-round." The adults oohed and aahed, the children cried, "I'm starved!" The waiters set down what

Ruth had ordered by phone: sweetly glazed phoenix-tail fish, vegetarian chicken made out of wrinkly tissues of tofu, and jellyfish, her mother's favorite, seasoned with sesame oil and sprinkled with diced green onions. "Tell me," Miriam said, "is that animal, vegetable, or mineral?"

"Here, Ma," Ruth said, holding the jellyfish platter, "you start since you're the oldest girl."

"No-no!" LuLing said automatically. "You help youself."

Ruth ignored this rite of first refusal and placed a heap of noodle-like strands of jellyfish on her mother's plate. LuLing immediately started to eat.

"What's that?" Ruth heard Boomer ask at the other table. He scowled at the jiggling mound of jellyfish as it swung by on the lazy Susan.

"Worms!" Dory teased. "Try some."

"Ewww! Take it away! Take it away!" Boomer screamed. Dory was hysterical with laughter. Art passed along the entire table's worth of jellyfish to Ruth, and Ruth felt her stomach begin to ache.

More dishes arrived, each one stranger than the last, to judge by the expressions on the non-Chinese faces. Tofu with pickled greens. Sea cucumbers, Auntie Gal's favorite. And glutinous rice cakes. Ruth had thought the kids would like those. She had thought wrong.

Halfway through the dinner, Nicky, Sally's six-year-old, spun the go-round, perhaps thinking he could launch it like a Frisbee, and the spout of a teapot knocked over a water glass. LuLing yelped and jumped up. Water dripped from her lap. "*Ai-ya!* Why you do this?"

Nicky crossed his arms, and tears started to well up in his eyes.

"It's okay, honey," Sally told him. "Say you're sorry, and next time spin it more slowly."

"She was mean to me." He aimed a pout in the direction of LuLing, who was now busy dabbing at her lap with a napkin.

"Sweetie, Grand-Auntie was just surprised, that's all. It's only that you're so strong—like a baseball player."

Ruth hoped her mother would not continue to berate Nicky. She remembered when her mother would enumerate all the times she had spilled food or milk, asking aloud to unseen forces why Ruth could not learn to behave. Ruth looked at Nicky and imagined what she would have been like if she had had children. Perhaps she too would have reacted like her mother, unable to restrain the impulse to scold until the child acted beaten and contrite.

More drinks were ordered. Ruth noticed Art was on his second glass of wine. He also seemed to be having an animated conversation with Miriam. Another round of dishes arrived, just in time to dissipate the tension. Eggplant sautéed with fresh basil leaves, a tender sable fish coated in a mantle of garlic chips, a Chinese version of polenta smothered in a spicy meat sauce, plump black mushrooms, a Lion's Head clay pot of meatballs and rice vermicelli. Even the "foreigners," LuLing reported, enjoyed the food. Above the noise, Auntie Gal leaned toward Ruth and said: "Your mother and I, we ate excellent dishes at Sun Hong Kong last week. But then we almost went to jail!" Auntie Gal liked to throw out zingers and wait for listeners to take the bait.

Ruth obliged. "Jail?"

"Oh, yes! Your mother got into a big fight with the waiter, said she already paid the bill." Auntie Gal shook her head. "The waiter was right, it was not yet paid." She patted Ruth's hand. "Don't worry! Later, when your mother was not looking, I paid. So you see, no jail, and here we are!" GaoLing took a few more bites of food, smacked her lips, then leaned toward Ruth again and whispered, "I gave your mother a big bag of ginseng root. This is good to cure confusion." She nodded, and Ruth nodded in turn. "Sometimes your mother calls me at the train station to say she's here, and I don't even know she's coming! Course, this is fine, I always welcome her. But at six in the morning? I'm not an early birdie!" She chuckled, and Ruth, her mind awhirl, gave out a hollow laugh.

What was wrong with her mother? Could depression cause confusion like this? The next week, when they had the follow-up visit with Dr. Huey, she would discuss it with him. If he ordered her mother to take antidepressants, maybe she would obey. Ruth knew she should visit her mother more often. LuLing often complained of loneliness, and she was obviously trying to fill a void by going to see GaoLing at odd hours.

During the lull before dessert, Ruth stood up and gave a brief speech. "As the years go on, I see how much family means. It reminds us of what's important. That connection to the past. The same jokes about being Young yet getting old. The traditions. The fact that we can't get rid of each other no matter how much we try. We're stuck through the ages, with the bonds cemented by sticky rice and tapioca pudding. Thank you all for being who you are." She left out individual tributes since she had nothing to say about Miriam and her party.

Ruth then passed out wrapped boxes of moon cakes and chocolate rabbits to the children. "Thank you!" they cried. "This is neat!" At last Ruth was somewhat becalmed. It was a good idea to host this dinner after all. In spite of the uneasy moments, reunions were important, a ritual to preserve what was left of the family. She did not want her cousins and her to drift apart, but she feared that once the older generation was gone, that would be the end of the family ties. They had to make the effort.

"More presents," Ruth called out, and handed out packages. She had found a wonderful old photo of LuLing and Auntie Gal as girls, flanking their mother. She had a negative made of the original, then ordered eight-by-tens and had those framed. She wanted this to be a meaningful tribute to her family, a gift that would last forever. And indeed, the recipients gave appreciative sighs.

"This is amazing," Billy said. "Hey, kids, guess who those two cute girls are?"

"Look at us, so young," Auntie Gal sighed wistfully.

"Hey, Auntie Lu," Sally teased. "You look kind of bummed-out in this picture."

LuLing answered: "This because my mother just die."

Ruth thought her mother had misheard Sally. "Bummed out" was not in LuLing's vocabulary. LuLing and GaoLing's mother had died in 1972. Ruth pointed to the photo. "See? Your mother is right there. And that's you."

LuLing shook her head. "That not my real mother."

Ruth's mind turned in loops, trying to translate what her mother meant. Auntie Gal gave Ruth a peculiar look, tightening her chin so as not to say anything. Others had quiet frowns of concern.

"That's Waipo, isn't it?" Ruth said to Auntie Gal, struggling to stay nonchalant. When GaoLing nodded, Ruth said happily to her mother, "Well, if that's your sister's mother, she must be yours as well."

LuLing snorted. "GaoLing *not* my sister!"

Ruth could hear her pulse pounding in her brain. Billy cleared his throat in an obvious bid to change the subject.

Her mother went on: "She my sister-in-*law*."

Everyone now guffawed. LuLing had delivered the punch line to a joke! Of course, they were indeed sisters-in-law, married to a pair of brothers. What a relief! Her mother not only made sense, she was clever.

Auntie Gal turned to LuLing and huffed with pretend annoyance. "Hey, why do you treat me so bad, hah?"

LuLing was fishing for something in her wallet. She pulled out a tiny photo, then handed it to Ruth. "There," she said in Chinese. "This one right here, she's my mother." A chill ran over Ruth's scalp. It was a photograph of her mother's nursemaid, Bao Bomu, Precious Auntie.

She wore a high-collared jacket and a strange headdress that looked as if it were made of ivory. Her beauty was ethereal. She had wide tilted eyes, with a direct and immodest stare. Her arched eyebrows suggested a questioning mind, her full lips a sensuality that was indecent for the times. The picture obviously had been taken before the accident that burned her face and twisted it into a constant expression of horror. As Ruth peered more closely at the photo, the woman's expression seemed even more oddly disturbing, as if she could see into the future and knew it was cursed. This was the crazy woman who had cared for her mother since birth, who had smothered LuLing with fears and superstitious notions. LuLing had told her that when she was fourteen, this nursemaid killed herself in a gruesome way that was "too bad to say." Whatever means the nursemaid used, she also made LuLing believe it was her fault. Precious Auntie was the reason her mother was convinced she could never be happy, why she always had to expect the worst, fretting until she found it.

Ruth quietly tried to steer her mother back to coherence. "That was your nursemaid," she coaxed. "I guess you're saying she was *like* a mother to you."

"No, *this* really my mother," LuLing insisted. "That one GaoLing mother." She held up the framed photo. In a daze, Ruth heard Sally asking Billy how the skiing was in Argentina the month before. Uncle Edmund was encouraging his grandson to try a black mushroom. Ruth kept asking herself, What's happening? What's happening?

She felt her mother tapping her arm. "I have present for you too. Early birthday, give you now." She reached into her purse and pulled out a plain white box, tied with ribbon.

"What's this?"

"Open, don't ask."

The box was light. Ruth slipped off the ribbon, lifted the lid, and saw a gleam of gray. It was a necklace of irregularly shaped black pearls, each as large as a gumball. Was this a test? Or had her mother really forgotten that Ruth had given her this as a gift years before? LuLing grinned knowingly—Oh yes, daughter cannot believe her luck!

"Best things take now," LuLing went on. "No need wait to I dead." She turned away before Ruth could either refuse or thank her. "Anyway, this not worth much." She was patting the back of her bun, trying to stuff pride back into her head. It was a gesture Ruth had seen many times. "If someone show-off give big," her mother would say, "this not really giving big." A lot of her admonitions had to do with *not* showing what you really meant about all sorts of things: hope, disappointment, and especially love. The less you showed, the more you meant.

"This necklace been in my family long time," Ruth heard her mother say. Ruth stared at the beads, remembered when she first saw the necklace in a shop on Kauai. "Tahiti-style black pearls," the tag said, a twenty-dollar bit of glassy junk to wear against sweaty skin on a tropically bright day. She had gone to the island with Art, the two of them newly in love. Later, when she returned home, she realized she had forgotten her mother's birthday, had not even thought to telephone while she was sipping mai-tais on a sandy beach. She had boxed the twice-worn trinket, and by giving her mother something that had crossed the ocean, she hoped she would also give the impression she had been thinking of her. Her downfall lay in being honest when she insisted the necklace was "nothing much," because LuLing mistook this modesty to mean the gift was quite expensive and thus the bona fide article, proof of a daughter's love. She wore it everywhere, and Ruth would feel the slap of guilt whenever she overheard her mother boast to her friends, "Look what my daughter Lootie buy me."

"Oh, very pretty!" GaoLing murmured, glancing at what Ruth held in her hand. "Let me see," and before Ruth could think, GaoLing snatched the box. Her lips grew tight. "Mmm," she said, examining the bauble. Had Auntie Gal seen this before? How many times had LuLing worn it to her house, bragging about its worth? And had GaoLing known all along that the necklace was fake, that Ruth, the good daughter, was also a fake?

"Let me see," Sally said.

"Careful," LuLing warned when Sally's son reached for the pearls, "don't touch. Cost too much."

Soon the pearls were making the rounds at the other table as well. Art's mother gave the necklace an especially critical eye, weighing it in her hand. "Just *lovely*," she said to LuLing, a bit too emphatically. Miriam simply observed, "Those beads are certainly large." Art gave the pearls a once-over and cleared his throat.

"Eh, what wrong?"

Ruth turned and saw her mother scrutinizing her face.

"Nothing," Ruth mumbled. "I'm just a little tired, I guess."

"Nonsense!" her mother said in Chinese. "I can see something is blocked inside and can't come out."

"Watch it! Spy talk!" Dory called from the other table.

"Something is wrong," LuLing persisted. Ruth was amazed that her mother was so perceptive. Maybe there was nothing the matter with her after all.

"It's that wife of Art's," Ruth finally whispered in her American-accented Mandarin. "I wish Art had not let her come."

"Ah! You see, I was right! I knew something was wrong. Mother always knows."

Ruth bit hard on the inside of her cheek.

"Now, now, don't worry anymore," her mother soothed. "Tomorrow you talk to Artie. Make him buy you a gift. He should pay a lot to show that he values you. He should buy you something like this." LuLing touched the necklace, which had been returned to Ruth's hands.

Ruth's eyes smarted with held-back tears.

"You like?" LuLing said proudly, switching back to the public language of English. "This real things, you know."

Ruth held up the necklace. She saw how the dark pearls glistened, this gift that had risen from the bottom of the sea.

FIVE

Ruth held LuLing's arm as they walked to the hospital parking garage. Her slack-skinned limb felt like the bony wing of a baby bird.

LuLing acted alternately cheerful and cranky, unchanged by what had just transpired in the doctor's office. Ruth, however, sensed that her mother was growing hollow, that soon she would be as light as driftwood. *Dementia.* Ruth puzzled over the diagnosis: How could such a beautiful-sounding word apply to such a destructive disease? It was a name befitting a goddess: Dementia, who caused her sister Demeter to forget to turn winter into spring. Ruth now imagined icy plaques forming on her mother's brain, drawing out moisture. Dr. Huey had said the MRI showed shrinkage in certain parts of the brain that were consistent with Alzheimer's. He also said the disease had probably started "years ago." Ruth had been too stunned to ask any questions at the time, but she now wondered what the doctor meant by "years ago." Twenty? Thirty? Forty? Maybe there was a reason her mother had been so difficult when Ruth was growing up, why she had talked about curses and ghosts and threats to kill herself. Dementia was her mother's redemption, and God would forgive them both for having hurt each other all these years.

"Lootie, what doctor say?" LuLing's question startled Ruth.

They were standing in front of the car. "He say I die soon?" she asked humorously.

"No." And for emphasis, Ruth laughed. "Of course not."

Her mother studied Ruth's face, then concluded: "I die, doesn't matter. I not afraid. You know this."

"Dr. Huey said your heart is fine," Ruth added. She tried to figure a way to translate the diagnosis into a condition her mother would accept. "But he said you may be having another kind of problem—with a balance of elements in your body. And this can give you troubles . . . with your memory." She helped LuLing into the front seat and snapped her seat belt in place.

LuLing sniffed. "Hnh! Nothing wrong my memory! I 'member lots things, more than you. Where I live little-girl time, place we call Immortal Heart, look like heart, two river, one stream, both dry-out. . . ." She continued talking as Ruth went to the other side of the car, got in, and started the engine. "What he know? That doctor don't even use telescope listen my heart. Nobody listen my heart! You don't listen. GaoLing don't listen. You know my heart always hurting. I just don't complain. Am I complain?"

"No—"

"See!"

"But the doctor said sometimes you forget things because you're depressed."

"Depress 'cause can *not* forgot! Look my sad life!"

Ruth pumped the brakes to make sure they would hold, then steered the car down the falling turns of the parking garage. Her mother's voice droned in rhythm with the engine: "Of course depress. When Precious Auntie die, all happiness leave my body. . . ."

Since the diagnosis three months before, LuLing had come to Art and Ruth's for dinner almost every night. Tonight Ruth watched her mother take a bite of salmon. LuLing chewed slowly, then choked. "Too salty," she gasped, as if she had been given deer lick for the main course.

"Waipo," Dory interjected, "Ruth didn't add any salt. I watched. *None.*"

Fia kicked Dory. She made an X with her index fingers, the symbolic cross that keeps movie Draculas at bay. Dory kicked her back.

Now that Ruth could no longer blame her mother's problems on the eccentricities of her personality, she saw the signs of dementia everywhere. They were so obvious. How could she not have noticed before? The time-shares and "free vacations" her mother ordered via junk mail. The accusations that Auntie Gal had stolen money from her. The way LuLing obsessed for days about a bus driver who accused her of not paying the fare. And there were new problems that caused Ruth to worry into the night. Her mother often forgot to lock the front door. She left food to defrost on the counter until it became rancid. She turned on the cold water and left it running for days, waiting for it to become hot. Some changes actually made life easier. For one thing, LuLing no longer said anything when Art poured himself another glass of wine, as he was doing tonight. "Why drink so much?" she used to ask. And Ruth had secretly wondered the same. She once mentioned to him that he might want to cut back before it became a habit. "You should take up juicing again." And he had calmly pointed out that she was acting like her mother. "A couple of glasses of wine at dinner is not a problem. It's a personal choice."

"Dad?" Fia asked. "Can we get a kitten?"

"Yeah," Dory jumped in. "Alice has the cutest Himalayan. That's what we want."

"Maybe," Art replied.

Ruth stared at her plate. Had he forgotten? She had told him she was not ready for another cat. She would feel disloyal to Fu-Fu. And when the time was right for another pet, an animal she inevitably would wind up feeding and cleaning, she preferred that it be a different species, a little dog.

"I once drive to Himalaya, long ways by myself," LuLing bragged. "Himalaya very high up, close to moon."

Art and the girls exchanged baffled looks. LuLing often issued what they considered non sequiturs, as free-floating as dust motes. But Ruth believed LuLing's delusions were always rooted in a deeper reason. Clearly this instance had to do with word association: Himalayan kitten, Himalayan mountains. But why did LuLing believe she had driven there by car? It was Ruth's job to untangle such puzzles. If she could find the source, she could help LuLing unclog the pathways in her brain and prevent more destructive debris from accumulating. With diligence, she could keep her from driving off a cliff in the Himalayas. And then it occurred to her: "My mother and I saw this really interesting documentary on Tibet last week," Ruth said. "They showed the road that leads to—"

But Dory interrupted her to say to LuLing, "You can't *drive* to the Himalayas from here."

LuLing frowned. "Why you say this?"

Dory, who like LuLing often acted on impulse, blurted, "You just can't. I mean, you're crazy if you think—"

"Okay I crazy!" LuLing sputtered. "Why you should believe me?" Her anger escalated like water in a teakettle—Ruth saw it, the rolling bubbles, the steam—and then LuLing erupted with the ultimate threat: "Maybe I die soon! Then everybody happy!"

Fia and Dory shrugged and gave each other knowing looks: Oh, this again. LuLing's outbursts were becoming more frequent, more abrupt. Fortunately, they quickly abated, and the girls were not that affected by them. Nor did they become more sensitive to the problem, it seemed to Ruth. She had tried to explain several times to them that they shouldn't contradict anything LuLing said: "Waipo sounds

illogical because she is. We can't change that. This is the disease talking, not her." But it was hard for them to remember, just as it was
hard for Ruth not to react to her mother's threats to die. No matter
how often she had heard them, they never ceased to grab her by the
throat. And now the threat seemed very real—her mother was dying, first her brain, then her body.

The girls picked up their plates. "I have homework," Fia said.
"Night, Waipo."

"Me, too," Dory said. "Bye, Waipo."

LuLing waved from across the table. Ruth had once asked the
girls to give LuLing kisses. But she had stiffened in response to their
pecks.

Art stood up. "I have some documents to look over for tomorrow. Better get started. Good night, LuLing."

When LuLing toddled off to the bathroom, Ruth went to the living room to speak to Art. "She's getting worse."

"I noticed." Art was shuffling papers.

"I'm afraid to leave her alone when we go to Hawaii."

"What are you going to do?"

She noted with dismay that he had asked what *she* would do, had
not said "we." Since the Full Moon Festival dinner, she had become
more aware of the ways she and Art failed to be a family. She had
tried to push this out of her mind, but it crept back, confirming to
her that it was not an unnecessary worry. Why did she feel she didn't
belong to anyone? Did she unconsciously choose to love people
who kept their distance? Was she like her mother, destined to be
unhappy?

She couldn't fault Art. He had always been honest about their relationship. From the beginning, he said he didn't want to marry
again. "I don't want us to operate by assumptions," he had told her,
cradling her in bed soon after they started to live together. "I want us
to look at each other every morning and ask, 'Who is this amazing

person I'm so lucky to love?' " At the time, she felt adored like a goddess. After the second year, he had spontaneously offered to give her a percentage ownership in the flat. Ruth had been touched by his generosity, his concern for her security. He knew how much she worried over the future. And the fact that they had not yet changed the deed? Well, that was more her fault than his. She was supposed to decide on the percentage interest she should have, then call the lawyer and set up the paperwork. But how could you express love as a percentage? She felt as she had when a college history professor of hers had told the students in the class to grade themselves. Ruth had given herself a B- and everyone else had taken an A.

"You could hire someone to check on your mother a few times a week," Art suggested. "Like a housekeeper."

"That's true."

"And call that service, Meals on Wheels. They might be able to deliver food while we're gone."

"That's an idea."

"In fact, why don't you start now, so she gets used to the food? Not that she isn't welcome to dinner here whenever she wants. . . . Listen, I really have to get some work done now. Are you going to take her home soon?"

"I guess."

"When you get back, we'll have some rum raisin ice cream." He named her favorite flavor. "It'll make you feel better."

LuLing had objected to the idea of having anyone come to her house to help clean. Ruth had anticipated she would. Her mother hated spending money on anything she believed she could do herself, from hair coloring to roof repairs.

"It's for an immigrant training program," Ruth lied, "so they won't have to go on welfare. And we don't have to pay anything. They're doing it free so they can put work experience on their résumé." LuLing readily accepted this reasoning. Ruth felt like a bad child. She would be caught. Or maybe she wouldn't, and that would be worse. Another reminder that the disease had impaired her mother's ability to know and see everything.

A few days after the first housekeeper started, LuLing called to complain: "She think come to America everything so easy. She want take break, then tell me, Lady, I don't do move furniture, I don't do window, I don't do iron. I ask her, You think you don't lift finger become millionaire? No, America not this way!"

LuLing continued to give the immigrant good advice until she quit. Ruth started interviewing new prospects, and until someone was hired, she decided she should go to LuLing's a few times a week to make sure the gas burners weren't on and water wasn't flooding the apartment. "I was in the neighborhood to drop off some work for a client," she explained one day.

"Ah, always for client. Work first, mother second."

Ruth went to the kitchen, carrying a bag of oranges, toilet paper, and other grocery essentials. While there, she checked for disasters and danger. The last time she'd been there, she found that LuLing had tried to fry eggs with the shells still on. Ruth did a quick sweep of the dining room table and picked up more junk mail offers LuLing had filled out. "I'll mail these for you, Mom," she said. She then went into the bathroom to make sure the faucets weren't running. Where were the towels? There was no shampoo, only a thin slice of cracked soap. How long had it been since her mother had bathed? She looked in the hamper. Nothing there. Was her mother wearing the same clothes every day?

The second housekeeper lasted less than a week. On the days she didn't visit, Ruth felt uneasy, distracted. She was not sleeping well

and had broken a molar grinding her teeth at night. She was too tired
to cook and ordered pizza several times a week, giving up her resolve to set a low-fat example for Dory, and then having to endure
LuLing's remarks that the pepperoni was too salty. Recently Ruth
had developed spasms across her shoulders that made it hard to sit at
her desk and work at her computer. She didn't have enough fingers
and toes to keep track of everything. When she found a Filipina who
specialized in elder care, she felt a huge burden removed. "I love old
people," the woman assured her. "They're not difficult if you take
time to get to know them."

But now it was night, and Ruth lay awake listening to the
foghorns warning ships to stay clear of the shallows. The day before, when she picked up her mother for dinner, Ruth learned that
the Filipina had quit.

"Gone," LuLing said, looking satisfied.

"When?"

"Never work!"

"But she was at your house until what? Two days ago? Three
days ago?"

After more questioning, Ruth deduced that the woman had not
been coming since the day after she started. Ruth would never be
able to find another person before she left for Hawaii. That was
only two days from now. A vacation across the ocean was out of the
question.

"You go," Ruth told Art in the morning. They had already paid
for the rental, and there was a no-refund policy.

"If you don't go, what fun would that be? What would I do?"

"Not work. Not get up. Not return phone calls."

"It won't be the same."

"You'll miss me dreadfully and tell me you were miserable."

Eventually, much to Ruth's chagrin, he agreed with her logic.

The next morning, Art left for Hawaii. The girls were at Miriam's for the week, and though Ruth was accustomed to working alone during the day, she felt empty and anxious. Soon after she settled in at her desk, Gideon called to say that the *Internet Spirituality* author had fired her—*fired,* a first in her career. Although she had finished his book earlier than scheduled, he had not liked what she had written. "I'm as pissed as you are," Gideon said. And Ruth knew she should be outraged, maybe even humiliated, but in fact, she was relieved. One less thing to think about. "I'll try to do damage control with the contract and HarperSanFrancisco," Gideon went on, "but I may also need for you to document your time spent and outline why his complaints were not in keeping with reality. . . . Hello? Ruth, are you still there?"

"Sorry. I was a little preoccupied. . . ."

"Hon, I've been meaning to talk to you about that. Not to imply that you're somehow at fault for what happened. But I am concerned that you haven't been your usual self. You seem—"

"I know, I know. I'm not going to Hawaii, so I can catch up."

"I think that's a good idea. By the way, I think we're going to hear about that other book project today, but frankly I don't think you'll get it. You should have told them you had an emergency appendectomy or something." Ruth had failed to show up at an interview because her mother had called in a panic, thinking her alarm clock was the smoke detector going off.

At four, Agapi called to discuss final edits for *Righting the Wronged Child.* An hour later, they were still talking. Agapi was eager to start a new book, which she wanted to call either *Past-Perfect Tension* or *The Embedded Self.* Ruth kept staring at the clock. She was supposed to pick up her mother at six for dinner at Fountain Court. "Habit, neuromusculature, and the limbic system, that's the basis . . ." Agapi was saying. "From babyhood and our first sense of insecurity, we clench, grasp, flail. We *embed* the response but forget the cause, the past that was imperfect. . . . Ruth, my dear, you seem to be somewhere else. Should you ring me later when you feel more refreshed?"

At five-fifteen, Ruth called her mother to remind her she was coming. No answer. She was probably in the bathroom. Ruth waited five minutes, then called again. Still no answer. Did she have constipation? Had she fallen asleep? Ruth tidied her desk, put the phone on speaker, and hit automatic redial. After fifteen minutes of unanswered ringing, she had run through all the possibilities, until they culminated in the inevitable worst possible thing. Flames leaping from a pot left on the stove. LuLing dousing the flames with oil. Her sleeve catching fire. As Ruth drove to her mother's, she braced herself to see a crackling blaze eating the roof, her mother lying twisted in a blackened heap.

Just as she feared, when Ruth arrived she saw lights flickering in the upper level, shadows dancing. She rushed in. The front door was unlocked. "Mom? Mommy! Where are you?" The television was on, blasting *Amor sin Límite* at high volume. LuLing had never figured out how to use the remote control, even though Ruth had taped over all but the Power, Channel Up, and Channel Down buttons. She turned off the TV, and the sudden silence frightened her.

She ran to the back rooms, flung open closets, looked out the windows. Her throat tightened. "Mommy, where are you?" she whimpered. "Answer me." She ran down the front steps and knocked on the tenant's door.

She tried to sound casual. "By any chance, have you seen my mother?"

Francine rolled her eyes and nodded knowingly. "She went charging down the sidewalk about two or three hours ago. I noticed because she was wearing slippers and pajamas, and I said to myself, 'Wow, she looks really flipped out.' . . . Like it's none of my business, but you should take her to the doctor and get her medicated or something. I mean that in the good sense."

Ruth raced back upstairs. With shaky fingers, she called a former client who was a captain in the police department. Minutes later, a Latino officer stood at the doorway. He was bulging with weapons and paraphernalia and his face was serious. Ruth's panic notched up. She stepped outside.

"She has Alzheimer's," Ruth jabbered. "She's seventy-seven but has the mind of a child."

"Description."

"Four-eleven, eighty-five pounds, black hair pulled into a bun, probably wearing pink or lilac pajamas and slippers . . ." Ruth was picturing LuLing as she said this: the puzzled look on her mother's face, her inert body lying in the street. Ruth's voice started to wobble. "Oh God, she's so tiny and helpless. . . ."

"Does she look anything like that lady there?"

Ruth looked up to see LuLing standing stock still at the end of the walkway. She was wearing a sweater over her pajamas.

"*Ai-ya!* What happen?" LuLing cried. "Robber?"

Ruth ran toward her. "Where were you?" She appraised her mother for signs of damage.

The officer walked up to the two of them. "Happy ending," he said, then turned toward his patrol car.

"Stay there," Ruth ordered her mother. "I'll be right back." She went to the patrol car and the officer rolled down his window. "I'm sorry for all the trouble," she said. "She's never done this before." And then she considered that maybe she had, but she just didn't know it. Maybe she did this every day, every night. Maybe she roamed the neighborhood in her underwear!

"Hey, no problem," the policeman said. "My mother-in-law did the same thing. Sundowning. The sun went down, she went wandering. We had to put alarm triggers on all the doors. That was one tough year, until we put her in a nursing home. My wife couldn't do it anymore—keeping an eye on her day and night."

Day and night? And Ruth thought she was being diligent by having her mother over for dinner and trying to hire a part-time housekeeper. "Well, thanks anyway," she said.

When she returned to her mother, LuLing complained right away: "Grocery store 'round the corner? I walk 'round and 'round, gone! Turn into bank. You don't believe, go see youself!"

Ruth wound up staying the night at her mother's, sleeping in her old bedroom. The foghorns were louder in this section of the city. She remembered listening to them at night when she was a teenager. She would lie in bed, counting the blasts, matching them to the number of years it would be before she could move out. Five years, then four, then three. Now she was back.

In the morning, Ruth opened the cupboards to look for cereal. She found dirty paper napkins folded and stacked. Hundreds. She opened the fridge. It was packed with plastic bags of black and greenish mush, cartons of half-eaten food, orange peels, cantaloupe rinds, frozen goods long defrosted. In the freezer were a carton of eggs, a pair of shoes, the alarm clock, and what appeared to have been bean sprouts. Ruth felt sick. This had happened in just one week?

She called Art in Kauai. There was no answer. She pictured him lying serenely on the beach, oblivious to all problems in the world. But how could he be on the beach? It was six in the morning there. Where was he? Hula dancing in someone's bed? Another thing to worry about. She could call Wendy, but Wendy would simply commiserate by saying her own mother was doing far crazier things. How about Gideon? He was more concerned about clients and contracts. Ruth decided to call Auntie Gal.

"Worse? How can she be worse?" GaoLing said. "I gave her ginseng, and she said she was taking it every day."

"The doctor said none of those things will help—"

"Doctor!" GaoLing snorted. "I don't believe this diagnosis, Alzheimer's. Your uncle said the same thing, and he's a dentist. Everybody gets old, everybody forgets. When you're old, there's too much to remember. I ask you, Why didn't anyone have this disease twenty, thirty years ago? The problem is, today kids have no time anymore to see parents. Your mommy's lonely, that's all. She has no one to talk to in Chinese. Of course her mind is a little rusted. If you stop speaking, no oil for the squeaky wheel!"

"Well, that's why I need your help. Can she come visit you, maybe for the week? It's just that I have a lot of work this week and can't spend as much time—"

"No need to ask. I'm already offering. I'll come get her in one hour. I need to do some shopping there anyway."

Ruth wanted to weep with relief.

After Auntie Gal left with her mother, Ruth walked a few blocks to the beach, to Land's End. She needed to hear the pummeling waves, their constancy and loudness drowning out her own pounding heart.

S·I X

As Ruth walked along the beach, the surf circled her ankles and
tugged. Go seaward, it suggested, where it is vast and free.

When Ruth was a teenager, her mother had once run off in the
middle of an argument, declaring she was going to drown herself in
the ocean. She had waded in to her thighs before her daughter's
screams and pleas had brought her back. And now Ruth wondered:
If she had not begged her mother to return, would LuLing have let
the ocean decide her fate?

Since childhood, Ruth had thought about death every day, sometimes many times a day. She thought everyone must secretly do the
same, but no one talked openly about it except her mother. She had
pondered in her young mind what death entailed. Did people disappear? Become invisible? Why did dead people become stronger,
meaner, sadder? That's what her mother seemed to think. When
Ruth was older, she tried to imagine the precise moment when she
could no longer breathe or talk or see, when she would have no feelings, not even fear that she was dead. Or perhaps she would have
plenty of fear, as well as worry, anger, and regrets, just like the
ghosts her mother talked to. Death was not necessarily a portal to the
blank bliss of absolute nothingness. It was a deep dive into the unknown. And that contained all sorts of bad possibilities. It was that

unknown which made her decide that no matter how terrible and un-solvable her life seemed, she would never willingly kill herself.

Although she remembered a time when she had tried.

It happened the year she turned eleven. Ruth and her mother had moved from Oakland to the flatlands of Berkeley, to a dark-shingled bungalow behind a butter-yellow cottage owned by a young couple in their twenties, Lance and Dottie Rogers. The bungalow had been a potting shed and garage that Lance's parents remodeled into an il-legal in-law unit during World War Two and rented to a series of brides whose husbands had departed for battle in the Pacific via the Alameda Naval Station.

The ceilings were low, the electricity often shorted out, and the back wall and one side abutted a fence on which alley cats howled at night. There was no ventilation, not even a fan over the two-burner gas stove, so that when LuLing cooked at night, they had to open the windows to let out what she called the "greasy smell." But the rent was cheap, and the place was in a neighborhood with a good interme-diate school attended by the smart and competitive sons and daugh-ters of university professors. That was why LuLing had moved there in the first place, she liked to remind Ruth, for her education.

With its small-paned windows and yellow shutters, the bungalow resembled a dollhouse. But Ruth's initial delight soon turned into peevishness. The new home was so small she had no privacy. She and her mother shared a cramped, sunless bedroom that allowed for nothing more than twin beds and a dresser. The combined living room, eating area, and efficiency kitchen afforded no place to hide. Ruth's only refuge was the bathroom, and perhaps for this reason she developed numerous stomach ailments that year. Her mother was usually in the same room as she was, doing her calligraphy, cooking, or knitting, activities that kept her hands busy but left her tongue all too free to interrupt Ruth when she was watching TV. "You hair getting too long. Hair cover your glasses like curtain, can't see. You think this good-looking, I telling you *not* good-looking! You tune off TV, I cut hair for you. . . . Eh, you hear me. Tune off TV. . . ."

Her mother took Ruth's television-watching as a sign that she had nothing better to do. And sometimes she would see this as a good opportunity for a talk. She would take down the sand tray from the top of the refrigerator and set it on the kitchen table. Ruth's throat would grow tight. *Not this again.* But she knew that the more she resisted, the more her mother would want to know why.

"Precious Auntie mad-it me?" her mother would say when Ruth had sat for several minutes without writing anything in the sand.

"It's not that."

"You feel something else matter? . . . Another ghost here?"

"It's not another ghost."

"Oh. Oh, I know. . . . I die soon. . . . I right? You can say, I not afraid."

The only time her mother didn't bother her was when she was doing her homework or studying for a test. Her mother respected her studies. If she interrupted her, all Ruth had to do was say, "Shh! I'm reading." And almost always, her mother fell quiet. Ruth read a lot.

On good-weather days, Ruth would take her book to the dwarf-sized porch of the bungalow, and there she'd sit with tucked legs on a bouncy patio chair with a clam-shaped back. Lance and Dottie would be in the yard, smoking cigarettes, pulling weeds out of the brick walkway or pruning the bougainvillea that covered one wall of their cottage like a bright quilt. Ruth would watch them surreptitiously, peering over the top of her book.

She had a crush on Lance. She thought he was handsome, like a movie star with his neatly cropped hair, square jaw, and lanky, athletic body. And he was so easygoing, so friendly to her, which made her even more shy. She had to pretend to be fascinated by her book or the snails that slimed the elephant plants, until finally he noticed her and said, "Hey there, squirt, you can go blind reading too much." His father owned a couple of liquor stores, and Lance helped with the family business. He often left for work in the late morning and returned at three-thirty or four, then took off again at nine and came back late, long after Ruth had given up listening for the sound of his car.

Ruth wondered how Dottie had been lucky enough to marry Lance. She wasn't even that pretty, though Ruth's new friend at school, Wendy, said that Dottie was cute in a beach-bunny way. How could she say that? Dottie was tall and bony, and about as huggable as a fork. Plus, as her mother had pointed out, Dottie had big teeth. Her mother had demonstrated to Ruth by pulling her own lips back with her fingers so that her gums showed on the top and bottom. "Big teeth, show too much inside out, like monkey." Later Ruth stared in the bathroom mirror and admired her own small teeth.

There was another reason Ruth thought Dottie did not deserve Lance: She was bossy and talked too loud and fast. Sometimes her voice was milky, as if she needed to clear her throat. And when she yelled, it sounded like rusty metal. On warm evenings, when their back windows were open, Ruth listened as Lance's and Dottie's garbled voices drifted across the yard and into the bungalow. On quite a few occasions, when they argued, she could hear clearly what they were saying.

"Damn it, Lance," she heard Dottie yell one night, "I'm going to throw out your dinner if you don't come right now!"

"Hey, gimme a break. I'm on the can!" he answered.

After that, whenever Ruth was in the bathroom, she imagined Lance doing the same, the two of them trying to avoid the people who nagged them without end.

Another night, as Ruth and her mother sat at the kitchen table with the sand tray between them, Dottie's husky voice rang out:

"I know what you did! Don't you play Mr. Innocent with me!"

"Don't tell me what the fuck I did, 'cause you don't know!"

This was followed by two door slams and the revving of the red Pontiac before it roared off. Ruth's heart was racing along with it. Her mother shook her head and clucked her tongue, then muttered in Chinese, "Those foreigners are crazy."

Ruth felt both thrilled and guilty over what she had heard. Dottie had sounded just like her mother, accusing and unreasonable. And Lance suffered as she did. The only difference was, he could talk back. He said exactly what Ruth wished she could tell her mother: Don't tell me what I think, 'cause you don't know!

In October, her mother asked her to give the rent check to the Rogerses. When Dottie opened the door, Ruth saw that she and Lance were busy unloading a huge box. Inside was a brand-new color television set, brought home in time to watch *The Wizard of Oz*, Dottie explained, which was going to air at seven o'clock that night. Ruth had never seen a color TV before, except in a store window.

"You know that part in the movie where everything is supposed to go from black-and-white to color?" Dottie said. "Well, on this set, it really does turn to color!"

"Hey, squirt," Lance said, "why'ncha come over and watch with us?"

Ruth blushed. "I don't know. . . ."

"Sure, tell your mom to come over too," said Dottie.

"I don't know. Maybe." Then Ruth rushed home.

Her mother did not think she should go. "They just polite, don't really mean."

"Yes, they do. They asked me twice." Ruth had left out the part about their inviting LuLing as well.

"Last year, report card, you get one Satisfactory, not even Good. Should be everything Excellent. Tonight better study more."

"But that was in PE!" Ruth wailed.

"Anyway, you already see this Ozzie show."

"It's *The Wizard of Oz*, not *Ozzie and Harriet*. And this one's a movie, it's *famous*!"

"Famous! Hnh! Everybody don't watch then no longer famous! Ozzie, Oz, Zorro, same thing."

"Well, Precious Auntie thinks I should watch it."

"What you mean?"

Ruth didn't know why she had said that. The words just popped out of her mouth. "Last night, remember?" She searched for an answer. "She had me write something that looked like a letter Z, and we didn't know what it meant?"

LuLing frowned, trying to recall.

"I think she wanted me to write O-Z. We can ask her now, if you don't believe me." Ruth went to the refrigerator, climbed the step stool, and brought down the sand tray.

"Precious Auntie," LuLing was already calling in Chinese, "are you there? What are you trying to say?"

Ruth sat with the chopstick poised for action. For a long time nothing happened. But that was because she was nervous she was about to trick her mother. What if there really was a ghost named Precious Auntie? Most of the time she thought the sand-writing was just a boring chore, that it was her duty to guess what her mother wanted to hear, then move quickly to end the session. Yet Ruth had also gone through times when she believed that a ghost was guiding her arm, telling her what to say. Sometimes she wrote things that turned out to be true, like tips for the stock market, which her mother started investing in to stretch the money she had saved over the years. Her mother would ask Precious Auntie to choose between two stocks, say IBM and U.S. Steel, and Ruth chose the shorter one to spell. No matter what she picked, LuLing profusely thanked Precious Auntie. One time, her mother asked where Precious Auntie's body was lying so she could find it and bury it. That question had given Ruth the creeps, and she tried to steer the conversation to a close. *The End*, she wrote, and this made her mother jump out of her chair and cry, "It's true, then! GaoLing was telling the truth. You're at the End of the World." Ruth had felt a cold breath blow down her neck.

Now she steadied her hand and mind, conjuring the wisdom Precious Auntie might impart like the Wizard. O-Z, she wrote, and then started to write *good* slowly and in large letters: G-O-O. And before she could finish, LuLing exclaimed, "Goo! *Goo* means 'bone' in Chinese. What about bone? This concern bone-doctor family?"

And so by luck all fell into place. *The Wizard of Oz*, Precious Auntie was apparently saying, was also about a bone doctor, and she would be happy for Ruth to see this.

At two minutes to seven, Ruth knocked on Lance and Dottie's door. "Who is it?" Lance yelled.

"It's me. Ruth."

"Who?" And then she heard him mutter, "God damn it."

Ruth was humiliated. Maybe he really had asked her only out of politeness. She bolted down the steps of the front porch. Now she'd have to hide in the backyard for two hours so her mother would not know about her mistake or her lie.

The door swung open. "Hey there, squirt," he said warmly, "come on in. We almost gave up on you. Hey, Dottie! Ruth's here! While you're in the kitchen, get her a soda, will you. Here, Ruth, sit yourself down here on the sofa."

During the movie, Ruth had a hard time paying attention to the television screen. She had to pretend to be comfortable. The three of them were sitting on a turquoise-and-yellow sofa that had the woven texture of twine and tinsel. It scratched the backs of Ruth's bare legs.

Besides that, Ruth kept noticing things that shocked her, like how Dottie and Lance put their feet up on the coffee table—without removing their shoes. If her mother saw that, she'd have more to talk about than Dottie's big teeth! What's more, Lance and Dottie were both drinking a golden-colored booze and they weren't even in a cocktail lounge. But what most bothered Ruth was the stupid way Dottie was acting, babyish, stroking her husband's left knee and thigh, while crooning things like, "Lancey-pants, could you turn up the volume a teensy-weensy smidge?"

During a commercial, Dottie untangled herself, stood up, and wobbled about tipsily like the scarecrow in the movie. "How about some pop-pop-pop popcorn, everybody?" And then with arms swinging widely, she took one step backward and loped out of the room, singing, "Ohhhh, we're off to see the kitchen. . . ."

Now Ruth found herself on the sofa alone with Lance. She stared ahead at the television, her heart thumping. She heard Dottie humming, the sound of cabinets being opened and shut.

"So what do you think?" Lance said, nodding toward the television.

"It's really neat," Ruth answered in a small, serious voice, her eyes trained on the screen.

She could smell the oil heating in the kitchen, hear the machine-gun spill of popcorn kernels into the pot. Lance swished the ice cubes in his glass and talked about the programs that he hoped were broadcasting in color: football, *Mister Ed*, *The Beverly Hillbillies*. Ruth felt like she was on a date. She turned slightly toward him. *Listen with a fascinated expression*. Wendy had told her this was what a girl should do to make a boy feel manly and important. But what came after that? Lance was so close to her. All at once, he patted her knee, stood up, and announced, "I guess I better use the can before the show comes back on." What he said was embarrassingly intimate. She was still blushing when he came back a minute later. This time he sat down even closer than before. He could have scooted over to where Dottie had been, so why hadn't he? Was it on purpose? The movie resumed. Was Dottie coming back soon? Ruth hoped not. She imagined telling Wendy how nervous she felt: "I thought I was going to pee in my pants!" That was just an expression, but now that she had thought it, she really did have to pee. This was terrible. How could she ask Lance if she could use the bathroom? She couldn't just get up and wander the house. Should she be casual like him and just say she had to use the can? She gripped her muscles, trying to hold on. Finally, when Dottie came in with the bowl of popcorn, Ruth blurted, "I have to wash my hands first."

"Through the back, past the bedroom," Dottie said.

Ruth tried to act casual, walking speedily while clenching the tops of her thighs together. As she flew past the bedroom, she smelled stale cigarettes, saw an unmade bed, pillows, towels, and Jean Naté bath oil at the foot of the bed. Once in the bathroom, she pulled down her pants and sat, groaning with relief. Here's where Lance had just been, she thought, and she giggled. And then she saw the bathroom was a mess. She was embarrassed for Lance. The grout between the pink tiles on the floor was grungy gray. A bra and panties lay mashed on top of the hamper. And car magazines were sloppily shoved into a built-in wall rack across from the toilet. If her mother could see this!

Ruth stood, and that's when she noticed the dampness on her bottom. The toilet seat had been wet! Her mother had always warned her not to sit on other people's toilets, even those at her friends' homes. Men were supposed to lift the seat, but they never did. "Every man forget," her mother had said, "they don't care. Leave germ there, put on you."

Ruth thought about rubbing off the pee with toilet paper. But then she decided it was a sign, like a pledge of love. It was Lance's pee, his germs, and leaving it on made her feel brave and romantic.

A few days later, Ruth saw a movie in gym class that showed how eggs floated in a female body, traveling along primordial paths, before falling out in a stream of blood. The movie was old and had been spliced in many places. A lady who looked like a nurse talked about the beginning of spring, and in the middle of describing the emergence of beautiful buds she disappeared with a *clack*, then reappeared in another room describing buds moving inside a branch. While she was explaining about the womb as a nest, her voice turned into a flapping-bird sound and she disappeared into the cloud-white screen. When the lights came on, all the girls squinted in embarrassment, for now they were thinking about eggs moving inside them. The teacher had to call in a slouching, slack-mouthed boy from the audiovisual department; this made Wendy and several other girls squeal that they wanted to curl up and die. After the boy spliced the reel back together, the movie took up again, to show a tadpole called a sperm traveling through a heart-shaped womb while a bus driver voice called out the destinations: "vagina," "cervix," "uterus." The girls shrieked and covered their eyes, until the boy swaggered out of the room, acting proud, as if he had seen them all naked.

The movie continued and Ruth watched the tadpole find the egg, which gobbled it up. A big-eyed frog began to grow. At the end of the movie, a nurse with a starched white cap handed a googly baby to a beautiful woman in a pink satin jacket, as her manly husband declared, "It's a miracle, the miracle of life."

When the lights came on, Wendy raised her hand and asked the teacher how the miracle got started in the first place, and the girls who knew the answer snorted and giggled. Ruth laughed as well. The teacher gave them a scolding look and said, "You have to get married first."

Ruth knew that wasn't entirely true. She had seen a Rock Hudson
and Doris Day movie. All it took was the right chemistry, which included love, and sometimes the wrong chemistry, which included
booze and falling asleep. Ruth was not quite sure how everything occurred, but she was pretty certain those were the main things that ac-
tivated a scientific change: it was similar to how Alka-Seltzer turned
plain water into bubbly. Plop, plop. Fizz, fizz. That wrong chemistry
was why some women had babies born out of wedlock, babies that
were illegitimate, one of the *b*-words.

Before the class ended, the teacher passed out white elastic belts
with clips, and boxes containing thick white pads. She explained that
the girls were due to have their first periods soon, and they should not
be surprised or frightened if they saw a red stain on their panties. The
stain was a sign that they had become women, and it was also an assurance that they were "good girls." A lot of the girls tittered. Ruth
thought the teacher was saying her period was due in the same way as
homework, meaning it was due tomorrow, the day after, or next week.

While she and Ruth walked home from school, Wendy explained
what the teacher had left out. Wendy knew things, because she hung
out with her brother's pals and their girlfriends, the hard girls who
wore makeup and stockings with nail polish dabbed over the runs.
Wendy had a big blond bubble hairdo that she teased and sprayed
during recess, while chewing gum she saved between classes in a wad
of tinfoil. She was the first girl to wear white go-go boots, and before
and after school she rolled up her skirt so that it was two inches
above her knees. She had been in detention three times, once for
coming to school late and twice for saying the other *b*-words, "bitch"
and "boner," to the gym teacher. On the way home, she bragged to
Ruth that she had let a boy kiss her during a basement make-out
party. "He had just eaten a neopolitan ice cream sandwich and his
breath tasted like barf, so I told him to kiss my neck but not to go be-

low. Below the neck and you're a goner." She peeled open her collar and Ruth gasped, seeing what looked like a huge bruise.

"What's that?"

"A hickey, you dummy. Course they didn't show that in that crummy movie. Hickeys, hard-ons, home runs, *it*. Speaking of *it*, there was an older girl at this party puking her guts out in the bathroom. A tenth-grader. She thought she was preggers from this boy who's in juvenile hall."

"Does she love him?"

"She called him a creep."

"Then she doesn't have to worry," Ruth said knowingly.

"What are you talking about?"

"It's the chemistry that gets you pregnant. Love is one of the ingredients," Ruth declared as scientifically as possible.

Wendy stopped walking. Her mouth hung open. Then she whispered: "Don't you know *anything*?" And she explained what Ruth's mother, the lady in the movie, and the teacher had not talked about: that the ingredient came from a boy's penis. And to ensure everything was now perfectly clear to Ruth, Wendy spelled it out: "The boy *pees* inside the girl."

"That's not true!" Ruth hated Wendy for telling her this, for laughing hysterically. She was relieved when they reached the block where she and Wendy went in opposite directions.

The last two blocks home, the truth of Wendy's words bounced in Ruth's head like pinballs. It made terrible sense, the part about the pee. That was why boys and girls had separate bathrooms. That's why boys were supposed to lift the seat, but they didn't, just to be bad. And that was why her mother always told her never to sit on the toilet seat in someone else's bathroom. What her mother had said about *germs* was really a warning about *sperms*. Why couldn't her mother learn to speak English right?

And then panic grabbed her. For now she remembered that three nights before she had sat on pee from the man she loved.

Ruth checked her underwear a dozen times a day. By the fourth day after the movie, her period had not come. Now look what's happened, she cried to herself. She walked around the bungalow, staring blankly. She had ruined herself and there was no changing this. Love, pee, booze, she counted the ingredients on her fingers over and over. She remembered how brave she had felt, falling asleep without wiping off the pee.

"Why you act so crazy?" her mother often asked. Of course, she could not tell her mother she was pregnant. Experience had taught her that her mother worried too much even when she had no reason to worry. If there was something *really* wrong, her mother would scream and pound her chest like a gorilla. She would do this in front of Lance and Dottie. She would dig out her eyes and yell for the ghosts to come take her away. And then she would really kill herself. This time for sure. She would make Ruth watch, to punish her even more.

Now whenever Ruth saw Lance, she breathed so hard and fast her lungs seized up and she nearly fainted from lack of air. She had a constant stomachache. Sometimes her stomach went into spasm and she stood over the toilet heaving, but nothing came out. When she ate, she imagined the food falling into the baby frog's mouth, and then her stomach felt like a gunky swamp and she had to run to the bathroom and make herself retch, hoping the frog would leap into the toilet and her troubles could be flushed away.

I want to die, she moaned to herself. Die, die, die. First she cried a lot in the bathroom, then sliced her wrist with a dinner knife. It left a row of plowed-up skin, no blood, and it hurt too much to cut any deeper. Later, in the backyard, she found a rusty tack in the dirt, poked her fingertip, and waited for blood poisoning to rise up her arm like liquid in a thermometer. That evening, still alive and miserable, she filled the tub and sat in it. As she sank under and was about to open her mouth wide, she remembered the water was now dirty with nasty stuff from her feet, her bottom, and the place between her legs. Still determined, she got out of the tub, dried off, and filled the sink, then lowered her face until it touched the water. She opened her mouth. How easy it was, drowning. It didn't hurt at all. It was like drinking water, which, after a while, she realized was what she was doing. So she pushed her face lower into the water and opened her mouth again. She took a deep breath, welcoming death at last. Her whole body backfired in stinging protest. She began coughing in such a loud and hacking way that her mother rushed in without knocking and pounded her back, put her hand on her forehead, and murmured in Chinese that she was sick and should go to bed right away. Having her mother comfort her so lovingly only made Ruth feel worse.

The first person Ruth finally confessed her secret to was Wendy. She knew things, she always knew what to do. Ruth had to wait until she saw her at school, because there was no way she could talk about this on the party-line phone without having her mother or someone else overhear.

"You have to tell Lance," Wendy said, then reached over and squeezed Ruth's hand.

That made Ruth cry even harder. She shook her head. The cruel world and its impossibility swam in front of her. Lance didn't love her. If she told him, he would hate her, Dottie would hate her. They would kick her mother and her out of the bungalow. The school would send Ruth to juvenile hall. And her life would be over.

"Well, if you don't tell Lance, I will," Wendy said.

"Don't," Ruth managed to choke out. "You can't. I won't let you."

"If I don't tell him, how else will he realize that he loves you?"

"He doesn't love me."

"Sure he does. Or he will. Lots of times it happens that way. The guy finds out a baby is coming, and them boom—love, marriage, baby carriage."

Ruth tried to imagine it. "Yep, it's yours," Wendy would say to Lance. She pictured Lance looking like Rock Hudson when he learned Doris Day was going to have his baby. He would look stunned, but slowly he would begin to smile, then grin like a fool and race into the street, unmindful of traffic or people he bumped into, people who shouted back that he was nuts. And he would yell, "I *am* nuts, nuts about her!" Soon he was by her side, on his knees, telling her he loved her, had always loved her, and now wanted to marry her. As for Dottie, well, she would soon fall in love with the postman or someone. Everything would work out. Ruth sighed. It was possible.

That afternoon, Wendy went home with Ruth. LuLing worked the afternoon shift at a nursery school and would not be home for another two hours. At four, while they were outside, they saw Lance stride to his car, whistling and jingling his keys. Wendy broke away from Ruth, and Ruth ran to the other side of the bungalow, where she could both hide and watch. She could hardly breathe. Wendy was walking toward Lance. "Hello?" she called to him.

"Hey there, girlie," he said. "What's up?"

And then Wendy turned around and fled. Ruth started to cry and when Wendy came back, she consoled Ruth, telling her she had a better plan. "Don't worry," she said. "I'll take care of it. I'll think of something." And she did. "Wait here," she said, smiling, and ran up to the back porch of the cottage. Ruth dashed into the bungalow. Five minutes later, the back door to the cottage flew open and Dottie raced down the porch steps. Through the window, Ruth saw Wendy wave to her before walking away quickly. Then came pounding on the door to the bungalow, and when Ruth answered, Dottie was there, grabbing her by both hands. She stared into her eyes with a stricken face and whispered hoarsely in her milk-and-metal voice, "Are you really——?"

Ruth started bawling, and Dottie put her arm around her shoulders, soothing her, then squeezing her so hard Ruth thought her bones would pop out of their sockets. It hurt but also felt good. "That bastard, that dirty, filthy bastard," Dottie kept saying through gritted teeth. Ruth was shocked to hear the *b*-word, but even more so to realize that Dottie was angry—not with her, but with Lance!

"Does your mommy know?" Dottie asked.

Ruth shook her head.

"All right. For now, we don't need to tell her, not yet. First, let me think how we're going to take care of this. Okay? It won't be easy, but I'll figure out what to do, don't worry. Five years ago, the same thing happened to me."

So that was why Lance had married her. But where was the baby?

"I know how you feel," Dottie went on. "I really do."

And Ruth cried even harder, bursting with more feelings than she ever thought a heart could hold. Someone was angry for her. Someone knew what to do.

That night, as her mother cooked with the windows cracked open, loud voices punctured the air above the sound of spitting oil. Ruth pretended to read *Jane Eyre*. Her ears were straining to hear the words from outside, but the only thing she could make out was Dottie's high-pitched shriek: "You filthy bastard!" Lance's voice was a low rumble, like the revving of his Pontiac.

Ruth went into the kitchen and reached under the sink. "I'm going to take out the garbage." Her mother gave her a raised eyebrow but kept cooking. As Ruth approached the cans by the side of the cottage, she slowed down to listen.

"You think you're so hot! How many others have you screwed? . . . You're nothing but a thirty-second wonder—yeah, wham, bam, thank you, ma'am!"

"What makes you the goddamn expert, I'd like to know!"

"I do know! I know what a *real* man is! . . . Danny . . . yeah, him, and he was good, Danny is a *real man*. But you! You gotta stick it up little girls who don't know any better."

Lance's voice rose and broke like a crying boy's: "You goddamn fucking whore!"

When Ruth went back into the house, she was still shaking. She had not expected everything to be so crazy and ugly. Being careless could cause terrible trouble. You could be bad without even meaning to be.

"Those people *huli-hudu*," her mother muttered. She set the steaming food on the table. "Crazy, argue over nothing." And then she closed the windows.

Hours later, as Ruth lay wide awake in bed, the muffled shouts and screams suddenly stopped. She listened for them to begin again, but all she detected were her mother's snores. She arose in the pitch dark and went into the bathroom. She climbed on the toilet seat and looked out the window across the yard. The cottage lights were burning. What was going on? And then she saw Lance walk out with a duffel bag and hurl it into the trunk of his car. A moment later, he spun the tires on the gravel and took off with a roar. What did that mean? Had he told Dottie he was going to marry Ruth?

The next morning, Saturday, Ruth barely touched the rice porridge her mother had heated up. She waited anxiously for the Pontiac to return, but everything remained quiet. She slumped onto the sofa with her book. Her mother was putting dirty clothes, towels, and sheets into a bag draped over a cart. She counted out the quarters and dimes needed for the laundromat, then said to Ruth, "Let's go. Wash-clothes time."

"I don't feel so good."

"Ai-ya, sick?"

"I think I'm going to throw up."

Her mother fussed over her, taking her temperature, asking her what she had eaten, what her stools looked like. She made Ruth lie down on the sofa and placed a bucket nearby, in case she really did get sick. At last her mother departed for the laundromat; she would be gone for at least three hours. She always pushed the cart to a place twenty minutes away, because the washers there were a nickel cheaper than those at the closer places and the dryers didn't burn the clothes.

Ruth put on a jacket and strayed outside. She slid into the chair on the porch, opened her book, and waited. Ten minutes later, Dottie opened the back door of the cottage, climbed down the four steps, and strode across the yard. Her eyes were puffy like a toad's, and when she smiled at Ruth, the upper half of her face looked tragic.

"How ya doin', kiddo?"

"Okay, I guess."

Dottie sighed, sat down on the porch, and dropped her chin onto her knees. "He's gone," she said. "But he's going to pay, don't you worry."

"I don't want any money," Ruth protested.

Dottie laughed once, then sniffed. "I mean he's going to jail."

Ruth was frightened. "Why?"

"Because of what he did to you, of course."

"But he didn't mean to. He just forgot—"

"Forgot you were only eleven? Jeez!"

"It was my fault too. I should have been more careful."

"Honey, no, no, no! You don't have to protect him. Really. It's not your fault or the baby's. . . . Now listen, you're going to have to talk to the police—"

"No! No! I don't want to!"

"I know you're scared, but what he did was wrong. It's called statutory rape, and he has to be punished for it. . . . Anyway, the police will probably ask you a lot of questions, and you just tell them the truth, what he did, where it happened. . . . Was it in the bedroom?"

"The bathroom."

"Jeez!" Dottie nodded bitterly. "Yeah, he always did like it in there. . . . So he took you to the bathroom—"

"I went by myself."

"All right, and then he followed you, and then what? Did he have his clothes on?"

Ruth was aghast. "He stayed in the living room, watching TV," she said in a tiny voice. "I was in the bathroom by myself."

"Then when did he do it?"

"Before me. He peed first, then I did."

"Wait a second. . . . He *what*?"

"He peed."

"On you?"

"On the toilet seat. Then I went in and sat on it."

Dottie stood up, her face twisted with horror. "Oh no, oh my God!" She grabbed Ruth by the shoulders and shook her. "That's *not* how babies are made. Pee on the toilet seat. How could you be so *stupid*? He has to stick his cock in you. He squirts sperm, not piss. Do you realize what you've done? You accused an innocent man of raping you."

"I didn't—" Ruth whispered.

"Yes, you did, and I believed you." Dottie stomped off, cursing.

"I'm sorry," Ruth cried after her. "I said I'm sorry." She was still not certain what she had done.

Dottie turned around and sneered. "You have no idea what sorry really is." Then she went inside and banged the door shut.

Though she was no longer pregnant, Ruth felt no relief. Everything was still awful, maybe even worse. When her mother returned from the laundromat, Ruth was lying under the covers in bed, pretending to be asleep. She felt stupid and scared. Would she go to jail? And though she knew now that she was not pregnant, she wanted to die more than ever. But how? She pictured herself lying under the wheels of the Pontiac, Lance starting the car and taking off, crushing her without even knowing it. If she died like her father, he would meet her in heaven. Or would he too think she was bad?

"Ah, good girl," her mother murmured. "You sleep, feel better soon."

Later that afternoon, Ruth heard the sounds of the Pontiac pulling into the driveway. She peeked out the window. Lance, grim-faced, carried out some boxes, two suitcases, and a cat from the cottage. Then Dottie came out, dabbing her nose with a tissue. She and Lance never looked at each other. And then they were gone. An hour later, the Pontiac returned, but only Lance got out. What had Dottie told Lance? Why did Dottie have to move out? Would Lance now march up to their door and tell her mother what Ruth had done and demand that they move out that same day as well? Lance hated her, Ruth was sure of that. She had thought being pregnant was the worst thing that could have happened to her. But this was far worse.

She stayed home from school on Monday. LuLing became increasingly fearful that a ghost was trying to take her daughter away. Why else was Ruth still sick? LuLing rambled about bony teeth from a monkey's jaw. Precious Auntie would know, she kept saying. She knew about the curse. This was punishment for something the family had done a long time ago. She put the sand tray on a chair by Ruth's twin bed, waiting. "Both us die," she asked, "or only me?"

No, Ruth wrote, *all o.k.*

"What okay-okay? Then why she sick, no reason?"

On Tuesday, Ruth could not stand her mother's fussing over her any longer. She said she was well enough to go to school. Before opening the door, she looked out the window, then down the driveway. Oh no, the Pontiac was still there. She was trembling so hard she feared her bones might break. After taking a deep breath, she darted out the door, scooted down the side of the driveway farther from the cottage, then edged past the Pontiac. She turned left, even though school was to the right.

"Hey, squirt! I've been waiting for you." Lance was on the porch, smoking a cigarette. "We need to talk." Ruth stood rooted to the sidewalk, unable to move. "I *said* we need to talk. Don't you think you owe me that? . . . Come here." He threw the burning cigarette onto the lawn.

Ruth's legs moved shakily forward. The top half of her was still running away. When she reached the top of the porch, she was numb. She looked up. "I'm sorry," she squeaked. The quiver in her chin shook open her mouth, and sobs burbled out.

"Hey, hey," Lance said. He looked nervously down the street. "Come on, you don't have to do that. I wanted to talk so we could have an understanding. I just don't want this to ever happen again. Okay?"

Ruth sniffed and nodded.

"All right, then. So settle down. Don't get all spooky on me."

Ruth wiped at her teary face with her sweater sleeve. The worst was over. She started to go down the stairs.

"Hey, where you going?"

Ruth froze.

"We still have to talk. Turn around." His voice was not quite so gentle. Ruth saw he had opened the door. She stopped breathing. "Inside," he ordered. She bit her lip and slowly climbed back up, then glided past him. She heard the door close and saw the room go dim.

The living room smelled like booze and cigarettes. The curtains were closed and there were empty TV-dinner trays on the coffee table.

"Sit down." Lance gestured toward the scratchy couch. "Want a soda?" She shook her head. The only light came from the TV, which was tuned to an old movie. Ruth was glad for the noise. And then she saw a commercial, a man selling cars. In his hand was a fake saber. "We've slashed our prices—so come on down to Rudy's Chevrolet and ask to see the slasher!"

Lance sat on the sofa, not as close as he had been that night. He took her books from her arms and she felt unprotected. Tears blurred her eyes, and she tried hard not to make any sounds as she cried.

"She left me, you know."

A sob burst out of Ruth's chest. She tried to say she was sorry, but she could make only mouselike sniffles.

Lance laughed. "Actually, I kicked her out. Yeah, in a way, you did me a favor. If it weren't for you, I wouldn't have found out she was screwing around. Oh sure, I kind of suspected it for a while. But I told myself, Man, you got to have trust. And you know what, she didn't trust me. Can you believe it? Me? Let me tell you something, you can't have a marriage if you don't have trust. You know what I mean?" He looked at her.

Ruth desperately nodded.

"Nah, you won't know for another ten years." He lit another cigarette. "You know, in ten years, you'll look back and say, 'Boy, I sure was dumb about how babies are made!'" He snorted, then cocked his head to get her reaction. "Aren't you going to laugh? I think it's kind of funny myself. Don't you?" He started to pat her arm and she flinched without intending to. "Hey, what's the matter? Uh-oh, don't tell me. . . . *You* don't trust me. What are you, like her? After what *you* did and what I certainly did *not* do, do you think I now *deserve* this kind of treatment from you?"

Ruth was quiet for a long time, trying to make her lips move right. Finally she said, in a cracked voice, "I trust you."

"Yeah?" He patted her arm again, and this time she didn't jerk stupidly. He continued talking in a weary but reassuring voice. "Listen, I'm not going to yell at you or nothing, okay? So just relax. Okay? Hey, I said 'Okay?'"

"Okay."

"Give me my smile."

She forced her lips to pull upward.

"There it is! Oops. Gone again!" He stubbed out his cigarette. "All right, are we friends again?" He stuck out his hand for her to shake. "Good. It'd be terrible if we couldn't be friends, since we live next to each other."

She smiled at him and this time it came naturally. She tried to breathe through her clogged nose.

"And being neighbors, we gotta help each other, not go around accusing someone innocent of doing wrong. . . ."

Ruth nodded and realized she was still gripping her toes. She relaxed. Soon this would be over. She saw that he had dark circles under his eyes, lines running from his nose to his jaw. Funny. He looked much older than she remembered, no longer as handsome. And then she realized it was because she was no longer in love with him. How strange. She had believed it was love, and it never was. Love was forever.

"So now you know the real way babies are made, don'cha?"

Ruth stopped breathing. She ducked her head.

"Well, do you or don't you?"

She nodded quickly.

"How? Tell me."

She squirmed, her mind turning around and around. She saw terrible pictures. A brown hot dog squirting yellow mustard. She knew the words: penis, sperm, vagina. But how could she say them? Then the nasty picture would be there in front of both of them. "You know," she whimpered.

He looked at her sternly. It was as if he had X-ray eyes. "Yeah," he finally said. "I know." He was silent for a few seconds, and then added in a friendlier voice. "Boy, were you dumb. Babies and toilet seats, Jeez." Ruth kept her head down, but her eyes glanced up at him. He was smiling. "I hope you one day do a better job teaching your kids about the facts of life. Toilet seat! Pee? Pee-*you*!"

Ruth giggled.

"Ha! I knew you could laugh." He poked his finger under her armpit and tickled her. She squealed politely. He tickled her again, lower along her ribs, and she spasmed as a reflex. Then suddenly, his other hand reached for her other armpit and she groaned with laughter, helpless, too scared to tell him to stop. He twirled his fingers around her back, along her stomach. She balled herself up like a sow bug and fell to the rug below with terrible gasping giggles.

"You think a lot of things are funny, don't you?" He twiddled his fingers up and down her ribs as if they were harp strings. "Yeah, I can see that now. Did you tell all your little girlfriends? Ha! Ha! I almost put that guy in jail."

She tried to cry no, stop, don't, but she was laughing too hard, unable to take a breath on her own, unable to control her arms or legs. Her skirt was tangled, but she couldn't pull it down. Her hands were like that of a marionette, twitching toward wherever he touched as she tried to keep his fingers away from her stomach, her breasts, her bottom. Tears poured out. He was pinching her nipples.

"You're just a little girl," he panted. "You don't even have any titties yet. Why would I want to mess around with you? Shit, I bet you don't even have any tushy hairs——" And when both of his hands shot down to pull off her flowered panties, her voice broke free and

blasted out as screeches. Over and over, she made a fierce, sharp
sound that came from an unknown place. It was as though another
person had burst out of her.

"Whoa! Whoa!" he said, holding up his hands like someone being robbed. "What are you doing? Get a hold of yourself. . . .
Would you just calm down, for chrissake!"

She continued the sirenlike wail, scuttling on her bottom away
from him, pulling up her panties, pushing down her dress.

"I'm not hurting you. I am *not* hurting you." He repeated this until she settled into whimpers and wheezes. And then there came just
fast breathing in the space between them.

He shook his head in disbelief. "Am I imagining things, or
weren't you just laughing a moment ago? One second we're having
fun, the next second you're acting like—well, I don't know, you tell
me." He squinted hard at her. "You know, maybe you have a big
problem. You start to get this funny idea in your head that people are
doing something wrong to you, and before you can see what's true,
you accuse them and go crazy and wreck everything. Is that what
you're doing?"

Ruth got up. Her legs were shaky. "I'm going to go," she whispered. She could hardly walk to the door.

"You're not going anywhere until you promise you're not going
to spread any more of your goddamn lies. You got that straight!" He
walked toward her. "You better not say I did something to you when
I didn't. 'Cause if you do, I'm going to get really mad and do something that'll make you sorrier than hell, you hear?"

She nodded dumbly.

He blew air out of his nose, disgusted. "Get out of here. Scram."

That night, Ruth tried to tell her mother what had happened.
"Ma? I'm scared."

"Why scare?" LuLing was ironing. The room had the smell of
fried water.

"That man Lance, he was mean to me——"

Her mother scowled, then said in Chinese: "This is because you're always bothering him. You think he wants to play with you—he doesn't! Why do you always make trouble? . . ."

Ruth felt sick to her stomach. Her mother saw danger where there wasn't. And now that something was truly really awful, she was blind. If Ruth told her the actual truth, she would probably go crazy. She'd say she didn't want to live anymore. So what difference did it make? She was alone. No one could save her.

An hour later, while LuLing was knitting and watching television, Ruth took down the sand tray by herself. "Precious Auntie wants to tell you something," she told her mother.

"Ah?" LuLing said. She immediately stood up and turned off the TV, and eagerly sat down at the kitchen table. Ruth smoothed the sand with the chopstick. She closed her eyes, then opened them, and began.

You must move, Ruth wrote. *Now.*

"Move?" her mother cried. "Ai-ya! Where we should move?"

Ruth had not considered this. *Far away,* she finally decided.

"Where far?"

Ruth imagined a distance as big as an ocean. She pictured the bay, the bridge, the long bus rides she had taken with her mother that made her fall asleep. *San Francisco,* she wrote at last.

Her mother still looked worried. "What part? Where good?"

Ruth hesitated. She did not know San Francisco that well, except for Chinatown and a few other places, Golden Gate Park, the Fun House at Land's End. And that was how it came to her, an inspiration that moved quickly into her hand: *Land's End.*

Ruth recalled the first day she had walked by herself along this stretch of beach. It had been nearly empty, and the sand in front of her had been clean, untrampled. She had escaped and reached this place. She had felt the waves, cold and shocking, grab at her ankles, wanting to pull her in. She remembered how she had cried with relief as the waves roared around her.

Now, thirty-five years later, she was that eleven-year-old child again. She had chosen to live. Why? As she now kept walking, she felt comforted by the water, its constancy, its predictability. Each time it withdrew, it carried with it whatever had marked the shore. She recalled that when her younger self stood on this same beach for the first time, she had thought the sand looked like a gigantic writing surface. The slate was clean, inviting, open to possibilities. And at that moment of her life, she had a new determination, a fierce hope. She didn't have to make up the answers anymore. She could ask.

Just as she had so long before, Ruth now stooped and picked up a broken shell. She scratched in the sand: *Help*. And she watched as the waves carried her plea to another world.

SEVEN

When Ruth returned to LuLing's apartment, she began to throw away what her mother had saved: dirty napkins and plastic bags, restaurant packets of soy sauce and mustard and disposable chopsticks, used straws and expired coupons, wads of cotton from medicine bottles and the empty bottles themselves. She emptied the cupboards of cartons and jars with their labels still attached. There was enough rotten food from the fridge and freezer to fill four large garbage sacks.

Cleaning helped her feel that she was removing the clutter from her mother's mind. She opened more closets. She saw hand towels with holly motifs, a Christmas present that LuLing never used. She put them in a bag destined for Goodwill. There were also scratchy towels and bargain-sale sheets she remembered using as a child. The newer linens were still in the department-store gift boxes they had come in.

But as Ruth reached for the old towels, she found she could not get rid of them any more than her mother could. These were objects suffused with a life and a past. They had a history, a personality, a connection to other memories. This towel in her hands now, for instance, with its fuchsia flowers, she once thought it was beautiful. She used to wrap it around her wet hair and pretend she was a queen wearing a turban. She took it to the beach one day and her mother scolded her for using "best things" instead of the green towel with frayed ends. By upbringing, Ruth could never be like Gideon, who bought thousands of dollars' worth of Italian linens each year and tossed out last year's collection as readily as last month's *Architectural Digest*. Perhaps she was not as frugal as her mother, but she was aware of the possibility that she might regret the loss of something.

Ruth went into LuLing's bedroom. On the dresser were bottles of toilet water, about two dozen, still in their cellophane-bound boxes. "Stinky water," her mother called it. Ruth had tried to explain to her that toilet water was not the same as water from a toilet. But LuLing said that how something sounded was what counted, and she believed these gifts from GaoLing and her family were meant to insult her.

"Well, if you don't like it," Ruth once said, "why do you always tell them it's just what you wanted?"

"How I cannot show polite?"

"Then be polite, but throw it away later if it bothers you so much."

"Throw away? How I can throw away? This waste money!"

"Then *give* it away."

"Who want such thing? *Toilet* water!—*peh!*—like I big insult them."

So there they sat, two dozen bottles, two dozen insults, some from GaoLing, some from GaoLing's daughter, who were unmindful that LuLing rose each morning, saw these gifts, and began the day feeling the world was against her. Out of curiosity, Ruth opened a box and twisted the cap of the bottle inside. Stinky! Her mother was right. Then again, what was the shelf life of scented water? It was not as though toilet water aged like wine. Ruth started to put the boxes into the Goodwill bag, then caught herself. Resolute but still feeling wasteful, she put them into the bag destined for the dump.

And what about this face powder? She opened a compact case of a gold-tone metal with fleur-de-lys markings. It had to be at least thirty years old. The powder inside was an oxidized orange, the cheek accent of ventriloquists' dummies. Whatever it was looked like it could cause cancer—or Alzheimer's. Everything in the world, no matter how apparently benign, was potentially dangerous, bulging with toxins that could escape and infect you when you least expected it. Her mother had taught her that.

She plucked out the powder puff. Its edges were still nubby, but the center was worn smooth from its once-daily skimming over the curves of LuLing's face. She threw the compact and powder puff in the trash bag. A moment later, she panicked, retrieved the compact and nearly cried. This was part of her mother's life! So what if she was being sentimental? She opened the compact again and saw her pained face in its mirror, then noticed the orange powder again. No, this wasn't being sentimental. It was morbid and disgusting. She stuffed the compact once more into the trash bag.

By nightfall, one corner of the living room was jammed with items Ruth had decided her mother would not miss: a rotary Princess phone, sewing patterns, piles of old utility bills, five frosted iced-tea glasses, a bunch of mismatched coffee mugs bearing slogans, a three-pod lamp missing one pod, the old rusted clam-shaped patio chair, a toaster with a frayed cord and curves like an old Buick fender, a kitchen clock with knife, fork, and spoon as hour, minute, and second hands, a knitting bag with its contents of half-finished purple, turquoise, and green slippers, medicines that had expired, and a spidery thatch of old hangers.

It was late, but Ruth felt even more energized, full of purpose. Glancing about the apartment, she counted on her fingers what repairs were needed to prevent accidents. The wall sockets needed to be brought up to code. The smoke detectors should be replaced. Get the water heater turned down so that her mother could not be scalded.

Was the brown stain on the ceiling the result of a leak? She followed where the water might be dripping, and her discerning eye skidded to a stop on the floor near the couch. She rushed over and peeled back the rug, and stared at the floorboard. This was one of her mother's hiding places, where she hoarded valuables that might be needed in time of war or, as LuLing said, "disaster you cannot even imagine, they so bad." Ruth pressed on one end of the board, and lo and behold, like a seesaw, the other end lifted. Aha! The gold serpentine bracelet! She plucked it out and laughed giddily as if she had just picked the right door on a game show. Her mother had dragged her into Royal Jade House on Jackson Street and bought the bracelet for a hundred twenty dollars, telling Ruth it was twenty-four-carat gold and could be weighed on a scale and traded for full value in an emergency.

And what about LuLing's other hiding spots? At the never used fireplace, Ruth lifted a basket containing photo albums. She pried at a loose brick, pulled it out, and—sure enough—it was still there, a twenty-dollar bill wrapped around four singles. Unbelievable! She felt giddy at finding this small treasure, a memento from her adolescent past. When they moved into this place, LuLing had put five twenty-dollar bills under the brick. Ruth would check every now and then, always noting that the bills lay in the same perfectly aligned wad. One day she put a piece of her hair on top of the money; she had seen this trick in a movie about a boy detective. Every time she looked after that, the hair was still there. When Ruth was fifteen, she began to borrow from the stash during times of her own emergencies—when she needed a dollar here and there for forbidden things: mascara, a movie ticket, and later, Marlboro cigarettes. At first she was always anxious until she could replace the bill. And when she did, she felt relieved and elated that she had not been caught. She rationalized that she *deserved* the money—for mowing the lawn, washing the dishes, being yelled at for no good reason. She replaced the missing twenties with tens, then fives, and eventually, just the singles wrapped with the one remaining twenty.

And now, thirty-one years afterward, in seeing the reminder of her small larceny, she was both the girl she once was and the observer of that younger version of herself. She remembered the unhappy girl who lived in her body, who was full of passion, rage, and sudden impulses. She used to wonder: Should she believe in God or be a nihilist? Be Buddhist or a beatnik? And whichever it should be, what was the lesson in her mother's being miserable all the time? Were there really ghosts? If not, did that mean her mother was really crazy? Was there really such a thing as luck? If not, why did Ruth's cousins live in Saratoga? At times, she became resolute in wanting to be exactly the opposite of her mother. Rather than complain about the world, she wanted to do something constructive. She would join the Peace Corps and go into remote jungles. Another day, she chose to become a veterinarian and help injured animals. Still later, she thought about becoming a teacher to kids who were retarded. She wouldn't point out what was wrong, as her mother did with her, exclaiming that half her brain must be missing. She would treat them as living souls equal to everyone else.

She gave vent to these feelings by writing them down in a diary that Auntie Gal had given her for Christmas. She had just finished reading *The Diary of Anne Frank* in sophomore English class, and like all the other girls, she was imbued with a sense that she too was different, an innocent on a path to tragedy that would make her posthumously admired. The diary would be proof of her existence, that she mattered, and more important, that someone somewhere would one day understand her, even if it was not in her lifetime. There was a tremendous comfort in believing her miseries weren't for naught. In her diary, she could be as truthful as she wanted to be. The truth, of course, had to be supported by facts. So her first entry included a list of the top ten songs on the radio hit list, as well as a

note that a boy named Michael Papp had a boner when he was dancing with Wendy. That was what Wendy had said, and at the time
Ruth thought *boner* referred to a puffed-up ego.

She knew her mother was sneaking looks at what she had written,
because one day she asked Ruth, "Why you like this song 'Turn,
Turn, Turn'? Just 'cause someone else like?" Another time her
mother sniffed and said, "Why smell like cigarette?" Ruth had just
written about going to Haight-Ashbury with friends and meeting
some hippies in the park who offered them a smoke. Ruth took some
glee in her mother's thinking it was cigarettes they were smoking and
not hashish. After that interrogation, she hid the diary in the bottom
of her closet, between her mattresses, behind her dresser. But her
mother always managed to find it, at least that was what Ruth figured, on the basis of what she was next forbidden to do: "No more
go beach after school." "No more see this Lisa girl." "Why you so
boy-crazy?" If she accused her mother of reading her diary, LuLing
would become evasive, never admitting that she had done so, while
also saying, "A daughter should have no secrets from a mother."
Ruth did not want to censor her writing, so she started recording it in
a combination of pig Latin, Spanish, and multisyllabic words that
she knew her mother would not understand. "Aquatic amusements
of the silica particulate variety," was her reference to the beach at
Land's End.

Didn't Mom ever realize, Ruth now mused, how her demands for
no secrets drove me to hide even more from her? Yet maybe her
mother did sense that. Maybe it made her hide certain truths from
Ruth about herself. *Things too bad to say.* They could not trust each
other. That was how dishonesty and betrayal started, not in big lies
but in small secrets.

Ruth now remembered the last place where she had hidden her
diary. She had forgotten about it all these years. She went to the
kitchen, hoisted herself onto the counter with less ease than she had

at sixteen. Patting along the top of the cabinet, she soon found it: the heart-patterned diary, some of the hearts coated with pink nail polish to obliterate the names of various boys she had immortalized as crushes of the moment. She climbed down with the dusty relic, leaned against the counter, and rubbed the red-and-gold cover.

She felt her limbs drain, felt unsure of herself, as if the diary contained an unalterable prediction of what would happen the rest of her life. Once again she was sixteen years old. She undid the clasp and read the words on the inside of the jacket, scrawled in two-inch block letters: STOP!!! PRIVATE!!! IF YOU ARE READING THIS YOU ARE GUILTY OF TRESPASSING!!! YES! I DO MEAN *YOU*!

But her mother had read it, had read and committed to heart what Ruth had written on the second-to-last page, the words that nearly killed them both.

The week before Ruth wrote those fateful words, she and LuLing had been escalating in their torment of each other. They were two people caught in a sandstorm, blasted by pain and each blaming the other as the origin of the wind. The day before the fight culminated, Ruth had been smoking in her bedroom, leaning out the window. The door was closed, and as soon as she heard her mother's footsteps coming toward her room, she dropped the cigarette outside, flopped onto her bed, and pretended to read a book. As usual, LuLing opened the door without knocking. And when Ruth looked up with an innocent expression, LuLing shouted, "You smoking!"

"No I wasn't!"

"Still smoking." LuLing pointed toward the window and marched over. The cigarette had landed on the ledge below the window, announcing its whereabouts with a plume of smoke.

"I'm an American," Ruth shouted. "I have a right to privacy, to pursue my own happiness, not yours!"

"No right! All wrong!"

"Leave me alone!"

"Why I have daughter like you? Why I live? Why I don't die long time 'go?" LuLing was huffing and snorting. Ruth thought she looked like a mad dog. "You want I die?"

Ruth was shaking but shrugged as nonchalantly as she could. "I really don't care."

Her mother panted a few more times, then left the room. Ruth got up and slammed the door shut.

Later, over sobs of righteous indignation, she began to write in her diary, knowing full well her mother would read the words: "I hate her! She's the worst mother a person could have. She doesn't love me. She doesn't listen to me. She doesn't understand anything about me. All she does is pick on me, get mad, and make me feel worse."

She knew that what she was writing was risky. It felt like pure evil. And the descending mantle of guilt made her toss it off with even more bravado. What she wrote next was even worse, such terrible words, which later—too late—she had crossed out. Ruth now looked at them, the blacked-out lines, and she knew what they said, what her mother had read:

"You talk about killing yourself, so why don't you ever do it? I wish you would. Just do it, do it, do it! Go ahead, kill yourself! Precious Auntie wants you to, and so do I!"

At the time, she was shocked that she could write such horrible feelings. She was shocked now to remember them. She had cried while writing the words, full of anger, fear, and a strange freedom of finally admitting so openly that she wanted to hurt her mother as much as her mother hurt her. And then she had hidden the diary in the back of her underwear drawer, an easy enough place to look. She had arranged the book just so, spine facing in, a pair of pink-flowered panties on top. That way Ruth would know for sure that her mother had been snooping in there.

The next day, Ruth had dawdled before coming home from school. She walked along the beach. She stopped at a drugstore and looked at makeup. She called Wendy from a phone booth. By the time she returned home, her mother would have read the words. She expected a huge fight, no dinner, just shouting, more threats, more rants about how Ruth wanted her dead so she could live with Auntie Gal. LuLing would wait for Ruth to admit that she wrote those hateful words.

Then Ruth imagined it another way. Her mother reading the words, pounding her chest with one fist to shove her suffering back into the private area of her heart, biting her lips to keep from crying. Later, when Ruth came home, her mother would pretend not to see her. She would fix dinner, sit down, and chew silently. Ruth would not give in and ask if she could have some dinner too. She would eat cereal from the box at every meal, if that's what it took. They would act like this for days, her mother torturing Ruth with her silence, her absolute rejection. Ruth would stay strong by not feeling any pain, until nothing mattered anymore, unless, of course, it went the way it usually did, and Ruth broke down, cried, and said she was sorry.

And then Ruth had no more time to imagine any other versions of what might happen. She was home. She steeled herself. Thinking about it was just as bad as going through with it. Just get it over with, she told herself. She walked up the stairs to the door, and as soon as she opened it, her mother ran to her and said in a voice choked with worry, "Finally you're home!"

Only she realized in the next moment that this was not her mother but Auntie Gal. "Your mother is hurt," she said, and grabbed Ruth by the arm to steer her back out the door. "Hurry, hurry, we're going to the hospital now."

"Hurt?" Ruth could not move. Her body felt airless, hollow and heavy at the same time. "What do you mean? How did she get hurt?"

"She fell out the window. Why she was leaning out, I don't know. But she hit the cement. The downstairs lady called the ambulance. Her body is broken, and something is wrong with her head—I don't know what—but it's very bad, the doctors say. I just hope there's no brain damage."

Ruth burst into sobs. She doubled over and began crying hysterically. She had wished for this, caused this to happen. She cried until she had dry heaves and was faint from hyperventilating. By the time they arrived at the hospital, Auntie Gal had to take Ruth to Emergency too. A nurse tried to make her breathe into a paper bag, which Ruth slapped away, and after that someone gave her a shot. She became weightless, all worries lifted from her limbs and mind. A dark, warm blanket was placed over her body, then pulled over her head. In this nothingness, she could hear her mother's voice pronouncing to the doctors that her daughter was quiet at last because they were both dead.

Her mother, as it turned out, had suffered a broken shoulder, a cracked rib, and a concussion. When she was released from the hospital, Auntie Gal stayed a few more days to help cook and set up the house so LuLing could learn to bathe and dress herself easily. Ruth was always standing off to the side. "Can I help?" she periodically asked in a weak voice. And Auntie Gal had her make rice or wash the tub or put fresh sheets on her mother's bed.

Over the following days, Ruth anguished over whether her mother had told Auntie Gal what she had read in Ruth's diary, why she had jumped out the window. She searched Auntie Gal's face for signs that she knew. She analyzed every word she said. But Ruth could not detect any anger or disappointment or false pity in how Auntie Gal spoke. Her mother was just as puzzling. She acted not angry but sad and defeated. There was *less* of something—but what was that? Love? Worry? There was a dullness in her mother's eyes, as if she did not care what was in front of her. All was equal, all was unimportant. What did that mean? Why didn't she want to fight anymore? LuLing accepted the bowls of rice porridge Ruth brought her. She drank her tea. They spoke, but the words were about meaningless facts, nothing that could lead to disputes or misunderstanding.

"I'm going to school now," Ruth would say.

"You have lunch money?"

"Yeah. You need more tea?"

"No more."

And each day, several times a day, Ruth wanted to tell her mother that she was sorry, that she was an evil girl, that everything was her fault. But to do so would be to acknowledge what her mother obviously wanted to pretend never existed, those words Ruth had written. For weeks, they walked on tiptoe, careful not to step on the broken pieces.

On her sixteenth birthday, Ruth came home from school and found her mother had bought some of her favorite foods: the sticky rice wrapped in lotus leaves, both kinds, one with meat filling, one with sweet red-bean paste, as well as a Chinese sponge cake stuffed with strawberries and whipped cream. "Cannot cook you better things," LuLing said. Her right side was still supported in a sling, and she could not lift anything with that arm. It was hard enough for her to haul bags of groceries from the market with her left hand. Ruth saw these offerings as a gesture of forgiveness.

"I like this stuff," Ruth said politely. "It's great."

"No time buy gift," her mother mumbled. "But I find some things, maybe you still like." She pointed to the coffee table. Ruth slowly walked over and picked up a lumpy package that was clumsily wrapped in tissue paper and tape, no ribbon. Inside she found a black book and a tiny purse of red silk, fastened with a miniature frog clasp. And within the purse was a ring Ruth had always coveted, with a thin gold band and two oval pieces of apple-green jade. It had been a gift from Ruth's father, who had received it from his mother to give to his future bride. Her mother never wore it. GaoLing had once hinted that the ring should belong to her, so it could be passed along to her son, who was also the only grandson. Forever after, LuLing brought up the ring in the context of that greedy remark of her sister's.

"Wow, wow, wow." Ruth stared at the ring in her palm.

"This is very good jade, don't loose," her mother warned.

"I won't lose it." Ruth slid the ring onto her middle finger. Too small for that one, but it did fit her ring finger.

Finally Ruth looked at the other gift. It was a pocket-sized book with black leather covers, a red ribbon for a place marker.

"You holding backward," her mother said, and flipped it so the back was the front but facing the wrong way. She turned the pages for Ruth, left to right. Everything was in Chinese. "Chinese Bible," her mother said. She opened it to a page with another place marker, a sepia-toned photograph of a young Chinese woman.

"This my mother." LuLing's voice sounded strangled. "See? I make copy for you." She pulled out a wax-paper sleeve with a duplicate of the photograph.

Ruth nodded, sensing this was important, that her mother was giving her a message about mothers. She tried to pay attention and not look at the ring on her finger. But she could not help imagining what the kids at school would say, how envious they would be.

"When I little-girl time, hold this Bible here." LuLing patted her chest. "Sleep time, think about my mother."

Ruth nodded. "She was pretty then." Ruth had seen other photos of LuLing and GaoLing's mother—Waipo is what Ruth called her. In those, Waipo had a doughy face with wrinkles as deep as cracks and a mouth as severe, straight, and lipless as a sword slash. LuLing

slipped the pretty picture into the Bible, then held one hand, palm up.
"Now give back."

"What?"

"Ring. Give back."

Ruth didn't understand. Reluctantly she put the ring in LuLing's
hand and watched as she returned it to the silk purse.

"Some things too good use right now. Save for later, 'preci-
ate more."

Ruth wanted to cry out, "No! You can't do that! It's *my* birthday
present."

But she said nothing, of course. She stood by, her throat tightening, as LuLing went to her vinyl easy chair. She pulled up the bottom
cushion. Underneath was a cutting board, and beneath that a flap,
which she lifted. Into this shallow cavern, her mother placed the
Bible and the ring in its purse. So that's where she also hid things!

"Someday I give you forever."

Someday? Ruth's throat ached. She wanted to cry. "When's forever?" But she knew what her mother meant—forever as in, "When
I forever dead, then you don't need listen me anymore." Ruth was a
mix of emotions, happy that her mother had given her such nice
presents, because this meant she still loved her, yet filled with a new
despair that the ring had been taken away so soon.

The next day, Ruth went to the easy chair, pulled back the cushion and cutting board, then reached her hand into the hollow to feel
for the silk purse. She extracted the ring and looked at it, now a forbidden object. She felt as if she had swallowed it and it was caught in
her throat. Maybe her mother had shown her the ring just to torture
her. That was probably it. Her mother knew exactly how to make
her miserable! Well, Ruth would not let her have the satisfaction. She
would pretend she didn't care. She would force herself never to look
at the ring again, to act as though it did not exist.

A few days after that, LuLing came into Ruth's room, accusing her of having gone to the beach. When Ruth lied and said she had not, LuLing showed Ruth the sneakers she had left by the front door. She banged them together and a storm of sand rained down.

"That's from the sidewalk!" Ruth protested.

And so the fights continued, and felt to Ruth both strange and familiar. They argued with increasing vigor and assurance, crossing the temporary boundaries of the last month, defending the old terrain. They flung out more pain, knowing already they had survived the worst.

Later, Ruth debated over throwing away her diary. She retrieved the dreaded book, still in the back of her underwear drawer. She turned the pages, reading here and there, weeping for herself. There was truth in what she had written, she believed, some of it, at least. There was a part of her in these pages that she did not want to forget. But when she arrived at the final entry, she was stricken with a sense that God, her mother, and Precious Auntie knew that she had committed near-murder. She carefully crossed out the last sentences, running her ballpoint pen over and over the words until everything was a blur of black ink. On the next page, the last page, she wrote: "I'm sorry. Sometimes I just wish you would say you're sorry too."

Though she could never show her mother those words, it felt good to write them. She was being truthful and neither good nor bad. She then tried to think of a place where her mother would never find her diary. She climbed onto the kitchen counter and stretched her arm way up and tossed the diary on top of the cabinet, so far out of reach that she too forgot about it over time.

Ruth now reflected that in all the years gone by, she and her mother had never talked about what had happened. She put down the diary. Forever did not mean what it once had. Forever was what changed inevitably over time. She felt a curious sympathy for her younger self, as well as an embarrassed hindsight in how foolish and egocentric she had been. If she had had a child, it would have been a daughter who grew up to make her just as miserable as she had made her mother. That daughter would have been fifteen or sixteen right about now, shouting that she hated Ruth. She wondered whether her mother had ever told her own mother that she hated her.

At that moment, she thought of the photos they had looked at during the Moon Festival dinner. Her mother had been around fifteen in the photo with Auntie Gal and Waipo. And there was another photo, the one of Precious Auntie, whom LuLing had mistakenly identified as her mother. A thought ran through her mind: The photo her mother kept in the Bible. She had also said that was her mother. Who was in that picture?

Ruth went to the vinyl chair, removed the cushion and the cutting board. Everything was still there: the small black Bible, the silk pouch, the apple-green-jade ring. She opened the Bible, and there it was, the wax-paper sleeve with the same photo her mother had shown her at the family reunion dinner. Precious Auntie, wearing the peculiar headdress and high-collared winter clothes. What did this mean? Was her mother demented thirty years before? Or was Precious Auntie really who her mother said she was? And if she was, did that mean her mother was *not* demented? Ruth stared at the photo again, searching the features of the woman. She couldn't tell.

What else was in the bottom of the chair? Ruth reached in and pulled out a package wrapped in a brown grocery bag and tied with red Christmas ribbon. Inside was a stack of paper, all written on in Chinese. At the top of certain sheets was a large character done in stylish brushed-drawn calligraphy. She had seen this before. But where? When?

And then it came to her. The other pages, the ones buried in her bottom right-hand desk drawer. "Truth," she recalled the top of that first page read. "These are the things I know are true." What did the next sentences say? The names of the dead, the secrets they took with them. What secrets? She sensed her mother's life was at stake and the answer was in her hands, had been there all along.

She looked at the top page of this new stack in her hands, the large calligraphed character. She could hear her mother scolding her, "Should study harder." Yes, she should have. The large character was familiar, a curved bottom, three marks over it—*heart!* And the first sentence, it was like the beginning of the page she had at home. "These are the things I—" And then it was different. The next word was *ying-gai*, "should." Her mother used that a lot. The next, that was *bu*, another word her mother often said. And the one after that . . . she didn't know. "These are the things I should not—" Ruth guessed what the next word might be: "These are the things I should not *tell*." "These are the things I should not *write*." "These are the things I should not *speak*." She went into her bedroom, to a shelf where her mother kept an English-Chinese dictionary. She looked up the characters for "tell," "write," "speak," but they did not match her mother's writing. She feverishly looked up more words, and ten minutes later, there it was:

"These are the things I should not forget."

Her mother had given her those other pages—what?—five or six years before. Had she written these at the same time? Did she know then that she was losing her memory? When did her mother intend to give her these pages, if ever? When she eventually gave her the ring to keep? When it was clear that Ruth was ready to pay attention? Ruth scanned the next few characters. But nothing except the one for "I" looked familiar, and there were ten thousand words that could follow "I." Now what?

Ruth lay down on the bed, the pages next to her. She looked at the photo of Precious Auntie and put that on her chest. Tomorrow she would call Art in Hawaii and see if he could recommend someone who could translate. That was One. She would retrieve the other pages from home. That was Two. She would call Auntie Gal and see what she knew. That was Three. And she would ask her mother to tell her about her life. For once, she would ask. She would listen. She would sit down and not be in a hurry or have anything else to do. She would even move in with her mother, spend more time getting to know her. Art would not be too happy about that. He might take her moving out as a sign of problems. But someone had to take care of her mother. And she wanted to. She wanted to be here, as her mother told her about her life, taking her through all the detours of the past, explaining the multiple meanings of Chinese words, how to translate her heart. Her hands would always be full, and finally, she and her mother could both stop counting.

PART TWO

HEART

These are the things I must not forget.

I was raised with the Liu clan in the rocky Western Hills south of Peking. The oldest recorded name of our village was Immortal Heart. Precious Auntie taught me how to write this down on my chalkboard. *Watch now, Doggie,* she ordered, and drew the character for "heart": *See this curving stroke? That's the bottom of the heart, where blood gathers and flows. And the dots, those are the two veins and the artery that carry the blood in and out.* As I traced over the character, she asked: *Whose dead heart gave shape to this word? How did it begin, Doggie? Did it belong to a woman? Was it drawn in sadness?*

I once saw the heart of a fresh-killed pig. It was red and glistening. And I had already seen plenty of chicken hearts in a bowl, waiting to be cooked. They looked like tiny lips and were the same color as Precious Auntie's scars. But what did a woman heart look like? "Why do we have to know whose heart it was?" I asked as I wrote the character.

And Precious Auntie flapped her hands fast: *A person should consider how things begin. A particular beginning results in a particular end.*

I remember her often talking about this, how things begin. Since then I have wondered about the beginning and end of many things. Like Immortal Heart village. And the people who lived there, myself

included. By the time I was born, Immortal Heart was no longer
lucky. The village lay between hills in a valley that dropped into a
deep limestone ravine. The ravine was shaped like the curved chamber of a heart, and the heart's artery and veins were the three streams
that once fed and drained the ravine. But they had gone dry. So had
the divine springs. Nothing was left of the waterways but cracked
gullies and the stench of a fart.

Yet the village began as a sacred place. According to legend, a
visiting emperor himself had planted a pine tree in the middle of the
valley. The tree was to honor his dead mother, and his respect for his
mother was so great he vowed that the tree would live forever. When
Precious Auntie first saw the tree, it was already more than three
thousand years old.

Rich and poor alike made a pilgrimage to Immortal Heart. They
hoped that the tree's vital energy would rub off on them. They
stroked the trunk, patted the leaves, then prayed for baby sons or big
fortunes, a cure for dying, an end to curses. Before leaving, they
chipped off some bark, snapped off some twigs. They took them
away as souvenirs. Precious Auntie said this was what killed the tree,
too much admiration. When the tree died, the souvenirs lost their
strength. And because the dead tree was no longer immortal, it was
no longer famous, nor was our village. That tree was not even ancient, people said afterward, maybe only two or three hundred years
old. As for the story about the emperor honoring his mother? That
was a fake feudal legend to make us think the corrupt were sincere.
Those complaints came out the same year that the old Ching Dynasty fell down and the new Republic sprang up.

The nickname of our village is easy for me to remember: Forty-
six Kilometers from Reed Moat Bridge. Reed Moat Bridge is the
same as Marco Polo Bridge, what people now call the turnoff point
to and from Peking. GaoLing's probably forgotten the old name, but

I have not. During my girlhood, the directions to get to Immortal Heart went like this: "First find the Reed Moat Bridge, then walk backward forty-six kilometers."

That joke made it sound as if we lived in a pitiful little hamlet of twenty or thirty people. Not so. When I was growing up, nearly two thousand people lived there. It was crowded, packed from one edge of the valley to the other. We had a brick maker, a sack weaver, and a dye mill. We had twenty-four market days, six temple fairs, and a primary school that GaoLing and I went to when we were not helping our family at home. We had all kinds of peddlers who went from house to house, selling fresh bean curd and steamed buns, twisted dough and colorful candies. And we had lots of people to buy those goods. A few coppers, that was all you needed to make your stomach as happy as a rich man's.

The Liu clan had lived in Immortal Heart for six centuries. For that amount of time, the sons had been inkstick makers who sold their goods to travelers. They had lived in the same courtyard house that had added rooms, and later wings, when one mother four hundred years ago gave birth to eight sons, one a year. The family home grew from a simple three-pillar house to a compound with wings stretching five pillars each. In later generations, the number of sons was less, and the extra rooms became run-down and were rented to squabbling tenants. Whether those people laughed at coarse jokes or screamed in pain, it did not matter, the sounds were the same, ugly to hear.

All in all, our family was successful but not so much that we caused great envy. We ate meat or bean curd at almost every meal. We had new padded jackets every winter, no holes. We had money to give for the temple, the opera, the fair. But the men of our family also had ambitions. They were always looking for more. They said that in Peking, more people wrote important documents. Those important documents required more good ink. Peking was where more of the big money was. Around 1920, Father, my uncles, and their sons went there to sell the ink. From then on, that was where they lived most of the time, in the back room of a shop in the old Pottery-Glazing District.

In our family, the women made the ink. We stayed home. We all worked—me, GaoLing, my aunts and girl cousins, everybody. Even the babies and Great-Granny had a job of picking out stones from the dried millet we boiled for breakfast. We gathered each day in the ink-making studio. According to Great-Granny, the studio began as a grain shed that sat along the front wall of the courtyard house. Over the years, one generation of sons added brick walls and a tile roof. Another strengthened the beams and lengthened it by two pillars. The next tiled the floors and dug pits for storing the ingredients. Then other descendants made a cellar for keeping the inksticks away from the heat and cold. "And now look," Great-Granny often bragged. "Our studio is an ink palace."

Because our ink was the best quality, we had to keep the tables and the floors clean year-round. With the dusty yellow winds from the Gobi, this was not easy to do. The window openings had to be covered with both glass and thick paper. In the summer, we hung netting over the doorways to keep out the insects. In the winter, it was sheep hides to keep out the snow.

Summer was the worst season for ink-making. Heat upon heat. The fumes burned our eyes and nostrils and lungs. From watching Precious Auntie tie her scarf over her marred face, we got the idea of putting a wet cloth over our mouths. I can still smell the ingredients of our ink. There were several kinds of fragrant soot: pine, cassia, camphor, and the wood of the chopped-down Immortal Tree. Father hauled home several big logs of it after lightning cracked the dead tree right down the middle, exposing its heart, which was nearly hollow because of beetles eating it inside out. There was also a glue of sticky paste mixed with many oils—serpentine, camphor, turpentine, and tung wood. Then we added a sweet poisonous flower that helped resist insects and rats. That was how special our ink was, all those lasting smells.

We made the ink a little at a time. If a fire broke out, as it had a couple of hundred years before, all the supplies and stock would not be lost at once. And if a batch was too sticky or too wet, too soft or not black enough, it was easier to find out who was to blame. Each of us had at least one part in a long list of things to do. First there was burning and grinding, measuring and pouring. Then came stirring and molding, drying and carving. And finally, wrapping and counting, storing and stacking. One season I had to wrap, only that. My mind could wander but my fingers still moved like small machines. Another season I had to use very fine tweezers to pluck bugs that had fallen onto the sticks. Whenever GaoLing did this, she left too many dents. Precious Auntie's job was to sit at a long table and press the sooty mixture into the stone molds. As a result, the tips of her fingers were always black. When the ink was dry, she used a long, sharp tool to carve the good-luck words and drawings into the sticks. Her calligraphy was even better than Father's.

It was boring work, but we were proud of our secret family recipe. It yielded just the right color and hardness. An inkstick of ours could last ten years or more. It did not dry out and crumble, or grow soggy with moisture. And if the sticks were stored in the coolness of a root cellar, as ours were, they could last from one great period of history to another. Those who used our ink said the same. It didn't matter how much heat or moisture or dirt from fingers soaked into the page, their words lasted, black and strong.

Mother claimed the ink was why our hair remained the blackest black. It was better for the hair than drinking black-sesame-seed soup. "Work hard all day making ink, look young at night while you sleep." That was our joke, and Great-Granny often boasted: "My hair is as black as the burnt shell of a horse chestnut and my face as wrinkly white as the meat inside." Great-Granny had a clever tongue. One time she added, "Better than having white hair and a burnt face," and everyone laughed, even though Precious Auntie was in the room.

In later years, however, Great-Granny's tongue was not so sharp or fast. Often she said with a worried brow, "Have you seen Hu Sen?" You could say yes, you could say no, and a moment later, she chirped like a bird, "Hu Sen? Hu Sen?" always requesting her dead grandson, very sad to hear.

Toward the end of her life, Great-Granny had thoughts that were like crumbling walls, stones without mortar. A doctor said her inner wind was cold and her pulse was slow, a shallow stream about to freeze. He advised foods with more heat. But Great-Granny only grew worse. Precious Auntie suspected that a tiny flea had crawled into her ear and was feasting on her brain. Confusion Itch was the name of the malady, Precious Auntie said. It is the reason people often scratch their heads when they cannot remember. Her father had been a doctor, and she had seen other patients with the same problem. Yesterday, when I could not remember Precious Auntie's name, I wondered if a flea had run in my ear! But now that I am writing down so many things, I know I don't have Great-Granny's disease. I can recall the smallest details even though they were long ago and far away.

The compound where we lived and worked—that comes back to me as if I were now standing before the gate. It was on Pig's Head Lane. The road started at the east, near the market square where pigs' heads were sold. From the square, it hooked to the north and ran past the former location of the once famous Immortal Tree.

Then it tightened into the little crooked alley where one compound bumped into another. The end of Pig's Head Lane was a narrow perch of earth above the deepest part of the ravine. Precious Auntie told me that the perch was originally made by a warlord thousands of years before. He dreamed that the insides of the mountain were made of jade. So he ordered everyone to dig, dig, don't stop. Men, women, and children dredged for his dream. By the time the warlord died, the children were old, with crooked backs, and half the mountain lay on its side.

Behind our compound, the perch became a cliff. And way down, if you fell head over toes, was the bottom of the ravine. The Liu family had once owned twenty *mu* of land behind the compound. But over the centuries, with each heavy rainfall, the walls of the ravine had collapsed and widened, rumbled and deepened. Each decade, those twenty *mu* of land grew smaller and smaller and the cliff crept closer to the back of our house.

The moving cliff gave us the feeling we had to look behind us to know what lay ahead. We called it the End of the World. Sometimes the men of our family argued among themselves whether we still owned the land that had crashed down into the ravine. One uncle said, "What you own is the spit that travels from your own mouth to the bottom of that wasteland." And his wife said, "Don't talk about this anymore. You're only inviting disaster." For what lay beyond and below was too unlucky to say out loud: unwanted babies, suicide maidens, and beggar ghosts. Everyone knew this.

I went to the cliff many times with my brothers and GaoLing when we were younger. We liked to roll spoiled melons and rotten cabbages over the edge. We watched them fall and splat, hitting skulls and bones. At least that was what we thought they had hit. But one time we climbed down, sliding on our bottoms, grabbing onto roots, descending into the underworld. And when we heard rustling sounds in the brush, we screamed so loud our ears hurt. The ghost turned out to be a scavenger dog. And the skulls and bones, they were just boulders and broken branches. But though we saw no bodies, all around were bright pieces of clothing: a sleeve, a collar, a shoe, and we were sure they belonged to the dead. And then we smelled it: the stink of ghosts. A person needs to smell that only once to know what it is. It rose from the earth. It wafted toward us on the wings of a thousand flies. The flies chased us like a storm cloud, and as we scrambled back up, First Brother kicked loose a stone that gouged out a piece of Second Brother's scalp. We could not hide this wound from Mother, and when she saw it, she beat us all, then told us that if we ever went down to the End of the World again, we might as well stand outside the walls of the compound forever and not bother to come in.

The walls of the Liu home were made of rocks exposed from the washed-down earth. The rocks were stacked and held together with a mud, mortar, and millet paste, then plastered over with lime. They were sweaty damp in summer, moldy damp in winter. And in the many rooms of that house, here and there was always another roof leak or drafty hole in the wall. And yet when I remember that house, I have a strange homesickness for it. Only there do I have a memory of secret places, warm or cool, of darkness where I hid and pretended I could escape to somewhere else.

Within those walls, many families of different positions and generations lived together at the same time, from landlord to tenants, Great-Granny to smallest niece. I guess we were thirty or more people, half of which was the Liu clan. Liu Jin Sen was the eldest of four sons. He was the one I called Father. My uncles and their wives called him Eldest Brother. My cousins called him Eldest Uncle. And by position my uncles were Big Uncle and Little Uncle, and their wives were Big Aunt and Little Aunt. When I was very small, I used to think Father and Mother were called Eldest because they were much taller than my uncles and aunts. First Brother and Second Brother were also large-boned, as was GaoLing, and for a long time I did not know why I was so short.

Baby Uncle was the fourth son, the youngest, the favorite. His name was Liu Hu Sen. He was my real father, and he would have married Precious Auntie, if only he had not died on their wedding day.

Precious Auntie was born in a bigger town down in the foothills, a place called Zhou's Mouth of the Mountain, named in honor of Emperor Zhou of the Shang Dynasty, whom everyone now remembers as a tyrant.

Our family sometimes went to the Mouth of the Mountain for temple fairs and operas. If we traveled by road, it was only about ten kilometers from Immortal Heart. If we walked through the End of the World, it was half that distance but a more dangerous way to go, especially in the summertime. That was when the big rains came. The dry ravine filled, and before you could run to the cliffs, climb up, and cry out, "Goddess of Mercy," the gullies ran by like thieves, grabbing you and whatever else was not deeply rooted in the soil. Once the rain stopped, the floodwaters drained fast and the mouths of the caves swallowed the dirt and the trees, the bodies and the bones. They went down the mountain's throat, into its stomach, intestines, and finally the bowels, where everything got stuck. *Constipated,* Precious Auntie once explained to me. *Now you see why there are so many bones and hills: Chicken Bone Hill, Old Cow Hill, Dragon Bone Hill. Of course, it's not just dragon bones in Dragon Bone Hill. Some are from ordinary creatures, bear, elephant, hippopotamus.* Precious Auntie drew a picture of each of these animals on my chalkboard, because we had never talked about them before.

I have a bone, probably from a turtle, she told me. She fished it from a tuck in her sleeve. It looked like a dried turnip with pockmarks. *My father almost ground this up for medicine. Then he saw there was writing on it.* She turned the bone over, and I saw strange characters running up and down. *Until recently, these kinds of bones weren't so valuable, because of the scratches. Bone diggers used to smooth them with a file before selling them to medicine shops. Now the scholars call these oracle bones, and they sell for twice as much. And the words on here? They're questions to the gods.*

"What does it say?" I asked.

Who knows? The words were different then. But it must be something that should have been remembered. Otherwise, why did the gods say it, why did a person write it down?

"Where are the answers?"

Those are the cracks. The diviner put a hot nail to the bone, and it cracked like a tree hit by lightning. Then he interpreted what the cracks meant.

She took back the divining bone. *Someday, when you know how to remember, I'll give this to you to keep. But for now you'll only forget where you put it. Later we can go looking for more dragon bones, and if you find one with writing on it, you can keep it for yourself.*

In the Mouth of the Mountain, every poor man collected dragon bones when he had a chance. So did the women, but if they found one, they had to say a man found it instead, because otherwise the bone was not worth as much. Later, middlemen went around the village buying the dragon bones, and then they took them to Peking and sold them to medicine shops for high prices, and the shops sold them to sick people for higher prices yet. The bones were well known for curing anything, from wasting diseases to stupidity. Plenty of doctors sold them. And so did Precious Auntie's father. He used bones to heal bones.

For nine hundred years, Precious Auntie's family had been bonesetters. That was the tradition. Her father's customers were mostly men and boys who were crushed in the coal mines and limestone quarries. He treated other maladies when necessary, but bonesetting was his specialty. He did not have to go to a special school to be a bone doctor. He learned from watching his father, and his father learned from his father before him. That was their inheritance. They also passed along the secret location for finding the best dragon bones, a place called the Monkey's Jaw. An ancestor from the time of the Sung Dynasty had found the cave in the deepest ravines of the dry riverbed. Each generation dug deeper and deeper, with one soft crack in the cave leading to another farther in. And the secret of the exact location was also a family heirloom, passed from generation to generation, father to son, and in Precious Auntie's time, father to daughter to me.

I still remember the directions to our cave. It was between the Mouth of the Mountain and Immortal Heart, far from the other caves in the foothills, where everyone else went to dig up dragon bones. Precious Auntie took me there several times, always in the spring or the autumn, never summer or winter. To get there, we went down into the End of the World and walked along the middle of the ravine, away from the walls, where the grown-ups said there were things that were too bad to see. Sometimes we passed by a skein of weeds, shards of a bowl, a quagmire of twigs. In my childish mind, those sights became parched flesh, a baby's skullcap, a soup of maiden bones. And maybe they were, because sometimes Precious Auntie put her hands over my eyes.

Of the three dry streambeds, we took the one that was the artery of the heart. And then we stood in front of the cave itself, a split in the mountain only as tall as a broom. Precious Auntie pulled aside the dead bushes that hid the cave. And the two of us took big breaths and went in. In words, it is hard to say how we made our way in, like trying to describe how to get inside an ear. I had to twist my body in an unnatural way far to the left, then rest a foot on a little ledge that I could reach only by crooking my leg close to my chest. By then I was crying and Precious Auntie was grunting to me, because I could not see her black fingers to know what she was saying. I had to follow her huffs and handclaps, crawling like a dog so I would not hit my head or fall down. When we finally reached the larger part of the cave, Precious Auntie lighted the candle lamp and hung it on a long pole with footrests, which had been left by one of her clan from long ago.

On the floor of the cave were digging tools, iron wedges of different sizes, hammers and claws, as well as sacks for dragging out the dirt. The walls of the cave were many layers, like an eight-treasure rice pudding cut in half, with lighter, crumbly things on top, then a thicker muddy part like bean paste below, and growing heavier toward the bottom. The highest layer was easiest to chip. The lowest was like rock. But that was where the best bones were found. And after centuries of people's digging through the bottom there was now an overhang waiting to crash down. The inside of the cave looked like the molars of a monkey that could bite you in two, which was why it was called the Monkey's Jaw.

While we rested, Precious Auntie talked with her inky hands. *Stay away from that side of the monkey's teeth. Once they chomped down on an ancestor, and he was ground up and gobbled with stone. My father found his skull over there. We put it back right away. Bad luck to separate a man's head from his body.*

Hours later, we would climb back out of the Monkey's Jaw with a sack of dirt and, if we had been lucky, one or two dragon bones. Precious Auntie held them up to the sky and bowed, thanking the gods. She believed the bones from this cave were the reason her family had become famous as bonesetters.

When I was a girl, she said once as we walked home, *I remember lots of desperate people coming to see my father. He was their last chance. If a man could not walk, he could not work. And if he could not work,*

*his family could not eat. Then he would die, and that would be the end
of his family line and all that his ancestors had worked for.*

For those desperate customers, Precious Auntie's father had
remedies of three kinds: modern, try-anything, and traditional. The
modern was the Western medicine of missionaries. The try-anything
was the spells and chants of rogue monks. As for the traditional, that
included the dragon bones, as well as seahorses and seaweed, insect
shells and rare seeds, tree bark and bat dung, all of the highest quality.
Precious Auntie's father was so talented that patients from the five
surrounding mountain villages traveled to the Famous Bonesetter
from the Mouth of the Mountain (whose name I will write down,
once I remember it).

Skilled and famous though he was, he could not prevent all tragedies. When Precious Auntie was four, her mother and older brothers
died of an intestine-draining disease. So did most of the other relatives from both sides of the family, dead just three days after they attended a red-egg ceremony and drank from a well infected with the
body of a suicide maiden. The bonesetter was so ashamed he could
not save his own family members that he spent his entire fortune and
went into a lifetime of debt to hold their funerals.

Because of grief, Precious Auntie said with her hands, *he spoiled
me, let me do whatever a son might do. I learned to read and write, to ask
questions, to play riddles, to write eight-legged poems, to walk alone and
admire nature. The old biddies used to warn him that it was dangerous
that I was so boldly happy, instead of shy and cowering around strangers.
And why didn't he bind my feet, they asked. My father was used to seeing pain of the worst kinds. But with me, he was helpless. He couldn't
bear to see me cry.*

So Precious Auntie freely followed her father around in his study
and shop. She soaked the splints and plucked the moss. She polished
the scales and tallied the accounts. A customer could point to any jar

in the shop and she could read the name of its contents, even the scientific words for animal organs. As she grew older, she learned to bleed a wound with a square nail, to use her own saliva for cleansing sores, to apply a layer of maggots for eating pus, and to wrap torn flaps with woven paper. By the time she passed from childhood to maidenhood, she had heard every kind of scream and curse. She had touched so many bodies, living, dying, and dead, that few families considered her for a bride. And while she had never been possessed by romantic love, she recognized the throes of death. *When the ears grow soft and flatten against the head,* she once told me, *then it's too late. A few seconds later, the last breath hisses out. The body turns cold.* She taught me many facts like that.

For the most difficult cases, she helped her father put the injured man on a light latticework pallet of rattan. Her father lifted and lowered this by pulleys and rope, and she guided the pallet into a tub filled with salt water. There the man's crushed bones floated and were fitted into place. Afterward, Precious Auntie brought her father rattan strips that had been soaked soft. He bent them into a splint so the limb could breathe but remain still. Toward the end of the visit, the bonesetter opened his jar of dragon bones and used a narrow chisel to chip off a sliver tiny as a fingernail clipping. Precious Auntie ground this into a powder with a silver ball. The powder went into a paste for rubbing or a potion for drinking. Then the lucky patient went home. Soon he was back in the quarries all day long.

One day, at dinnertime, Precious Auntie told me a story with her hands that only I could understand. *A rich lady came to my father and told him to unbind her feet and mold them into more modern ones. She said she wanted to wear high-heeled shoes. "But don't make the new feet too big," she said, "not like a slave girl's or a foreigner's. Make them naturally small like hers." And she pointed to my feet.*

I forgot that Mother and my other aunts were at the dinner table, and I said aloud, "Do bound feet look like the white lilies that the ro-

mantic books describe?" Mother and my aunts, who still had bound
feet, gave me a frowning look. How could I talk so openly about a
woman's most private parts? So Precious Auntie pretended to scold
me with her hands for asking such a question, but what she really
said was this: *They're usually crimped like flower-twist bread. But if
they're dirty and knotty with calluses, they look like rotten ginger roots
and smell like pig snouts three days dead.*

In this way, Precious Auntie taught me to be naughty, just like
her. She taught me to be curious, just like her. She taught me to be
spoiled. And because I was all these things, she could not teach me to
be a better daughter, though in the end, she tried to change my faults.

I remember how she tried. It was the last week we were together.
She did not speak to me for days. Instead she wrote and wrote and
wrote. Finally she handed me a bundle of pages laced together with
cord. *This is my true story,* she told me, *and yours as well.* Out of spite,
I did not read most of those pages. But when I did, this is what I
learned.

One late-autumn day, when Precious Auntie was nineteen by her
Chinese age, the bonesetter had two new patients. The first was a
screaming baby from a family who lived in Immortal Heart. The
second was Baby Uncle. They would both cause Precious Auntie
everlasting sorrow, but in two entirely different ways.

The bawling baby was the youngest son of a big-chested man
named Chang, a coffinmaker who had grown rich in times of
plagues. The carvings on the outside of his coffins were of camphor
wood. But the insides were cheap pine, painted and lacquered to look
and smell like the better golden wood.

Some of that same golden wood had fallen from a stack and
knocked the baby's shoulder out of its socket. That's why the baby
was howling, Chang's wife reported with a frightened face. Precious

Auntie recognized this nervous woman. Two years before, she had sat in the bonesetter's shop because her eye and jaw had been broken by a stone that must have fallen out of the open sky. Now she was back with her husband, who was slapping the baby's leg, telling him to stop his racket. Precious Auntie shouted at Chang: "First the shoulder, now you want to break his leg as well." Chang scowled at her. Precious Auntie picked up the baby. She rubbed a little bit of medicine inside his cheeks. Soon the baby quieted, yawned once, and fell asleep. Then the bonesetter snapped the small shoulder into place.

"What's the medicine?" the coffinmaker asked Precious Auntie. She didn't answer.

"Traditional things," the bonesetter said. "A little opium, a little herbs, and a special kind of dragon bone we dig out from a secret place only our family knows."

"Special dragon bone, eh?" Chang dipped his finger in the medicine bowl, then dabbed inside his cheek. He offered some to Precious Auntie, who sniffed in disgust, and then he laughed and gave Precious Auntie a bold look, as if he already owned her and could do whatever he pleased.

Right after the Changs and their baby left, Baby Uncle limped in.

He had been injured by his nervous horse, he explained to the bonesetter. He had been traveling from Peking to Immortal Heart, and during a rest, the horse startled a rabbit, then the rabbit startled the horse, and the horse stepped on Baby Uncle's foot. Three broken toes resulted, and Baby Uncle rode his bad horse to the Mouth of the Mountain, straight to the Famous Bonesetter's shop.

Baby Uncle sat in the blackwood examination chair. Precious Auntie was in the back room and could see him through the parted curtain. He was a thin young man of twenty-two. His face was refined but he did not act pompous or overly formal, and while his gown was not that of a rich gentleman, he was well groomed. She heard him joke about his accident: "My mare was so crazy with fright I thought she was going to gallop straight to the underworld with me stuck astride." When Precious Auntie stepped into the room, she said, "But fate brought you here instead." Baby Uncle fell quiet. When she smiled, he forgot his pain. When she put a dragon bone poultice on his naked foot, he decided to marry her. That was Precious Auntie's version of how they fell in love.

I have never seen a picture of my real father, but Precious Auntie told me that he was very handsome and smart, yet also shy enough to make a girl feel tender. He looked like a poor scholar who could rise above his circumstances, and surely he would have qualified for the imperial examinations if they had not been canceled several years before by the new Republic.

The next morning, Baby Uncle came back with three stemfuls of lychees for Precious Auntie as a gift of appreciation. He peeled off the shell of one, and she ate the white-fleshed fruit in front of him. The morning was warm for late autumn, they both remarked. He asked if he could recite a poem he had written that morning: "You speak," he said, "the language of shooting stars, more surprising than sunrise, more brilliant than the sun, as brief as sunset. I want to follow its trail to eternity."

In the afternoon, the coffinmaker Chang brought a watermelon to the bonesetter. "To show my highest appreciation," he said. "My baby son is already well, able to pick up bowls and smash them with the strength of three boys."

Later that week, unbeknownst one to the other, each man went to a different fortune-teller. The two men wanted to know if their combination of birthdates with Precious Auntie's was lucky. They asked if there were any bad omens for a marriage.

The coffinmaker went to a fortune-teller in Immortal Heart, a man who walked about the village with a divining stick. The marriage signs were excellent, the fortune-teller said. See here, Precious

Auntie was born in a Rooster year, and because Chang was a Snake, that was nearly the best match possible. The old man said that Precious Auntie also had a lucky number of strokes in her name (I will write the number down here when I remember her name). And as a bonus, she had a mole in position eleven, near the fatty part of her cheek, indicating that only sweet words fell from her obedient mouth. The coffinmaker was so happy to hear this that he gave the fortune-teller a big tip.

Baby Uncle went to a fortune-teller in the Mouth of the Mountain, an old lady with a face more wrinkled than her palm. She saw nothing but calamity. The first sign was the mole on Precious Auntie's face. It was in position twelve, she told Baby Uncle, and it dragged down her mouth, meaning that her life would always bring her sadness. Their combination of birth years was also inharmonious, she a fire Rooster and he a wood Horse. The girl would ride his back and peck him apart piece by piece. She would consume him with her insatiable demands. And here was the worst part. The girl's father and mother had reported the date of her birth was the sixteenth day of the seventh moon. But the fortune-teller had a sister-in-law who lived near the bonesetter, and she knew better. She had heard the newborn's wails, not on the sixteenth day, but on the fifteenth, the only day when unhappy ghosts are allowed to roam the earth. The sister-in-law said the baby sounded like this: *"Wu-wu, wu-wu,"* not like a human but like a haunted one. The fortune-teller confided to Baby Uncle that she knew the girl quite well. She often saw her on market days, walking by herself. That strange girl did fast calculations in her head and argued with merchants. She was arrogant and headstrong. She was also educated, taught by her father to know the mysteries of the body. The girl was too curious, too questioning, too determined to follow her own mind. Maybe she was possessed. Better find another marriage match, the fortune-teller said. This one would lead to disaster.

Baby Uncle gave the fortune-teller more money, not as a tip, but to make her think harder. The fortune-teller kept shaking her head. But after Baby Uncle had given a total of a thousand coppers, the old lady finally had another thought. When the girl smiled, which was often, her mole was in a luckier position, number eleven. The fortune-teller consulted an almanac, matched it to the hour of the girl's birth. Good news. The Hour of the Rabbit was peace-loving. Her inflexibility was just a bluff. And any leftover righteousness could be beaten down with a strong stick. It was further revealed that the fortune-teller's sister-in-law was a gossip known for exaggeration. But just to make sure the marriage went well, the fortune-teller sold Baby Uncle a Hundred Different Things charm that covered bad dates, bad spirits, bad luck, and hair loss. "But even with this, don't marry in the Dragon Year. Bad year for a Horse."

The first marriage proposal came from Chang's matchmaker, who went to the bonesetter and related the good omens. She boasted of the coffinmaker's respect, as an artisan descended from noted artisans. She described his house, his rock gardens, his fish ponds, the furniture in his many rooms, how the wood was of the best color, purple like a fresh bruise. As to the matter of a dowry, the coffinmaker was willing to be more than generous. Since the girl was to be a second wife and not a first, couldn't her dowry be a jar of opium and a jar of dragon bones? This was not much, yet it was priceless, and therefore not insulting to the girl's worth.

The bonesetter considered the offer. He was growing old. Where would his daughter go when he died? And what other man would want her in his household? She was too spirited, too set in her ways. She had no mother to teach her the manners of a wife. True, the coffinmaker would not have been his first choice of son-in-law, if he had had another, but he did not want to stand in the way of his daughter's future happiness. He told Precious Auntie about the generous offer from the coffinmaker.

To this, Precious Auntie huffed. "The man's a brute," she said. "I'd rather eat worms than be his wife."

The bonesetter had to give Chang's matchmaker an awkward answer: "I'm sorry," he said, "but my daughter cried herself sick, unable to bear the thought of leaving her worthless father." The lie would have been swallowed without disgrace, if only the offer from Baby Uncle's matchmaker had not been accepted the following week.

A few days after the future marriage was announced, the coffin-maker went back to the Mouth of the Mountain and surprised Precious Auntie as she was returning from the well. "You think you can insult me, then walk away laughing?"

"Who insulted whom? You asked me to be your concubine, a servant to your wife. I'm not interested in being a slave in a feudal marriage."

As she tried to leave, Chang pinched her neck, saying he should break it, then shook her as if he truly might snap off her head like a winter twig. But instead he threw her to the ground, cursing her and her dead mother's private parts.

When Precious Auntie recovered her breath, she sneered, "Big words, big fists. You think you can scare a person into being sorry?"

And he said these words, which she never forgot: "You'll soon be sorry every day of your miserable life."

Precious Auntie did not tell her father or Hu Sen what had happened. No sense in worrying them. And why lead her future husband to wonder if Chang had a reason to feel insulted? Too many people had already said she was too strong, accustomed to having her own way. And perhaps this was true. She had no fear of punishment or disgrace. She was afraid of almost nothing.

A month before the wedding, Baby Uncle came to her room late at night. "I want to hear your voice in the dark," he whispered. "I want to hear the language of shooting stars." She let him into her *k'ang* and he eagerly began the nuptials. But as Baby Uncle caressed her, a wind blew over her skin and she began to tremble and shake. For the first time, she was afraid, she realized, frightened by unknown joy.

The wedding was supposed to take place in Immortal Heart village, right after the start of the new Dragon Year. It was a bare spring day. Slippery pockets of ice lay on the ground. In the morning, a traveling photographer came to the bonesetter's shop in the Mouth of the Mountain. He had broken his arm the month before, and his payment was a photograph of Precious Auntie on her wedding day. She wore her best winter jacket, one with a high fur-lined collar, and an embroidered cap. She had to stare a long time into the camera, and as she did so, she thought of how her life would soon change forever. Though she was happy, she was also worried. She sensed danger, but she could not name what it was. She tried to look far into the future, but she could see nothing.

For the journey to the wedding, she changed her clothes to her bridal costume, a red jacket and skirt, the fancy headdress with a scarf that she had to drape over her head once she left her father's home. The bonesetter had borrowed money to rent two mule carts, one to carry gifts for the groom's family, the other for the bride's trunks of blankets and clothes. There was an enclosed sedan chair for the bride herself, and the bonesetter also had to hire four sedan carriers, two carters, a flute player, and two bodyguards to watch out for bandits. For his daughter, he had procured only the best: the fanciest sedan chair, the cleanest carts, the strongest guards with real pistols and gunpowder. In one of the carts was the dowry, the jar of opium and the jar of dragon bones, the last of his supply. He assured his daughter many times not to worry about the cost. After her wedding, he could go to the Monkey's Jaw and gather more bones.

Halfway between the villages, two bandits wearing hoods sprang out of the bushes. "I'm the famous Mongol Bandit!" the larger one bellowed. Right away, Precious Auntie recognized the voice of Chang the coffinmaker. What kind of ridiculous joke was this? But before she could say anything, the guards threw down their pistols, the carriers dropped their poles, and Precious Auntie was thrown to the floor of the sedan and knocked out.

When she came to, she saw Baby Uncle's face in a haze. He had lifted her out of the sedan. She looked around and saw that the wedding trunks had been ransacked and the guards and carriers had fled. And then she noticed her father lying in a ditch, his head and neck at an odd angle, the life gone from his face. Was she in a dream? "My father," she moaned. "I want to go to him." As she bent over the body, unable to make sense of what had happened, Baby Uncle picked up a pistol that one of the guards had dropped.

"I swear I'll find the demons who caused my bride so much grief," he shouted, and then he fired the pistol toward heaven, startling his horse.

Precious Auntie did not see the kick that killed Baby Uncle, but she heard it, a terrible crack, like the opening of the earth when it was born. For the rest of her life she was to hear it in the breaking of twigs, the crackling of fire, whenever a melon was cleaved in the summer.

That was how Precious Auntie became a widow and an orphan in the same day. "This is a curse," she murmured, as she stared down at the bodies of the men she loved. For three sleepless days after their deaths, Precious Auntie apologized to the corpses of her father and Baby Uncle. She talked to their still faces. She touched their mouths, though this was forbidden and caused the women of the house to fear that the wronged ghosts might either possess her or decide to stay.

On the third day, Chang arrived with two coffins. "He killed them!" Precious Auntie cried. She picked up a fire poker and tried to

strike him. She beat at the coffins. Baby Uncle's brothers had to
wrestle her away. They apologized to Chang for the girl's lunacy,
and Chang replied that grief of this magnitude was admirable. Because Precious Auntie continued to be wild with admirable grief, the
women of the house had to bind her from elbows to knees with strips
of cloth. Then they laid her on Baby Uncle's *k'ang*, where she wiggled and twisted like a butterfly stuck in its cocoon until Great-
Granny forced her to drink a bowl of medicine that made her body
grow limp. For two days and nights, she dreamed she was with Baby
Uncle, lying on the *k'ang* as his bride.

When she revived, she was alone in the dark. Her arms and legs
had been unbound, but they were weak. The house was quiet. She
went searching for her father and Baby Uncle. When she reached the
main hall, the bodies were gone, already buried in Chang's wooden
handiwork. Weeping, she wandered about the house and vowed to
join them in the yellow earth. In the ink-making studio, she went
looking for a length of rope, a sharp knife, matches she could swal-
low, anything to cause pain greater than she felt. And then she saw a
pot of black resin. She lowered a dipper into the liquid and put it in
the maw of the stove. The oily ink became a soup of blue flames. She
tipped the ladle and swallowed.

Great-Granny was the first to hear the thump-bumping sounds in
the studio. Soon the other women of the household were there as
well. They found Precious Auntie thrashing on the floor, hissing air
out of a mouth blackened with blood and ink. "Like eels are swimming in the bowl of her mouth," Mother said. "Better if she dies."

But Great-Granny did not let this happen. Baby Uncle's ghost
had come to her in a dream and warned that if Precious Auntie died,
he and his ghost bride would roam the house and seek revenge on
those who had not pitied her. Everyone knew there was nothing
worse than a vengeful ghost. They caused rooms to stink like corpses.
They turned bean curd rancid in a moment's breath. They let wild

creatures climb over the walls and gates. With a ghost in the house, you could never get a good night's sleep.

Day in and day out, Great-Granny dipped cloths into ointments and laid these over Precious Auntie's wounds. She bought dragon bones, crushed them, and sprinkled them into her swollen mouth. And then she noticed that another part of Precious Auntie had become swollen: her womb.

Over the next few months, Precious Auntie's wounds changed from pus to scars, and her womb grew like a gourd. She had once been a fine-looking girl. Now all except blind beggars shuddered at the sight of her. One day, when it was clear she was going to survive, Great-Granny said to her speechless patient: "Now that I've saved your life, where will you and your baby go? What will you do?"

That night, the ghost of Baby Uncle came once again to Great-Granny, and the next morning, Great-Granny told Precious Auntie: "You are to stay and be nursemaid to this baby. First Sister will claim it as hers and raise it as a Liu. To those you meet, we'll say you're a distant relation from Peking, a cousin who lived in a nunnery until it burned down and nearly took you with it. With that face, no one will recognize you."

And that's what happened. Precious Auntie stayed. I was the reason she stayed, her only reason to live. Five months after my birth in 1916, GaoLing was born to Mother, who had been forced by Great-Granny to claim me as her own. How could Mother say she had two babies five months apart? That was impossible. So Mother decided to wait. Exactly nine months after my birth, and on a very lucky date in 1917, GaoLing was born for sure.

The grown-ups knew the truth of our births. The children knew only what they were supposed to pretend. And though I was smart I was stupid. I did not ever question the truth. I did not wonder why Precious Auntie had no name. To others she was Nursemaid. To me, she was Precious Auntie. And I did not know who she really was until I read what she wrote.

"I am your mother," the words said.

I read that only after she died. Yet I have a memory of her telling me with her hands, I can see her saying this with her eyes. When it is dark, she says this to me in a clear voice I have never heard. She speaks in the language of shooting stars.

CHANGE

In the year 1929, my fourteenth year, I became an evil person.

That was also the year the scientists, both Chinese and foreign, came to Dragon Bone Hill at the Mouth of the Mountain. They wore sun hats and Wellington boots. They brought shovels and poking sticks, sorting pans and fizzing liquids. They dug in the quarries, they burrowed in the caves. They went from medicine shop to medicine shop, buying up all the old bones. We heard rumors that the foreigners wanted to start their own dragon bone factories, and a dozen villagers went to the quarries with axes to chase them away.

But then some of the Chinese workers who dug for the scientists passed along the rumor that two of the dragon bones might have been teeth from a human head. And everyone thought they meant a recently dead one. From whose grave? Whose grandfather? Whose grandmother? Some people stopped buying dragon bones. Big signs in the medicine shops declared: "None of our remedies contains human parts."

At the time, Precious Auntie still had four or five dragon bones left from our visits to the family cave, not counting the oracle bone her father had given her long ago. The others she had used as medicine for me over the years, and those, she assured me, were not human. Soon after she said this, her father, the Famous Bonesetter, came to her in a dream. "The bones you have are not from dragons," he said. "They are from our own clan, the ancestor who was crushed in the Monkey's Jaw. And because we stole them, he's cursed us. That's why nearly everyone in our family has died, your mother, your brother, myself, your future husband—because of this curse. And it doesn't stop with death. Ever since I arrived in the World of Yin, his shadow has been jumping on me from every turn. If I were not already dead, I would have died of fright a thousand times."

"What should we do?" Precious Auntie asked in her dream.

"Return the bones. Until they're reunited with the rest of his body, he'll continue to plague us. You'll be next, and any future generations of our family will be cursed, too. Believe me, daughter, there is nothing worse than having your own relative out for revenge."

The next morning, Precious Auntie rose early, and she was gone almost the entire day. When she returned, she seemed more at ease. But then the workmen from Dragon Bone Hill passed along this news: "The teeth," they said, "are not only human but belong to a piece of skullcap from our oldest ancestors, one million years old!" "Peking Man" was what the scientists decided to call the skullcap. They just needed to find more pieces to make a whole skullcap, and a few more after that to connect his skull to his jaw, his jaw to his neck, his neck to his shoulders, and so on, until he was a complete man. That meant a lot of pieces had to be found, and that was why the scientists were asking the villagers to bring all the dragon bones they had lying around their houses and medicine shops. If the dragon bones proved to be from ancient humans, the owner would receive a reward.

One million years! Everyone kept saying this. One day they had no need to say this number, the next day they could not say it enough. Little Uncle guessed that a person might earn a million coppers for a single piece of dragon bone. And Father said, "Coppers are worth nothing these days. A million silver taels are more likely."

By guesses and arguments, the amount grew to be a million gold ingots. The whole town was talking about this. "Old bones grow new fat," became the saying people had on their lips. And because dragon bones were now worth so much, at least in people's wild imaginations, no one could buy them for medicine anymore. Those folks with life-draining ailments could no longer be cured. But what did that matter? They were the descendants of Peking Man. And he was famous.

Naturally, I thought about the dragon bones that Precious Auntie had put back in the cave. They were human, too—her father had said so in her dream. "We could sell them for a million ingots," I told her. I reasoned I was not just thinking selfishly. If Precious Auntie made us rich, my family might respect her more.

A million or ten million, she scolded with her moving hands, *if we sell them, the curse will return. A ghost will then come and take us and our miserable bones with it. Then we'll have to wear the weight of those million ingots around our dead necks to bribe our way through hell.* She poked my forehead. *I tell you, the ghosts won't rest until all of our family is dead. The entire family, gone.* She knocked her fist against her chest. *Sometimes I wish I were already dead. I wanted to die, really I did, but I came back for you.*

"Well, I'm not afraid," I answered. "And since the curse is on you and not me, I can go get the bones."

Suddenly Precious Auntie slapped the side of my head. *Stop this talk!* Her hands sliced the air. *You want to add to my curse? Never go back. Never touch them. Say you won't, say it now!* She grabbed my shoulders and rattled me until a promise fell out of my clacking mouth.

· Later I daydreamed of sneaking to the cave. How could I sit by while everyone in the Mouth of the Mountain and the surrounding villages went looking for immortal relics? I knew where the human bones were, and yet I could say nothing. I had to watch as others gouged where their sheep chewed grass, gutted where their pigs wal-

lowed in the mud. Even First Brother and Second Brother, along
with their wives, dredged the remaining land between our compound and the cliff. From the muck they yanked out roots and
worms. They guessed that these might be ancient men's fingers and
toes, or even the fossilized tongue that spoke the first words of our
ancestors. The streets filled with people trying to sell all kinds of
dried-up relics, from chicken beaks to pig turds. In a short while, our
village looked worse than a burial ground dug up by grave robbers.

Day and night the family talked of Peking Man and almost nothing else. "Million years?" Mother wondered aloud. "How can anyone know the age of someone who has been dead that long? Hnh,
when my grandfather died, no one knew if he was sixty-eight or
sixty-nine. Eighty was how long he should have lived, if only he had
had better luck. So eighty was what our family decided he was—
luckier, yes, but still dead."

I, too, had something to say on the new discovery: "Why are they
calling him Peking Man? The teeth came from the Mouth of the
Mountain. And now the scientists are saying that skullcap was a
woman's. So it should be called Woman from the Mouth of the
Mountain." My aunts and uncles looked at me, and one of them said:
"Wisdom from a child's lips, simple yet true." I was embarrassed to
hear such high words. Then GaoLing added, "I think he should be
called Immortal Heart Man. Then our town would be famous and so
would we." Mother praised her suggestion to the skies, and the others did as well. To my mind, however, her idea made no sense, but I
could not say this.

I was often jealous when GaoLing received more attention from
the mother we shared. I still believed I was the eldest daughter. I was
smarter. I had done better in school. Yet GaoLing always had the
honor of sitting next to Mother, of sleeping in her *k'ang*, while I had
Precious Auntie.

When I was younger, that did not bother me. I felt I was lucky to have her by my side. I thought the words "Precious Auntie" were the same as what others meant by "Ma." I could not bear to be separated from my nursemaid for even one moment. I had admired her and was proud that she could write the names of every flower, seed, and bush, as well as say their medicinal uses. But the bigger I grew, the more she shrank in importance. The smarter I thought I had become, the more I was able to reason that Precious Auntie was only a servant, a woman who held no great position in our household, a person no one liked. She could have made our family rich, if only she did not have crazy thoughts about curses.

I began to increase my respect for Mother. I sought her favor. I believed favor was the same as love. Favor made me feel more important, more content. After all, Mother was the number-one-ranking lady of the house. She decided what we ate, what colors we should wear, how much pocket money we received for those times she allowed us to go to the market. Everyone both feared her and wanted to please her, all except Great-Granny, who was now so feeble-minded she could not tell ink from mud.

But in Mother's eyes, I had no charms. To her ears, my words had no music. It did not matter how obedient I was, how humble or clean. Nothing I did satisfied her. I became confused as to what I must do to please her. I was like a turtle lying on its back, struggling to know why the world was upside down.

Often I complained to Precious Auntie that Mother did not love me. *Stop your nonsense,* Precious Auntie would answer. *Didn't you hear her today? She said your sewing stitches were sloppy. And she mentioned your skin was getting too dark. If she didn't love you, why did she bother to criticize you for your own good?* And then Precious Auntie went on to say how selfish I was, always thinking about myself. She said my face looked ugly when I pouted. She criticized me so much I did not consider until now that she was saying she loved me even more.

One day—I remember this was sometime before Spring Festival—Old Cook came back from the market and said big news was flying through Immortal Heart. Chang the coffinmaker had become famous and was soon to be very rich. Those dragon bones he had given to the scientists? The results had come back: They were human. How old was not certain yet, but everyone guessed they were at least a million years, maybe even two.

We were in the ink-making studio, all the women, girls, and babies, except for Precious Auntie, who was in the root cellar, counting the inksticks she had already carved. I was glad she wasn't in the studio, because whenever anyone mentioned Chang's name, she spat. So when he delivered wood, she was sent to her room, where she cursed him by banging on a pail so long and loud that even the tenants yelled back.

"What a peculiar coincidence," Big Aunt now said. "The same Mr. Chang who sells us wood. His luck could have been ours just as easily."

"The association goes back even farther than that," Mother boasted. "He was the man who stopped his cart to help after Baby Brother was killed by the Mongol bandits. A man of good deeds, that Mr. Chang."

It seemed there was no end to the many ways we were connected to the now famous Mr. Chang. Since Mr. Chang would soon be even richer than before, Mother thought he would surely reduce the price of his leftover wood. "He should share his luck," Mother agreed with herself. "The gods expect him to do no less."

Precious Auntie came back to the ink studio, and in a short while she realized who it was everyone was talking about. She stamped her feet and punched the air with her fists. *Chang is evil,* she said, her arms flailing. *He killed my father. He is the reason Hu Sen is dead.* She made a rasping sound as if the whole of her throat would slough off.

That was not true, I thought. Her father had fallen off a wagon when he was drunk, and Baby Uncle had been kicked by his own horse. Mother and my aunts had told me so.

Precious Auntie grabbed my arm. She looked into my eyes, then talked fast with her hands, *Tell them, Doggie, tell them what I'm saying is true. And the dragon bones Chang has,* and she poured imaginary ones into her palm, *I realize now that they probably are the ones that belonged to my father, my family. Chang stole them from us on my wedding day. They were my dowry. They are bones from the Monkey's Jaw. We need to get them back from Chang, return them to the cave or the curse will go on and on. Hurry, tell them.*

Before I could, Mother warned: "I don't want to hear any more of her crazy stories. Do you hear me, Daughter?"

Everyone stared at me, including Precious Auntie. *Tell them,* she signaled. But I turned to Mother, nodded, and said, "I heard." Precious Auntie ran out of the ink studio with a choking sound that twisted my heart and made me feel evil.

For a while, it was very quiet in the studio. Then Great-Granny went up to Mother and said with a worried face: "Eh, have you seen Hu Sen?"

"He's in the courtyard," Mother answered. And Great-Granny shuffled out.

My uncles' wives began to cluck their tongues. "Still crazy from what happened," Little Aunt muttered, "and that was almost fifteen years ago." For a moment, I did not know if they were talking about Great-Granny or Precious Auntie.

Big Aunt added, "Good thing she can't talk. It would be a terrible embarrassment to our family if anyone knew what she was trying to say."

"You should turn her out of the house," Little Aunt said to Mother. And then Mother nodded toward Great-Granny, who was now wandering about, scratching at a bloody spot on the back of her ear. "It's because of old Granny," she said, "that the lunatic nursemaid has stayed all these years." And I knew then what Mother really meant but could not say. When Great-Granny died, she could finally tell Precious Auntie to go. All at once, I felt tender toward my nursemaid. I wanted to protest that Mother must not do this. But how could I argue against something that had not yet been said?

A month later, Great-Granny fell and hit her head on the brick edge of her *k'ang*. Before the Hour of the Rooster she was dead. Father, Big Uncle, and Little Uncle returned home from Peking, though the roads had become dangerous. A lot of shooting among warlords was going on between Peking and the Mouth of the Mountain. Lucky for us, the only fighting we saw was among the tenants. We had to ask them several times not to scream and shout while we were paying respects to Great-Granny as she lay in the common hall.

When Mr. Chang delivered the coffin, Precious Auntie stayed in her room and cursed him with her banging pail. I was sitting on a bench in the front courtyard, watching as Father and Mr. Chang unloaded the cart.

I thought to myself, Precious Auntie is wrong. Mr. Chang didn't look like a thief. He was a large man with friendly manners and an open face. Father was eagerly discussing with him his "important contribution to science, history, and all of China." To this, Mr. Chang acted both modest and pleased. Then Father left to get Mr. Chang's money for the coffin.

Though it was a cold day, Mr. Chang was sweating. He wiped his brow with his sleeve. After a while, he noticed I was staring at him. "You've certainly grown big," he called to me. I blushed. A famous man was talking to me.

"My sister is bigger," I thought to say. "And she's a year younger."

"Ah, that's good," he said.

I had not intended for him to praise GaoLing. "I heard that you had pieces of Peking Man," I then said. "What parts?"

"Oh, only the most important."

And I, too, wanted to seem important, so I blurted without thinking, "I once had some bones myself," before I slapped my hand over my mouth.

Mr. Chang smiled, waiting for me to continue. "Where are they?" he said after a while.

I could not be impolite. "We took them back to the cave," I answered.

"Where's that?"

"I can't say where. My nursemaid made me promise. It's a secret."

"Ah, your nursemaid. She's the one with the ugly face." Mr. Chang stiffened his fingers like a crab and held them over his mouth.

I nodded.

"The crazy person." He looked toward the sounds of the banging pail. I said nothing.

"And she found bones from this place you can't talk about?"

"We found them together, she took them back," I answered quickly. "But I can't say where."

"Of course. You shouldn't tell a stranger."

"Oh, you're not a stranger! Our family knows you very well. We all say so."

"Still, you shouldn't tell me. But surely you've told your own father and mother."

I shook my head. "No one. If I did, they would want to dig them out. Precious Auntie said so. She said the bones have to stay in the cave or she would suffer the consequences."

"What consequences?"

"A curse. She'll die if I say."

"But she is already quite old, is she not?"

"I don't know. I don't think so."

"Often women die at all sorts of ages and it's not because of a curse. Illness or accident, that's often the cause. My first wife died ten years ago. She was always clumsy and one day she fell off a roof. Now I have a new wife and she's even better than the last. If your nursemaid dies, you can get a new one, too."

"I'm too old for another," I said. I did not like our conversation anymore. Soon Father returned with Mr. Chang's money. They chatted a few more minutes in a friendly manner, and then Mr. Chang called to me, "Next time I see you, we'll talk again," and he left with his empty cart. Father seemed pleased that Mr. Chang, who was now such a well-known man in our town, had found me worthy of attention.

A few days later, we had a proper funeral for Great-Granny. Everyone wailed loudly, but Mother was the loudest, as was the custom, she being the number-one-ranking lady of the house. She did a very good job sounding sad beyond hope. And I, too, cried, sad but also afraid. And when the funeral was over, I became nervous of what would happen next: Mother would make Precious Auntie leave.

But she did not, and this was why.

Mother believed Great-Granny was still around, haunting the outhouse and making sure everyone still followed her rules. Every time Mother squatted over the hole, she heard a voice asking, "Have you seen Hu Sen?" When she told us this, Third Aunt said, "The sight of your bare bottom should have scared away any ghost." And we all laughed, but Mother became angry and announced she was cutting off everyone's allowance for the next month. "To teach you to have more respect for Great-Granny," she said. For the ghost in the outhouse, Mother went to the village temple every day and gave special offerings. She went to Great-Granny's grave and burned silver paper, so Great-Granny could buy her way to a better level. After ninety days of constipation, Mother went back to the funerary ship and bought a paper automobile large as life, complete with chauffeur. Great-Granny had seen a real one once at a temple fair in the Mouth of the Mountain. It was in the parking lot where carts and donkeys were kept, and when the automobile roared away, she said, it was loud enough to scare the devil and fast enough to fly to heaven.

So the paper auto went up in flames, and Great-Granny's ghost traveled from the latrine to the World of Yin. And then our household went back to its normal, noisy ways. For the rest of the family, the concerns were on little daily matters: mold in the millet, a crack in the glass, nothing at all of lasting importance.

And only I worried about what would happen to Precious Auntie.

I remember the day Mother received a surprise letter from Peking. It was the period of Great Heat, when mosquitoes were their happiest and fruit left outside rotted in less than an hour under the sun. Great-Granny had been dead for more than ninety days. We sat in the shade of the big tree in the courtyard, waiting to hear the news.

We all knew the letter writer, Old Widow Lau. She was a cousin, within eight degrees of kinship on Father's side and five degrees on Mother's side, close enough to follow the mourning rituals of family. She had come to Great-Granny's funeral and had wailed as loudly as the rest of us.

Since Mother could not read, she asked GaoLing, and I had to hide my disappointment that she had been chosen for this important task. GaoLing smoothed her hair, cleared her throat, licked her lips, then read: " 'Dear Cousin, I send greetings from all those who have asked after you with deep feeling.' " GaoLing then stumbled through a long list of names, from those of brand-new babies to people Mother was sure were already dead. On the next page, our old cousin wrote something like this: "I know you are still in mourning and barely able to eat because of grief. So it is not a good time to invite everyone to come visit in Peking. But I have been thinking about what you and I discussed when we last saw each other at the funeral."

GaoLing broke off reading and turned to Mother. "What did you discuss?" I, too, was wondering this.

Mother slapped GaoLing's hand. "Don't be nosy. You just read, and I'll tell you what you should know."

The letter continued: " 'I wish to humbly suggest that your number-one daughter' "—she was speaking of me, and my heart swelled—" 'come to Peking and accidentally meet a distant relation of mine.' " GaoLing threw me a scowl, and I was pleased she was jealous. " 'This relation,' " GaoLing went on reading in a less enthusiastic voice, " 'has four sons, who are seventh cousins of mine, three times removed, with a different surname. They live in your same village, but are barely related to you, if at all.' "

When I heard the words "barely related," I knew this accidental meeting meant she wanted to see whether I might be a marriage match for a certain family. I was fourteen (this was by my Chinese age), and most of the girls my age were already married. As to which family, Old Widow Lau did not want to say, unless she knew for certain that our family believed such an accident could be beneficial. "To be honest," she wrote, "I would not have thought of this family on my own. But the father came to me and asked about LuLing. They have apparently seen the girl and are impressed with her beauty and sweet nature."

My face flushed. At last Mother knew what others were saying about me. Perhaps she might see these good qualities in me as well.

"I want to go to Peking, too," GaoLing said like a complaining cat.

Mother scolded her: "Did anyone invite you? No? Well, then,

you only look stupid for saying you want to go." When she whined
again, Mother yanked her braid and said, "Shut your mouth," before
handing me the letter to finish reading.

I sat up straight, facing Mother, and read with much expression:
" 'The family suggests a meeting at your family's ink shop in
Peking.' " I stopped a moment and smiled at GaoLing. I had never
seen the shop, nor had she. " 'In this way,' " I continued, " 'if there is
any disharmony of interest, there will be no public embarrassment to
either family. If both families are in agreement about the match, then
this will be a blessing from the gods for which I can take no credit.' "

"No credit," Mother said with a snort, "just a lot of gifts."

The next part of the letter went like this: "A good daughter-in-
law is hard to find, I'm sure you will agree. Perhaps you remember
my second daughter-in-law? I am ashamed to admit that she has
turned out to be coldhearted. Today she suggested that your daughter's nursemaid should not accompany her to Peking. She said that if
a person were to see the two together, he would remember only the
shocking ugliness of the nursemaid and not the emerging beauty of
the maiden. I told her that was nonsense. But as I write this letter, I
realize now that it would be inconvenient to accommodate another
servant, since mine already complain that there is not enough room
for them to sleep in one bed. So perhaps it would be better if the
nursemaid does not come after all. I apologize that nothing can be
done about the poverty of our household. . . ."

Only when I was done reading did I look up at Precious Auntie,
embarrassed. *Never mind,* she signed to me quietly. *I'll tell her later
that I can sleep on the floor.* I turned to Mother, waiting to hear what
more she had to say.

"Write a letter back. Tell Old Widow Lau that I will have you go
in a week. I'd take you myself, but it's the ink season and we have
too much to do. I'll ask Mr. Wei to take you in his cart. He always

makes a medical delivery to Peking on the first and won't mind an extra passenger in exchange for a little cash."

Precious Auntie flapped her hands for my attention. *Now is the time to tell her you can't go alone. Who will make sure it's a good marriage? What if that busybody idiot cousin tries to barter you off as a second wife to a poor family? Ask her to consider that.*

I shook my head. I was afraid to anger Mother with a lot of unnecessary questions and ruin my chances to visit Peking. Precious Auntie tugged my sleeve. I ignored her. Lately I had done this a few times, and it infuriated Precious Auntie. Since she could not speak and Mother could not read, when I refused to talk for her, she was left wordless, powerless.

Back in our room, Precious Auntie beseeched me. *You are too young to go to Peking by yourself. This is more dangerous than you can imagine. You could be killed by bandits, your head chopped off and put on a stake. . . .* I did not answer her, I did not argue, I gave her no ground on which to keep her footing. On and on she went that day, the next, and the day after that. At times, she expressed anger at what Old Widow Lau had written. *That woman does not care about what's best for you. She sticks her nose in other people's business for money. Soon she'll stink like the bottoms she's been smelling.*

Later Precious Auntie handed me a letter, which I was supposed to give to GaoLing so she could read it to Mother. I nodded, and as soon as I was out of the room and around the corner, I read it: "Besides all the shooting and unrest, the summer air there is full of diseases. And in Peking, there are strange ailments we have never even experienced here, maladies that could make the tips of LuLing's nose and fingers fall off. Luckily, I know the remedies to treat such problems so that LuLing does not return home bringing with her an epidemic. . . ."

When Precious Auntie asked me if I had given Mother the letter,

I made my face and heart a stone wall. "Yes," I lied. Precious Auntie sighed, relieved. This was the first time she had believed a lie of mine. I wondered what had changed within her that she could no longer sense if I was telling the truth. Or was it I who had changed?

The night before I was to leave, Precious Auntie stood before me with the letter, which I had wadded into a little ball and stuffed in a pocket of my trousers. *What is the meaning of this?* She grabbed my arm.

"Leave me alone," I protested. "You can't tell me what to do anymore."

You think you're so smart? You're still a silly baby.

"I'm not. I don't need you anymore."

If you had a brain then you wouldn't need me.

"You want to keep me here only so you won't lose your position as nursemaid."

Her face turned dark, as if she were choking. *Position? You think I am here only for a lowly position as your nursemaid? Ai-ya! Why am I still alive to hear this child say such things?*

Our chests were heaving. And I shouted back what I had often heard Mother and my aunts say: "You're alive because our family was good and took pity on you and saved your life. We didn't have to. And Baby Uncle never should have tried to marry you. It was bad luck that he tried. That's why he was killed by his own horse. Everyone knows it."

Her whole body slumped, and I thought she was acknowledging that I was right. At that moment, I pitied her in the same way I pitied beggars I could not look in the eye. I felt I had grown up at last and she had lost her power over me. It was as if the old me was looking at the new me, admiring how much I had changed.

The next morning, Precious Auntie did not help me with my bundle of clothes. She did not prepare a lunch I could take along. Instead, she sat on the edge of the *k'ang*, refusing to look at me. The sun was not up yet, but I could see that her eyes were red and puffy. My heart wobbled, but my mind was firm.

Two hours before daybreak, Mr. Wei came by with his donkey loaded with cages of snakes for medicine shops. I tied on a scarf to keep the sun off my face. As I climbed into the cart next to him, everyone except Precious Auntie was standing at the gate to see me off. Even GaoLing was there with her unwashed face. "Bring me back a doll," she shouted. At thirteen, she was still such a baby.

The day was a long ride of never-ending dust. Whenever the donkey stopped to drink water, Mr. Wei dipped a large rag into the stream and wrapped it around his head to keep himself cool. Soon I was doing the same with my scarf. At lunchtime, Mr. Wei pulled out a tin with dumplings inside. I had nothing. I had not wanted to ask Old Cook to fix me a tin, for fear he would tell Mother that it was too much of a nuisance to send me to Peking. Of course, Mr. Wei offered me some of his food. And naturally, I pretended that I was not hungry. And then he offered only twice more; the last offer never came. So I had to ride the rest of the way with an empty stomach and eight cages of ugly snakes.

In the late afternoon, we approached Peking. I instantly revived from the listlessness of the heat and my hunger. When we entered the inspection station, I worried that we would be refused permission to go on. A policeman with a cap poked through my small bundle and looked inside the cages with Mr. Wei's snakes.

"What is your reason for being in Peking?" the policeman asked.

"Delivery of medicine." Mr. Wei nodded to the snake cages.

"Marriage," I answered truthfully, and the policeman turned to another and called out my answer and they both laughed. After that, they let us go in. Soon I saw a tall memorial archway in the distance, its gold letters glinting like the sun. We passed through this and entered a roadway as wide as the greatest of rivers. Rickshaws raced by, more in one glance than I had seen in a lifetime. And over there, an automobile, like the paper one Mother had burned for Great-Granny. I began to measure all the sights in comparison with my life before. The markets were larger and louder. The streets were filled with busier crowds. I saw men in loose-weave long jackets, others in Western suits. Those men looked more impatient, more important. And there were many girls in floating dresses, wearing hairstyles exactly like those of famous actresses, the fringe in front crimped like dried noodles. I thought they were prettier than any of the girls in Immortal Heart. We passed walkways lined with peddlers selling every kind of bird, insect, and lizard on a stick, and they were ten times more expensive than the best snack we could buy in our own town. Farther on, I saw persimmons that were more golden, peanuts that were fatter, and sugar-coated haws that were a shinier red. I heard a crisp crack, saw the freshly opened gut of a more delicious-looking melon. And those who could not resist a slice looked more satisfied than any other melon-eaters I had ever seen.

"If you gawk any more, your head will twist right off," Mr. Wei said. I kept tallying the sights in my head so I could tell everyone all that I had seen. I was imagining their awe, Mother's admiration, GaoLing's envy. I could also see the disappointment in Precious Auntie's face. She would not want me to have a good time. So I pushed her out of my mind.

Mr. Wei stopped several times to ask for directions to a certain shop near Lantern Market Street, then went looking for a particular alleyway, and finally we stood in front of the gate that led into the cramped courtyard of Old Widow Lau's house. Two dogs ran toward me, barking.

"Ai! Are you a girl or a yellow mud statue!" Old Widow Lau said in greeting. Dirt ringed my neck, my hands, every place where my body had a crease or a bend. I stood in a four-walled courtyard compound that was so chaotic my arrival raised almost no notice. Right away, Old Widow Lau told me dinner was almost ready so I'd better hurry and wash up. She handed me a beaten bucket and told me where the well pump was. As I filled the bucket, I recalled that Mother had said Peking water was sweet. I took a sip, but it was brackish, terrible-tasting. No wonder Precious Auntie had told me that Peking was once the wasteland of the bitter sea. Just then, I realized this was the first time she was not there to help me with my bath. Where was the tub? Where was the stove for warming the water? I was too scared to touch anything. I squatted behind a mat shed and poured cold water over my neck, angry with Precious Auntie for turning me into such a stupid girl, one now afraid to show everyone how stupid I really was.

After I finished, I realized I had not thought to bring a comb for my hair or wooden sticks for cleaning under my nails. Precious Auntie always remembered those things for me. *She* was the reason I forgot! At least I had brought a clean shirt-jacket and trousers. But of course, these were wrinkled and dusty when I pulled them out from my bundle.

During the evening meal, another thought came to me. This was the first time I did not have Precious Auntie telling me which things I should and should not eat. For that I was glad. "Not too many greasy-spicy things," she would have warned, "or you'll break out in boils and other dampness diseases." So I ate several helpings of spicy pork. But later I had a queasy feeling and worried that my stomach was blistering inside out.

After dinner, I sat in the courtyard with Old Widow Lau and her daughters-in-law, listening to the buzz of mosquitoes and gossiping voices. I slapped the insects away, recalling the big fan Precious Auntie used to chase the heat and the bugs from both of us. When my eyes kept falling down, Old Widow Lau told me to go find my bed. So I went to the sad little shed that held my bundle and a rope-cot. As I fingered the holes of the cot's rattan weave, I realized yet another thing: This was the first time I had to sleep by myself. I lay down and closed my eyes. As I tumbled into thoughtlessness, I heard rats scratching along the wall. I leaned over to see if cups of turpentine had been placed under the legs of the cot. They had not. And again, rather than be grateful that Precious Auntie had always done all these things for me, I blamed her for keeping me so stupid.

When I awoke, I found I had no one to fix my hair or inspect my ears and nails. Having no comb, I used my fingers to undo the tangles. The shirt-jacket and trousers I had worn to bed were sweaty, and no fresh clothes lay in their place. They were not suitable to wear for my accidental meeting that day. And the costume that I had chosen to wear now did not look quite right, but that was all I had thought to bring. I was a grown girl, and there I was, helpless and stupid beyond belief. That was how well Precious Auntie had raised me.

When I appeared before Old Widow Lau, she exclaimed, "Is your head just an empty eggshell? Why are you wearing a padded jacket and winter trousers? And what's the matter with your hair?"

How could I answer? That Precious Auntie had refused to advise me? The truth was, when I had chosen these clothes, I was thinking only that I should bring my best things with the nicest embroidery. And my best had not seemed too uncomfortable when I had put them in my bundle during the cooler hours of the morning the day before.

"What a disaster!" Old Widow Lau muttered as she flung about all the clothing I had brought. "Pity the family that takes in this stupid girl for a daughter-in-law." She hurried to her trunks to search among the slim dresses of her youth. At last she settled on a dress borrowed from one of her daughters-in-law, a lightweight *chipao* that was not too old-fashioned. It had a high collar, short sleeves, and was woven in the colors of summer foliage, lilac for the body and leafy green for the trim and frog clasps. Old Widow Lau then undid my messy braids and dragged a wet comb through my hair.

At noon she announced we were leaving for the ink shop. She informed her servant we would not eat our lunch at home. She was certain her cousin the inkmaker was preparing a special meal at his place. "If the other family is also there," she warned me, "eat a little of each dish to show you are not picky, but don't be greedy. Let others be served first and act like you are the least important."

Lantern Market Street was not far from the Pottery-Glazing District, perhaps a thirty-minute rickshaw ride. But Old Widow Lau was afraid we might accidentally miss our accidental meeting if we did not allow for a few extra minutes to ensure that we arrived on time. "After all," she fretted aloud, "what if the rickshaw driver is old and lame? What if it begins to rain?"

Sometime after the noon hour, I found myself standing before our family's ink shop, anxious to see Father. Old Widow Lau was paying the rickshaw driver—or rather, arguing with him that he should not charge us so much for an extra passenger since I was still a small child. "Small child?" the driver said with a huff. "Where are your eyes, old woman?" I stared at the lap of the lilac dress I had borrowed, patted the neatly knotted bun at the back of my head. I was embarrassed but also proud that the driver thought I was a grown-up woman.

Almost every door on the street led to a shop, and flanking each door were red banners with good-luck couplets. The couplet by our family's shop was particularly fine. It had been written in a cursive style, the one Precious Auntie was teaching me to copy. The manner was more like a painting than writing, very expressive, running down like cloud-swept branches. You could tell that whoever had written this was an artist, cultured and deserving of respect. Reluctantly, I admitted to myself that this calligraphy must have been Precious Auntie's.

At last, Old Widow Lau was done haggling with the driver and we stepped inside Father's shop. It was north-facing, quite dim inside, and perhaps this was why Father did not see us at first. He was busy with a customer, a man who was distinguished-looking, like the scholars of two decades before. The two men were bent over a glass case, discussing the different qualities of inksticks. Big Uncle welcomed us and invited us to be seated. From his formal tone, I knew he did not recognize who we were. So I called his name in a shy voice. And he squinted at me, then laughed and announced our arrival to Little Uncle, who apologized many times for not rushing over sooner to greet us. They rushed us to be seated at one of two tea tables for customers. Old Widow Lau refused their invitation three times, exclaiming that my father and uncles must be too busy for visitors. She made weak efforts to leave. On the fourth insistence, we finally sat. Then Little Uncle brought us hot tea and sweet oranges, as well as bamboo latticework fans with which to cool ourselves.

I tried to notice everything so I could later tell GaoLing what I had seen, and tease out her envy. The floors of the shop were of dark wood, polished and clean, no dirty footprints, even though this was during the dustiest part of the summer. And along the walls were display cases made of wood and glass. The glass was very shiny and not one pane was broken. Within those glass cases were our silk-wrapped boxes, all our hard work. They looked so much nicer than they had in the ink-making studio at Immortal Heart village.

I saw that Father had opened several of the boxes. He set sticks and cakes and other shapes on a silk cloth covering a glass case that served as a table on which he and the customer leaned. First he pointed to a stick with a top shaped like a fairy boat and said with graceful importance, "Your writing will flow as smoothly as a keel cutting through a glassy lake." He picked up a bird shape: "Your mind will soar into the clouds of higher thought." He waved toward a row of ink cakes embellished with designs of peonies and bamboo: "Your ledgers will blossom into abundance while bamboo surrounds your quiet mind."

As he said this, Precious Auntie came back into my mind. I was remembering how she taught me that everything, even ink, had a purpose and a meaning: Good ink cannot be the quick kind, ready to pour out of a bottle. You can never be an artist if your work comes without effort. That is the problem with modern ink from a bottle. You do not have to think. You simply write what is swimming on the top of your brain. And the top is nothing but pond scum, dead leaves, and mosquito spawn. But when you push an inkstick along an inkstone, you take the first step to cleansing your mind and your heart. You push and you ask yourself, What are my intentions? What is in my heart that matches my mind?

I remembered this, and yet that day in the ink shop, I listened to what Father was saying, and his words became far more important than anything Precious Auntie had thought. "Look here," Father said to his customer, and I looked. He held up an inkstick and rotated it in the light. "See? It's the right hue, purple-black, not brown or gray like the cheap brands you might find down the street. And listen to this." And I heard a sound as clean and pure as a small silver bell. "The high-pitched tone tells you that the soot is very fine, as smooth as the sliding banks of old rivers. And the scent—can you smell the balance of strength and delicacy, the musical notes of the ink's perfume? Expensive, and everyone who sees you using it will know that it was well worth the high price."

I was very proud to hear Father speak of our family's ink this way. I sniffed the hot air. The smell of spices and camphor was very strong.

"This soot," Father continued, "is far better than Anhui pine. We make it from a kind of tree so rare that it's now forbidden to chop it down. Luckily, we have a supply felled by lightning, blessed by the gods." Father asked the customer if he had heard about the ancient human skullcap recently unearthed from the quarry at Dragon Bone Hill. The old scholar nodded. "Well, we're from the village one hill over," Father explained. "And the trees in our village are said to be *more* than a million years old! How do we know? Think about it. When those million-year-old folks roamed the earth around Dragon Bone Hill, didn't they need trees to sit under? Trees for shade? Trees to make fires? Trees to build stools and tables and beds? Aha, am I right? Well then, we, the people from the village next to Dragon Bone Hill, supplied that need. And now we're the ones who own the remains of those ancestral trees. We call them Immortal Heart wood."

Father motioned to the shelves. "Now, look here, on this shelf there's only a pinch per stick, so the cost is less. In this row, two pinches. And in this case, it is almost entirely the soot of Immortal Tree wood. The ink draws easily into the brush, like nectar into a butterfly's nostril."

In the end, the customer bought several of the most expensive sticks and left the shop. I wanted to clap, as if I had just seen a play for the gods. And then Father was coming toward us, toward me. I rose from the chair with a leaping heart. I had not seen him since Great-Granny's funeral more than three months before. I wondered if he would say anything about my more grown-up appearance.

"What! Is it already five o'clock in the evening?" he asked.

This caused Old Widow Lau to jump up and cry, "We're too early! We should leave and come back later!"

That was how I learned what time we were supposed to come, five o'clock, not one. Old Widow Lau was so upset by this open announcement of her mistake that my father had to insist five times that she be seated again. And then my uncles brought more tea and more oranges, but still everything was awkward.

After a while, Father expressed his care and his concern for me. "You look too thin," he said. Or perhaps he said I was looking quite plump. Next he asked after the health of my mother, then that of GaoLing and my younger brothers, then that of the various aunts and in-laws. Good, well, fine, I chattered like a duck. Wearing those new clothes, it was hard for me to answer in a natural way. Finally he asked if I had eaten yet. And although I was hungry enough to faint, I had no chance to answer, for Old Widow Lau was crying: "We've eaten, we're full enough to burst! Please don't let us be any more trouble. Go on with your work."

"We're not busy at all," Father answered out of politeness, "not too busy for family."

And Old Widow Lau answered even more politely, "Really, we must go . . . but before we leave, have you heard what happened to . . . ?" And she started talking nervously of some distant relations. After Old Widow Lau had mentioned at least five or six more relatives, my father set down his teacup and stood up.

"Cousin Lau, where are my manners? I shouldn't force you to entertain me any longer. I know you came early so you and my daughter could wander the city streets and become lost in marvelous sights." He handed me a few coins for sweets and dumplings, warning me I should treat Elder Aunt well and not wear her out. "Take your time," he told her. "No need to rush back for our sake."

Old Widow Lau was embarrassed to be dismissed in this clever way. I was overjoyed. And soon we were outside in the festering heat.

Down the lane we found a dumpling stall where we could sit on outdoor benches. As I gobbled down my dumplings, Old Widow Lau complained that the hot dampness was swelling her feet: "Soon they'll be as soft and useless as rotted bananas." She was too frugal to take a rickshaw home to Lantern Market Street, only to have to turn around and come back. But she worried aloud that when we returned to the shop at five o'clock, we would have our accidental meeting with someone important, and there we would be, mouths open, tongues out, panting like worm-infested gutter dogs. "Don't sweat," she warned me.

We started walking, searching for shade. I listened to Old Widow Lau's complaints with one ear as I watched people pass us on the streets: Young men who appeared to be students or apprentices. Old Manchu women with heavy bundles. Girls with short modern hair-styles and Western clothes. Everyone walked with purpose, a quick step that was not the style of people back home. Now and then, Old Widow Lau pushed my shoulder and snapped, "Eh! Don't gawk like you're an old greasy-hat from the countryside."

And so we continued our ramble, two streets east, then two streets north, then two streets east again. That was the method my old cousin took to avoid our getting lost. Soon we found ourselves in a park with weeping willows and walkways over a pond covered with floating flowers and twitching larvae. Old Widow Lau sat down on a bench under the shade of a tree and began to fan herself vigor-ously, complaining that she was going to explode like an overbaked yam. In a short while, her jaw dropped onto her chest and she was asleep.

Close by was an open-air pavilion made of dark wood lattice screens and rows of column posts supporting its heavy tiled roof. I went to a corner of the pavilion and squeezed against a post, trying to make myself still and unseen like a lizard. From there, I watched a man mastering his mind over his sword. I saw an old man blowing musical notes out of a metal comb, while the old woman beside him peeled an orange and tried to catch a butterfly that dipped and swooped toward the rind. Down a flight of stairs, a young couple sat by a small pond, pretending to admire ducks while the tips of their fingers secretly touched. There was also a foreigner, although I did not recognize him as such at first, for he was dressed in the clothes of a scholar, a long summer gown and trousers. His eyes were gray like muddy water. Around another pillar, a nursemaid was cooing to a baby, trying to get him to look at her, but the baby was screaming, trying to look back at the foreigner. And then another man, very elegant in his dress and manners, walked to a tree and parted the curtains of a cage I had not even noticed before. Birds immediately began to sing. I felt that I had entered a world a thousand years old and that I had always been there, but only just now had opened my eyes to see it.

I stayed until the pavilion was nearly empty. And then I heard Old Widow Lau bellowing my name. "You scared my body right out of my skin," she scolded, and pinched my arm hard.

As we walked back to my father's shop, I was a different girl. My head was a sandstorm, ideas and hopes whirling about freely. I was wondering all the while what those people at the pavilion would remember the next day and the day after that. Because I knew I would never forget a moment of that day, the day I was to begin my new life.

Just as Old Widow Lau had planned, my prospective mother-in-law accidentally passed by the shop promptly at five o'clock. The woman was younger than Mother. She had a stern countenance and was critical-looking. On her wrists she wore much gold and jade, to show how valuable she was. When Old Widow Lau called to her, she acted puzzled at first, then delighted.

"What luck that we should run into you here," Old Widow Lau cried in a high voice. "When did you arrive in Peking? . . . Oh, visiting a cousin? How are things back in Immortal Heart?" After we had recovered from our fake surprise, Old Widow Lau introduced the woman to Father and my uncles. I was concentrating so hard on not showing any expression whatsoever that I did not hear the woman's name.

"This is my cousin's Eldest Daughter, Liu LuLing," Old Widow Lau said. "She is fifteen."

"I'm fourteen," I corrected, and Old Widow Lau gave me a scolding glance before adding, "Almost fifteen. She is visiting Peking this week. The family lives in Immortal Heart village as well but they sell their ink in Peking. And as you can see," she said, sweeping her hand out to indicate the shop, "their business is doing not too bad."

"In part, we have your husband to thank," Father then said. "We buy much of our excellent wood from him."

"Really?" Old Widow Lau and the woman said at once. My ears turned toward him, curious now that our family knew this family.

"That's correct. We get the camphor wood from Mr. Chang," Father continued. "And he has also supplied us with coffins on less fortunate occasions, and always of the best quality."

Chang the coffinmaker. As exclamations of more surprise and pleasure rang out, I could imagine Precious Auntie pounding the air with her fists. She would never allow me to marry into this family. And then I reminded myself that this was not her decision to make.

"We, too, are thinking of starting a business in Peking," Mrs. Chang said.

"Is that so? Perhaps we can help you in some way," Father said politely.

"We wouldn't want to trouble you," Mrs. Chang said.

"No trouble at all," Father countered.

"You should get together and discuss the possibility," Old Widow Lau suggested, at just the right moment.

As Mrs. Chang paused to think of the excellence of this idea, Father added: "In any case, I've been eager to talk to your husband more about the dragon bones he contributed to the great scientific discovery of Peking Man."

Mrs. Chang nodded. "We were astonished that those ugly little bones were so valuable. Lucky we didn't eat them up as medicine."

I was thinking what it would mean if I married into this rich and famous family. GaoLing would be spitting with envy. Mother would treat me with special fondness. Of course, the Changs probably would not allow Precious Auntie to come as nursemaid to their future grandchildren, especially if she kept spitting and thrashing whenever their name was mentioned.

At the end, it was decided that Old Widow Lau, my father, and I should visit a house in Peking belonging to Chang's cousin, where we could see some unusual rocks in the garden. This was good news to Old Widow Lau, for it meant that the signs were good that the Changs considered me a prospect. And I was glad, for this meant I could stay longer in Peking.

Two evenings later, we went to the cousin's house for a Viewing the Moon party. I wore another borrowed dress. I sat quietly and did not eat too much and talked even less. Mr. Chang had come up from Immortal Heart, and he and Father discussed Peking Man.

"All the pieces of the skull must stay in China," Father said. "That is not only proper, it's the agreement with the foreigners."

"Those foreigners," Chang said, "you can't trust them to keep their word. They'll find a way to sneak out some pieces. They'll find excuses, make new treaties, put up pressure."

"No treaty can change that Peking Man is a Chinese man and should stay where he lived and died."

Suddenly Mr. Chang saw me sitting on a garden stool. "Maybe one day you and I can collect more Peking Man together. How would you like that?"

I nodded eagerly.

The next day, I was a contented girl as I rode home. I had never felt such importance. I had not shamed Old Widow Lau or my family. In fact, I had been a great success. My father had criticized me in small ways about unimportant matters. So I knew he was proud of me. Old Widow Lau had bragged to her daughters-in-law that I had looks and manners to warrant ten marriage proposals. She was certain I would receive a marriage offer from the Changs within the week.

Though I had yet to meet the Changs' fourth son, who was back in Dragon Bone Hill, I knew he was two years older than I was. Like the other sons, he was an apprentice in his father's coffin-making business. What's more, there had been talk that he, the youngest son, might expand the coffin-making business to Peking, just as our family had done with the ink business. That meant I would live in Peking.

During all these discussions, I did not ask if my future husband was smart, if he was educated, if he was kind. I did not think about romantic love. I knew nothing of that. But I did know that marriage had to do with whether I improved my station in life or made it worse. And to judge by the Changs' manners and the jewelry the Chang wife wore, I, too, was about to become a more important person. What could be wrong with that?

Mr. Wei had come before dawn to take me back. The sky was dark and the air was still clear of summer's rotting smells. In the cart, I began to dream of all the ways I had to change my life. Of course, I needed new clothes right away. And I should be more careful to keep my face out of the sun. I did not want to look like a dark little peasant girl. After all, we were artisans and merchants from an old clan, very respected.

By the time the stars faded and the sun rose, Peking had disappeared from the horizon, and the landscape before me returned to the same dusty dull.

Hours later, the cart climbed the last hill that hid Immortal Heart. I could hear the crowing of cocks, the yowling of dogs, all the familiar sounds of our village.

Mr. Wei started bellowing a peasant love song loud enough to burst his lungs. As we turned the bend, we came upon Sheepherder Wu gathering his flock. The late-afternoon sun sliced through the trees and fell on the backs of the sheep. Wu lifted his stick and called a greeting to Mr. Wei and me. Just then his herd turned in one motion, one direction, like a cloud bringing a storm, and I sensed a great danger. I recalled that Mother had once spoken quietly of this sheepherder's being a widower, who needed a new wife to help him run the looms for his wool. I could practically feel the graininess of yellow Gobi dust as my fingers picked through the wool. I could smell the lamb stink seeping into my fingers, my bones. And now that I stared at the sheepherder with his grin and his upraised stick, I was even more determined that I should marry the son of the Changs. Perhaps that son would turn out to be a one-eyed idiot. So be it. I would still be daughter-in-law to a famous family who ran a business in Peking.

As quickly as it takes to snap a twig—that's how fast the mind can turn against what is familiar and dear. There I was, about to arrive at my old home, and I was not filled with sentimental fondness for all I had grown up with. Instead I noticed the ripe stench of a pig pasture, the pockmarked land dug up by dragon-bone dreamseekers, the holes in the walls, the mud by the wells, the dustiness of the unpaved roads. I saw how all the women we passed, young and old, had the same bland face, sleepy eyes that were mirrors of their sleepy minds. Each person's life was the same as the next person's. Each family was as important as the next, which was to say, not very

important. They were country people, both naive and practical, slow
to change but quick to think that a disturbance of ants on the ground
was a sign of bad luck from the gods high above. Even Precious
Auntie had become this way in my mind, a sleepy-headed greasy-hat
from the country.

I remembered a funny saying about life in a slow village: When
you have nothing else to do, you can always busy yourself picking
maggots out of rice. Once I had laughed at that saying. Now I saw
that it was true.

Mr. Wei was still singing his loud folk songs as we rode into the
town square. And then we came to Pig's Head Lane. I passed all the
familiar faces and listened to their harsh, dust-choked greetings. As
we came closer to the bend of the neck where our house stood, my
heart began to drum in my ears. I saw the family gateway, the arch
with its peeling timber, the fading red couplet banners that hung on
the pillars.

But just as I pushed open the gate, my heart flew back into my
chest, and I was filled with a longing to see Precious Auntie. She
would be glad to see me. She had cried when I left. I dashed into the
front courtyard: "I'm home! I'm home already!" I went into the ink
studio, where I saw Mother and GaoLing. "Ah, back so soon?"
Mother said, not bothering to stop her work. "Cousin Lau sent me
a note that the meeting went well, and the Changs will probably
take you."

I was bursting to tell them about my adventures, the pleasures
I had enjoyed. But Mother stopped me: "Hurry and clean up, so
you can help your little sister and me grind this up." And GaoLing
wrinkled her nose and said, "*Cho!* You smell like the hind end of a
donkey."

I went to the room I shared with Precious Auntie. Everything
was in its usual place, the quilt folded just so at the bottom of the
k'ang. But she was not there. I wandered from room to room, from

little courtyard to little courtyard. With each passing moment, I felt more anxious to see her.

And then I heard a pot banging. She was in the root cellar, eager that I should know she was there. I peered down the steep ladder and into the tunnel. She waved, and as she climbed up from the shadows, I saw that she still had the figure of a girl. In the brief moment of seeing only half of her face lit by the sun, she was again as beautiful as she had seemed to me when I was a small child. When she emerged from the hole, she put the pot down and stroked my face, then said with her hands, *Have you really come back to me, my Doggie?* She pulled my tangled braid and snorted. *Didn't take your comb? No one to remind you? Now you know why you need me. You have no brains!* She jabbed the side of my head, and this made me irritable. With spit on her finger, she rubbed dirt from my cheek, then felt my forehead. *Are you sick? You seem feverish.*

"I'm not sick," I said. "I'm hot." She went back to unraveling the mats of my hair. I glanced at her ropy scars, her twisted mouth.

I pulled away. "I can clean myself," I said.

She began to make hissing sounds. *Gone one week and now you're so grown-up?*

I snapped back: "Of course. After all, I'm about to be a married woman."

I heard. And not as a concubine but as a wife. That's good. I raised you well, and everyone can see that.

I knew then that Mother had not told her the name of the family. She had to hear it sooner or later. "The family is the Changs," I said, watching the words cut her in two. "That's right, Chang the coffinmaker."

She sounded as if she were drowning. She rocked her head like a clanging bell. And then she told me with slashing hands, *You cannot. I forbid you.*

"It's not for you to decide!" I shouted back.

She slapped me, then pushed me against the wall. Again and again, she beat me on my shoulders, around my head, and at first I whimpered and cowered, trying to protect myself. But then I·became angry. I pushed her back and stood tall. I drained all expression out of my face and this surprised her. We stared at each· other, breathing hard and fast, until we no longer recognized each other. She dropped onto her knees, pounding her chest over and over, her sign for *useless*.

"I need to go help Mother and GaoLing," I said, then turned from her and walked away.

GHOST

Just as expected, the Changs asked our family if I could join theirs as a daughter-in-law. If I went there right away, Old Widow Lau added, my family would receive a money gift and I would immediately be known as a daughter-in-law during all the family and town ceremonies, including the special one that would happen during the Moon Festival, honoring Mr. Chang for his scientific achievements.

"She should go now," Big Aunt and Little Aunt advised Mother. "Otherwise, they might later change their minds. What if they discover something wrong with her background and want to end the marriage contract?" I thought they were talking about my poor sewing skills or some naughtiness I had forgotten but they had not. But of course, they were talking about my birth. They knew whose daughter I really was. The Changs and I did not.

Mother decided I would join the Chang family in a few weeks, before the town ceremony at the Moon Festival. She assured me that would give her and my aunts enough time to sew together quilts and clothes suitable for my new life. After Mother announced this news, she cried for joy. "I've done well by you," she said proudly. "No one can complain." GaoLing cried as well. And though I shed some tears, not all of them were for joy. I would leave my family, my familiar house. I would change from a girl to a wife, a daughter to a

daughter-in-law. And no matter how happy I was sure to be, I would
still be sad to say good-bye to my old self.

Precious Auntie and I continued to share the same room, the
same bed. But she no longer drew my bath or brought me sweet water from the well. She did not help me with my hair or worry over
my daily health and the cleanliness of my fingernails. She gave no
warnings, no advice. She did not talk to me with her hands.

We slept at the farthest ends of the *k'ang* away from each other.
And if I found myself huddled next to her familiar form, I quietly
moved away before she awoke. Every morning she had red eyes, so I
knew she had been crying. Sometimes my eyes were red, too.

When Precious Auntie was not working in the ink-making studio, she was writing, sheet after sheet after sheet. She sat at her table,
grinding the inkstick into the inkstone, thinking what, I could not
guess. She dipped her brush and wrote, paused and dipped again.
The words flowed without blots or cross-outs or backward steps.

A few days before I was supposed to leave to join the Changs, I
awoke to find Precious Auntie sitting up, staring at me. She raised
her hands and began to talk. *Now I will show you the truth.* She went
to the small wooden cupboard and removed a package wrapped in
blue cloth. She put this in my lap. Inside was a thick wad of pages,
threaded together with string. She stared at me with an odd expression, then left the room.

I looked at the first page. "I was born the daughter of the Famous
Bonesetter from the Mouth of the Mountain," it began. I glanced
through the next few pages. They concerned the tradition of her
family, the loss of her mother, the grief of her father, all the things
she had already told me. And then I saw where it said: "Now I will
tell how bad this man Chang really is." Right away, I threw those
pages down. I did not want Precious Auntie poisoning my mind anymore. So I did not read to the end where she said she was my mother.

During our evening meal, Precious Auntie acted as if I were once again helpless. She pinched pieces of food with her chopsticks and added these to my bowl. *Eat more,* she ordered. *Why aren't you eating? Are you ill? You seem warm. You forehead is hot. Why are you so pale?*

After dinner, we all drifted to the courtyard as usual. Mother and my aunts were embroidering my bridal clothes. Precious Auntie was repairing a hole in my old trousers. She put down the needle and tugged my sleeve. *Did you already read what I wrote?*

I nodded, not wishing to argue in front of the others. My cousins, GaoLing, and I were playing weaving games with strings looped around our fingers. I was making lots of mistakes, which caused GaoLing to howl with glee that the Changs were getting a clumsy daughter-in-law. Upon hearing this, Precious Auntie threw me stern looks.

The evening wore on. The sun went down, the sounds of darkness came, the chirp, creak, and flap of unseen creatures. All too soon it was time for bed. I waited for Precious Auntie to go first. After a long while, when I thought she might already be asleep, I went into the dark room.

Immediately Precious Auntie sat up and was talking to me with her hands.

"I can't see what you're saying," I said. And when she went to light the kerosene lamp, I protested, "Don't bother, I'm sleepy. I don't want to talk right now." She lit the lamp anyway. I went to the *k'ang* and lay down. She followed me and set the lamp on the ledge, crouched, and stared at me with a glowing face. *Now that you have read my story, what do you feel toward me? Be honest.*

I grunted. And that little grunt was enough for her to clasp her hands, then bow and praise the Goddess of Mercy for saving me from the Changs. Before she could give too many thanks, I added: "I'm still going."

For a long time, she did not move. Then she began to cry and beat her chest. Her hands moved fast: *Don't you have feelings for who I am?*

And I remember exactly what I said to her: "Even if the whole Chang family were murderers and thieves, I would join them just to get away from you."

She slapped her palms against the wall. And then she finally blew out the lamp and left the room.

In the morning, she was gone. But I was not worried. A few times in the past, when she had become angry with me, she left but always came back. She was not at the table for breakfast, either. So I knew her anger was greater than in the past. Let her be angry, then, I said to myself. She doesn't care about my future happiness. Only Mother does. That is the difference between a nursemaid and a mother.

These were my very thoughts as my aunts, GaoLing, and I followed Mother to the ink-making studio to begin our work. As we entered the dim room, we all saw the mess. Stains on the walls. Stains on the bench. Long spills along the floor. Had a wild animal broken in? And what was that rotten sweet smell? Then Mother began to wail, "She's dead! She's dead!"

Who was dead? In the next moment, I saw Precious Auntie, the top half of her face limestone white, her wild eyes staring at me. She was sitting crooked against the far wall. "Who's dead?" I called to Precious Auntie. "What happened?" I walked toward her. Her hair was unbound and matted, and then I saw that her neck was clotted with flies. She kept her eyes on me, but her hands were still. One held a knife used to carve the inkstones. Before I could reach her, a tenant pushed me aside so she could better gawk.

Of that day, that was all I remembered. I didn't know how I came to be in my room, lying on the *k'ang*. When I awoke in the dark, I thought it was still the morning before. I sat up and shuddered, shaking off my nightmare.

Precious Auntie was not in the *k'ang*. Then I remembered she was angry with me and had left to sleep elsewhere. I tried to fall back asleep, but now I could not lie still. I got up and stepped outside. The sky was thick with stars, no lamp burned in any room, and even the old rooster did not rustle in alarm. It was not morning but still night, and I wondered if I was dreamwalking. I made my way across the courtyard, toward the ink-making studio, thinking that Precious Auntie might be sleeping on a bench. And then I remembered more of the bad dream: black flies feasting on her neck, crawling along her shoulders like moving hair. I was scared to see what was inside the studio, but my shaking hands were already lighting the lamp.

The walls were clean. So was the floor. Precious Auntie was not there. I was relieved, and returned to bed.

When I woke up the next time, it was morning and GaoLing was on the edge of the *k'ang*. "No matter what," she said with a tearful face, "I promise to always treat you like a sister." Then she told me what had happened, and I listened as if I were still in a bad dream.

The day before, Mrs. Chang had come over with a letter from Precious Auntie clutched in her hand. It had arrived in the middle of the night. "What is the meaning of this?" the Chang woman wanted to know. The letter said that if I joined the Chang household, Precious Auntie would come to stay as a live-in ghost, haunting them forever. "Where is the woman who sent this?" Mrs. Chang demanded, slapping the letter. And when Mother told her that the nursemaid had just killed herself, the Chang wife left, scared out of her wits.

After that, Mother rushed over to the body, GaoLing said. Precious Auntie was still leaning on the wall in the studio. "This is how you repay me?" Mother cried. "I treated you like a sister. I treated your daughter like my own." And she kicked the body, again and again, for not saying thank you, sorry, I beg your pardon a thousand times. "Mother was crazy with anger," GaoLing said. "She told Precious Auntie's body, 'If you haunt us, I'll sell LuLing as a whore.' " After that, Mother ordered Old Cook to put the body in a pushcart and throw it over the cliff. "She's down there," GaoLing said, "your Precious Auntie is lying in the End of the World."

When GaoLing left, I still did not understand everything she had said, and yet I knew. I found the pages Precious Auntie had written for me. I finished reading them. At last, I read her words. *Your mother, your mother, I am your mother.*

That day I went to the End of the World to look for her. As I slid down, branches and thorns tore at my skin. When I reached the bottom, I was feverish to find her. I heard the drumming of cicadas, the beating of vulture wings. I walked toward the thick brush, to where trees grew sideways just as they had fallen with the crumbling cliff. I saw moss, or was that her hair? I saw a nest high in the branches, or was that her body stuck on a limb? I came upon branches, or were those her bones, already scattered by wolves?

I turned and went the other direction, following the turns of the cliff's wall. I glimpsed tatters of cloth—her clothes? I saw crows carrying shreds—pieces of her flesh? I came to a wasteland with rocky mounds, ten thousand pieces of her skull and bones. Everywhere I looked, it was as if I were seeing her, torn and smashed. I had done this. I was remembering the curse of her family, *my* family, the dragon bones that had not been returned to their burial place. Chang, that terrible man, he wanted me to marry his son only so I would tell him where to find more of those bones. How could I be so stupid not to have realized this before?

I searched for her until dusk. By then, my eyes were swollen with dust and tears. I never found her. And as I climbed back up, I was a girl who had lost part of herself in the End of the World.

For five days I could not move. I could not eat. I could not even cry. I lay in the lonely *k'ang* and felt only the air leaving my chest. When I thought I had nothing left, my body still continued to be sucked of breath. At times I could not believe what had happened. I refused to believe it. I thought hard to make Precious Auntie appear, to hear her footsteps, see her face. And when I did see her face, it was in dreams and she was angry. She said that a curse now followed me and I would never find peace. I was doomed to be unhappy. On the sixth day, I began to cry and did not stop from morning until night. When I had no more feeling left, I rose from my bed and went back to my life.

No more mention was ever made of my going to live with the Changs. The marriage contract had been canceled, and Mother no longer pretended I was her daughter. I did not know where I belonged in that family anymore, and sometimes when Mother was displeased with me, she threatened to sell me as a slave girl to the tubercular old sheepherder. No one spoke of Precious Auntie, either once living or now dead. And though my aunts had always known I was her bastard daughter, they did not pity me as her grieving child. When I could not stop myself from crying, they turned their faces, suddenly busy with their eyes and hands.

Only GaoLing talked to me, shyly. "Are you hungry yet? If you don't want that dumpling, I'll eat it." And I remember this: Often, when I lay on my *k'ang*, she came to me and called me Big Sister. She stroked my hand.

Two weeks after Precious Auntie killed herself, a figure ran through our gate, looking like a beggar chased by the devil. It was Little Uncle from Peking. His clothes and the hollows of his eyes were full of soot. When he opened his mouth, choking cries came out. "What's wrong? What's wrong?" I heard Mother shout as I climbed out of the root cellar. The others stumbled out of the ink-making studio. Some of the tenants rushed over as well, trailed by crawling babies and noisy dogs.

"Gone," Little Uncle said. His teeth chattered as if he were cold. "Everything's burnt up. We're finished."

"Burnt?" Mother cried. "What are you saying?"

Little Uncle collapsed onto a bench, his face bunched into knots. "The shop on the lane, the sleeping quarters in back, everything gone to cinders." GaoLing clasped my arm.

Bit by bit, Mother and the aunts pulled the story out of him. Last night, he said, Precious Auntie came to Father. Her hair was unbound, dripping tears and black blood, and Father instantly knew she was a ghost and not an ordinary dream.

"Liu Jin Sen," Precious Auntie had called. "Did you value camphor wood more than my life? Then let the wood burn as I do now."

Father swung out his arm to chase her away and knocked over the oil lamp, which was not in his dream but on a table next to his cot. When Big Uncle heard the crash, he sat up and lit a match to see what had spilled onto the floor. Just then, Little Uncle said, Precious Auntie knocked the match out of his fingertips. Up burst a fountain of flames. Big Uncle shouted to Little Uncle to help him douse the fire. By Precious Auntie's trickery, Little Uncle said, he poured out a jar of *pai gar* wine instead of the pot of cold tea. The fire jumped higher. Father and the two uncles rousted their sons from the next room; then all the men of our family stood in the courtyard, where they watched the flames eat up the bedding, the banners, the walls. The more the fire ate, the hungrier it became. It crept to the ink shop to hunt for more food. It devoured the scrolls of famous scholars who had used our ink. It licked the silk-wrapped boxes holding the most expensive inksticks. And when the resin of those sticks leaked out, it roared with joy, its appetite increased. Within the hour, our family's fortunes wafted up to the gods as incense, ashes, and poisonous smoke.

Mother, Big Aunt, and Little Aunt clapped their hands over their ears, as if this was the only way to keep their senses from dribbling out. "The fates have turned against us!" Mother cried. "Could there be anything worse?" Little Uncle then cried and laughed and said indeed there was.

The buildings next to our family's ink shop also began to burn, he said. The one on the east sold old scholar books, the one on the west was filled to the rafters with the works of master painters. In the middle of the orange-colored night, the shopkeepers dumped their goods into the ashy lane. Then the fire brigade arrived. Everyone joined in and tossed so many buckets of water into the air it looked like it was raining. And then it really did rain, shattering down hard, ruining the saved goods, but saving the rest of the district from being burned.

By the time Little Uncle finished telling us this, Mother, my aunts, and GaoLing had stopped wailing. They looked as though their bones and blood had drained out of the bottoms of their feet. I think they felt as I did when I finally understood that Precious Auntie was dead.

Mother was the first to regain her senses. "Take the silver ingots out of the root cellar," she told us. "And whatever good jewelry you have, gather it up."

"Why?" GaoLing wanted to know.

"Don't be stupid. The other shopkeepers will make our family pay for the damages." And then Mother pushed her. "Get up. Hurry." She pulled a bracelet off GaoLing's wrist. "Sew jewelry into the sleeves of your worst-looking jackets. Hollow out the hardest crab apples and put the gold inside those. Pile them in the cart and put more apples on top, rotten ones. Old Cook, see if the tenants have any wheelbarrows they can sell us, and don't bargain too hard. Everyone put a bundle together, but don't bother with trifles. . . ." I was amazed at how Mother's mind flowed, as if she were accustomed to running two paces ahead of a flood.

The next day Father, Big Uncle, and their sons came home. They already looked like paupers with their unwashed faces, their smoky clothes. Big Aunt and Little Aunt went to them, jabbering:

"Will we lose the house?"

"Will we starve?"

"Do we really have to run away?"

The smaller children began to cry. Father was like a deaf mute. He sat in his elmwood chair, rubbing its arm, declaring it the finest thing he had ever owned and lost. That night, nobody ate. We did not gather in the courtyard for the evening breezes. GaoLing and I spent the night together, talking and crying, swearing loyalty to die together as sisters. We exchanged hairpins to seal our pledge. If she felt that Precious Auntie was to blame for our disasters, she did not say so as the others had continued to do. She did not blame my birth for bringing Precious Auntie into their lives. Instead, GaoLing told me that I should feel lucky that Precious Auntie had already died and would therefore not suffer the slow death of starvation and shame that awaited the rest of us. I agreed yet wished she were with me. But she was at the End of the World. Or was she really wandering the earth, seeking revenge?

The next day, a man came to our gate and handed Father a letter with seals. A complaint had been made about the fire and our family's responsibility for the damages. The official said that as soon as the owners of the affected shops had tallied their losses, the figure would be given to the magistrate, and the magistrate would tell us how the debt should be settled. In the meantime, he said, our family should present the deed for our house and land. He warned us that he was posting a notice in the village about this matter, and thus people would know to report us if we tried to run away.

After the official left, we waited to hear from Father what we should do. He sagged into his elmwood chair. Then Mother announced, "We're finished. There's no changing fate. Today we'll go to the market and tomorrow we'll feast."

Mother gave all of us more pocket money than we had held in our entire lives. She said we should each buy good things to eat, fruits and sweets, delicacies and fatty meats, whatever we had always denied ourselves but longed for. The Moon Festival was coming up, and so it was not unusual that we would be shopping like the rest of the crowd for the harvest meal.

Because of the holiday, it was a bigger market day, with a temple fair, jugglers and acrobats, vendors of lanterns and toys, and more than the usual numbers of tricksters and hucksters. As we pushed through the hordes, GaoLing and I clung to each other's hands. We saw crying lost children and rough-looking men who stared at us openly. Precious Auntie had constantly warned me of hooligans from the big cities who stole stupid country girls and sold them as slaves. We stopped at a stall selling mooncakes. They were stale. We turned up our noses at pork that was gray. We looked into jars of fresh bean curd, but the squares were gooey and stunk. We had money, we had permission to buy what we wanted, yet nothing looked good, everything seemed spoiled. We wandered about in the thick crowd, pressed one to the other like bricks.

And then we found ourselves in Beggars Lane, a place I had never been. There we saw one pitiful sight after another: A shaved head and a limbless body that rocked on its back like a tortoise on its shell. A boneless boy whose legs were wrapped around his neck. A dwarf with long needles poked through his cheeks, belly, and thighs. The beggars had the same laments: "Please, little miss, I beg you, big brother, have pity on us. Give us money, and in your next life you won't have to suffer like us."

Some passing boys laughed, most other people turned away their eyes, and a few old grannies, soon bound for the next world, threw down coins. GaoLing clawed at my arm and whispered: "Is that what we're destined to become?" As we turned to leave, we bumped into a wretch. She was a girl, no older than we were, dressed in shredded rags, strips tied onto strips, so that she looked as if she were wearing an ancient warrior's costume. Where the orbs of her eyes should have been, there were two sunken puckers. She began to chant: "My eyes saw too much, so I plucked them out. Now that I can't see, the unseen come to me."

She shook an empty bowl in front of us. "A ghost is now waiting to speak to you."

"What ghost?" I asked right away.

"Someone who was like a mother to you," the girl answered just as fast.

GaoLing gasped. "How did she know Precious Auntie was your mother?" she whispered to me. And then she said to the girl, "Tell us what she says."

The blind girl held up her empty bowl again and shook it. Gao-Ling threw in a coin. The girl tipped the bowl and said, "Your generosity does not weigh much."

"Show us what you can do first," GaoLing said.

The girl crouched on the ground. From one tattered sleeve she pulled out a sack, then untied it and poured its contents on the ground. It was limestone silt. From her other sleeve she removed a long, slender stick. With the flat length of the stick, she smoothed the silt until its surface was as flat as a mirror. She pointed the stick's sharp end to the ground, and with her sightless eyes aimed toward

heaven, she began to write. We crouched next to her. How did a beggar girl learn to do this? This was no ordinary trick. Her hand was
steady, the writing was smooth, just like a skilled calligrapher's. I
read the first line.

A dog howls, the moon rises, it said. "Doggie! That was her nickname for me," I told the girl. She smoothed the silt and wrote more:
In darkness, the stars pierce forever. Shooting stars, that was in the
poem Baby Uncle wrote for her. Another sweep, another line: *A
rooster crows, the sun rises.* Precious Auntie had been a Rooster. And
then the girl write the last line: *In daylight, it's as if the stars never existed.* I felt sad, but did not know why.

The girl smoothed the dirt once more and said, "The ghost has
no more to say to you."

"That's it?" GaoLing complained. "Those words make no sense."

But I thanked the girl and put all the coins from my pocket into
her bowl. As we walked home, GaoLing asked me why I had given
the money for nonsense about a dog and a rooster. At first I could
not answer her. I kept repeating the lines in my head so I would not
forget them. Each time I did, I grew to understand what the message
was and I became more miserable. "Precious Auntie said I was the
dog who betrayed her," I told GaoLing at last. "The moon was the
night I said I would leave her for the Changs. The stars piercing forever, that is her saying this is a lasting wound she can never forgive.
By time the rooster crowed, she was gone. And until she was dead, I
never knew she was my mother, as if she had never existed."

GaoLing said, "That is one meaning. There are others."

"What, then?" I asked. But she could not think of anything else
to say.

When we returned home, Mother and Father, as well as our aunts
and uncles, were bunched in the courtyard, talking in excited voices.

Father was relating how he had met an old Taoist priest at the market, a remarkable and strange man. As he passed by, the priest had called out to him: "Sir, you look as if a ghost is plaguing your house."

"Why do you say that?" Father asked.

"It's true, isn't it?" the old man insisted. "I feel you've had a lot of bad luck and there's no other reason for it. Am I right?"

"We had a suicide," Father admitted, "a nursemaid whose daughter was about to be married."

"And bad luck followed."

"A few calamities," Father answered.

The young man standing next to the priest then asked Father if he had heard of the Famous Catcher of Ghosts. "No? Well, this is he, the wandering priest right before you. He's newly arrived in your town, so he's not yet as well known as he is in places far to the north and south. Do you have relatives in Harbin? No? Well, then! If you had, you'd know who he is." The young man, who claimed to be the priest's acolyte, added, "In that city alone, he is celebrated for having already caught one hundred ghosts in disturbed households. When he was done, the gods told him to start wandering again."

When Father finished telling us how he had met these two men, he added, "This afternoon, the Famous Catcher of Ghosts is coming to our house."

A few hours later, the Catcher of Ghosts and his assistant stood in our courtyard.

The priest had a white beard, and his long hair was piled like a messy bird's nest. In one hand he carried a walking stick with a carved end that looked like a flayed dog stretched over a gateway. In the other, he held a short beating stick. Slung over his shoulders was a rope shawl from which hung a large wooden bell. His robe was not the sand-colored cotton of most wandering monks I had seen. His

was a rich-looking blue silk, but the sleeves were grease-stained, as if he had often reached across the table for more to eat.

I watched hungrily as Mother offered him special cold dishes. It was late afternoon, and we were sitting on low stools in the court-yard. The monk helped himself to everything—glass noodles with spinach, bamboo shoots with pickled mustard, tofu seasoned with sesame seed oil and coriander. Mother kept apologizing about the quality of the food, saying she was both ashamed and honored to have him in our shabby home. Father was drinking tea. "Tell us how it's done," he said to the priest, "this catching of ghosts. Do you seize them in your fists? Is the struggle fierce or dangerous?"

The priest said he would soon show us. "But first I need proof of your sincerity." Father gave his word that we were indeed sincere. "Words are not proof," the priest said.

"How do you prove sincerity?" Father asked.

"In some cases, a family might walk from here to the top of Mount Tai and back, barefoot and carrying a load of rocks." Everyone, especially my aunts, looked doubtful that any of us could do that.

"In other cases," the monk continued, "a small offering of pure silver can be enough and will cover the sincerity of all members of the immediate family."

"How much might be enough?" Father asked.

The priest frowned. "Only *you* know if your sincerity is little or great, fake or genuine."

The monk continued eating. Father and Mother went to another room to discuss the amount of their sincerity. When they returned, Father opened a pouch and pulled out a silver ingot and placed this in front of the Famous Catcher of Ghosts.

"This is good," the priest said. "A little sincerity is better than none at all."

Mother then drew an ingot from the sleeve of her jacket. She slid this next to the first so that the two made a clinking sound. The monk nodded and put down his bowl. He clapped his hands, and the assistant took from his bundle an empty vinegar jar and wad of string.

"Where's the girl that the ghost loved best?" asked the priest.

"There," Mother said, and pointed to me. "The ghost was her nursemaid."

"Her mother," Father corrected. "The girl's her bastard."

I had never heard this word said aloud, and I felt as if blood was going to pour out of my ears.

The priest gave a small grunt. "Don't worry. I've had other cases just as bad." Then he said to me: "Fetch me the comb she used for your hair."

My feet were locked to the ground until Mother gave me a little knock on the head to hurry. So I went to the room Precious Auntie and I had shared not so long before. I picked up the comb she used to run through my hair. It was the ivory comb she never wore, its ends carved with roosters, its teeth long and straight. I remembered how Precious Auntie used to scold me for my tangles, worrying over every hair on my head.

When I returned, I saw the assistant had placed the vinegar jar in the middle of the courtyard. "Run the comb through your hair nine times," he said. So I did.

"Place it in the jar." I dropped the comb inside, smelling the escape of cheap vinegar fumes. "Now stand there perfectly still." The Catcher of Ghosts beat his stick on the wooden bell. It made a deep *kwak, kwak* sound. He and the acolyte walked in rhythm, circling me, chanting, and drawing closer. Without warning, the Catcher of Ghosts gave a shout and leapt toward me. I thought he was going to squeeze me into the jar, so I closed my eyes and screamed, as did GaoLing.

When I opened my eyes, I saw the acolyte was pounding a tight-fitting wooden lid onto the jar. He wove rope from top to bottom, bottom to top, then all around the jar, until it resembled a hornet's nest. When this was done, the Catcher of Ghosts tapped the jar with his beating stick and said, "It's over. She's caught. Go ahead. Try to open it, you try. Can't be done."

Everyone looked, but no one would touch. Father asked, "Can she escape?"

"Not possible," said the Catcher of Ghosts. "This jar is guaranteed to last more than several lifetimes."

"It should be more," Mother grumbled. "Stuck in a jar forever wouldn't be too long, considering what she's done. Burned down our shop. Nearly killed our family. Put us in debt." I was crying, unable to speak on Precious Auntie's behalf. I was her traitor.

The next day, our family held its banquet, the best dishes, food we would never again enjoy in this lifetime. But no one except the youngest children had any appetite. Mother had also hired a man to take photographs, so we could remember the days when we had plenty. In one, she wanted a picture of just her and GaoLing. At the last moment, GaoLing insisted I come and stand near Mother as well, and Mother was not pleased but did not say anything. The following day, Father and my two uncles went to Peking to hear what the damages would be against our family.

While they were gone, we learned to eat watery rice porridge flavored with just a few bites of cold dishes. Want less, regret less, that was Mother's motto. About a week later, Father stood in the courtyard, bellowing like a madman.

"Make another banquet," he shouted.

Then our uncles followed: "Our bad luck has ended! No damages! That was the magistrate's decision—no damages at all!"

We rushed toward them, children, aunts, tenants, and dogs.

How could this be? And we listened as Father explained. When the other shop owners brought in their damaged goods for inspection, the magistrate discovered that one had rare books that had been stolen from the Hanlin Academy thirty years before. Another, who claimed he had works of master calligraphers and painters, was actually selling forgeries. The judges then decided the fire was fitting punishment to those two thieves.

"The Catcher of Ghosts was right," Father concluded. "The ghost is gone."

That evening everyone ate well, except me. The others laughed and chatted, all worries gone. They seemed to forget that our inksticks had returned to charcoal, that the ink shop was just floating ash. They were saying their luck had changed because Precious Auntie was now knocking her head on the inside of a stinky vinegar jar.

The next morning, GaoLing told me Mother needed to talk to me right away. I had noticed that since Precious Auntie had died, Mother no longer called me Daughter. She did not criticize me. She almost seemed afraid I, too, would turn into a ghost. As I walked toward her room, I wondered if she had ever felt warmly toward me. And then I was standing in front of her. She seemed embarrassed to see me.

"In times of family misfortune," she began in a sharp voice, "personal sadness is selfish. Still, I am sad to tell you we are sending you to an orphanage." I was stunned, but I did not cry. I said nothing.

"At least we are not selling you as a slave girl," she added.

Without feeling, I said, "Thank you."

Mother went on: "If you remain in the house, who can tell, the ghost might return. I know the Catcher of Ghosts guaranteed this would not happen, but that's like saying drought is never followed by drought, or flood by flood. Everyone knows that isn't true."

I did not protest. But still she became angry. "What is that look on your face? Are you trying to shame me? Just remember, all these years I treated you like a daughter. Would any other family in this town have done the same? Maybe your going to the orphanage will teach you to appreciate us more. And now you'd better get ready. Mr. Wei is already waiting to take you in his cart."

I thanked her again and left the room. As I packed my bundle, GaoLing ran into the room with tears streaming down her cheeks. "I'll come find you," she promised, and gave me her favorite jacket.

"Mother will punish you if I take it," I said.

"I don't care."

She followed me to Mr. Wei's cart. As I left the courtyard and the house for the last time, she and the tenants were the only ones to see me off.

When the cart turned down Pig's Head Lane, Mr. Wei began to sing a cheerful tune about the harvest moon. And I thought about what Precious Auntie had told the beggar girl to write:

A dog howls, the moon rises.
In darkness, the stars pierce forever.
A rooster crows, the sun rises.
In daylight, it's as if the stars never existed.

I looked at the sky, so clear, so bright, and in my heart I was howling.

DESTINY

The orphanage was an abandoned monastery near Dragon Bone Hill, a hard climb up a zigzag road from the railway station. To spare the donkey, Mr. Wei made me walk the last kilometer. When he let me off and said good-bye, that was the start of my new life.

It was autumn, and the leafless trees looked like an army of skeletons guarding the hill and the compound at the top. When I walked through the gate, nobody greeted me. Before me was a temple of dried-out wood and peeling lacquer, and in the bare open yard stood rows of girls in white jackets and blue trousers, lined up like soldiers. They bent at the waist—forward, side, back, side—as if obedient to the wind. There was another strange sight: two men, one foreign, one Chinese. It was only the second time I had seen a foreigner so close. They walked across this same courtyard, carrying maps, followed by a troop of men with long sticks. I was afraid I had stumbled upon a secret army for the Communists.

As I stepped over the threshold, I nearly jumped out of my skin. Dead bodies in shrouds, twenty or thirty. They stood in the middle of the hall, along the sides, some tall, some short. Immediately, I thought they were the Returning Dead. Precious Auntie had once told me that in her childhood some families would hire a priest to put a dead body under a spell and make it walk back to its ancestral home. The priest led them only at night, she said, so the dead wouldn't meet any living people they could possess. By day, they rested in temples. She didn't believe the story herself until she heard a priest banging a wooden bell late at night. And rather than run away like the other villagers, she hid behind a wall to watch. *Kwak, kwak,* and then she saw them, six of them, like giant maggots, leaping forward ten feet into the air. *What I saw I can't say for certain,* Precious Auntie told me. *All I know is that for a long time afterward, I was not the same girl.*

I was about to run out the door when I saw the glint of golden feet. I looked more carefully. They were statues of gods, not dead people. I walked toward one and pulled off the cloth. It was the God of Literature with his horned head, a writing brush in one hand, a valedictorian's cap in the other. "Why did you do that?" a voice called out, and I turned around and saw a little girl.

"Why is he covered?"

"Teacher said he is not a good influence. We should not believe in the old gods, only Christian ones."

"Where is your teacher?"

"Who have you come to see?"

"Whoever arranged to take Liu LuLing as an orphan." The girl ran off. A moment later, two lady foreigners were standing before me.

The American missionaries had not been expecting me, and I had not expected them to be Americans. And because I had never talked to a foreigner, I could not speak, only stare. They both had short hair, one white, the other curly red, and they also wore glasses, which made me think they were equally old.

"Sorry to say, no arrangements have been made," the white-haired lady told me in Chinese.

"Sorry to say," the other added, "most orphans are much younger."

When they asked my name, I was still unable to talk, so I used my finger to paint the characters in the air. They talked to each other in English voices.

"Can you read that, can you?" one of them asked me, pointing to a sign in Chinese.

" 'Eat until full, but do not hoard,' " I read.

One of the ladies gave me a pencil and a sheet of paper. "Can you write those same words down?" I did, and they both exclaimed: "She didn't even look back at the sign." More questions flew at me: Could I also use a brush? What books had I read? Afterward, they again spoke to each other in foreign talk, and when they were done, they announced that I could stay.

Later I learned I had been welcomed so that I could be both student and tutor. There were only four teachers, former students of the school, who now lived in one of the thirty-six rooms and buildings in the compound. Teacher Pan taught the older girls. I was his helper. When he had been a student fifty years before, the school was for boys only. Teacher Wang taught the younger girls, and her widowed sister—we called her Mother Wang—took care of the babies in the nursery, as did older girls she assigned as helpers. Then there was Sister Yu, a tiny woman with a bony hunched back, a hard hand, and a sharp voice. She was in charge of Cleanliness, Neatness, and Proper Behavior. Besides scheduling our baths and our tasks for the week, she liked to boss around the cook and his wife.

The missionary ladies, I found out, were not equally old. Miss Grutoff, the curly-haired one, was thirty-two, half the age of the other. She was the nurse and headmistress of the school. Miss Towler was the director of the orphanage, and she begged donations from people who should have pity on us. She also led our Sunday chapel, conducted dramas of Christian history, and played the piano while teaching us to sing "like the angels." At the time, of course, I did not know what an angel was. I also could not sing.

As for the foreign men, they were not Communists but scientists who worked the quarry where the bones of Peking Man had been found. Two foreign and ten Chinese scientists lived in the north end of the monastery compound, and they ate their morning and evening meals in the temple hall with us. The quarry was nearby, about a twenty-minute walk down and up and down a winding path.

Altogether, there were seventy or so children: thirty big girls, thirty little girls, and ten babies, more or less, depending on how many grew up and how many died. Most of the girls were like me, the love children of suicides, singsong girls, and unmarried maidens. Some were like the entertainers GaoLing and I had seen on Beggars Lane—girls without legs or arms, a cyclops, a dwarf. And there were also half-breed girls, all of them fathered by foreigners, one English, one German, one American. I thought they were strangely beautiful, but Sister Yu was always mocking them. She said they had inherited haughtiness in the Western part of their blood and this had to be diluted with humility. "You can have pride in what you do each day," said Sister Yu, "but not arrogance in what you were born with." She also often reminded us that self-pity was not allowed. That was an indulgence.

If a girl wore a long face, Sister Yu would say, "Look at Little Ding over there. No legs, and still she smiles all day long." And Little Ding's fat cheeks rose and nearly swallowed her eyes, she was that glad to have buds instead of limbs. According to Sister Yu, we could find immediate happiness by thinking of someone else whose situation was much worse than our own.

I acted as big sister to this same Little Ding without legs, and Little Ding was big sister to a younger girl named Little Jung who had only one hand. Everyone had a relationship like that, being responsible to someone else, just like in a family. The big and small girls shared the same living quarters, three rooms of twenty girls each, three rows of beds in each room. The first row was for the youngest girls, the second row was for the in-between girls, and the third row was for the oldest girls. In this way, Little Ding's bed was below mine, and Little Jung's was below Little Ding's, everyone positioned by her level of responsibility and respect.

To the missionaries, we were Girls of New Destiny. Each classroom had a big red banner embroidered with gold characters that proclaimed this. And every afternoon, during exercise, we sang our destiny in a song that Miss Towler had written, in both English and Chinese:

We can study, we can learn,
We can marry whom we choose.
We can work, we can earn,
And bad fate is all we lose.

Whenever special visitors came by the school, Miss Grutoff had us perform a skit and Miss Towler played piano music, very dramatic to hear, like the kind in silent movies. One group of girls held up signs that were connected to Old Fate: opium, slaves, the buying of charms. They stumbled around on bound feet and fell down helpless. Then the New Destiny girls arrived as doctors. They cured the opium smokers. They unbound the feet of the fated ones and picked up brooms to sweep away the useless charms. In the end, they thanked God and bowed to the special guests, the foreign visitors to China, thanking them as well for helping so many girls overcome bad fate and move forward with their New Destiny. In this way, we raised a lot of money, especially if we could make the guests cry.

During chapel, Miss Towler always told us that we had a choice to become Christians or not. No one would ever force us to believe in Jesus, she said. Our belief had to be genuine and sincere. But Sister Yu, who had come to the orphanage when she was seven, often reminded us of her old fate. She had been forced to beg as a child, and if she did not collect enough coins, she was given nothing but curses to eat. One day when she protested she was hungry, her sister's husband threw her away like a piece of garbage. In this school, she said, we could eat as much as we wanted. We never had to worry that someone would kick us out. We could choose what we wanted to believe. However, she added, any student who did not choose to believe in Jesus was a corpse-eating maggot, and when this unbeliever died, she would tumble into the underworld, where her body would be pierced by a bayonet, roasted like a duck, and forced to suffer all kinds of tortures that were worse than what was happening in Manchuria.

Sometimes I wondered about the girls who could not choose. Where would they go when they died? I remember seeing a baby even the missionaries did not think had a New Destiny, a baby that had been fathered by her own grandfather. I saw her in the nursery, where I worked every morning. No one gave her a name, and Mother Wang told me not to pick her up, even if she cried, because something was wrong with her neck and head. She never made a sound. She had a face as flat and round as a large platter, two big eyes, and a tiny nose and mouth stuck in the middle. Her skin was as pale as rice paste, and her body, which was too small for her head, was as still as a wax flower. Only her eyes moved, back and forth, as if watching a mosquito drift across the ceiling. And then one day, the crib where she once lay was empty. Miss Grutoff said the baby was now a child of God, so I knew she had died. Over the years that I lived at the orphanage, I saw six other babies that looked the same, always fathered by a grandfather, born with the same "universal face," as Mother Wang called it. It was as though the same person had come back into the same body for someone else's mistake. Each time, I welcomed that baby back like an old friend. Each time, I cried when she left the world again.

Because I came from a family of inkmakers, I was the best

calligraphy student the school had ever had. Teacher Pan said so. He often recounted to us the days of the Ching, how everything had become corrupt, even the examination system. Yet he also spoke of those old times with a sentimental fondness. He said to me, "LuLing, if you had been born a boy back then, you could have been a scholar." Those were his exact words. He also said I was a better calligrapher than his own son, Kai Jing, whom he taught himself.

Kai Jing, who was a geologist, was actually a very good calligrapher, especially for someone whose right side had been weakened by polio when he was a child. Lucky for him, when he fell ill, the family spent a great deal of money, their entire savings, to hire the best Western and Chinese doctors. As a result, Kai Jing recovered with only a small limp and a drooped shoulder. The missionaries later helped him get a scholarship at the famous university in Peking where he studied to become a geologist. After his mother died, he returned home to take care of his father and work with the scientists in the quarry.

Every day he rode his bicycle from the orphanage to the quarry and back, pedaling right to the door of his father's classroom. Teacher Pan would perch sideways on the back of the bicycle, and as his son pedaled off to their rooms at the other end of the compound, we students and teachers called out, "Be careful! Don't fall off!"

Sister Yu admired Kai Jing a great deal. She once pointed him out to the children and said, "See? You, too, can set a goal to help others rather than remain a useless burden." Another time I heard her say, "What a tragedy that a boy so handsome has to be lame." Perhaps this was supposed to comfort the students as well. But to my mind she was saying Kai Jing's tragedy was greater than that of others simply because he had been born more pleasing to the eye. How could Sister Yu, of all people, think such a thing? If a rich man loses his house, is that worse than if a poor man loses his?

I asked an older girl about this, and she said, "What a stupid question. Of course! The handsome and the rich have more to lose." Yet this did not seem right to me.

I thought of Precious Auntie. Like Kai Jing, she had been born with a natural beauty, and then her face was ruined. I heard people say all the time, "How terrible to have a face like that. It would have been better if she had died." Would I have felt the same if I had not loved her? I thought of the blind beggar girl. Who would miss her?

Suddenly I wanted to find that beggar girl. She could talk to Precious Auntie for me. She could tell me where she was. Was she wandering in the End of the World or was she stuck in the vinegar jar? And what about the curse? Would it find me soon? If I died this moment, who would miss me in this world? Who would welcome me in the next?

When the weather was good, Teacher Pan took us older girls to the quarry at Dragon Bone Hill. He was proud to do so, because his son was one of the geologists. The quarry had started as a cave like the one that belonged to Precious Auntie's family, but when I saw it, it was a giant pit about one hundred fifty feet deep. From top to bottom and side to side, the walls and floor had been painted with white lines, so that it looked like a giant's fishnet had been placed inside. "If a digger finds a piece of an animal, a person, or a hunting tool," Kai Jing explained to us, "he can write down that it came from this square of the quarry and not that one. We can calculate the age of the piece by where it was found, the eighth layer being the oldest. And then the scientists can go back to that spot and dig some more."

We girls always brought thermoses of tea and small cakes for the scientists, and when they saw us arrive, they quickly climbed up from the bottom, refreshed themselves, and said with grateful sighs,

"Thank you, thank you. I was so thirsty I thought I would turn into another one of these dried-up bones." Every now and then, a rickshaw made its way up the steep road, and a pipe-smoking foreigner with thick glasses stepped out and asked if anything new had been found. Usually the scientists pointed this way and that, and the man with glasses nodded but seemed disappointed. But sometimes he became very excited, and sucked on his pipe faster and faster as he talked. Then he got back in the rickshaw and went down the hill, where a shiny black car would be waiting to take him back to Peking. If we ran to a lookout point on the hill, we could see to the far end of the flat basin, and there was the black car, running along the narrow road, sending up streams of dust.

When winter came, the scientists had to hurry before the ground grew too hard and the season of digging came to an end. They let some of us girls climb down and help put the dug-up dirt in boxes, or repaint the white lines on the quarry floor, or carefully sift what had already been sifted ten times. We were not allowed in any of the places where there were ropes—that was where human bones had been found. To an inexperienced eye, it was easy to mistake the bones for rocks or bits of pottery, but I knew the difference from all those times I had collected bones with Precious Auntie. I also knew that Peking Man was the bones not just from one person, but from many—men, women, children, babies. The pieces were small, not enough to make even one whole person. I did not say these things to the other girls. I did not want to show off. So like them, I helped only where the scientists said we could be, where there were mostly animal bones, deer horns, and turtle shells.

I remember the day Teacher Pan's son gave me special praise. "You are a careful worker," Kai Jing said. After that, sifting dirt carefully was my favorite job. But then the weather turned icy cold and we could no longer feel our fingers or cheeks. So that was the end of that kind of work and praise.

My next-favorite job was tutoring the other students. Sometimes I taught painting. I showed the younger students how to use the brush to make cat ears, tails, and whiskers. I painted horses and cranes, monkeys, and even a hippopotamus. I also helped the students improve their calligraphy and their minds. I recalled for them what Precious Auntie had taught me about writing characters, how a person must think about her intentions, how her *ch'i* flowed from her body into her arm, through the brush, and into the stroke. Every stroke had meaning, and since every word had many strokes, it also had many meanings.

My least favorite job was whatever Sister Yu assigned me to do for the week: sweeping the floors, cleaning the basins, or lining up the benches for chapel and putting them back at the tables for lunch. These jobs would not have been so bad if Sister Yu had not always picked apart what I had done wrong. One week, for a change, she put me in charge of crawling insects. She complained that the monks had never killed them, thinking they might have been former mortals and holy ones. "Former landlords is what these bugs likely were," Sister Yu grumbled, then told me: "Step on them, kill them, do whatever you must to keep them from coming in." The doors to most of the rooms, except those belonging to the foreigners, were never closed except in the winter, so the ants and cockroaches marched right over the thresholds. They also came in through any crack or hole in the wall, as well as through the large wooden latticed panels that allowed breezes and light to come in. But I knew what to do. Precious Auntie had taught me. I glued paper over the lattices. And then I took a stick of chalk from the schoolroom and drew a line in front of all the thresholds and around the cracks. The ants would sniff that chalk line and get confused, then turn around and leave. The cockroaches were braver. They walked right through the chalk, and the dust went into their joints and under their shells, and the next day they lay upside down, with their legs in the air, choked to death.

That week Sister Yu did not criticize me. Instead I received an award for Remarkable Sanitation, two hours free to do anything I wanted, as long as it was not evil. In that crowded place, there was no room to be alone. So that was what I chose to do with my prize. For a long time, I had not reread the pages Precious Auntie had written to me before she died. I had resisted because I knew I would cry if I saw those pages again, and then Sister Yu would scold me for allowing self-pity in front of Little Ding and the other younger girls. On a Sunday afternoon, I found an abandoned storeroom, smelling of must and filled with small statues. I sat on the floor against one wall near a window. I unfolded the blue cloth that held the pages. And for the first time I saw that Precious Auntie had sewn a little pocket into the cloth.

In that pocket were two wondrous things. The first one was the oracle bone she had shown me when I was a girl, telling me I could have it when I had learned to remember. She had once held this, just as her father had once held this. I clutched that bone to my heart. And then I pulled out the second thing. It was a small photograph of a young woman wearing an embroidered headwrap and a padded winter jacket with a collar that reached up to her cheeks. I held the picture up to the light. Was it . . . ? I saw that it was indeed Precious Auntie before she had burned her face. She had dreamy eyes, daring eyebrows that tilted upward, and her mouth—such plump pouting lips, such smooth skin. She was beautiful, but she did not look the way I remembered her, and I was sorry it was not her burnt face in the photo. The more I looked, however, the more she became familiar. And then I realized: Her face, her hope, her knowledge, her sadness—they were mine. Then I cried and cried, glutting my heart with joy and self-pity.

Once a week, Miss Grutoff and the cook's wife went to the railway station to pick up packages and mail. Sometimes there were letters from their friends at other missionary schools in China or from the scientists at Peking Union Medical College. Other times there would be letters with pledges of money. These came from far away: San Francisco in California, Milwaukee in Wisconsin, Elyria in Ohio. Miss Grutoff would read the letters aloud at Sunday chapel. She would show us on a globe, "Here we are, there they are. And they are sending you love and lots of money." Then she would spin the globe so we could become dizzy with this idea.

I used to wonder, Why would a stranger love another stranger? Mother and Father were like strangers to me now. They did not love me. To them, I no longer existed. And what about GaoLing's promises to find me? Had she tried? I did not think so.

One afternoon, after I had been at the orphanage for two years, Miss Grutoff handed me a letter. I recognized the handwriting immediately. It was noontime, and in that noisy main hall, I became deaf. The girls nearest me clamored to know what the letter said and who had written it. I ran away from them, guarding my treasure like a starved dog. I still have it, and this is what I read:

"My dearest sister, I apologize for not writing sooner. Not one day has passed that I don't think of you. But I could not write. Mr. Wei would not tell me where he had taken you. Neither would Mother. I finally heard in the market last week that the quarries at Dragon Blue Hill were becoming busy again, and that the American and Chinese scientists were living in the old monastery, along with the students of the orphanage. The next time I saw First Brother's Wife, I said, 'I wonder if LuLing has met the scientists, since she lives so close to them.' And she answered, 'I was wondering the same.' So then I knew.

"Mother is well, but she complains that she is so busy her fingertips are always black. They are still working hard to replenish the inksticks lost in the fire. And Father and our uncles had to rebuild the shop in Peking. They borrowed the money and lumber from Chang the coffinmaker, who now owns most of the business. They received part of the business when I married Chang Fu Nan, the fourth son, the boy you were supposed to marry.

"Mother said we were lucky the Changs wanted any of the girls in our family at all. But I don't think I'm lucky. I think you are lucky that you did not become a daughter-in-law to this family. Every day, with each bite I eat, I am reminded of the Changs' position over our family. We are in debt to them for the wood, and the debt keeps growing. In a hundred years, the Liu clan will still be working for them. The inksticks no longer sell as well or for as much money. To be honest, the quality is no longer as good, now that the ingredients are inferior and Precious Auntie is no longer here to do the carvings. As reminder of our family's debt, I receive no spending money of my own. To buy a stamp for this letter, I had to barter away a hairpin.

"You should also know that the Chang family is not as rich as we believed when we were children. Much of their fortune has been drained away by opium. One of the other son's wives told me that the problem began when Fu Nan was a baby and tore his shoulder out of the socket. His mother began feeding him opium. Later, the mother died, beaten to death, some say, although Chang claims she fell off the roof by accident. Then Chang took another wife, who used to be the girlfriend of a warlord who had been trading opium for coffins. The second wife had the habit, too. The warlord told Chang that if he ever harmed her, he would turn him into a eunuch. And Chang knew this could happen, because he had seen other men who were missing parts of their body for failing to pay their opium debts.

"This household is a misery of shouting and madness, a constant search for money for more opium. If Fu Nan could sell pieces of me for his smoke, he would do so. He's convinced I know where to find more dragon bones. He jabbers that I should tell him, so we will all be rich. If only I did know, I would sell them to leave this family. I would even sell myself. But where would I go?

"Sister, I am sorry for any suffering or worry this letter causes you. I write this only so you know why I have not come to see you and why you are lucky to be where you are. Please do not write back to me. This would only cause me trouble. Now that I know where you are, I will try to write again. In the meantime, I hope your health is good and you are content. Your sister, Liu GaoLing."

When I finished, the letter was still shaking in my hands. I remembered that I had once been jealous of GaoLing. Now her fate was worse than mine. Sister Yu had said we could find happiness in our own situation when we thought of people whose lives were much worse. But I was not happy.

Yet in time, I did become less unhappy. I accepted my life. Maybe it was the weakness of memory that made me feel less pain. Perhaps it was my life force growing stronger. All I knew was, I had become a different girl from the one who had arrived at the orphanage.

Of course, by then even the gods in the monastery had changed their minds. Over the years, Miss Towler had been removing the coverings from the statues, one by one, as cloth was needed for making clothes or quilts. Eventually, all the statues revealed themselves, mocking Miss Towler, so she said, with their red faces, three eyes, and bare bellies. And there were many, many statues, both Buddhist and Taoist, because the monastery had been occupied by both kinds of monks in different centuries, depending on which warlord was in charge of the land. One day, before Christmas, when it was too cold to go anywhere, Miss Grutoff decided that we should convert the Chinese gods into Christians. We would baptize them with paint. The girls who had grown up in the orphanage since they were babies thought this would be a lot of fun. But some of the students who had come later did not want to deface the gods and tempt their wrath. They were so scared that when they were dragged to the statues they screamed and foamed at the mouth, then fell to the ground as if possessed. I was not afraid. I believed that if I was respectful to both the Chinese gods and the Christian one, neither would harm me. I reasoned that Chinese people were polite and also practical about life. The Chinese gods understood that we were living in a Western household run by Americans. If the gods could speak, they, too, would insist that the Christian deities have the better position. Chinese people, unlike foreigners, did not try to push their ideas on others. Let the foreigners follow their own ways, no matter how strange they were, that was their thinking. As my brush ran over their gold-and-red faces, I said, "Pardon me, Jade Ruler, forgive me, Chief of the Eight Immortals, I am only making a disguise for you, in case the Communists or the Japanese come and recruit statues for a bonfire." I was a good artist. With some of the gods, I glued on sheep's hair for beards, noodles for long hair, feathers for wings. In this way, Buddha became fat Jesus, the Goddess of Mercy was Mary of the Manger, the Three Pure Ones, boss gods of the Taoists, turned into the Three Wise Men, and the Eighteen Lohan of Buddha were converted to the Twelve Apostles with six sons. Any small figures in hell were promoted to angels. The following year, Miss Grutoff decided we should also paint the little Buddha carvings throughout the compound. There were hundreds of those.

The year after that, Miss Grutoff found the musty storeroom where I had gone to reread Precious Auntie's pages. The statues there, Sister Yu said, were for a Taoist diorama that showed what would happen if a person went to the underworld. There were dozens of figures, very realistic and scary to see. One was a kneeling man with horned animals feeding on his entrails. Three figures dangled from a pole like pigs on a spit. Four people sat in a vat of boiling oil. And there were giant devils, red-faced with pointed skulls, ordering the dead to go into battle. When we finished painting those, we had a complete nativity scene, Baby Jesus, Mother Mary, Father Joseph, everybody including Santa Claus. Even so, the mouths on the statues were still wide open in screaming fright. No matter what Miss Grutoff said, most of the girls did not think the nativity statues were singing "Joy to the World."

After we finished with those statues, there were no more idols to be changed to angels. By then, I too had changed, from tutor to teacher, from lonely girl to one who was in love with Teacher Pan's son.

The way we started was this.

Every year, during the small New Year, the students painted good-luck banners for the temple fair in the Mouth of the Mountain. And so I was with Teacher Pan and our students in the classroom one day, painting the long red strips, which covered the desks and floors.

As usual, Kai Jing came by on his bicycle to take his father to his rooms. The ground at Dragon Bone Hill was frozen hard, so most of Kai Jing's time was devoted to drawing diagrams, writing reports, and making casts of different spots where bones were found. On this particular day, Kai Jing came early, and Teacher Pan was not ready to leave. So Kai Jing offered to help us paint banners. He stood next to me at my table. I was glad for the extra hands.

But then I noticed what he was doing. Whatever character or figure I drew, he would make the same. If I drew "fortune," he drew "fortune." If I wrote "abundance," he wrote "abundance." If I painted "all that you wish," he painted the same, stroke by stroke. He used almost the same rhythm, so that we were like two people performing a dance.

That was the beginning of our love, the same curve, the same dot, the same lifting of the brush as our breath filled as one.

A few days later, the students and I took the banners to the fair. Kai Jing accompanied me, walking alongside, talking quietly. He held a little book of brush paintings done on mulberry paper. On the cover it said: *The Four Manifestations of Beauty.* "Would you like to know what's inside?" he asked. I nodded. Anyone who overheard us would have thought we were speaking of school lessons. But really, he was speaking of love.

He turned the page. "With any form of beauty, there are four levels of ability. This is true of painting, calligraphy, literature, music, dance. The first level is Competent." We were looking at a page that showed two identical renderings of a bamboo grove, a typical painting, well done, realistic, interesting in the detail of double lines, conveying a sense of strength and longevity. "Competence," he went on, "is the ability to draw the same thing over and over in the same strokes, with the same force, the same rhythm, the same trueness. This kind of beauty, however, is ordinary.

"The second level," Kai Jing continued, "is Magnificent." We looked together at another painting, of several stalks of bamboo. "This one goes beyond skill," he said. "Its beauty is unique. And yet it is simpler, with less emphasis on the stalk and more on the leaves. It conveys both strength and solitude. The lesser painter would be able to capture one quality but not the other."

He turned the page. This painting was of a single stalk of bamboo. "The third level is Divine," he said. "The leaves now are shadows blown by an invisible wind, and the stalk is there mostly by suggestion of what is missing. And yet the shadows are more alive than the original leaves that obscured the light. A person seeing this would be wordless to describe how this is done. Try as he might, the same painter could never again capture the feeling of this painting, only a shadow of the shadow."

"How could beauty be more than divine?" I murmured, knowing I would soon learn the answer.

"The fourth level," Kai Jing said, "is greater than this, and it is within each mortal's nature to find it. We can sense it only if we do not try to sense it. It occurs without motivation or desire or knowledge of what may result. It is pure. It is what innocent children have. It is what old masters regain once they have lost their minds and become children again."

He turned the page. On the next was an oval. "This painting is called *Inside the Middle of a Bamboo Stalk*. The oval is what you see if you are inside looking up or looking down. It is the simplicity of being within, no reason or explanation for being there. It is the natural wonder that anything exists in relation to another, an inky oval to a page of white paper, a person to a bamboo stalk, the viewer to the painting."

Kai Jing was quiet for a long time. "This fourth level is called Effortless," he said at last. He put the booklet back in his jacket and looked at me thoughtfully. "Recently I have felt this beauty of Effortlessness in all things," he said. "How about you?"

"It's the same for me," I said, and began to cry.

For we both knew we were speaking about the effortlessness with which one falls in love without intending to, as if we were two stalks of bamboo bent toward each other by the chance of the wind. And then we bent toward each other and kissed, lost in the nowhere of being together.

EFFORTLESS

The first night Kai Jing and I tried forbidden joy, it was summer-time, a bright-moon night. We had slipped into a dark storage room at the abandoned end of a corridor, far from the eyes and ears of others. I had no shame, no guilty feelings. I felt wild and new, as though I could swim the heavens and fly through waves. And if this was bad fate, let it be. I was the daughter of Precious Auntie, a woman who also could not control her desires, who then gave birth to me. How could this be bad when the skin on Kai Jing's back was so smooth, so warm, so fragrant? Was it also fate to feel his lips on my neck? When he unbuttoned the back of my blouse and it fell to the floor, I was ruined, and I was glad. Then the rest of my clothing slipped off, piece by piece, and I felt I was growing lighter and darker. He and I were two shadows, black and airy, folding and blending, weak yet fierce, weightless, mindless of others—until I opened my eyes and saw that a dozen people were watching us.

Kai Jing laughed. "No, no, they're not real." He tapped one. They were the painted-over theater of hell, now converted to Merry Christmas.

"They're like an audience at a bad opera," I said, "not so pleased." There was Mother Mary with a screaming mouth, the sheepherders with pointed heads, and Baby Jesus, whose eyes stuck out like a frog's.

Kai Jing draped my blouse over the head of Mary. He covered Joseph with my skirt, while Baby Jesus received my slip. Then Kai Jing put his own clothes over the Three Wise Men and turned the sheepherders around. When all their eyes faced the wall, Kai Jing guided me to lie down in the straw, and once more we became shadows.

But what happened after that was not like a poem or a painting of the fourth level. We were not like nature, as beautifully harmonious as a leafy tree against the sky. We had expected all these things. But the straw made us itch and the floor stank of urine. A rat stumbled out of its nest, and this caused Kai Jing to roll off me and knock Baby Jesus out of his crib. The frog-eyed monster lay next to us, as if it were our love child. Then Kai Jing stood up and lighted a match, searching for the rat. And when I looked at Kai Jing's private parts, I saw he was no longer possessed. I also saw he had ticks on his thigh. A moment later, he pointed out three on my bottom. I jumped up and was dancing to shake them off. I had to try very hard not to laugh and cry as Kai Jing turned me around and inspected me, then burned off the ticks with the tip of a match. When I took back my blouse from Mary's head, she looked glad that I was ashamed, even though we had not fulfilled our desires.

As we quickly dressed, Kai Jing and I were too embarrassed to talk. He also said nothing as he walked me to my room. But at the door, he told me, "I'm sorry. I should have controlled myself." My heart hurt. I didn't want to hear his apology, his regrets. I heard him add: "I should have waited until we're married." And then I gasped and began to cry, and he embraced me and uttered promises that we would be lovers for ten thousand lifetimes, and I vowed the same, until we heard a loud "Shhhh!" Even after we quieted, Sister Yu, whose room was next to mine, kept grumbling: "No consideration for others. Worse than roosters . . ."

The next morning, I felt like a different person, happy but also worried. Sister Yu had once said that you could tell which girls in the

lanes were prostitutes because they had eyes like chickens. What she
meant by this, I didn't know. Did the eyes become redder or smaller?
Would others see in my eyes that I had a new kind of knowledge?
When I arrived in the main hall for breakfast, I saw that almost
everyone was there, gathered in a circle, talking in serious voices. As
I walked in, it seemed that all the teachers lifted their eyes to stare at
me, shocked and sad. Then Kai Jing shook his head. "Bad news," he
said, and the blood drained from my limbs so that even if I had
wanted to run away I was too weak to do so. Would I be kicked out?
Had Kai Jing's father refused to let him marry me? But how did they
know? Who told? Who saw? Who heard? Kai Jing pointed to the
shortwave radio that belonged to the scientists, and the others turned
back to listen. And I wondered: Now the *radio* is announcing what
we did? In English?

When Kai Jing finally told me, I didn't have even one moment to
be relieved that the bad news was not about me. "The Japanese attacked last night," he said, "close to Peking, and everyone is saying it
is war for sure."

Maku polo this, *maku polo* that, I heard the radio voice say. I
asked: "What is this *maku* thing?"

Sister Yu said, "The *Maku Polo* Bridge. The island dwarves have
captured it." I was surprised to hear her use this slur for the Japanese. In the school, she was the one who taught the girls not to use
bad names, even for those we hated. Sister Yu went on: "Shot their
rifles in the air—just for practice, they said. So our army shot back to
teach the liars a lesson. And now one of the dwarves is missing.
Probably the coward ran away, but the Japanese are saying one missing man is enough reason to declare war." With Sister Yu translating
the English into Chinese, it was hard to tell which was the news and
which were her opinions.

"This Maku Polo Bridge," I said, "how far away is it?"

"North of here, in Wanping," Miss Grutoff said, "close to the railway station."

"But that's the Reed Moat Bridge, forty-six kilometers from my village," I said. "When did they start calling it something else?"

"More than six hundred years ago," Miss Grutoff said, "when Marco Polo first admired it." And as everyone continued to talk about the war, I was wondering why no one in our village knew the bridge had changed its name so long before. "Which way are the Japanese advancing?" I asked. "North to Peking or south to here?"

Everyone stopped talking at once. A woman stood in the doorway. With the bright sun behind her, she was a shadow, and I could not make out who she was, only that she wore a dress. "Is Liu LuLing still living here?" I heard her say. I squinted. Who was asking this? I was already confused about so many things, now this as well. As I walked toward her, my confusion turned into a guess, then the guess into a certainty. *Precious Auntie.* I had often dreamed that her ghost would come back. As in dreams, she could talk and her face was whole, and as in dreams, I rushed toward her. And at last, this time she did not push me away. She threw open her arms and cried: "So you still recognize your own sister!"

It was GaoLing. We spun each other around, danced and slapped each other's arms, taking turns to cry, "Look at you." I had not heard from her since she wrote me the letter four or five years before. In minutes, we were treating each other like sisters once again. "What's happened to your hair?" I joked, grabbing her messy curls. "Was it an accident, or did you do this on purpose?"

"Do you like it?"

"Not bad. You look modern, no longer the country girl."

"No flies circling your head, either. I heard rumors you're now a high-and-mighty intellectual."

"Only a teacher. And you, are you still—"

"Wife to Chang Fu Nan. Six years already, hard to believe."

"But what's happened to you? You look terrible."

"I haven't eaten since yesterday."

I jumped up, went to the kitchen, and brought her back a bowl of millet porridge, some pickles and steamed peanuts, and little cold dishes. We sat in a corner of the hall, away from news of the war, she eating with much noise and speed. "We've been living in Peking, Fu Nan and I, no children," she said between thick mouthfuls. "We have the back rooms of the ink shop. Everything's been rebuilt. Did I tell you this in my letter?"

"Some."

"Then you know that the Changs own the business, our family owns only the debt. Father and our uncles are back in Immortal Heart village, churning out ink till it sweats from their pores. And now that they're home all the time, they have bad tempers and argue constantly among themselves about who is to blame for this, that, and the weather."

"What about First Brother and Second Brother?" I asked. "Home, too?"

"The Nationalists conscripted First Brother five years ago. All the boys his age had to go. And Second Brother ran off to join the Communists two years after that. Big Uncle's sons followed, then Big Uncle cursed that all three should never come back. Mother didn't speak to him until the United Front was formed and Uncle apologized, saying now it didn't matter which side they were on."

"And Mother, how's her health?"

"Remember how black her hair used to be? Now it's like an old man's beard, white and wiry. She no longer dyes it."

"What? I thought it was naturally black from working with the ink."

"Don't be stupid. They all dyed their hair—Great-Granny, the aunts. But these days Mother doesn't care what she looks like. She claims she hasn't slept in two years. She's convinced the tenants are stealing from us at night and rearranging the furniture. And she also believes Great-Granny's ghost has returned to the latrine. She hasn't had a bowel movement bigger than a bean sprout in months. The shit's hardened to mortar, she says, that's why she's distended like a summer gourd."

"This is terrible to hear." Though this was the same Mother who had kicked me out, I took no pleasure in hearing about her difficulties. Perhaps a little bit of me still thought of Mother and Father as my parents.

"What about Precious Auntie's ghost? Did she ever come back?"

"Not a wail or a whimper, which is strange, since that Catcher of Ghosts turned out to be a fake, not a monk at all. He had a wife and three brats, one of whom was the assistant. They were using the same vinegar jar to catch other ghosts, just opened the lid, sealed it up, over and over. They caught a lot of foolish customers that way. When Father heard this, he wanted to stuff the crook in the jar and plug it up with pony dung. I said to him, 'If Precious Auntie's ghost never came back, what does it matter?' But ever since, he's been muttering about the two ingots he lost, tallying their worth, which according to him was enough to purchase the sky."

My mind was a sandstorm: If the monk was a fake, did that mean Precious Auntie had escaped? Or was she never put in the jar? And then I had another thought.

"Maybe there never was a ghost because she never died," I said to GaoLing.

"Oh, she died for sure. I saw Old Cook throw her body in the End of the World."

"But perhaps she was not entirely dead and she climbed back up. Why else didn't I find her? I searched for hours, from side to side and top to bottom."

GaoLing looked away. "What a terrible day that was for you. . . .

You didn't find her, but she was there. Old Cook felt sorry that
Precious Auntie didn't get a proper burial. He pitied her. When
Mother wasn't looking, he went down there and piled rocks on top of
the body."

And now I pictured Precious Auntie struggling up the ravine, a
rock rolling toward her, striking her, then another and another, as
she tumbled back down. "Why didn't you tell me this sooner?"

"I didn't know until Old Cook died, two years after Precious
Auntie. His wife told me. She said he did good deeds that no one
even knew about."

"I need to go back and find her bones. I want to bury them in a
proper place."

"You'll never find them," GaoLing said. "The cliff broke off
again last year during the rainstorms, a ledge the length of five men.
Collapsed all at once and buried everything along that side of the
ravine with rocks and dirt three stories deep. Our house will be the
next to go."

And I mourned uselessly: "If only you had come and told me
sooner."

"What a pity, I know. I didn't think you'd still be here. If it
weren't for Mr. Wei's gossipy wife, I wouldn't have known you were
a teacher here. She told me when I came home for a visit during
Spring Festival."

"Why didn't you come see me then?"

"You think my husband gives me permission to take a holiday
when I want? I had to wait for the way of heaven to throw me a
chance. And then it came at the worst time. Yesterday Fu Nan told
me to go to Immortal Heart village to beg more money from his father. I said to him, 'Didn't you hear? The Japanese are parading
their army along the railway.' *Fff.* He didn't care. His greed for
opium is greater than any fear that his wife could be run through
with a bayonet."

"Still eating the opium?"

"That's his life. Without it, he's a rabid dog. So I went to Wan-ping, and sure enough, the trains stopped and went no further. All the passengers got off and milled around like sheep and ducks. We had soldiers poking us to keep moving. They herded us into a field, and I was certain we were going to be executed. But then we heard *pau-pau-pau*, more shooting, and the soldiers ran off and left us there. For a minute, we were too afraid to move. The next I thought, Why should I wait for them to come back and kill me? They can chase me. So I ran away. And soon everyone did, scattering every which way. I must have walked for twelve hours."

GaoLing took off her shoes. The heels were broken, the sides were split, and her soles had bleeding blisters. "My feet hurt so much I thought they would kill me with the pain." She snorted. "Maybe I should let Fu Nan think I was killed. Yes, make him feel he is to blame. Though probably he'd feel nothing. He'd just go back to his cloudy dreams. Every day is the same to him, war or no war, wife or no wife." She laughed, ready to cry. "So Big Sister, what do you say? Should I go back to him?"

What could I do except insist four times that she stay with me? And what could she do except insist three times that she did not want to be a burden? Finally, I took her to my room. She wiped her face and neck with a wet cloth, then lay on my cot with a sigh, and fell asleep.

Sister Yu was the only one who objected to GaoLing's living with me at the school. "We're not a refugee camp," she argued. "As it is, we have no cots to take any more children."

"She can live in my room, stay in my bed."

"She is still a mouth to feed. And if we allow one exception, then others will want an exception, too. In Teacher Wang's family alone, there are ten people. And what about the former students and their families? Should we let them in as well?"

"But they're not asking to come here."

"What? Is moss growing on your brain? If we are at war, *every-one* will soon ask. Think about this: Our school is run by the Americans. The Americans are neutral on the Japanese. They are neutral on the Nationalists and the Communists. Here you don't have to worry which side wins or loses from day to day. You can just watch. That's what it means to be neutral."

For all these years, I had bitten back my tongue when Sister Yu was bossy. I had shown her respect when I felt none. And even though I was now a teacher, I still did not know how to argue with her. "You talk about kindness, you say we should have pity"—and before I could tell her what I really thought of her, I said, "and now you want to send my sister back to an opium addict?"

"My eldest sister also had to live with one," she replied. "When her lungs were bleeding, her husband refused to buy any medicine. He bought opium for himself instead. That's why she's dead—gone forever, the only person with deep feeling for me." It was no use. Sister Yu had found yet another misery to compare as greater than anyone else's. I watched her hobble out of the room.

When I found Kai Jing, we walked out the gate and around the back wall of the orphanage to snuggle. And then I told him my complaints about Sister Yu.

"You may not think so, but she really does have a good heart," he said. "I've known her since we were children together."

"Maybe you should marry her, then."

"I prefer a woman with ticks on her pretty bottom."

I slapped his hands away. "You mean to be loyal," he went on. "She means to be practical. Don't fight differences of meaning. Find where you mean the same. Or simply do nothing for now. Wait and see." I can honestly say I admired Kai Jing as much as I loved him. He was kind and sensible. If he had a fault, it was his foolishness in loving me. And as my head floated in the pleasure of this mystery and his caresses, I forgot about big wars and small battles.

When I returned to my room, I was startled to see Sister Yu there, shouting at GaoLing: "As hollow as a worm-eaten tree trunk!"

GaoLing shook her fist and said: "The morals of a maggot."

Then Sister Yu laughed. "I hate that man to the very marrow of my bones!"

GaoLing nodded. "Exactly my feeling, too."

After a while, I understood that they were not fighting with each other but in a contest to name the worst insult for the devils who had wronged them. For the next two hours, they tallied their grievances. "The desk that was in my father's family for nine generations," GaoLing said, "gone in exchange for a few hours of pleasure."

"No food, no coal, no clothes in winter. We had to huddle so tightly together we looked like one long caterpillar."

Later that night, GaoLing said to me, "That Sister Yu is very wise, also a lot of fun." I said nothing. She would soon learn this woman could also be like a stinging wasp.

The next day, I found them seated together in the teacher's dining room. Sister Yu was talking in a quiet voice, and I heard GaoLing answer her, "This is unbearable to even hear. Was your sister pretty as well as kind?"

"Not a great beauty, but fair," Sister Yu answered. "Actually, you remind me of her—the same broad face and large lips."

And GaoLing acted honored, not insulted at all. "If only I could be as brave and uncomplaining."

"She *should* have complained," Sister Yu said. "You, too. Why must those who suffer also be quiet? Why accept fate? That's why I agree with the Communists! We have to struggle to claim our worth. We can't stay mired in the past, worshipping the dead."

GaoLing covered her mouth and laughed. "Careful what you

say, or the Japanese and Nationalists will take turns whacking off your head."

"Whack away," Sister Yu said. "What I say, I mean. The Communists are closer to God, even though they don't believe in Him. Share the fish and loaves, that's what they believe. It's true, Communists are like Christians. Maybe they should form a united front with Jesus worshippers rather than with the Nationalists."

And GaoLing put her hand over Sister Yu's mouth. "Are all Christians as stupid as you are?" They were freely insulting each other, as only good friends can.

A few days after this, I found the two of them sitting in the courtyard before dinner, reminiscing like comrades stuck together through the ages like glue and lacquer. GaoLing waved me over to show me a letter with a red seal mark and the emblem of the rising sun. It was from the "Japanese Provisional Military Police."

"Read it," Sister Yu said.

The letter was to Chang Fu Nan, announcing that his wife, Liu GaoLing, had been arrested at Wanping as an anti-Japanese spy. "You were arrested?" I cried.

GaoLing slapped my arm. "You melonhead, read more."

"Before she escaped from the detention center, where she was awaiting execution," the letter said, "Liu GaoLing confessed that it was her husband, Chang Fu Nan, who sent her to the railway station to conduct her illegal mission. For this reason, the Japanese agents in Peking wish to speak to Chang Fu Nan of his involvement in her spying activities. We will be coming soon to Chang Fu Nan's residence to discuss the matter."

"I typed the words," Sister Yu boasted.

"And I carved the seals," GaoLing said.

"It's very realistic," I told them. "My heart went *peng-peng-peng* when I read it."

"Fu Nan will think firecrackers have exploded in his chest," said GaoLing. She and Sister Yu squealed like schoolgirls.

"But won't Mother and Father be in agony when they hear you're missing?"

"I'll go see them next week if the roads are safe."

And that's what GaoLing did, went to Immortal Heart, where she discovered that Fu Nan had told no one about the letter. About a month later, she returned to the school as Sister Yu's helper. "Mother and Father knew only what the Chang father told him," she reported. " 'That husband of yours,' Father said to me. 'I thought he was all boast and no backbone. And then we hear he's joined the army—didn't even wait to be forced to go.'

"I also told Mother and Father that I ran into you at the railway station at the Mouth of the Mountain," GaoLing said. "I bragged you were an intellectual, working side by side with the scientists—and you'd soon be married to one."

I was glad she had said this. "Were they sorry about what they did to me?"

"Ha! They were proud," GaoLing said. "Mother said, 'I always knew we did well by her. Now you see the result.' "

The dew turned to frost, and that winter we had two kinds of weddings, American and Chinese. For the American part, Miss Grutoff gave me a long white dress she had made for her own wedding but never wore. Her sweetheart died in the Great War, so it was a bad-luck dress. But she had such happy tears when she gave me the gown, how could I refuse? For the Chinese banquet, I wore a red wedding skirt and head scarf that GaoLing had embroidered.

Since GaoLing had already told Mother and Father I was to be married, I invited them out of politeness. I hoped they would use the convenient excuse of war to not come. But Mother and Father did come, as did the aunts and uncles, big and little cousins, nephews and nieces. No one talked of the great embarrassment of what we all knew. It was very awkward. I introduced Mother and Father as my aunt and uncle, which would have been a true fact if I had not been a love child without proper claim to any family. And most everyone at the school acted politely toward them. Sister Yu, however, gave them critical stares. She muttered to GaoLing, loud enough for Mother to hear: "They threw her away, and now they stuff their mouths at her table." All day long, I felt confused—happy in love, angry with my family, yet strangely glad that they were there. And I was also worried about the white wedding dress, thinking this was a sign that my happiness would not last for long.

Only two of the scientists, Dong and Chao, came to our party. Because of the war, it was too dangerous for anyone to work in the quarry anymore. Most of the scientists had fled for Peking, leaving behind almost everything except the relics of the past. Twenty-six of the local workers stayed, as did Kai Jing, Dong, and Chao, who also lived on the former monastery grounds. Someone needed to keep an eye on the quarry, Kai Jing reasoned. What if the Japanese decided to blow up the hill? What if the Communists used the quarry as a machine-gun trench? "Even if they used it as an open pit toilet," I said to him, "how can you stop them?" I was not arguing that he and I should run to Peking as well. I knew he would never separate from his old father, and his old father would never separate from the school and the orphan girls. But I did not want my husband to go into the quarry as hero and come out as martyr. So much was uncertain. So many had already gone away. And many of us felt left behind. As a result, our wedding banquet was like the celebration of a sad victory.

After the banquet, the students and friends carried us to our bedchamber. It was the same storeroom where Kai Jing and I had gone for that disaster of a first night. But now the place was clean: no rats, no urine, no ticks or straw. The week before, the students had painted the walls yellow, the beams red. They had pushed the statues to one side. And to keep the Three Wise Men from watching us, I had made a partition of ropes and cloth. On our wedding night, the students remained outside our door for many hours, joking and teasing, laughing and setting off firecrackers. Finally they tired and left, and for the first time Kai Jing and I were alone as husband and wife. That night, nothing was forbidden, and our joy was effortless.

The next day, we were supposed to visit the houses of our in-laws. So we went to the two rooms at the other end of the corridor, where Teacher Pan lived. I bowed and served him tea, calling him "Baba," and we all laughed over this formality. Then Kai Jing and I went to a little altar I had made with the picture of Precious Auntie in a frame. We poured tea for her as well, then lighted the incense, and Kai Jing called her "Mama" and promised he would take care of my entire family, including the ancestors who had come before me. "I am your family now, too," he said.

All at once, a cold breath poured down my neck. Why? I thought of our ancestor who died in the Monkey's Jaw. Was that the reason? I remembered the bones that were never brought back, the curse. What was the meaning of this memory?

"There are no such things as curses," Kai Jing later told me. "Those are superstitions, and a superstition is a needless fear. The only curses are worries you can't get rid of."

"But Precious Auntie told me this, and she was very smart."

"She was self-taught, exposed to only the old ideas. She had no chance to learn about science, to go to a university like me."

"Then why did my father die? Why did Precious Auntie die?"

"Your father died because of an accident. Precious Auntie killed herself. You said so yourself."

"But why did the way of heaven lead to these things?"

"It's not the way of heaven. There is no reason."

Because I loved my husband very much, I tried to abide by the new ideas: no curses, no bad luck, no good luck, either. When I worried over dark clouds, I said there was no reason. When wind and water changed places, I tried to convince myself that there was no reason for this as well. For a while, I had a happy life, not too many worries.

Every evening after dinner, Kai Jing and I paid a visit to his father. I loved to sit in his rooms, knowing this was my family home, too. The furnishings were plain, old, and honest, and everything had its place and purpose. Against the west wall, Teacher Pan had placed a cushioned bench that was his bed, and above that, he had hung three scrolls of calligraphy, one hundred characters each, as if done in one breath, one inspiration. By the south-facing window, he kept a pot of flowers in season, bright color that drew the eye away from shadows. Against the east wall were a simple desk and a chair of dark polished wood, a good place for thought. And on the desk were precious scholar-objects arranged like a still-life painting: a lacquered leather box, ivory brush holders, and an inkstone of *duan*, the best kind of stone, his most valuable possession, a gift from an old missionary who had taught him in his boyhood.

One night Teacher Pan gave me that *duan* inkstone. I was about to protest, but then I realized that he was my father now, and I could accept it openly with my heart. I held that circle of *duan* and ran my fingers over its silky smoothness. I had admired that inkstone since the days when I first came to the school as his helper. He had brought it to class once to show to the students. "When you grind ink against stone you change its character, from ungiving to giving, from a single hard form to many flowing forms. But once you put the ink to paper, it becomes unforgiving again. You can't change it back. If you make a mistake, the only remedy is to throw away the whole thing." Precious Auntie had once said words that were similar. *You should think about your character. Know where you are changing, how you will be changed, what cannot be changed back again.* She said that when I first learned to grind ink. She also said this when she was angry with me, during the last days we were together. And when I heard Teacher Pan talking about this same thing, I promised myself I would change and become a better daughter.

Much had changed, and I wished Precious Auntie could see how good my life was. I was a teacher and a married woman. I had both a husband and a father. And they were good people, unlike GaoLing's in-laws, the Changs. My new family was genuine and sincere to others, the same inside as they showed outside. Precious Auntie had taught me that was important. Good manners are not enough, she had said, they are not the same as a good heart. Though Precious Auntie had been gone for all these years, I still heard her words, in happy and sad times, when it was important.

After the Japanese attacked the Mouth of the Mountain, GaoLing and I climbed to the hilltop whenever we heard distant gunfire. We looked for the direction of the puffs of smoke. We noticed which way the carts and trucks were moving along the roads. GaoLing joked that we brought news faster than the ham radio that Kai Jing and Miss Grutoff sat in front of for half the day, hoping to hear a word from the scientists who had gone to Peking. I did not understand why they wanted the radio to talk back to them. It spoke only about bad things—which port city was taken, how nearly everyone in this or that town was killed to teach the dead people a lesson not to fight against the Japanese.

"The Japanese won't win here," GaoLing would say in the evenings. "They may be fast in the sea, but here in the mountains they're like fish flopping on the sand. Our men, on the other hand, are like goats." Every night she said this to convince herself it was true. And for a while, it was true. The Japanese soldiers could not push their way up the mountain.

While water couldn't run uphill, money did. All kinds of vendors from down below sneaked past the barricades and brought their goods up the mountain so that people from the hill towns could spend their money before they were killed. GaoLing, Kai Jing, and I would walk along the ridge road to buy luxuries. Sometimes I filled my tin with *shaoping*, the savory flaky buns coated with sesame seeds that I knew Teacher Pan loved so much. Other days I bought fried peanuts, dried mushrooms, or candied melon. There were many shortages during wartime, so any delicacies we could find were always an excuse for little parties.

We held them in Teacher Pan's sitting room. GaoLing and Sister Yu always joined us, as did the scientists—Dong, the older man with a gentle smile, and Chao, the tall young one whose thick hair hung in front of his face. When we were pouring the tea, Teacher Pan would wind his phonograph. And as we savored our treats, we listened to a song by Rachmaninoff called "Oriental Dance." I can still see Teacher Pan, waving his hand like a conductor, telling the invisible pianist and cello players where to quiet down, where to come back with full feeling. At the end of the party, he would lie on the cushioned bench, close his eyes, and sigh, grateful for the food, Rachmaninoff, his son, his daughter-in-law, his dear old friends. "This is the truest meaning of happiness," he would tell us. Then Kai Jing and I would go for an evening stroll before we returned to our own room, grateful ourselves for the joy that exists only between two people.

Those were the small rituals we had, what comforted us, what we loved, what we could look forward to, what we could be thankful for and remember afterward.

Even in wartime and poverty, people must have plays and opera. "They are the speech and music of the soul," Kai Jing told me. Every Sunday afternoon, the students performed for us, and they were very enthusiastic. But to be honest, the acting and music were not very good, painful sometimes to listen to and see, and we had to be very good actors ourselves to pretend this was enjoyment beyond compare. Teacher Pan told me that the plays were just as bad when I was a student and performed in them. How long ago that seemed. Now Miss Towler was bent over with old age, almost as short as Sister Yu. When she played the piano, her nose nearly touched the keys. Teacher Pan had cataracts and worried that soon he would not be able to paint anymore.

When winter came, we heard that many of the Communist soldiers were falling sick and dying of diseases before they had a chance to fire a single bullet. The Japanese had more medicine, warmer clothes, and they took food and supplies from whatever villages they occupied. With fewer Communist troops to defend the hills, the Japanese were crawling up, and with each step, they chopped down trees so no one could hide and escape. Because they were coming closer, we could no longer safely walk the ridge road to buy food.

Yet Kai Jing and his colleagues still went to the quarry, and this made me crazy with anxiety. "Don't go," I always begged him. "Those old bones have been there for a million years. They can wait until after the war." That quarry was the only reason we had arguments, and sometimes when I remember this, I think I should have argued more, argued until he stopped going. Then I think, no, I should have argued less, or not at all. Then maybe his last memories of me would not have been those of a complaining wife.

When Kai Jing was not at the quarry, he taught the girls in my class about geology. He told them stories about ancient earth and ancient man, and I listened, too. He drew pictures on the chalkboard of icy floods and fiery explosions from underneath, of the skull of Peking Man and how it was different from a monkey's, higher in the forehead, more room for his changing brain. If Miss Towler or Miss Grutoff were listening, Kai Jing did not draw the monkey or talk about the ages of the earth. He knew that his ideas about life before and everlasting were different from theirs.

One day, Kai Jing told the girls how humans grew to be different from monkeys: "Ancient Peking Man could stand up and walk. We see this by the way his bones are formed, the footprints he left in the mud. He used tools. We see this by the bones and rocks he shaped to cut and smash. And Peking Man probably also began to speak in words. At least his brain was capable of forming a language."

A girl asked, "What words? Were they Chinese?"

"We don't know for certain," Kai Jing said, "because you cannot leave behind spoken words. There was no writing in those days. That happened only thousands of years ago. But if there was a language, it was an ancient one that likely existed only in that time. And we can only guess what Peking Man tried to say. What does a person need to say? What man, woman, or child does he need to say it to? What do you think was the very first sound to become a word, a meaning?"

"I think a person should always say her prayers to God," another girl said. "She should say thank you to those who are nice to her."

That night, when Kai Jing was already asleep, I was still thinking about these questions. I imagined two people without words, unable to speak to each other. I imagined the need: The color of the sky that meant "storm." The smell of fire that meant "Flee." The sound of a tiger about to pounce. Who would worry about such things?

And then I realized what the first word must have been: *ma*, the sound of a baby smacking its lips in search of her mother's breast. For a long time, that was the only word the baby needed. Ma, ma, ma. Then the mother decided that was her name and she began to speak, too. She taught the baby to be careful: sky, fire, tiger. A mother is always the beginning. She is how things begin.

One spring afternoon, the students were performing a play. I remember it well, a scene from *The Merchant of Venice*, which Miss Towler had translated into Chinese. "Fall down on your knees and pray," they were chanting. And right then, my life changed. Teacher Pan burst into the hall, panting and shouting, "They've seized them."

Between broken breaths, he told us that Kai Jing and his friends had gone to the quarry for their usual inspection. Teacher Pan had gone along for the fresh air and small talk. At the quarry they found soldiers waiting. They were Communists, and since they were not Japanese, the men were not concerned.

The leader of the soldiers approached them. He asked Kai Jing, "Hey, why haven't you joined us?"

"We're scientists not soldiers," Kai Jing explained. He started to tell them about the work with Peking Man, but one of the soldiers cut him off: "No work has been going on here in months."

"If you've worked to preserve the past," the leader said, trying to be more cordial, "surely you can work to create the future. Besides, what past will you save if the Japanese destroy China?"

"It's your duty to join us," another soldier grumbled. "Here we are spilling our own blood to protect your damn village."

The leader waved for him to be quiet. He turned to Kai Jing. "We're asking all men in the villages we defend to help us. You don't need to fight. You can cook or clean or do repairs." When no one said anything, he added in a less friendly voice: "This isn't a request, it's a requirement. Your village owes us this. We order you. If you don't come along as patriots, we'll take you as cowards."

It happened that quickly, Teacher Pan said. The soldiers would have taken him as well, but they decided an old man who was nearly blind was more trouble than help. As the soldiers led the men away, Teacher Pan called out, "How long will they be gone?"

"You tell me, comrade," the leader said. "How long will it take to drive out the Japanese?"

Over the next two months, I grew thin. GaoLing had to force me to eat, and even then I could not taste anything. I could not stop thinking of the curse from the Monkey's Jaw, and I told GaoLing this, though no one else. Sister Yu held Praying for a Miracle meetings, asking that the Communists defeat the Japanese soon, so that Kai Jing, Dong, and Chao could return to us quickly. And Teacher Pan wandered the courtyards, his eyes misty with cataracts. Miss Grutoff and Miss Towler would not allow the girls to go outside the compound anymore, even though the fighting took place in other areas of the hills. They had heard terrible stories of Japanese soldiers raping girls. They found a large American flag and hung this over the gateway, as if this were a charm that would protect them from evil.

Two months after the men disappeared, Sister Yu's prayers were half answered. Three men walked through the gateway early in the morning, and Miss Grutoff beat the gong of the Buddha's Ear. Soon everyone was shouting that Kai Jing, Dong, and Chao had returned. I ran so fast across the courtyard I tripped and nearly broke my ankle. Kai Jing and I grabbed each other and gave in to happy sobs. His face was thinner and very brown; his hair and skin smelled of smoke. And his eyes—they were different. I remember thinking that at the time. They were faded, and I now think some part of his life force had already gone.

"The Japanese now occupy the hills," he told us. "They drove off our troops." That was how Sister Yu learned that the other half of her miracle prayer had not come true. "They'll come looking for us."

I heated water, made a bath, and washed his body with a cloth as he sat in the narrow wooden tub. And then we went to our bedchamber and I pinned a cloth over the lattice window so it would be dark. We lay down, and as he rocked me, he talked to me in soft murmurs, and it took all of my senses to realize that I was in his arms, that his eyes were looking at mine. "There is no curse," he said. I was listening hard, trying to believe that I would always hear him speak. "And you are brave, you are strong," he went on. I wanted to protest that I didn't want to be strong, but I was crying too much to speak. "You cannot change this," he said. "This is your character."

He kissed my eyes, one at a time. "This is beauty, and this is beauty, and you are beauty, and love is beauty and we are beauty. We are divine, unchanged by time." He said this until I promised I believed him, until I agreed it was enough.

The Japanese came for Kai Jing, Dong, and Chao that evening. Miss Grutoff was brave and declared that she was an American and they had no right to enter the orphanage. They paid no attention to her, and when they started to walk toward the rooms where the girls were hiding under their beds, Kai Jing and the other men came forward and said they did not need to look any further. I tried to follow.

A few days later, I heard wailing in the main hall. When GaoLing came to me with red eyes, I stopped her from saying what I already knew. For a month more, I tried to keep Kai Jing alive in my heart and mind. For a while longer, I tried so much to believe what he had said: "There is no curse." And then finally I let GaoLing say the words.

Two Japanese officers questioned the men day and night, tried to force them to say where the Communist troops had gone. On the third day, they lined them up, Kai Jing, Dong, and Chao, as well as thirty other villagers. A soldier stood nearby with a bayonet. The Japanese officer said he would ask them once again, one at a time. And one by one, they shook their heads, one by one they fell. In my mind, sometimes Kai Jing was first, sometimes he was last, sometimes he was in between.

I was not there when this happened, yet I saw it. The only way I could push it out of my mind was to go into my memory. And there in that safe place, I was with him, and he was kissing me when he told me, "We are divine, unchanged by time."

CHARACTER

GaoLing said the Japanese would soon come for all of us, so I should not bother to kill myself right away. Why not wait and die together? Less lonely that way.

Teacher Pan said I should not leave him for the other world. Otherwise, who would he have left as family to give him comfort in his last days?

Miss Grutoff said the children needed me to be an inspiration of what an orphan girl could become. If they knew I had given up hope, then what hope could they have?

But it was Sister Yu who gave me the reason to stay alive and suffer on earth. Kai Jing, she said, had gone to the Christian heaven, and if I did suicide, I would be forbidden by God to go see him. To me, the Christian heaven was like America, a land that was far away, filled with foreigners, and ruled by their laws. Suicide was not allowed.

So I stayed and waited for the Japanese to come back and get me. I visited Teacher Pan and brought him good things to eat. And every afternoon, I walked outside the school to the part of the hillside with many little piles of rocks. That was where the missionaries buried the babies and girls who had died over the years. That was where Kai Jing lay as well. In our room, I found a few dragon bones he had dug up in the last few months. They were nothing too valuable, just those of old animals. I picked up one and with a thick needle carved words into it to make an oracle bone like the one Precious Auntie had given me. I wrote: "You are beauty, we are beauty, we are divine, unchanged by time." When I finished one, I began another, unable to stop. Those were the words I wanted to remember. Those were the morsels of grief I ate.

I put those oracle bones at Kai Jing's grave. "Kai Jing," I said each time I placed them there. "Do you miss me?" And after a long silence, I told him what had happened that day: who was sick, who was smart, how we had no more medicine, how it was too bad he wasn't there to teach the girls more about geology. One day I had to tell him that Miss Towler had not awakened in the morning and soon she would be lying next to him. "She went gently to God," Miss Grutoff had said at breakfast, and she acted glad that it was this way. But then she clamped her mouth shut and two deep lines grew down the sides, so I knew she was pitifully sad. To Miss Grutoff, Miss Towler had been mother, sister, and oldest friend.

After Miss Towler's death, Miss Grutoff began to make American flags. I think she made those flags for the same reason I made oracle bones for Kai Jing's grave. She was saving some memory, afraid of forgetting. Every day she would sew a star or a stripe. She would dye scraps of cloth red or blue. She had the girls in the school make flags, as well. Soon there were fifty flags waving along the outside wall of the old monastery building, then a hundred, two hundred. If a person did not know this was an orphanage for Chinese girls, he would think many, many Americans were inside having a patriotic party.

One cold morning, Japanese soldiers finally flocked onto the grounds. We were in the main hall for Sunday worship, although it was not Sunday. We heard gun sounds, *pau-pau*. We ran to the door and saw Cook and his wife lying facedown in the dirt, and the chickens squabbling nearby, pecking at a bucket of grain that had tipped over. The big American flag that used to hang over the gateway was now lying on the ground. The girls began to cry, thinking that Cook and his wife were dead. But then we saw Cook move a little, turn his head to the side, carefully looking to see who was around them. Miss Grutoff pushed past us to the front. I think we all wondered if she would order the Japanese soldiers to leave us alone, since she was an American. Instead, she asked us to be quiet. No one moved or talked after that. And then we watched, hands covering our mouths to keep from screaming, as the Japanese soldiers shot down the rest of those hundreds of flags, *pau-pau, pau-pau,* taking turns, criticizing if anyone missed. When all the flags were in pieces, they began to shoot at the chickens, which flapped and squawked and fell to earth. Finally, they took the dead chickens and left. Cook and his wife stood up, the remaining chickens clucked quietly, and the girls let out the wails they had kept locked inside.

Miss Grutoff asked everyone to return to the main hall. There she informed us in a shaky voice what she had learned on the ham and shortwave radios several days before: Japan had attacked the United States, and the Americans had declared war on Japan. "With America on our side, now China will be able to win the war more quickly," she said, and she led us to join her in clapping. To please her, we smiled to pretend we believed this good news. Later that night, when the girls had gone to their rooms, Miss Grutoff told the teachers and the cook and his wife what else she had heard from her friends at Peking Union Medical College.

"The bones of Peking Man are lost."

"Destroyed?" Teacher Pan asked.

"No one knows. They've disappeared. All the pieces of forty-one ancient people. They were supposed to be taken by train to be loaded on an American boat sailing from Tientsin to Manila, but the ship was sunk. Some say the boxes were never loaded onto the boat. They say the Japanese stopped the trains. They thought the boxes contained only the possessions of American soldiers, so they threw

them on the tracks to let them get smashed by other trains. Now no
one knows what to think. It's not good, either way." As I listened, I
felt my own bones grow hollow. All of Kai Jing's work, his sacrifice,
his last trip to the quarry—all was for nothing? I imagined those little pieces of skulls floating among the fish in the harbor, sinking
slowly to the bottom, sea eels swimming over them, covering them
with sand. I saw other fragments of bones thrown off the train like
garbage, the tires of army trucks crushing them until the pieces were
no bigger than grains of Gobi sand. I felt as if those bones were Kai
Jing's.

The next day, the Japanese returned to take Miss Grutoff to a
prisoner-of-war camp. She had known this would happen, and yet
she had not tried to escape. "I would never willingly leave my girls,"
she told us. Her suitcases were already packed, and she was wearing
her travel hat with a scarf that wrapped around her neck. Fifty-six
weeping girls stood at the gate to say good-bye. "Teacher Pan, don't
forget the lessons of the apostles," she called out, just before she
boarded the back of the truck. "And please be sure to tell the others
so they can pass on the good word." I thought it was a strange
farewell. So did the others, until Teacher Pan showed us what she
meant.

He took us to the main hall, to the statue of an apostle. He
twisted off its hand. Inside was a hole that he and Miss Grutoff had
carved out, where they had hidden silver, gold, and a list of names of
former students in Peking. For the past month he and Miss Grutoff
had been doing this, late at night. Each apostle had only part of her
personal savings, so if the Japanese found money in one, as heathens
they might not know which of hundreds of statues to search to find
the rest.

If things became dangerous around the orphanage, we were supposed to use the money to take the girls to Peking, four or five at a

time. There they could stay with former students and friends of the school. Miss Grutoff had already contacted these people, and they agreed that if the time came, they would willingly help us. We needed only to tell them by the ham radio when we were coming.

Teacher Pan assigned each of us—teachers, helpers, and four older students—to an apostle for our share of the refugee money. And from the day that Miss Grutoff left, Teacher Pan had us practice and memorize which apostle was which and where the wood had been dug out of its body. I thought it was enough that we recognized which was our own statue, but Sister Yu said, "We should say all the names out loud. Then the apostles will protect our savings better." I had to say those names so many times they are still in my head: *Pida, Pa, Matu, Yuhan, Jiama yi, Jiama er, Andaru, Filipa, Tomasa, Shaimin, Tadayisu,* and *Budalomu.* The traitor, *Judasa,* did not have a statue.

About three months after Miss Grutoff left us, Teacher Pan decided it was time for us to go. The Japanese had become angry that the Communists were hiding in the hills. They wanted to draw them out by slaughtering people in the nearby villages. Sister Yu also told GaoLing and me that the Japanese were doing unspeakable acts with innocent girls, some as young as eleven or twelve. That was what had happened in Tientsin, Tungchow, and Nanking. "Those girls they didn't kill afterward tried to kill themselves," she added. So we knew what she was saying just by using the frightened parts of our imaginations.

Counting four older students who had stayed on through the war, we had twelve chaperones. We radioed Miss Grutoff's friends in Peking, who said the city was occupied, and although the situation was calm, we should wait to hear from them. The trains did not always run, and it would not be good for us to be stuck for days waiting at different cities along the way. Teacher Pan determined the order in which the groups would leave: first that led by Mother

Wang, who could tell us how the journey went, then those of the four older girls, then those of Cook's wife, Teacher Wang, Cook, GaoLing, me, Sister Yu, and last, Teacher Pan.

"Why should you be last?" I asked him.

"I know how to use the radio."

"You can teach me just as easily."

"And me," said Sister Yu and GaoLing.

We argued, taking turns at being brave. And to do that, we had to be a little unkind and criticize each other. Teacher Pan's eyes were too poor for him to be left alone. Sister Yu was too deaf. GaoLing had bad feet and a fear of ghosts that made her run the wrong way. Plenty was wrong with me, as well, but in the end, I was allowed to go last so I could visit Kai Jing's grave as long as possible.

And now I can confess how scared I was those last few days. I was responsible for four girls: six years, eight, nine, and twelve. And while it was still comforting to think about killing myself, it made me nervous to wait to be killed. As each group of girls left, the orphanage seemed to grow larger and the remaining footsteps louder. I was afraid the Japanese soldiers would come and find the ham radio, then accuse me of being a spy and torture me. I rubbed dirt on the girls' faces and told them that if the Japanese came, they should scratch their heads and skin, pretending to have lice. Almost every hour, I prayed to Jesus and Buddha, whoever was listening. I lighted incense in front of Precious Auntie's photo, I went to Kai Jing's grave and was honest with him about my fears. "Where is my character?" I asked him. "You said I was strong. Where is that strength now?"

On the fourth day of our being alone, we heard the message on the radio: "Come quickly. The trains are running." I went to tell the girls, and then I saw that a miracle had happened, but whether this came from the Western God or the Chinese ones, I don't know. I was simply thankful that all four girls had swollen eyes, green pus coming out of the corners. They had an eye infection, nothing serious, but it was awful to see. No one would want to touch them. As for myself, I thought quickly and had an idea. I took some of the left-overs of the rice porridge we had eaten that morning, and drained off the watery portion and smeared this liquid onto my skin, my cheeks, forehead, neck, and hands, so that when it dried I had the leathery, cracked appearance of an old country woman. I put some more of the sticky rice water into a thermos and to that I added chicken blood. I told the girls to gather all the chicken eggs left in the pens, even the rotten ones, and put them in sacks. Now we were ready to walk down the hill to the railway station.

When we were about a hundred paces down the road, we saw the first soldier. I slowed my pace and took a sip from the thermos. The soldier remained where he was, and stopped us when we reached him.

"Where are you going?" he asked. We five looked up and I could see an expression of disgust pass over his face. The girls started to scratch their heads. Before I answered, I coughed into a hand-kerchief, then folded it so he could see the blood-streaked mucus. "We are going to market to sell our eggs," I said. We lifted our sacks. "Would you like some as a gift?" He waved us on.

When we were a short distance away, I took another sip of the rice water and chicken blood to hold in my mouth. Twice more we were stopped, twice more I coughed up what looked like the bloody sputum of a woman with tuberculosis. The girls stared with their green oozing eyes.

When we arrived in Peking, I saw from the train window that GaoLing was there to meet us. She squinted to make sure it was I getting off the train. Slowly she approached, her lips spread in hor-ror. "What happened to you?" she asked. I coughed blood one last time into my handkerchief. "Ai-ya!" she cried, and jumped back. I showed her my thermos of "Japanese chase-away juice." And then I began to laugh and couldn't stop. I was crazy-happy, delirious with relief.

GaoLing complained: "The whole time I've been worried sick, and you just play jokes."

We settled the girls in homes with former students. And over the next few years, some married, some died, some came to visit us as their honorary parents. GaoLing and I lived in the back rooms of the old ink shop in the Pottery-Glazing District. We had Teacher Pan and Sister Yu join us. As for GaoLing's husband, we all hoped he was dead.

Of course, it made me angry beyond belief that the Chang family now owned the ink shop. For all those years since Precious Auntie died, I had not had to think about the coffinmaker too much. Now he was ordering us to sell more ink, sell it faster. This was the man who killed my grandfather and father, who caused Precious Auntie so much pain she ruined her life. But then I reasoned that if a person wants to strike back, she must be close to the person who must be struck down. I decided to live in the ink shop because it was practical. In the meantime, I thought of ways to get revenge.

Luckily, the Chang father did not bother us too much about the business. The ink was selling much, much better than before we came. That was because we used our heads. We saw that not too many people had a use for inksticks and ink cakes anymore. It was wartime. Who had the leisure and calm to sit around and grind ink on an inkstone, meditating over what to write? We also noted that the Chang family had lowered the quality of the ingredients, so the sticks and cakes crumbled more easily. Teacher Pan was the one who suggested we make quick-use ink. We ground up the cheap ink, mixed it with water, and put it in small jars that we bought for almost nothing at a medicine shop that was going out of business.

Teacher Pan also turned out to be a very good salesman. He had the manners and writing style of an old scholar, which helped convince customers that the quality of our quick-use ink was excellent, though it was not. To demonstrate it, however, he had to be careful not to write anything that could be interpreted as anti-Japanese or pro-feudal, Christian or Communist. This was not easy to do. Once he decided he should simply write about food. There was no danger in that. So he wrote, "Turnips taste best when pickled," but GaoLing worried that this would be taken either as a slur against the Japanese or as siding with the Japanese, since turnips were like radishes and radishes were what the Japanese liked to eat. So then he wrote, "Father, Mother, Brother, Sister." Sister Yu said that this looked like a listing of those who had died, that this was his way of protesting the occupation. "It could also be a throwback to Confucian principles of family," GaoLing added, "a wish to return to the time of emperors." Everything had dangers, the sun, the stars, the directions of the wind, depending on how many worries we each had. Every number, color, and animal had a bad meaning. Every word sounded like another. Eventually I came up with the best idea for what to write, and it was settled: "Please try our Quick Ink. It is cheap and easy to use."

We suspected that many of the university students who bought our ink were Communist revolutionaries making propaganda posters that would appear on walls in the middle of the night. "Resist Together," the posters said. Sister Yu managed the accounts, and she was not too strict when some of the poorer students did not have enough money to pay for the ink. "Pay what you can," she told them. "A student should always have enough ink for his studies." Sister Yu also made sure we kept some money for ourselves without the Chang father's noticing that anything was missing.

When the war ended in 1945, we no longer had to think about secret meanings that could get us in trouble with the Japanese. Firecrackers burst in the streets all day long and this made everyone nervously happy. Overnight the lanes grew crowded with vendors of every delicious kind of thing and fortune-tellers with only the best news. GaoLing thought this was a good day to ask her fortune. So Sister Yu and I went wandering with her.

The fortune-teller GaoLing chose could write three different words at one time with three different brushes held in one hand. The first brush he put between the tip of his thumb and one finger. The second rested in the web of his thumb. The third was pinched at the bend of his wrist. "Is my husband dead?" GaoLing asked him. We were all surprised by her bluntness. We held our breath as the three characters formed at once: "Return Lose Hope."

"What does that mean?" Sister Yu said.

"For another small offering," the fortune-teller answered, "the heavens will allow me to explain." But GaoLing said she was satisfied with this answer, and we went on our way.

"He's dead," GaoLing announced.

"Why do you say that?" I asked. "The message could also mean he's not dead."

"It clearly said all hope is lost about his returning home."

Sister Yu suggested: "Maybe it means he'll return home, then we'll lose hope."

"Can't be," GaoLing said, but I could see a crack of doubt running down her forehead.

The next afternoon, we were sitting in the courtyard of the shop, enjoying a new sense of ease, when we heard a voice call out, "Hey, I thought you were dead." A man was looking at GaoLing. He wore a soldier's uniform.

"Why are you here?" GaoLing said as she rose from the bench.

He sneered. "I live here. This is my house."

Then we knew it was Fu Nan. It was the first time I saw the man who might have been my husband. He was large like his father, with a long, wide nose. GaoLing rose and took his bundle and offered him her seat. She treated him extra politely, like an unwanted guest.

"What happened to your fingers?" she asked. Both of his little fingers were missing.

He seemed confused at first, then laughed. "I'm a damn war hero," he said. He glanced at us. "Who are they?" GaoLing gave our names and said what each of us did to run the business. Fu Nan nodded, then gestured toward Sister Yu and said, "We don't need that one anymore. I'll manage the money from now on."

"She's my good friend."

"Who says?" He glared at GaoLing, and when she did not look away, he said, "Oh, still the fierce little viper. Well, you can argue with the new owner of this shop from now on. He arrives tomorrow." He threw down a document covered with the red marks of name seals. GaoLing snatched it.

"You sold the shop? You had no right! You can't make my family work for someone else. And the debt—why is it now even bigger? What did you do, gamble the money away, eat it, smoke it, which one?"

"I'm going to sleep now," he said, "and when I wake up, I don't want to see that woman with the hunchback. The way she looks makes me nervous." He waved one hand to dismiss any further protests. He left, and soon we smelled the smoke of his opium clouds. GaoLing began to curse.

Teacher Pan sighed. "At least the war is over and we can see if our friends at the medical school might know of rooms where we can squeeze in."

"I'm not going," GaoLing said.

How could she say this after all she had told me about her husband? "You'd stay with that demon?" I exclaimed.

"This is our family's ink shop. I'm not walking away from it. The war is over, and now I'm ready to fight back."

I tried to argue and Teacher Pan patted my arm. "Give her time. She'll come to her senses."

Sister Yu left that afternoon for the medical school, but soon she returned. "Miss Grutoff is back," she told us, "released from the war camp. But she is very, very sick." The four of us immediately left for the house of another foreigner, named Mrs. Riley. When we went in, I saw how thin Miss Grutoff had become. We used to joke that foreign women had big udders because of the cow's milk they drank. But now Miss Grutoff looked drained. And her color was poor. She insisted on standing up to greet us, and we insisted she sit and not bother to be polite with old friends. Loose skin hung from her face and arms. Her once red hair was gray and thin. "How are you?" we asked.

"Not bad," she said, cheerful and smiling. "As you can see, I'm alive. The Japanese couldn't starve me to death, but the mosquitoes almost had their way with me. Malaria."

Two of the little girls at the school had had malaria and died. But I did not tell Miss Grutoff. There would be plenty of time for bad news later.

"You must hurry and get well," I said. "Then we can reopen the school."

Miss Grutoff shook her head. "The old monastery is gone. Destroyed. One of the other missionaries told me."

We gasped.

"The trees, the building, everything has been burned to the ground and scattered." The other foreigner, Mrs. Riley, nodded.

I wanted to ask what had happened to the graves, but I could not speak. I felt as I had that day when I knew Kai Jing had been killed. Thinking about him caused me to try to remember his face. But I saw more clearly the stones under which he lay. How long had I loved him when he was alive? How long had I grieved for him since he had died?

Mrs. Riley then said: "We're going to open a school in Peking once we find a building. But now we need to help Miss Grutoff get well, don't we, Ruth?" And she patted Miss Grutoff's hand.

"Anything," we took turns saying. "Of course we'll help. We love Miss Grutoff. She is mother and sister to us all. What can we do?" Mrs. Riley then said Miss Grutoff had to return to the United States to see the doctors in San Francisco. But she would need a helper to accompany her to Hong Kong and then across the ocean.

"Would one of you be willing to go with me? I think we can arrange for a visa."

"We can all go!" GaoLing answered at once.

Miss Grutoff became embarrassed. I could see this. "I wouldn't want to trouble more than one of you," she said. "One is enough, I think." And then she sighed and said she was exhausted. She needed to lie down.

When she left the room, we looked at one another, uncertain how to begin the discussion of who should be the one to help Miss Grutoff. America? Miss Grutoff did not ask this only as a favor. We all knew she was also offering a great opportunity. A visa to America. But only one of us could take it. I thought about this. In my heart, America was the Christian heaven. It was where Kai Jing had gone, where he was waiting for me. I knew this was not actually true, but there was a hope that I could find happiness that had stayed hidden from me. I could leave the old curse, my bad background.

Then I heard GaoLing say, "Teacher Pan should go. He's the oldest, the most experienced." She had jumped in with the first suggestion, so I knew she wanted to go, as well.

"Experienced at what?" he said. "I can't be of much help, I'm afraid. I'm an old man who can't even read and write unless the words are as large and close as my shaky hands. And it would not be proper for a man to accompany a lady. What if she needs help during the night?"

"Sister Yu," GaoLing said. "You go, then. You're smart enough to overcome any obstacle." Another suggestion! GaoLing was desperate to go, to have someone argue that it should be she who went.

"If people don't trample me first," Sister Yu said. "Don't be ridiculous. Besides, I don't want to leave China. To be frank, while I have Christian love for Miss Grutoff and our foreign friends, I don't care to be around other Americans. Civil war or not, I'd rather stay in China."

"Then LuLing should go," GaoLing said.

What could I do? I had to argue: "I could never leave my father-in-law or you."

"No, no, you don't have to keep this old man company," I heard my father-in-law say. "I've been meaning to tell you that I may marry again. Yes, me. I know what you're thinking. The gods are laughing, and so am I."

"But who?" I asked. I could not imagine he had any time to court a woman. He was always at the shop, except when he went on brief errands.

"She lives next door to us, the longtime widow of the man who ran the bookshop."

"Wah! The man who sued my family?" GaoLing said.

"The books were fake," I reminded her. "The man lost the lawsuit, remember?" And then we remembered our manners and congratulated Teacher Pan by asking if she was a good cook, if she had a pleasant face, a kind voice, a family that was not too much trouble. I was happy for him but also glad that I no longer had to argue that I could not go to America.

"Well, it's clear to me LuLing should be the one to go to America with Miss Grutoff," Sister Yu said. "Teacher Pan will soon be bossed around by a new wife, so LuLing has less need to stay."

GaoLing hesitated a moment too long before saying, "Yes, that's the best. It's settled, then."

"What do you mean?" I said, trying to be bighearted. "I can't leave my own sister."

"I'm not even your real sister," GaoLing said. "You go first. Later, you can sponsor me."

"Ah, see! That means you want to go!" I could not help rubbing it in. But now that everything had been decided, I felt I could safely do this.

"I didn't say that," GaoLing said. "I meant only if things change and later I *need* to come."

"Why don't you go first, and later you can sponsor me? If you stay, that husband of yours will put you under his thumb and grind you to pieces." I was really being generous.

"But I can't leave my sister, any more than she can leave me," GaoLing said.

"Don't argue," I told her, "I'm older than you. You go first, then I'll go to Hong Kong in a month or so and wait for the sponsorship papers to come through."

GaoLing was supposed to argue that she should be the one to wait in Hong Kong. But instead she asked, "Is that how long it takes to sponsor another person? Only one month?"

And though I had no idea how long it took, I said, "Maybe it's even quicker than that." I still thought she was going to agree to wait.

"That fast," GaoLing marveled. "Well, if it's that quick, I might as well go first, but only so I can leave that demon of a husband right away."

Just then Mrs. Riley came back to the room. "We've agreed," Sister Yu announced. "GaoLing will accompany Miss Grutoff to San Francisco."

I was too stunned to say anything. That night, I went over in my head how I had lost my chance. I was angry that GaoLing had tricked me. Then I had sisterly feelings and was glad she was going so she could get away from Fu Nan. Back and forth I went, between these two feelings. Before I fell asleep, I decided this was fate. Now whatever happened, that was my New Destiny.

Three days later, just before we left for Hong Kong, we had a little party. "There's no need for tears and good-byes," I said. "Once we're settled in the new country, we'll invite you all to come visit."

Teacher Pan said that he and his new wife would enjoy that very much, a chance to visit another country before their life was over. Sister Yu said she had heard much about dancing in America. She confessed that she had always wanted to learn how to dance. And for the rest of the evening, which was the last time we ever saw them, we took turns guessing and joking. Miss Grutoff would be healed, then come back to China, where she would make more orphan girls act in more bad plays. GaoLing would be rich, having finally found the right fortune-teller, one who could write with four brushes at once. And I would be a famous painter.

We toasted one another. Soon, maybe in a year or less, Sister Yu and Teacher Pan with his new wife would sail to America for a holiday. GaoLing and I would come to the harbor in San Francisco and wait for them in our new automobile, a shiny black one with many comfortable seats and an American driver. Before we drove them to our mansion on top of a hill, we would stop at a ballroom. And to celebrate our reunion, we all agreed, we would dance and dance and dance.

FRAGRANCE

Each night when I returned to the rooming house in Hong Kong, I lay on a cot with wet towels over my chest. The walls were sweating because I couldn't open the windows for fresh air. The building was on a fishy street on the Kowloon side. This was not the part where the fish were sold. There it smelled of the morning sea, salty and sharp. I was living in Kowloon Walled City, along the low point in a wide gutter, where the scales and blood and guts gathered, swept there by the fishmongers' buckets of water at night. When I breathed the air, it was the vapors of death, a choking sour stink that reached like fingers into my stomach and pulled my insides out. Forever in my nose, that is the fragrance of Fragrant Harbor.

The British and other foreigners lived on the Hong Kong Island side. But in Kowloon Walled City, it was almost all Chinese, rich and raggedy, poor and powerful, everyone different, but we all had this in common: We had been strong, we had been weak, we had been desperate enough to leave behind our motherland and families.

And there were also those who made money from people's despair. I went to many blind seers, the *wenmipo* who claimed they were ghost writers. "I have a message from a baby," they called. "A message from a son." "A husband." "An ancestor who is angry." I sat down with one and she told me, "Your Precious Auntie has already been reincarnated. Go three blocks east, then three blocks north. A beggar girl will cry out to you, 'Auntie, have pity, give me hope.' Then you will know it is she. Give her a coin and the curse will be ended." I did exactly as she said. And on that exact block, a girl said those exact words. I was so overjoyed. Then another girl said those words, another and another, ten, twenty, thirty little girls, all without hope. I gave them coins, just in case. And for each of them, I felt pity. The next day, I saw another blind lady who could talk to ghosts. She also told me where to find Precious Auntie. Go here, go there. The next day was the same. I was using up my savings, but I didn't think it mattered. Soon, any day now, I would leave for America.

After I had lived a month in Hong Kong, I received a letter from GaoLing:

"My Own True Sister, Forgive me for not writing you sooner. Teacher Pan sent your address to me, but I did not receive it right away, because I was moving from one church lady's house to another. I'm also sorry to tell you that Miss Grutoff died a week after we arrived. Right before she flew to heaven, she said she made a mistake coming back to America. She wanted to return to China so her bones could rest there, next to Miss Towler's. I was glad to know how much she loved China, and sorry because it was too late to send her back. I went to her funeral, but not too many people knew her. I was the only one who cried, and I said to myself, She was a great lady.

"My other news is not so good, either. I learned I cannot sponsor you, not yet. The truth is, I almost was not able to stay myself. Why we thought it would be so easy, I don't know. I see now we were foolish. We should have asked many more questions. But now I have asked the questions, and I know of several ways for you to come later. How much later depends.

"One way is for you to apply as a refugee. The quota for Chinese, however, is very low, and the number who want to get in is beyond count. To be honest, your chances are like a leak moving against a flood.

"Another way is for me to be a citizen first so I can sponsor you as my sister. You will have to claim that Mother and Father are your real mother and father, since I cannot sponsor a cousin. But as a relative, you would be in a different line, ahead of ordinary refugees. For me to become a citizen, however, means I have to learn English first and get a good job. I promise you I am studying very hard, in case this is the means I have to turn to.

"There is a third way: I can marry a citizen and then become a citizen faster. Of course, it is inconvenient that I am already married to Chang Fu Nan, but I think no one needs to know this. On my visa papers, I did not mention it. Also, you should know that when I applied for the visa, the visa man asked for documents as proof of my birth, and I said, 'Who has documents for such things?' He said, 'Oh, were they burned during the war like everyone else's?' I thought that was the correct answer, so I agreed this was true. When you prepare your visa papers, you must say the same thing. Also make yourself five years younger, born 1921. I already did, born 1922, but in the same month as the old birthday. This will give you extra time to catch up.

"Mother and Father have already written to ask me to send them my extra money. I have had to write back and say I have none. If I do in the future, of course, I will send some to you. I feel so guilty that you insisted I come first and I gave in to your demands. Now it is you who are stuck, not knowing what to do. Don't mistake my meaning. Life here is not so easy. And making money is not like we imagined. All those stories of instant riches, don't believe them. As for dancing, that is only in the movies. Most of the day, I clean houses. I am paid twenty-five cents. That may sound like a lot, but it costs that much to eat dinner. So it is hard to save money. For you, of course, I am willing to starve.

"In his last letter, Father said he almost died of anger when he learned that Fu Nan lost the ink business in Peking. He said Fu Nan has returned to Immortal Heart and is lying around useless, but the Chang father is not being critical, saying Fu Nan is a big war hero, lost two fingers, saved lives. You know what I was thinking when I read that. Most terrible of all, our family still has to supply the inksticks and ink cakes, and we receive none of the profit, only a lesser debt. Everyone has had to take on various home businesses, weaving baskets, mending, doing menial labor that makes Mother complain that we have fallen as low as the tenants. She asks me to hurry and become rich, so I can pull her out of the bowels of hell.

"I feel a great burden of guilt and responsibility."

When I finished reading GaoLing's letter, I felt as if an ax were chopping my neck when I was already dead. I had waited in Hong Kong for nothing. I could wait a year, ten years, or the rest of my life, in this crowded city among desperate people with stories sadder than mine. I knew no one and I was lonely for my friends. There was no America for me. I had lost my chance.

The next day, I gathered my things and went to the train station to return to Peking. I put down my remaining money at the ticket booth. "The fare is higher now, miss," said the ticket man. How could this be? "Money is worth less now," he told me, "everything costs more." I then asked for a lower-class ticket. That's the lowest, he said, and pointed to a wall with fares written on a blackboard.

Now I was stuck. I wondered if I should write to Teacher Pan or perhaps Sister Yu. But then I thought, Oh, to give so much trouble to someone. No, you fix this problem yourself. I would pawn my valuables. But when I looked at them, I saw that these were treasures only to me: a notebook of Kai Jing's, the jacket GaoLing gave me before I went to the orphanage, the pages of Precious Auntie's and her photograph.

And there was also the oracle bone.

I unwrapped it from its soft cloth and looked at the characters scratched on one side. Unknown words, what should have been remembered. At one time, an oracle bone was worth twice as much as a dragon bone. I took my treasure to three shops. The first belonged to a bonesetter. He said the bone was no longer used as medicine, but as a strange curiosity it was worth a little money. He then offered me a price that surprised me, for it was almost enough to buy a second-class ticket to Peking. The next shop sold jewelry and curios. That shopkeeper took out a magnifying glass. He examined the oracle bone very carefully, turning it several times. He said it was genuine, but not a good example of an oracle bone. He offered me the price of a first-class ticket to Peking. The third place was an antique shop for tourists. Like the jeweler, this man examined the oracle bone with a special glass. He called another man over to take a look. Then he asked me many questions. "Where did you find this? . . . What? How did a girl like you find such a treasure? . . . Oh, you are the granddaughter of a bonesetter? How long have you been in Hong Kong? . . . Ah, waiting to go to America? Did someone else leave for America without this? Did you take it from him? There are plenty of thieves in Hong Kong these days. Are you one? Miss, you come back, come back, or I'll call the police."

I left that store, angry and insulted. But my heart was going *poom-poom-poom*, because now I knew that what was in my hand was worth a lot of money. Yet how could I sell it? It had belonged to my mother, my grandfather. It was my connection to them. How could I hand it over to a stranger so I could abandon my homeland, the graves of my ancestors? The more I thought these things, the stronger I became. Kai Jing had been right. This was my character.

I made a plan. I would find a cheaper place to live—yes, even cheaper than the stinky-fish house—and find a job. I would save my money for a few months, and if the visa still had not come through, I would return to Peking. There at least I could get a job at another orphanage school. I could wait there in comfort and companionship. If GaoLing got me the visa, fine, I would make my way back to Hong Kong. If she did not, fine, I would stay and be a teacher.

That day, I moved to a cheaper place to live, a room I shared with two women, one snoring, one sick. We took turns sleeping on the cot, the snoring girl in the morning, me in the afternoon, the sick one after me. Whichever two were not sleeping wandered outside, looking for take-home work: mending shoes, hemming scarves, weaving baskets, embroidering collars, painting bowls, anything to make a dollar. That's how I lived for a month. And when the sick girl didn't stop coughing, I moved away. "Lucky you didn't get TB like the other girl did," a melon vendor later told me. "Now they're both coughing blood." And I thought: TB! I had pretended to have this same sickness to escape from the Japanese. And would I now escape from getting sick?

Next I lived with a Shanghai lady who had been very, very rich but was no longer. We shared a hot little room above a place where we worked boiling laundry, dipping the clothes and plucking them out with long sticks. If she got splashed she yelled at me, even if it was not my fault. Her husband had been a top officer with the Kuomintang. A girl in the laundry told me he had been jailed for collaborating with the Japanese during the war. "So why does she act so uppity," the girl said, "when everyone looks down on her?" The uppity lady made a rule that I could not make any sounds at night—not a cough or a sneeze or a burst of gas. I had to walk softly, pretend my shoes were made of clouds. Often she would cry, then wail to the Goddess of Mercy what a terrible punishment it was that she had to be with such a person, meaning me. I told myself, Wait and see, maybe your opinion of her will change, as it did with Sister Yu. But it did not.

After that awful woman, I was glad to move in with an old lady who was deaf. For extra money, I helped her boil and shell peanuts all night long. In the morning, we sold the peanuts to people who would eat them with their breakfast rice porridge. During the heat of the afternoon, we slept. This was a comfortable life: peanuts and sleep. But one day a couple arrived, claiming to be relatives of the deaf lady's: "Here we are, take us in." She didn't know who they were, so they traced a zigzag relationship, and sure enough, she had to admit, maybe they were related. Before I left, I counted my money and saw I had enough for the train ticket to Peking at the lowest, lowest price.

Again I went to the railway station. Again I found out that the money value had gone down, down and the price of the ticket had gone up and up, to twice as much as before. I was like a little insect scurrying up a wall with the water rising faster.

This time I needed a better plan to change my situation, my *siqing*. In English and in Chinese, the words sound almost the same. On every street corner, you could hear people from everywhere talking about this: "My situation is this. This is how I can improve my situation." I realized that in Hong Kong, I had come to a place where everyone believed he could change his situation, his fate, no more staying stuck with your circumstances. And there were many ways to change. You could be clever, you could be greedy, you could have connections.

I was clever, of course, and if I had been greedy, I would have sold the oracle bone. But I decided once again I could not do that. I was not that poor in body and respect for my family.

As for connections, I had only GaoLing, now that Miss Grutoff was dead. And GaoLing was of no use. She did not know how to be resourceful. If I had been the one to go first to America, I would have used my strength, my character, to find a way to get a visa within a few weeks at the most. Then I wouldn't be facing the troubles I had simply because GaoLing didn't know what to do. That was the problem: GaoLing was strong, but not always in the right ways. She had forever been Mother's favorite, spoiled by pampering. And all those years in the orphanage, she had forever lived the easy life. I had helped her so much, as had Sister Yu, that she never had to think for herself. If the river turned downstream, she would never think to swim upstream. She knew how to get her way, but only if others helped her.

By the next morning, I had devised a new plan. I took my little bit of money and bought the white smock and trousers of a *majie*. British people were crazy for that kind of maid—pious, refined, and clean. That was how I found a job with an English lady and her ancient mum. Their last name was Flowers.

They had a house in the Victoria Peak area. It was smaller than the others nearby, more like a cottage, with a twisty narrow path and green ferns that led to the front door. The two old English ladies lived on top, and I lived in a room on the basement floor of the cottage.

Miss Patsy was the daughter, seventy years old, born in Hong Kong. Her mother must have been at least ninety, and her name was Lady Ina. Her husband had been a big success in shipping goods from India to China to England. Sir Flowers was how Miss Patsy called him in memory, even though he was her father. If you ask me, the Flowers part of their name stood for the flowers that made opium. That was what the shipping business was a long time ago between India and Hong Kong, and that was how lots of Chinese people found the habit.

Because Miss Patsy had always lived in Hong Kong, she could speak Cantonese just like the local people. It was a special dialect. When I first went to live there, she spoke to me in the local talk, which I could not understand except for the words that sounded a little like Mandarin. Later she mixed in a bit of English, some of which I knew from living at the orphanage school. But Miss Patsy spoke English like a British person, and at first it was very hard for me to understand.

Lady Ina's words were also hard to understand. The sounds

spilled out as soft and lumpy as the porridge she ate every day. She
was so old she was like a baby. She made messes in her panties, both
kinds, stinky and wet. I know, because I had to clean her. Miss Patsy
would say to me, "Lady Ina needs to wash her hands." And then I
would lift Lady Ina from the sofa or bed or dining room chair. Lucky
for me she was tiny like a child. She also had a temper like one. She
would shout, "No, no, no, no, no," as I walked her to the bathroom,
inch by inch, so slow we were like two turtles glued at the shells. She
kept shouting this while I washed her, "No, no, no, no, no," because
she did not like any water to touch her body and especially not her
head. Three or four times a day, I changed and cleaned her and her
panties, her other clothes, too. Miss Patsy did not want her mummy
to wear diapers because that would be a big insult. So I had to wash,
wash, wash, so many clothes, every day. At least Miss Patsy was a
nice lady, very polite. If Lady Ina threw her temper, Miss Patsy had
to say only three words in a happy voice, "Visitors are here!" and
Lady Ina suddenly stopped what she was doing. She would sit down,
her crooked back now very straight, her hands folded in her lap.
That was how she had been taught from the time she was a young
girl. In front of visitors, she had to be a lady, even if it was just
pretend.

In that house, there was also a parrot, a big gray bird named
Cuckoo—Cuckoo like the clock bird. At first I thought Miss Patsy
was calling him *ku-ku*, like the Chinese word for crying, which is
what he sometimes did, *ku! ku! ku!* as if he were wounded to near-
death. And sometimes he laughed like a crazy woman, long and
loud. He could copy any kind of sound—man, woman, monkey,
baby. One day I heard a teakettle whistle. I went running, and the
teakettle was Cuckoo rocking on his branch, stretching his neck, so
delighted that he had fooled me. Another time I heard a Chinese girl
cry, "Baba! Baba! Don't beat me! Please don't beat me!" and then she
screamed and screamed, until I thought my skin would peel off.

Miss Patsy said, "Cuckoo was already bad when Sir Flowers bought him for my tenth birthday. And for sixty years, he has learned only what he wants, like so many men." Miss Patsy loved that parrot like a son, but Lady Ina always called him the devil. Whenever she heard that bird laugh she would waddle to his cage, shake her finger, and say something like, "*Ooh shh-duh,* you shut up." Sometimes she would raise her finger, but before any sounds could come out of her mouth, the bird would say, *"Ooh shh-duh,"* exactly like Lady Ina. Then Lady Ina would get confused. Wah! Had she already spoken? I could see these thoughts on her face, her head twisting this way, then that, as if two sides of her mind were having a fight. Sometimes she would go all the way to the end of the room, inch by inch, then turn around and walk back, inch by inch, raise her finger, and say, *"Ooh shh-duh!"* And then the bird would say the same. Back and forth they went: "You shut up! You shut up!" One day Lady Ina went up to the bird, and before she could say anything, Cuckoo said in Miss Patsy's singsong happy voice, "Visitors are here!" Right away, Lady Ina went to a nearby chair, sat down, took out a lacy handkerchief from her sleeve, crossed her hands in her lap, closed her lips, and waited, her blue eyes turned toward the door.

So that's how I learned to speak English. To my way of thinking, if a bird could speak good English, I could, too. I had to pronounce the words exactly right, otherwise Lady Ina would not follow my directions. And because Miss Patsy talked to her mother in simple words, it was easy for me to learn other new things to say: *Stand up, Sit down, Lunch is served, Time for tea, Horrid weather, isn't it.*

For the next two years or so, I thought my situation would never change. Every month, I went to the train station, only to find the fares had gone up again. Every month, I received a letter from GaoLing. She told me of her new life in San Francisco, how hard it was to be a burden on strangers. The church that sponsored her had found her a room with an old grandmother named Mrs. Wu who spoke Mandarin. "She is very rich but acts very cheap," GaoLing wrote. "She saves everything that she thinks is too good to eat right away—fruit, chocolates, cashews. So she puts them on top of her refrigerator, and when they are finally too rotten to eat, that's when she puts them in her mouth and says, 'Why does everyone say this tastes so good? What's so good about it?' " This was GaoLing's way of telling me how hard her life was.

One month, though, I received a letter from GaoLing that did not start with her complaints. "Good news," she wrote. "I have met two bachelors and I think I should marry one of them. They are both American citizens, born in this country. According to my passport with the new birth year, one is a year older than I am, the other is three years older. So you know what that means. The older one is studying to be a doctor, the younger a dentist. The older is more serious, very smart. The younger is more handsome, full of jokes. It is very hard for me to decide which one I should put all my attentions on. What do you think?"

When I read that letter, I had just finished cleaning up Lady Ina's bottom twice in one hour. I wanted to reach across the ocean and shake GaoLing by the shoulders and shout, "Marry the one who takes you the fastest. How can you ask which one, when I am wondering how I can live from day to day?"

I did not answer GaoLing at once. I had to go to the bird market that afternoon. Miss Patsy said that Cuckoo needed a new cage. So I went down the hill and crossed over the harbor in the ferry to the Kowloon side. Every day it was becoming more crowded there as people came in from China. "The civil war is growing worse," Sister Yu had written me, "with battles as fierce as those during the war with Japan. Even if you had enough money to return to Peking right now, you should not. The Nationalists would say you are a Communist because Kai Jing is now called one of their martyrs, and the Communists would say you are a Nationalist because you lived in an

American orphanage. And whichever is worse changes with each town you pass through."

When I read this, I no longer had the worry of how to get back to Peking. I exchanged that for a worry over Sister Yu and Teacher Pan and his new wife. They, too, could be counted as enemies on either side. As I walked toward the bird market, these were the only thoughts I had. And then I felt a cold breeze run down my back, though it was a warm day. Like a ghost is right behind me, I thought. I kept walking, turning one corner, then another, and this feeling that someone was following me grew stronger. Suddenly I stopped and turned around, and a man said to me, "So it really is you."

There stood Fu Nan, GaoLing's husband, and now he was missing not only two fingers but his entire left hand. His face had a bad color, and his eyes were yellow and red. "Where's my wife?" he asked.

I stirred the question in my head. What was the danger in answering him one way or another? "Gone," I finally told him, and I was glad to be able to say these words: "Gone to America."

"America?" He looked astonished at first, and then he smiled. "I knew that. I just wanted to see if you would tell me the truth."

"I have nothing to hide."

"Then you aren't hiding the fact that you are trying to go to America, too?"

"Who says that?"

"The entire Liu family. They're panting like dogs for an opportunity to follow their daughter. Why should you go first, they say, when you aren't even really her sister? Only true relatives can be sponsored, not bastards." He gave me a smile of false apology, then added: "Husbands, of course, should be number one."

I began to walk away and he grabbed me. "You help me, I help you," he said. "Give me her address, that's all I want. If she doesn't want me to come, that's that, and you can be next in line. I won't tell the Liu family."

"I already know she doesn't want you to come. She went to America to run away from you."

"Give me her address, or I'll go to the authorities and tell them you aren't really sisters. Then you'll lose your chance to go to America as well, same as me."

I stared at that terrible man. What was he saying? What would he really do? I hurried away, weaving in and out of the busy crowds, until I was certain I had lost him. At the bird market, I watched from the corner of my eye. I did not spend too much time bargaining, and when I had bought the cage, I quickly made my way back to the Hong Kong side, holding on tight to my documents that showed where I lived. What would Fu Nan do? Would he really tell the authorities? How smart was he? Which authorities would he tell?

That night, I wrote GaoLing a letter, telling her of Fu Nan's threats. "Only you know how tricky he is," I said. "He might also tell the authorities you are already married, and then you'll be in trouble, especially if you marry an American."

The next day, I left the house to post the letter. As soon as I stepped into the street, I felt the sudden chill again. I stuffed the letter in my blouse. Around the next corner, there he was, waiting for me.

"Give me some money," he said. "You can do this for your brother-in-law, can't you? Or aren't you really my wife's sister?"

For the next few weeks he popped up like that, every time I left the house. I could not call the police. What could I say? "My brother-in-law who is not really my brother-in-law is following me, asking me for money and the address of my sister who is not my true sister"? And then one day when I stepped outside to go to the market, he was not there. The entire time I was out, I expected I would

see him, and I was prepared to be miserable. Nothing. When I returned home, I was puzzled and felt a strange relief. Perhaps he died,
I allowed myself to hope. For the next week, I saw no sign of him. I
felt no sudden cold breeze. Could it be that my luck had changed?
When I opened the next letter from GaoLing, I was convinced this
was true.

"I was so angry to hear that Fu Nan has been bothering you," she
wrote. "That turtle spawn will stop at nothing to satisfy himself. The
only way to get rid of him for a few days is to give him money for his
opium. But soon this will no longer be a problem for you. Happy
news has arrived! I have found another way you can come. Do you
remember the brothers I told you about—one is studying to be a
dentist, the other a doctor? Their family name is Young and the father said a person like you can come if a person like him sponsors
you as a Famous Visiting Artist. This is like a tourist with special visiting privileges. The family is very kind to do this, since I am not yet
related to them. Of course, I cannot ask them to pay your way. But
they have already completed the application and supplied the documents. The next step is for me to earn more money so we can buy the
boat passage. In the meantime, you must prepare yourself to leave at
any moment. Obtain the boat schedules, have a doctor's examination
for parasites. . . ."

I read the long list she provided, and was surprised at how smart
she truly was. She knew so much, and I felt like a child now being
guided by a worried mother. I was so happy I let tears fall right there
as I rode the ferry home. And because I was on the ferry, I did not
think to be afraid when I felt a breeze. To me it was a comfort. But
then I looked up.

There was Fu Nan. One of his eyes was missing.

I nearly jumped off the boat I was so scared. It was as if I were
seeing what would happen to me. "Give me some money," he said.

That night, I put Precious Auntie's picture on a low table and lighted some incense. I asked her forgiveness and that of her father. I said that the gift she had given me would now buy me my freedom and that I hoped she would not be angry with me for this, as well.

The next day, I sold the oracle bone to the second shop I had gone to all those months ago. With my savings as a maid, I had enough money to buy a ticket in steerage. I got the boat schedules and sent GaoLing a telegram. Every few days, I gave Fu Nan money for his habit, enough to put him into dreams. And then finally the visa was approved. I was a Famous Visiting Artist.

I sailed for America, a land without curses or ghosts. By the time I landed, I was five years younger. Yet I felt so old.

PART THREE

Mr. Tang was in love with LuLing, though he had never met her. Ruth could sense this. He talked as if he knew her better than anyone else, even her own daughter. He was eighty years old, a survivor of World War Two, the civil war in China, the Cultural Revolution, and a triple coronary bypass. He had been a famous writer in China, but here his work remained untranslated and unknown. A linguistics colleague of Art's had given Ruth his name.

"She is a woman of strong character, very honest," he said to Ruth on the telephone after he began to translate the pages Ruth had mailed to him. "Could you send me her picture, one when she was a young woman? Seeing her would help me say her words in English the way she has expressed them in Chinese."

Ruth thought that was an odd request, but she complied, mailing him scanned copies of the photo of LuLing and GaoLing with their mother when they were young, and another taken when LuLing first arrived in the United States. Later, Mr. Tang asked Ruth for a picture of Precious Auntie. "She was unusual," he remarked. "Self-educated, forthright, quite a rebel for her time." Ruth was bursting to ask him: Did he know whether Precious Auntie was indeed her mother's real mother? But she held off, wanting to read his translation all at one time, not piecemeal. Mr. Tang had said he would need about two months to finish the job. "I don't like to just transliterate word for word. I want to phrase it more naturally, yet ensure these are your mother's words, a record for you and your children for generations to come. They must be just right. Don't you agree?"

While Mr. Tang translated, Ruth lived at LuLing's house. She had told Art of her decision when he returned from Hawaii.

"This seems sudden," he said as he watched her pack. "Are you sure you're not being rash? What about hired help?"

Had she downplayed the problems over the past six months? Or had Art simply not been paying attention? She was frustrated by how little they seemed to know each other.

"I think it would be easier if you hired help to take care of you and the girls," Ruth said.

Art sighed.

"I'm sorry. It's just that the housekeepers I get for my mother keep quitting, and I can't get Auntie Gal or anyone else to take care of her except for an occasional day here and there. Auntie Gal said that the one week she spent with her was worse than running after her grandkids when they were babies. But at least she finally believes the diagnosis is real and that ginseng tea isn't a cure-all."

"Are you sure something else isn't going on?" he asked, following Ruth into the Cubbyhole.

"What do you mean?" She took down diskettes and notebooks from the shelves.

"Us. You and me. Do we need to talk about something more than just your mother's mind falling apart?"

"Why do you say that?"

"You seem—I don't know—distant, maybe even a little angry."

"I'm tense. Last week I saw how she really is, and it frightened me. She's a danger to herself. She's far worse than I thought. And I realize the disease is further along than I first thought. She's probably had it six or seven years already. I don't know why I never noticed—"

"So your going to live there has nothing to do with us?"

"No," Ruth said firmly. And then in a softer voice, "I don't know." And after a long silence, she added, "I remember you asked me once what I was going to do about *my* mother. And it struck me. Yes, what am *I* going to do? I felt it was all up to me. I've tried to handle it the best I can, and this is it. Maybe my moving out does have to do with us, but now, if there's anything wrong with us, it's secondary to what's wrong with my mom. That's all I can handle right now."

Art looked uncertain. "Well, when you feel you're ready to talk . . ." He drifted off, so miserable, it seemed to Ruth, she was almost tempted to assure him that nothing was really wrong.

LuLing was also suspicious as to why Ruth needed to live with her.

"Someone asked me to write a children's book, with illustrations of animals," Ruth said. She was now accustomed to telling lies without feeling guilty. "I was hoping you'd do the drawings, and if you did, it would be easier if we worked together here, less noisy that way."

"How many animal? What kind?" LuLing was as excited as a child going to the zoo.

"Anything we want. You get to decide what to draw, Chinese style."

"All right." Her mother looked pleased at the prospect of being vital to her daughter's success. Ruth sighed, relieved yet sad. Why hadn't she ever asked her mother to make drawings before? She should have done it when her mother's hand and mind were still steady. It broke her heart to see her mother trying so hard, being so conscientious, so determined to be valuable. Making her mother happy would have been easy all along. LuLing simply wanted to be essential, as a mother should be.

Each day, she went to her desk and spent fifteen minutes grinding her inkstick. Luckily, many of the drawings she did were of subjects she had drawn many times for scroll paintings—fish, horse, cat, monkey, duck—and she executed them and the characters from a neuromotor memory of the strokes. The results were shaky yet recognizable renditions of what she once had done perfectly. But the moment LuLing attempted the unfamiliar, her hand flailed in synchrony with her confusion, and Ruth became as distressed as her mother, though she tried not to show it. Every time LuLing finished a drawing, Ruth praised it, took it away, then suggested a new animal to draw.

"Hippo?" LuLing puzzled over the word. "How you say in Chinese?"

"Never mind," Ruth said. "How about an elephant? Do an elephant, you know, the one with a long nose and big ears."

But LuLing was still frowning. "Why you give up? Something hard maybe worth more than easy. Hippo, what look like? Horn right here?" She tapped the top of her head.

"That's a rhinoceros. That's good too. Do a rhinoceros, then."

"Not hippo?"

"Don't worry about it."

"I not worry! You worry! I see this. Look your face. You not hiding from me. I know. I your mother! Okay-okay, you don't worry hippo anymore. I worry for you. Later I remember, then tell you, you be happy. Okay now? Don't cry anymore."

Her mother was good at being quiet when Ruth was working. "Study hard," she would whisper. But if Ruth was watching television, LuLing, as she always had, figured she was not doing anything important. Her mother then gabbed about GaoLing, rehashing her sister's greatest insults to her over the years. "She want me to go love-boat cruise to Hawaii. I ask her, Where I have this kind money? My Social Security only seven hundred fifty dollar. She tell me, You too cheap! I tell her, This not cheap, this *poor*. I not rich widow. Hnh! She forget she once want marry my husband. Tell me when he die, *lucky* she choose other brother. . . ."

Sometimes Ruth listened with interest, trying to determine how much of the story LuLing changed in each retelling, feeling reassured when she repeated the same story. But other times Ruth was simply irritated by having to listen, and this irritation made her feel strangely satisfied, as if everything was the same, nothing was wrong.

"That girl downstair eat popcorn almost every night! Burn it, fire alarm go off. She don't know, I can smell! Stink! Popcorn all she eat! No wonder skinny. Then she tell me, this not work right, that not right. Always complaining, threat me 'lawsuit *in*-jury, code vio-*la*-tion' . . ."

At night, as Ruth lay in her old bed, she felt she had come back to her adolescence in the guise of an adult. She was the same person and yet she was not. Or perhaps she was two versions of herself, Ruth$_{1969}$ and Ruth$_{1999}$, one more innocent and the other more perceptive, one needier, the other more self-sufficient, both of them fearful. She was her mother's child, and mother to the child her mother had become. So many combinations, like Chinese names and characters, the same elements, seemingly simple, reconfigured in different ways. This was the bed from her childhood, and still within were those youthful moments before dreams, when she ached and wondered alone: What's going to happen? And just as in childhood, she listened to her breathing and was frightened by the idea that her mother's might one day stop. When she was conscious of it, each inhalation was an effort. Expiration was simply a release. Ruth was afraid to let go.

Several times a week, LuLing and Ruth would talk to ghosts. Ruth pulled out the old sand tray stored on top of the refrigerator and offered to write to Precious Auntie. Her mother reacted politely, the way people do when offered a box of chocolates: "Oh! . . . Well, maybe just little." LuLing wanted to know if the children's book was going to make Ruth famous. Ruth had Precious Auntie say that LuLing would be.

LuLing also asked for updates on the stock market. "Dow Jones go up or down?" she asked one day.

Ruth drew an upward arrow.

"Sell Intel, buy Intel?"

Ruth knew her mother watched the stock market mostly just for fun. She had not found any letters, junk mail or otherwise, from brokerage firms. *Buy on sale,* she decided to write.

LuLing nodded. "Oh, wait till down. Precious Auntie very smart."

One night, as Ruth held the chopstick in her hand, ready to divine more answers, she heard LuLing say: "Why you and Artie argue?"

"We're not arguing."

"Then why you not live together? This because me? My fault?"

"Of course not." Ruth said this a bit too loudly.

"I think maybe so." She gave Ruth her all-knowing look. "Long time 'go, you first meet him, I tell you, Why you live together first? You do this, he never marry you. You remember? Oh, now you thinking, Ah, Mother right. Live together, now I just leftover, easy throw away. Don't be embarrass. You be honest."

Her mother had said those things, Ruth recalled with chagrin. She busied her hands, brushing off stray grains of sand from the edges of the tray. She was both surprised by the things her mother remembered and touched by her concern. What LuLing had said about Art was not exactly right, yet she had pierced the heart of it, the fact that Ruth felt like a leftover, last in line to get a helping of whatever was being served.

Something was terribly wrong between Art and her. She had

sensed that more strongly during their trial separation—wasn't that what this was? She saw more clearly the habits of emotion, her trying to accommodate herself to him even when he didn't need her to. At one time she had thought that adjustment was what every couple, married or not, did, willingly or out of grudging necessity. But had Art also accommodated to her? If so, she didn't know how. And now that they had been apart, she felt unweighted, untethered. This was what she had predicted she might feel when she lost her mother. Now she wanted to hang on to her mother as if she were her life preserver.

"What bothers me is that I don't feel lonelier without Art," she told Wendy over the phone. "I feel more myself."

"Do you miss the girls?"

"Not that much, at least not their noise and energy. Do you think my feelings are deadened or something?"

"I think you're worn out."

Twice a week, Ruth and her mother went to Vallejo Street for dinner. On those days, Ruth had to finish her work early and shop for groceries. Since she did not want to leave her mother alone, she took her along to the store. While they shopped, LuLing commented on the cost of every item, questioning whether Ruth should wait until it was cheaper. Once Ruth arrived home—and yes, she reminded herself, the flat on Vallejo Street was still her home—she seated LuLing in front of the television, then sorted through mail addressed to her and Art as a couple. She saw how little of that there was, while most of the repair bills were in her name. At the end of the night, she was frazzled, saddened, and relieved to go back to her mother's house, to her little bed.

One night, while she was in the kitchen cutting vegetables, Art sidled up to her and patted her bottom. "Why don't you get GaoLing to baby-sit your mom? Then you can stay over for a conjugal visit."

She flushed. She wanted to lean against him, wrap her arms around him, and yet the act of doing so was as scary as leaping off a cliff.

He kissed her neck. "Or you can take a break right now and we can sneak into the bathroom for a quickie."

She laughed nervously. "They'll all know what we're doing."

"No they won't." Art was breathing in her ear.

"My mother knows everything, she sees everything."

With that, Art stopped, and Ruth was disappointed.

During the second month of their living apart, Ruth told Art, "If you really want to have dinner together, maybe you should come over to my mother's for a change, instead of my schlepping over here all the time for dinner. It's exhausting to do that all the time."

So Art and the girls started to go twice a week to LuLing's house. "Ruth," Dory whined one night as she watched her making a salad, "when are you coming home? Dad is like really boring and Fia is all the time like, 'Dad, there's nothing to do, there's nothing good to eat.' "

Ruth was pleased that they missed her. "I don't know, honey. Waipo needs me."

"We need you too."

Ruth felt her heart squeeze. "I know, but Waipo's sick. I have to stay with her."

"Then can I come and stay here with you?"

Ruth laughed. "I'd like that, but you'll have to ask your dad."

Two weekends later, Fia and Dory came with an inflatable mattress. They stayed in Ruth's room. "Girls only," Dory insisted, so Art had to go home. In the evening, Ruth and the girls watched television and drew mehndi tattoos on each other's hands. The next weekend, Art asked if it was boys' night yet.

"I think that can be arranged," Ruth said coyly.

Art brought his toothbrush, a change of clothes, and a portable boombox with a Michael Feinstein CD, Gershwin music. At night, he squeezed into the twin bed with Ruth. But she did not feel amorous with LuLing in the next room. That was the explanation she gave Art.

"Let's just cuddle, then," he suggested. Ruth was glad he did not press her for further explanations. She nestled against his chest. Deep into the night, she listened to his sonorous breathing and the foghorns. For the first time in a long while, she felt safe.

Mr. Tang called Ruth at the end of two months. "Are you sure there aren't any more pages?"

"Afraid not. I've been cleaning out my mother's house, drawer by drawer, room by room. I even discovered she put a thousand dollars under a floorboard. If there was anything else, I'm sure I would have found it."

"Then I've finished." Mr. Tang sounded sad. "There were a few pages with some writing on them, the same sentences over and over, saying she was worried that she was already forgetting too many things. The script on those was pretty shaky. I think they were more recent. It may upset you. I'm just telling you now, so you know."

Ruth thanked him.

"May I come over now to deliver my work to you?" he asked formally. "Would that be all right?"

"Is it too much trouble?"

"It would be an honor. To be honest, I would dearly like to meet your mother. After all this time of reading her words, day and night, I feel I know her like an old friend and miss her already."

Ruth warned him: "She won't be the same woman who wrote those pages."

"Perhaps . . . but somehow I think she will be."

"Would you like to come for dinner tonight?"

Ruth joked with her mother that an admirer was coming to see her and she should put on her pretty clothes.

"No! No one coming."

Ruth nodded and smiled.

"Who?"

Ruth answered vaguely. "An old friend of an old friend of yours in China."

LuLing pondered hard. "Ah, yes. I remember now."

Ruth helped her bathe and dress. She tied a scarf around her neck, combed her hair, added a touch of lipstick. "You're beautiful," Ruth said, and it was true.

LuLing looked at herself in the mirror. "Buddha-full. Too bad GaoLing not pretty like me." Ruth laughed. Her mother had never expressed vanity about her looks, but with the dementia, the modesty censors must not have been working. Dementia was like a truth serum.

At seven exactly, Mr. Tang arrived with LuLing's pages and his translation. He was a slender man with white hair, deep smile lines, a very kind face. He brought LuLing a bag of oranges.

"No need to be so polite," she said automatically as she inspected the fruit for soft spots. She scolded Ruth in Chinese: "Take his coat. Ask him to sit down. Give him something to drink."

"No need to trouble yourself," Mr. Tang said.

"Oh, your Chinese is the Beijing dialect, very elegant," LuLing said. She became girlish and shy, which amused Ruth. And Mr. Tang in turn poured on the charm, pulling out LuLing's chair to seat her, serving her tea first, filling her cup when it was half empty. She and Mr. Tang continued to speak in Chinese, and to Ruth's ear, her mother began to sound more logical, less confused.

"Where in China are you from?" LuLing asked.

"Tianjin. Later I went to school at Yenching University."

"Oh, my first husband went there, a very smart boy. Pan Kai Jing. Did you know him?"

"I've heard of him," Ruth heard Mr. Tang answer. "He studied geology, didn't he?"

"That's right! He worked on many important things. Have you ever heard of Peking Man?"

"Of course, Peking Man is world-famous."

LuLing looked wistful. "He died watching over those old bones."

"He was a great hero. Others admired his bravery, but you must have suffered."

Ruth listened with fascination. It was as if Mr. Tang had known her mother years before. He easily guided her to the old memories, to those that were still safeguarded from destruction. And then she heard her mother say, "My daughter Luyi also worked with us. She was at the same school where I lived after Precious Auntie died."

Ruth turned, startled then touched that her mother included her in the past.

"Yes, I was sorry to hear about your mother. She was a great lady. Very smart."

LuLing tilted her head and seemed to be struggling with sadness. "She was the daughter of a bonesetter."

Mr. Tang nodded. "A very famous doctor."

At the end of the evening, Mr. Tang thanked LuLing elaborately for some delightful hours of remembering the old times. "May I have the honor of visiting you again soon?"

LuLing tittered. She raised her eyebrows and looked at Ruth.

"You're welcome to come anytime," Ruth said.

"Tomorrow!" LuLing blurted. "Come tomorrow."

Ruth stayed up all night to read the pages Mr. Tang had translated. "Truth," the account began. She started to enumerate all the true things she was learning, but soon lost count, as each fact led to

more questions. Her mother was really five years older than Ruth
had always thought. So that meant she had told Dr. Huey the truth
about her age! And the part about not being GaoLing's sister, that
was true as well. Yet her mother and GaoLing *were* sisters, more so
than Ruth had ever thought. They had had more reason than most
sisters to disavow their relationship, yet they had been fiercely loyal,
had remained irrevocably bound to each other by grudges, debt, and
love. She was elated to know this.

Parts of her mother's story saddened her. Why did she feel she
could never tell Ruth that Precious Auntie was her mother? Did she
fear that her own daughter would be ashamed that LuLing was illegitimate? Ruth would have assured her that there was no shame, that
it was practically fashionable these days to be born a love child. But
then Ruth remembered that as a girl she had been terrified of Precious Auntie. She had resented her presence in their lives, had
blamed her for her mother's quirkiness, her feelings of doom. How
misunderstood Precious Auntie had been—by both her daughter
and her granddaughter. Yet there were moments when Ruth sensed
that Precious Auntie had been watching her, that she knew when
Ruth was suffering.

Ruth mused over this, lying in her childhood bed. She understood more clearly why her mother had always wanted to find Precious Auntie's bones and bury them in the proper place. She wanted
to walk through the End of the World and make amends. She wanted
to tell her mother, "I'm sorry and I forgive you, too."

The next day, Ruth telephoned Art to tell him what she had read. "It
feels like I've found the magic thread to mend a torn-up quilt. It's
wonderful and sad at the same time."

"I'd like to read it. Would you let me?"

"I want you to." Ruth sighed. "She should have told me these things years ago. It would have made such a difference——"

Art interrupted: "There are things I should have said years ago too."

Ruth fell silent, waiting.

"I've been thinking about your mother, and I've also been thinking about us."

Ruth's heart started to race.

"Remember what you said when we first met, about not wanting to have assumptions about love?"

"I didn't say that, you did."

"I did?"

"Absolutely. I remember."

"Funny, I thought you did."

"Ah, you assumed!"

He laughed. "Your mother isn't the only one with memory problems. Well, if I said it, then I was wrong, because I do think it's important to have certain assumptions—for one thing, that the person who's with you is there for the long haul, that he'll take care of you and what comes with you, the whole package, mother and everything. For whatever reason—my having said that about assumptions, and your going along with it—well, I guess I thought it was great at the time, that I had love on a free ride. I didn't know what I was going to lose until you moved out."

Art paused. Ruth knew he was waiting for her to respond. In part, she wanted to shout with gratitude that he had said what she had been feeling and could not express. Yet she was scared that he was saying this too late. She felt no joy in hearing his admission. She felt sad.

"I don't know what to say," she finally admitted.

"You don't have to say anything. I just wanted you to know. . . . The other thing is, I really am worried about your taking care of your mother over the long term. I know you want to do this, that it's important, and she needs someone around. But you and I know she's going to get worse. She'll require more and more care, and she can't do it alone, and neither can you. You have your work and a life too, and your mother would be the last person to see you give that up for her sake."

"I can't keep hiring new housekeepers."

"I know. . . . That's why I've been reading up on Alzheimer's, stages of the disease, medical needs, support groups. And I've thought of an idea, a possible solution . . . an assisted-living residence."

"That's not a solution." Ruth felt as she had when her mother showed her the ten-million-dollar check from the magazine sweepstakes.

"Why not?"

"Because my mother would never go for it. *I* wouldn't go for it. She'd think I was sending her to the dog pound. She'd threaten to kill herself every single day—"

"I'm *not* talking about a nursing home and bedpans. This is assisted living. They're the latest concept, the wave of the baby-boomer future, like senior Club Meds—meals, maid service, laundry, transportation, organized outings, exercise, even dancing. And it's supervised, twenty-four hours. It's upscale, not depressing at all. I've already looked at a bunch of residences, and I've found a great one, not far from where your mother lives now—"

"Forget it. Upscale or not, she would never live in a place like that."

"All she has to do is try it."

"I'm telling you, forget it. She won't do it."

"Whoa, whoa. Before you dismiss the idea outright, tell me the specific objections. Let's see if we can move forward from there."

"There's nothing to move forward. But if you must know, for one thing, she'd never leave her own home. And second, there's the cost. I assume these places aren't free, which is what it would have to be for her to even consider it. And if it *were* free, she'd think it was welfare, so she'd refuse on those grounds."

"All right. I can deal with those factors. What else?"

Ruth took a deep breath. "She'd have to love it. She would have to *want* to live there as her choice, not yours or mine."

"Done. And she can come stay with you and me anytime she wants."

Ruth noted that he said "you and me." She let down her guard. Art was trying. He was telling her he loved her in the best way he knew possible.

Two days later, LuLing showed Ruth an official-looking notice from the California Department of Public Safety, on letterhead generated from Art's computer.

"Radon leak!" LuLing exclaimed. "What this mean, radon leak?"

"Let me see," Ruth said, and scanned the letter. Art had been very clever. Ruth played along. "Mm. It's a heavy gas, it says, radioactive, dangerous to your lungs. The gas company detected it when they did a routine inspection for earthquake dangers. The leakage isn't from a pipe. It comes from the soil and rocks under the house, and they need to have you move out for three months while they do an environmental assessment and hazard removal via intensive ventilation."

"Ai-ya! How much cost?"

"Hm. Nothing, it says. The city does it for free. Look, they even pay for the place where you stay while they do the ventilation. Three months' free rent ... including food. The Mira Mar Manor— 'located near your current residence,' it says, 'with amenities typical of a five-star hotel.' That's the highest rating, five stars. They're asking you to go there as soon as possible."

"Free five-star? For two people?"

Ruth pretended to search the fine print. "No. Looks like it's just for one person. I can't go." She sighed, sounding disappointed.

"Hunh! I don't mean you!" her mother exclaimed. "What about that girl downstair?"

"Oh, right." Ruth had forgotten about the tenant. So had Art, evidently. But her mother, brain disease and all, hadn't let that slip by.

"I'm sure she got a similar notice. They wouldn't let anyone remain in the building, not if it can give them lung disease."

LuLing frowned. "Then she live my *same* hotel?"

"Oh! . . . No, it's probably different, a place that isn't as nice, I'm sure, since you're the owner and she's only the renter."

"But she still pay *me* rent?"

Ruth looked at the letter again. "Of course. That's the law."

LuLing nodded with satisfaction. "Okay, then."

By phone, Ruth told Art that his plan seemed to have worked. She was glad that he didn't sound smug.

"It's kind of scary how easily fooled she was," he said. "That's how a lot of old people get swindled out of their homes and savings."

"I feel like a spy right now," Ruth added. "Like we succeeded at a covert mission."

"I guess she and a lot of other people will buy into any idea that involves getting something for nothing."

"Speaking of which, how much will this Mira Mar place cost?"

"Don't worry about it."

"Come on. Tell me."

"I'll take care of it. If she likes it and stays, we'll figure it out later. If she hates it, the three months are on me. She can move back into her old place, and we'll think of something else."

Ruth liked that he was thinking "we" again. "Well, we'll share the cost of the three months, then."

"Just let me do this, okay?"

"Why should I?"

"Because it feels like the most important thing I've done in a long time. Call it a Boy Scout good deed for the day. Mitzvah-gathering, mensch remedial training. Temporary insanity. It makes me feel good, like a human being. It makes me happy."

Happy. If only her mother could be happy as well, living in a place like the Mira Mar. Ruth wondered what made people happy. Could you find happiness in a place? In another person? What about happiness for herself? Did you simply have to know what you wanted and reach for it through the fog?

As they parked in front of the three-story shingled building, Ruth was relieved to see that it did not look like an asylum. LuLing was at her sister's for the weekend, and it was Art's idea that they visit Mira Mar Manor without her, so that they could anticipate what objections she might raise. Mira Mar Manor was flanked by windswept cypress trees and looked out on the ocean. The wrought-iron fence held a plaque declaring that this was a San Francisco landmark, erected as an orphanage after the Great Earthquake.

Ruth and Art were ushered into an oak-paneled office and told that the director of care services would be with them soon. They sat stiffly on a leather sofa, facing a massive desk. Framed diplomas and health certifications hung on the wall, as well as old photographs of the building in its original incarnation, with beaming girls posed in white frocks.

"Sorry to keep you waiting," she heard someone say in a British accent. Ruth turned and was surprised to see a polished-looking young Indian man in suit and tie. "Edward Patel," he said, smiling warmly. He shook hands and handed them each a business card. He must be in his early thirties, Ruth thought. He looked like a stockbroker, not someone who concerned himself with laxatives and arthritis medication.

"I'd like to start here," Patel said, taking them back to the foyer, "because this is what our seniors first see when they arrive." He began what sounded like an oft recited spiel: "Here at Mira Mar Manor, we believe home is more than a bed. It's a whole concept."

Concept? Ruth looked at Art. This would never work.

"What does the 'P and F' in P and F HealthCare stand for?" Art asked, looking at the business card.

"Patel and Finkelstein. One of my uncles was a founding partner. He's been in the hospitality business a long time, hotels. Morris Finkelstein is a doctor. His own mother is a resident here."

Ruth marveled that a Jewish mother would allow her son to put her in a place like this. Now *that* was an endorsement.

They stepped through French doors into a garden surrounded by hedges. On each side was a shady arbor with a latticed covering of jasmine. Underneath were cushioned chairs and opaque glass-topped tables. Several women glanced up from their conversations.

"Hello, Edward!" three of them sang out in turn.

"Morning, Betty, Dorothy, Rose. Wow, Betty, that's a spectacular color on you!"

"You watch it, young lady," the old woman said sternly to Ruth. "He'll sell the pants off you, if he can." Patel laughed easily, and Ruth wondered whether the woman was only joking. Well, at least he knew their names.

Down the middle of the garden was a reddish pathway lined with benches, some shaded by awnings. Patel pointed out amenities that might have gone unnoticed to an untrained eye. His voice was resonant, familiar, and knowledgeable, like that of an English teacher Ruth had once had. The strolling path, he explained, had the same covering used for indoor running tracks, no loose bricks or stones to catch a feeble walker off guard, no hard concrete. Of course, if a senior fell, she could still break a hip, he said, but it was less likely to shatter into a million pieces. "And studies show that's what is so deadly to this population. One fall, boom!" Patel snapped his fingers. "Happens a lot when the elderly live alone and in the old family home that hasn't been adapted to their needs. No rampways, no handrails."

Patel gestured to the flowers in the garden. "All thorn-free and non-toxic, no deadly oleander or foxglove that a confused person might nibble on." Each plant was identified by staked marker at eye level—no bending down necessary. "Our seniors really love naming the herbs. On Mondays, the afternoon activity is herb collecting. There's rosemary, parsley, oregano, lemon thyme, basil, sage. The word 'echinacea' gives them a hard time, though. One lady calls it 'the China Sea.' Now we all call it that."

The herbs from the garden, Patel added, were used in the meals. "The ladies still pride themselves on their cooking abilities. They love to remind us to add only a pinch of oregano, or to rub the sage on the inside not the outside of the chicken, that sort of thing." Ruth could picture dozens of old ladies complaining about the food, and her mother yelling above the rest that everything was too salty.

They continued walking along the path toward a greenhouse at the back of the garden. "We call this the Love Nursery," Patel said, as they stepped into a blast of color—shocking pink and monk-robe saffron. The air was moist and cool.

"Each resident has an orchid plant. The flower pots are painted with the names they've given their orchids. As you may have already noticed, about ninety percent of our residents are women. And no matter how old they are, many still have a strong maternal instinct. They adore watering their orchids every day. We use a dendrobium orchid known as *cuthbertsonii*. Blooms nearly year-round, nonstop, and unlike most orchids, it can take daily watering. Many of our residents have named their orchids after their husbands or children or other family members who've already passed. They often talk to their plants, touch and kiss the petals, fuss and worry over them. We give them tiny eyedroppers and a bucket of water we call 'Love Potion.' 'Mother's coming, Mother's coming,' you'll hear them say. It's quite touching to watch them feeding their orchids."

Ruth's eyes welled up. Why was she crying? Stop this, she told herself, you're being stupid and maudlin. He's talking about a business plan, for God's sake, concept-sanctioned forms of happiness. She turned away as if to inspect a row of orchids. When she had collected herself, she said, "They must love it here."

"They do. We've tried to think of everything that a family would think about."

"Or wouldn't," Art said.

"There's a lot to think about," Patel said with a modest smile.

"Do you ever find any of them reluctant to be here, especially in the beginning?"

"Oh, yes indeed. That's expected. They don't want to move out of their old homes, because that's where all the memories are. And they don't want to spend down their kids' inheritance. Nor do they think they're old—certainly not *that* old, they'll say. I'm sure we'll be saying the same thing when we're their age."

Ruth laughed to be polite. "We may have to trick my mother into coming here."

"Well, you won't be the first family members to do so," Patel said. "The subterfuges people have used to get their parents here—wow, pretty ingenious. It could fill a book."

"Like what?" Ruth asked.

"We have quite a few folks here who don't know it costs anything to live here."

"Really!" Art exclaimed, and gave Ruth a wink.

"Oh, yes. Their sense of economy is strictly Depression-era. Paying rent is money down the drain. They're used to owning a house, paid free and clear."

Ruth nodded. Her mother's building had been paid up last year. They continued along the walkway and went inside and down a hall toward the dining room.

"One of our residents," Patel added, "is a ninety-year-old former sociology professor, still fairly sharp. But he thinks he's here on a fellowship from his alma mater to study the effects of aging. And another woman, a former piano teacher, thinks she's been hired to play music every night after dinner. She's not too bad, actually. We direct-bill most families, so their parents don't even know what the fees are."

"Is that legal?" Ruth asked.

"Perfectly, as long as the families have conservatorship or power of attorney over the finances. Some of them take out loans against the principal on the house, or they've sold their parents' homes and use the money in trust to make the payments. Anyway, I know all about the problems of getting seniors to accept the idea of even considering living in a place like this. But I guarantee you, once your mother has lived here for a month, she'll never want to leave."

"What do you do," Ruth joked, "spike the food?"

Patel misunderstood. "Actually, because of all the dietary needs of our population, we can't prepare anything too spicy. We do have a nutritionist who makes up the monthly menu. Many of the choices are low-fat, low-cholesterol. We also offer vegan. The residents receive printed-out menus every day." He picked one off a nearby table.

Ruth scanned it. The choice today was turkey meatloaf, tuna casserole, or tofu fajitas, accompanied by salad, rolls, fresh fruit, mango sorbet, and macaroons. Suddenly another problem loomed: No Chinese food.

But when she brought it up, Patel was ready with an answer: "We've encountered that issue in the past. Chinese, Japanese, kosher food, you name it. We have a delivery service from approved restaurants. And since we have two other Chinese residents who get takeout twice a week, your mother can share the selections we get for them. Also, one of our cooks is Chinese. She makes rice porridge on the weekends for breakfast. Several of our non-Chinese residents go for that as well." Patel returned smoothly to his rehearsed patter: "Regardless of special diets, they all love the waiter service, table-cloths at the meals, just like a fine restaurant. And no tipping is necessary or allowed." Ruth nodded. LuLing's idea of a big tip was a dollar.

"It's really a carefree life, which is how it should be when you're this age, don't you agree?" Patel looked at Ruth. He must have picked her as the stumbling block. How could he tell? Did she have a crease in the middle of her brow? It was obvious that Art thought the place was great.

Ruth decided she should get hard-nosed. "Are any of the people here, you know, like my mother? Do any of them have, well, memory problems of some sort?"

"It's safe to assume that half the general population over age eighty-five likely has some memory problems starting to show. And after all, our average age here is eighty-seven."

"I don't mean just memory problems. What if it's something more . . ."

"You mean like Alzheimer's? Dementia?" Patel motioned them into another large room. "I'll get back to your question in just a minute. This is the main activity hall."

Several people looked up from a bingo game being conducted by a young man. Ruth noticed that most were nicely dressed. One was wearing a powder-blue pantsuit, a pearl necklace and earrings, as if she were going to Easter services. A beak-nosed man in a jaunty beret winked at her. She imagined him at thirty, a brash businessman, confident of his position in the world and with the ladies.

"Bingo!" a woman with almost no chin shouted.

"I haven't called enough numbers yet, Anna," the young man said patiently. "You need at least five to win. We've only done three so far."

"Well, I don't know. Just call me stupid, then."

"No! No! No!" a woman in a shawl yelled. "Don't you dare use that word in here."

"That's right, Loretta," the young man added. "No one here is stupid. Sometimes we get a little confused, that's all."

"Stupid, stupid, stupid," Anna muttered under her breath, as if she was cursing. She gave Loretta the evil eye. "Stupid!"

Patel did not seem perturbed. He quietly led Ruth and Art out of the room and to an elevator. As they ascended, he spoke. "To answer your question, most of the residents are what we call 'frail elderly.' They may have problems seeing or hearing or getting around without a cane or a walker. Some are sharper than you or I, others are easily confused and have signs of dementia due to Alzheimer's or what have you. They tend to be a little forgetful about taking their pills, which is why *we* dispense all medications. But they always know what day it is, whether it's movie Sunday or herb-picking Monday. And if they don't remember the year, why should they? Some notions of time are irrelevant."

"We might as well tell you now," Art said. "Mrs. Young thinks she's coming here because of a radon leak in her home." He presented a copy of the letter he had created.

"That's a new one," Patel conceded with an appreciative chuckle. "I'll keep that in mind for other family members whose parents need a nudge. Ah yes, free rent, courtesy of the California Department of Public Safety. Quite good to make it official, mark of authority, like a summons." He swung open a door. "This is the unit that just became available." They walked into an apartment overlooking the garden: a compact living room, bedroom, and bathroom, empty of furnishings, smelling of fresh paint and new carpets. It occurred to Ruth that what Patel meant by "just became available" was that the last resident had died. The cheeriness of the place now seemed ominous, a façade hiding a darker truth.

"This is one of the nicest units," Patel said. "There are smaller, less expensive rooms, studios, and some without an ocean or garden view. We should have one of those available, oh, in about another month."

My God! He expected someone else to die soon. And he said it so casually, so matter-of-factly! Ruth felt trapped, frantic to escape. This place was like a death sentence. Wouldn't her mother feel the same way? She'd never stay here for a month, let alone three.

"We can provide the furniture at no extra charge," Patel said. "But usually the residents like to bring their own things. Personalize it and make it their home. We encourage that. And each floor is assigned the same staff, two caretakers per floor, day and night. Everyone knows them by name. One of them even speaks Chinese."

"Cantonese or Mandarin?" Ruth asked.

"That's a good question." He pulled out a digital recorder and spoke into it: "Find out if Janie speaks Cantonese or Mandarin."

"By the way," Ruth asked, "how much are the fees?"

Patel answered without hesitation: "Thirty-two to thirty-eight hundred a month, depending on the room and level of services needed. That includes an escort to a monthly medical appointment. I can show you a detailed schedule downstairs."

Ruth couldn't keep from gasping over the cost. "Did you know that?" she asked Art. He nodded. She was both shocked at the expense and amazed that Art would be willing to pay that for three months, nearly twelve thousand dollars. She stared at him, open-mouthed.

"It's worth it," he whispered.

"That's crazy."

She repeated this later, as he drove her to her mother's.

"You can't think of it the same way you think of rent," Art replied. "It includes food, the apartment, a twenty-four-hour nurse, help with medication, laundry——"

"Right, and a very expensive orchid! I can't let you pay that, not for three months."

"It's worth it," he told her again.

Ruth exhaled heavily. "Listen, I'll pay half, and if it works out, I'll pay you back."

"We already went through this. No halves and there's nothing to pay back. I have some money saved and I want to do this. And I don't mean it as a condition for us getting back together or getting rid of your mother or any of that. It's not a condition for anything. It's not pressure for you to make a decision one way or the other. There are no expectations, no strings attached."

"Well, I appreciate the thought, but——"

"It's more than a thought. It's a gift. You have to learn to take them sometimes, Ruth. You do yourself wrong when you don't."

"What are you talking about?"

"The way you want something from people, some kind of proof of love or loyalty or belief in you. But you expect it won't come. And when it's handed to you, you don't see it. Or you resist, refuse."

"I do not——"

"You're like someone who has cataracts and wants to see, but you refuse to have an operation because you're afraid you'll go blind. You'd rather go blind slowly than take a chance. And then you can't see that the answer is right in front of you."

"That's not true," she protested. Yet she knew there was some validity to what Art was saying. It was not exactly right, but parts of it were as familiar as the tidal wave in her dreams. She turned. "Have you always thought this of me?"

"Not in so many words. I didn't really think about it until these past few months you've been gone. And then I started wondering if what you said about me was true. I realized I *am* self-centered, that I'm used to thinking about me first. But I also realized that you tend to think about you second. It's as though I had permission from you to be less responsible. I'm not saying it's your fault. But you have to learn to take back, grab it when it's offered. Don't fight it. Don't get all tense thinking it's complicated. Just take it, and if you want to be polite, say thank you."

Ruth was tumbling in her head. She was being swept and tossed, and she was scared. "Thank you," she finally said.

To Ruth's surprise, her mother seemed to have no objection to staying at Mira Mar Manor. Then again, why would she? LuLing thought it was temporary—and free. After she had toured the place, Ruth and Art took her to a nearby deli to have lunch and hear her reactions.

"So many old people have radon leak," she murmured with awe.

"Actually, not all of them are staying there because of radon leaks," Art said. Ruth wondered where this was leading to.

"Oh. Other problem their house?"

"No problem at all. They just like living there."

LuLing snorted. "Why?"

"Well, it's comfortable, convenient. They have plenty of company. In a way, it's like a cruise ship."

LuLing's face broke into a look of disgust. "Cruise ship! Gao-Ling always want me go cruise ship. You too cheap, she tell me. I not cheap! I poor, I don't have money throw in ocean. . . ."

Ruth felt Art had blown it. Cruise ship. If he had been listening to her mother's complaints these last few years, he'd have known this was precisely the wrong comparison to make.

"Who can afford cruise ship?" her mother groused.

"A lot of people find staying at the Mira Mar cheaper than living at home," Art said.

One of LuLing's eyebrows rose. "How cheap?"

"About a thousand dollars a month."

"T'ousand! Ai-ya! Too much!"

"But that includes housing, food, movies, dancing, utilities, *and* cable TV. That's thrown in for free."

LuLing did not have cable TV. She often talked about getting it, but changed her mind when she found out how much it cost.

"Chinese channel too?"

"Yep. Several of them. And there are no property taxes."

This also captured LuLing's interest. Her property taxes were in fact low, stabilized by a state law that protected the holdings of the elderly. Nonetheless, each year when LuLing received her tax bill, the sum seemed agonizingly huge to her.

Art went on: "Not all of the units are a thousand a month. Yours is more expensive because it's the number-one unit, the best view, top floor. We're lucky that we got it for free."

"Ah, best unit."

"Number one," Art emphasized. "The smaller units are cheaper. . . . Honey, what did Mr. Patel say they were?"

Ruth was taken by surprise. She pretended to recollect. "I think he said seven hundred fifty."

"That how much I get Social Security!" LuLing said smugly.

And Art added: "Mr. Patel also said people who eat less can get a discount."

"I eat less. Not like American people, always take big helping."

"You'd probably qualify, then. I think you're supposed to weigh less than a hundred and twenty pounds—"

"No, Art," Ruth interrupted. "He said the cutoff was a hundred."

"I only eighty-five."

"Anyway," Art said offhandedly, "someone like you could live in the number-one unit for the same as what you get each month for Social Security. It's like living there for free."

As they continued with lunch, Ruth could see her mother's mind adding up the *free* cable TV, the *big discounts*, the *best* unit—all irresistible concepts.

When LuLing next spoke, she gloated: "Probably GaoLing think I got lots money live this place. Just like cruise ship."

TWO

They were celebrating Auntie Gal's seventy-seventh birthday—her eighty-second if the truth be known, but only she, LuLing, and Ruth knew that.

The Young clan was gathered at GaoLing and Edmund's ranch-style house in Saratoga. Auntie Gal was wearing a silk-flower lei and a hibiscus-patterned muumuu, in keeping with the luau theme of the party. Uncle Edmund had on an aloha shirt printed with ukuleles. They had just returned from their twelfth cruise to the Hawaiian Islands. LuLing, Art, Ruth, and various cousins were sitting poolside in the backyard—or lanai, as Auntie Gal referred to it—where Uncle Edmund had fired up a grill to barbecue enough slabs of spare ribs to give everyone indigestion. The outdoor gas-fueled tiki torches were wafting warmth, making the outdoors seem balmy. The kids weren't fooled. They decided the pool was too cold and improvised a game of soccer on the lawn. Every few minutes they had to use the long-handled net to fish the ball out of the water. "Too much splash," LuLing complained.

When GaoLing went to the kitchen to prepare the last side dishes, Ruth followed. She had been waiting for an opportunity to talk to her aunt privately. "Here's how you make tea eggs," Auntie Gal said, as Ruth shelled the hard-boiled eggs. "Use two big pinches black tea leaves. It must be black, not Japanese green, and not the herbal kind all you kids like to drink for health purposes. Put the leaves in the cheesecloth, tie it tight.

"Now put these cooked eggs in the pot with the tea leaves, a half-cup soy sauce for twenty eggs, and six star anise," GaoLing continued. She sprinkled the mixture with liberal amounts of salt. Her longevity was obviously a tribute to her genetics and not her diet. "Cook for one hour," she said, and set the pot on the stove to simmer. "When you were a little girl, you loved to eat these. Lucky eggs, we called them. That's why your mommy and I made them. All the kids liked them better than anything else. One time, though, you ate five and got very sick. Big mess all over my sofa. After that, you said no eggs, no more eggs. You wouldn't eat them the next year either, not you. But the year after that, eggs were okay again, yum-yum."

Ruth didn't remember any of this, and wondered whether Gao-Ling was confusing her with her daughter. Was her aunt also showing signs of dementia?

She went to the refrigerator and took out a bowl of scalded celery, cut into strips. Without measuring, she doused the celery with sesame oil and soy sauce, chatting as if she were on a talk show for cooks.

"I've been thinking one day I might write a book. The title is this, *Culinary Road to China*—what do you think, good? Easy recipes. Maybe if you're not too busy, you can help me write it. I don't mean for free, though. Course, most of the words are already in my head, right here. I just need someone to write them down. Still, I'd pay you, doesn't matter that I'm your auntie."

Ruth did not want to encourage this line of thinking. "Did you make those same eggs when you lived in the orphanage with Mom?"

GaoLing stopped stirring. She looked up. "Ah, your mother told you about that place." She tasted a piece of celery and added more soy sauce. "Before, she never wanted to tell anyone why she went to the orphan school." GaoLing paused and pursed her lips, as if she had already divulged too much.

"You mean that Precious Auntie was her mother."

GaoLing clucked her tongue. "Ah, so she told you. Good, I'm glad. Better to tell the truth."

"I also know both you and Mom are five years older than what we always thought. And that your real birthday is what, four months earlier?"

GaoLing tried to laugh, but she also looked evasive. "I always wanted to be honest. But your mommy was afraid of so many things—oh, she said the authorities would send her back to China if they knew she wasn't my real sister. And maybe Edwin wouldn't marry her, because she was too old. Then later you might be ashamed if you knew who your real grandmother was, unmarried, her face ruined, treated like a servant. Me? Over the years, I've become more modern-thinking. Old secrets? Here nobody cares! Mother not married? Oh, just like Madonna. But still your mommy said, No, don't tell, promise."

"Does anyone else know? Uncle Edmund, Sally, Billy?"

"No, no, no one at all. I promised your mother. . . . Of course Uncle Edmund knows. We don't keep secrets. I tell him everything. . . . Well, the age part, he doesn't know. But I wasn't lying. I forgot. It's true! I don't even feel like I'm seventy-seven. In my mind, the most is sixty. But now you remind me, I'm even older—how old?"

"Eighty-two."

"Wah." Her shoulders slumped as she pondered this fact. "Eighty-two. It's like less money in the bank than I thought."

"You still look twenty years younger. Mom does too. And don't worry, I won't tell anyone, not even Uncle Edmund. Funny thing is, last year when she told the doctor she was eighty-two, I thought that was a sure sign something was wrong with her mind. And then it turned out she did have Alzheimer's, but she was right all along about her age. She just forgot to lie—"

"Not lying," GaoLing corrected. "It was a secret."

"That's what I meant. And I wouldn't have known her age until I read what she wrote."

"She wrote this down—about her age?"

"About a lot of things, a stack of pages this thick. It's like her life story, all the things she didn't want to forget. The things she couldn't talk about. Her mother, the orphanage, her first husband, yours."

Auntie Gal looked increasingly uncomfortable. "When did she write this?"

"Oh, it must have been seven, eight years ago, probably when she first started worrying that something was wrong with her memory. She gave me some of the pages a while back. But it was all in Chinese, so I never got around to reading them. A few months ago, I found someone to translate."

"Why didn't you ask me?" GaoLing pretended to be insulted. "I'm your auntie, she's my sister. We are still blood-related, even though we don't have the same mother."

The truth was, Ruth had feared her mother might have written unflattering remarks about GaoLing. And it occurred to her now that GaoLing might have also censored the parts that dealt with her own secrets, her marriage to the opium addict, for instance. "I didn't want to bother you," Ruth said.

Her aunt sniffed. "What are relatives for if you can't bother them?"

"That's true."

"You call me anytime, you know this. You want Chinese food, I cook for you. Translate Chinese writing, I can do this too. You need me to watch your mommy, no need to ask, just drop her off."

"Actually, remember how we talked about Mom's future needs? Well, Art and I looked at a place, Mira Mar Manor, it's assisted living, really nice. They have staff twenty-four hours a day, activities, a nurse who helps with medication—"

GaoLing frowned. "How can you put your mommy in a nursing home? No, this is not right." She clamped her mouth shut and shook her head.

"It's not what you think—"

"Don't do this! If you can't take care of your mommy, let her come live here with me."

Ruth knew that GaoLing was barely able to handle LuLing for a couple of days at a time. "Nearly gave me a heart attack," was how she had described LuLing's last visit. Still, Ruth was ashamed that her aunt saw her as neglectful, uncaring. All the doubts she had about the Mira Mar bobbed to the surface, and she felt unsteady about her intentions. Was this really the best solution for her mother's safety and health? Or was she abandoning her mother for convenience' sake? She wondered whether she was simply going along with Art's rationale, as she had with so many aspects of their relationship. It seemed she was always living her life through others, for others.

"I just don't know what else to do," Ruth said, her voice full of the despair she had kept pent up. "This disease, it's awful, it's progressing more quickly than I thought. She can't be left alone. She wanders away. And she doesn't know if she's eaten ten minutes ago or ten hours ago. She won't bathe by herself. She's afraid of the faucets—"

"I know, I know. Very hard, very sad. That's why I'm saying, you can't take it anymore, you just bring her here. Part-time my place, part-time your place. Easier that way."

Ruth ducked her head. "Mom already went for a tour of the Mira Mar. She thought it was nice, like a cruise ship."

GaoLing gave a doubting sniff.

Ruth wanted her aunt's approval. She also sensed that GaoLing wanted her to ask for it. She and her mother had taken turns protecting each other. Ruth met GaoLing's eyes. "I won't make any decision until you think it's the right thing. But I would like you to look at the place. And when you do, I can give you a copy of what Mom wrote."

That got GaoLing's interest.

"Speaking of which," Ruth went on, "I was wondering whatever happened to those people you and Mom knew in China. Mom didn't say anything about her life after she left Hong Kong. What happened to that guy you were married to, Fu Nan, and his father? Did they keep the ink shop?"

GaoLing looked to the side to make sure no one was close enough to hear. "Those people were *awful.*" She made a face. "So bad you can't even imagine how bad. The son had many problems. Did your mother write about this?"

Ruth nodded. "He was hooked on opium."

GaoLing looked momentarily taken aback, realizing that LuLing had been thorough in her account. "This is true," she conceded. "Later he died, maybe in 1960, though no one is sure-for-sure. But that was when he stopped writing and calling different people, threatening this and that to get them to send money."

"Uncle Edmund knows about him?"

GaoLing huffed. "How could I tell him that I was still married? Your uncle would then question if we are really married, if I am a bigamist, if our children are—well, like your mother. Later, I forgot to tell him, and when I heard my first husband was probably dead, it was too late to go back and explain what should be forgotten anyway. You understand."

"Like your age."

"Exactly. As for the Chang father, well, in 1950, the Communists cracked down on all the landlords. They put the Chang father in jail and beat a confession from him for owning many businesses, cheating people, and trading in opium. Guilty, they said, and shot him, public execution."

Ruth pictured this. She was against the death penalty in principle, but felt a secret satisfaction that the man who had caused her grandmother and mother so much misery had met a fitting end.

"The people also confiscated his house, made his wife sweep the streets, and all his sons were sent to work outdoors in Wuhan, where it's so hot most people would rather bathe in a vat of boiling oil than go there. My father and mother were glad they were already poor and didn't have to suffer that kind of punishment."

"And Sister Yu, Teacher Pan. Did you hear from them?"

"My brother did—you know, Jiu Jiu in Beijing. He said Sister Yu was promoted many times, until she was a high-position Communist Party leader. I don't know her title, something to do with good attitude and reforms. But during the Cultural Revolution, everything got turned around, and she became an example of bad attitude because of her background with the missionaries. The revolutionaries put her in jail for a long time and treated her pretty hard. But when she came out, she was still happy to be a Communist. Later, I think she died of old age."

"And Teacher Pan?"

"Jiu Jiu said the country one year held a big ceremony for the Chinese workers who helped discover Peking Man. The newspaper article he sent me said Pan Kai Jing—the one your mother married—died as a martyr protecting the whereabouts of the Communist Party, and his father, Teacher Pan, was present to receive his honorable-mention award. After that, I don't know what happened to Teacher Pan. By now, he must be dead. So sad. We once were like family. We sacrificed for each other. Sister Yu could have come to America, but she let your mommy and me have this chance. That's why your mommy named you after Sister Yu."

"I thought I was named after Ruth Grutoff."

"Her too. But your Chinese name comes from Sister Yu. Yu Luyi. Luyi, it means 'all that you wish.' "

Ruth was amazed and gratified that her mother had put so much heart into naming her. For most of her childhood, she had hated both her American and her Chinese names, the old-fashioned sound of "Ruth," which her mother could not even pronounce, and the way "Luyi" sounded like the name of a boy, a boxer, or a bully.

"Did you know your mommy also gave up her chance to come to America so I could come first?"

"Sort of." She dreaded the day GaoLing would read the pages describing how she had wangled her way to the States.

"Many times I've thanked her, and always she said, 'No, don't talk about this or I'll be mad at you.' I've tried to repay her many times, but she always refused. Each year we invite her to go to Hawaii. Each year she tells me she doesn't have the money."

Ruth nodded. How many times she had had to suffer listening to her mother complain about that.

"Each time I tell her, I'm inviting you, what money do you need? Then she says she can't let me pay. Forget it! So I tell her, 'Use the money in the Charles Schwab account.' No, she doesn't want that money. She *still* won't use it."

"What Charles Schwab account?"

"*This* she didn't tell you? Her half of the money from your grandparents when they died."

"I thought they just left her a little bit."

"Yes, that was wrong of them to do. Very old-fashioned. Made your mommy so angry. That's why she wouldn't take the money, even after your Uncle Edmund and I said we could divide it in half anyway. Long time ago, we put her half in T-bills. Your mommy always pretended she didn't know about it. But then she'd say something like, 'I hear you can make more money investing in the stock market.' So we opened a stock market account. Then she said, 'I hear this stock is good, this one is bad.' So we knew to tell the stockbroker what to buy and sell. Then she said, 'I hear it's better to invest yourself, low fees.' So we opened a Charles Schwab account."

A chill ran down Ruth's arms. "Did some of those stocks she mentioned include IBM, U.S. Steel, AT&T, Intel?"

GaoLing nodded. "Too bad Uncle Edmund didn't listen to her advice. He was always running after this IPO, that IPO."

Ruth now recalled the many times her mother had asked Precious Auntie for stock tips via the sand tray. It never occurred to her that the answers mattered that much, since her mother didn't have any real money to gamble with. She thought LuLing followed the stock market the way some people followed soap operas. And so when her mother presented her with a choice of stocks, Ruth chose whichever was the shortest to spell out. That was how she decided. Or had she? Had she also received nudges and notions from someone else?

"So the stocks did well?" Ruth asked with a pounding heart.

"Better than S and P, better than Uncle Edmund—she's like a Wall Street genius! Every year it's grown and grown. She hasn't touched one penny. She could have gone on lots of cruises, bought a fancy house, nice furniture, big car. But no. I think she has been saving it all for you. . . . Don't you want to know how much?"

Ruth shook her head. This was already too much. "Tell me later." Instead of feeling excited about the money, Ruth was hurt to know that her mother had denied herself pleasure and happiness. Out of love, she had stayed behind in Hong Kong, so GaoLing could have a chance at freedom first. Yet she would not take love back from people. How did she become that way? Was it because of Precious Auntie's suicide?

"By the way," Ruth now thought to ask, "what was Precious Auntie's real name?"

"Precious Auntie?"

"Bao Bomu."

"Oh, oh, oh, *Bao Bomu*! You know, only your mother called her that. Everyone else called her Bao Mu."

"What's the difference, 'Bao Bomu' and 'Bao Mu'?"

"*Bao* can mean 'precious,' or it can mean 'protect.' Both are third tone, *baaaaooo*. And the *mu* part, that stands for 'mother,' but when it's written in *bao mu*, the *mu* has an extra piece in front, so that the meaning is more of a female servant. *Bao mu* is like saying 'baby-sitter,' 'nursemaid.' And *bomu*, that's 'auntie.' I think her mother taught her to say and write it this way. More special."

"So what was her real name? Mom can't remember, and it really bothers her."

"I don't remember either. . . . I don't know."

Ruth's heart sank. Now she would never know. No one would ever know the name of her grandmother. She had existed, and yet without a name, a large part of her existence was missing, could not be attached to a face, anchored to a family.

"We all called her Bao Mu," GaoLing went on, "also lots of bad nicknames because of her face. Burnt Wood, Fried Mouth, that sort of thing. People weren't being mean, the nicknames were a joke. . . . Well, now that I think of this, they were mean, very mean. That was wrong."

It pained Ruth to hear this. She felt a lump growing in her throat. She wished she could tell this woman from the past, her grandmother, that her granddaughter cared, that she, like her mother, wanted to know where her bones were. "The house in Immortal Heart," Ruth asked, "is it still there?"

"Immortal Heart? . . . Oh, you mean our village—I only know the Chinese name." She sounded out the syllables. "*Xian Xin*. Yes, I guess that's how it might translate. The immortal's heart, something like that. Anyway, the house is gone. My brother told me. After a few drought years, a big rainstorm came. Dirt washed down the mountain, flooded the ravine, and crumbled the sides. The earth holding up our house broke apart and fell, bit by bit. It took with it the back rooms, then the well, until only half the house was left. It stood like that for several more years, then in 1972, all at once, it sank and the earth folded on top of it. My brother said that's what killed our mother, even though she had not lived in that house for many years."

"So the house is now lying in the End of the World?"

"What's that—end of what?"

"The ravine."

She sounded out more Chinese syllables to herself, and laughed. "That's right, we called it that when we were kids. End of the World. That's because we heard our parents saying that the closer the edge came to our house, the faster we'd reach the end of this world. Meaning, our luck would be gone, that was it. And they were right! Anyway, we had many nicknames for that place. Some people called it 'End of the Land,' just like where your mommy lives in San Francisco, Land's End. And sometimes my uncles joked and called that cliff edge *momo meiyou*, meaning 'rub sink gone.' But most people in the village just called it the garbage dump. In those days, no one came by once a week to take away your garbage, your recycling, no such thing. Course, people then didn't throw away too much. Bones and rotten food, the pigs and dogs ate that. Old clothes we mended and gave to younger children. Even when the clothes were so bad they couldn't be repaired, we tore them into strips and weaved them into liners for winter jackets. Shoes, the same thing. You fixed the holes, patched up the bottoms. So you see, only the worst things were thrown away, the most useless. And when we were little and bad, our parents made us behave by threatening to throw us in the ravine—as if we too were the most useless things! When we were older and wanted to play down there, then it was a different story. Down there, they said, was everything we were afraid of—"

"Bodies?"

"Bodies, ghosts, demons, animal spirits, Japanese soldiers, whatever scared us."

"Were bodies really thrown in there?"

GaoLing paused before she answered. Ruth was sure she was editing a bad memory. "Things were different then. . . . You see, not everyone could afford a cemetery or funeral. Funerals, those cost ten times more than weddings. But it wasn't just cost. Sometimes you couldn't bury someone for other reasons. So to put a body down there, well, this was bad, but not the same way you think, not as though we didn't care about who died."

"What about Precious Auntie's body?"

"Ai-ya. Your mommy wrote everything! Yes, that was very bad what my mother did. She was crazy when she did that, afraid that Bao Mu put a curse on our whole family. After she threw the body in there, a cloud of black birds came. Their wings were big, like umbrellas. They nearly blocked out the sun, there were so many. They flapped above, waiting for the wild dogs to finish with the body. And one of our servants—"

"Old Cook."

"Yes, Old Cook, he was the one who put the body there. He thought that the birds were Bao Mu's spirit and her army of ghosts and that she was going to pick him up with her claws and snatch him up if he did not bury her properly. So he took a large stick and chased the wild dogs away, and the birds stayed there above him, watching as he piled rocks on top of her body. But even after he did all that, our household was still cursed."

"You believed that?"

GaoLing stopped to think. "I must have. Back then I believed whatever my family believed. I didn't question it. Also, Old Cook died only two years later."

"And now?"

GaoLing was quiet for a long time. "Now I think Bao Mu left a lot of sadness behind. Her death was like that ravine. Whatever we didn't want, whatever scared us, that's where we put the blame."

Dory flew into the kitchen. "Ruth! Ruth! Come quick! Waipo fell in the pool. She almost drowned."

By the time Ruth reached the backyard, Art was carrying her mother up the steps of the shallow end. LuLing was coughing and shivering. Sally ran from the house with a pile of towels. "Wasn't anyone watching her?" Ruth cried, too upset to be more tactful.

LuLing looked at Ruth as though she were the one being chastised. "Ai-ya, so stupid."

"We're okay," Art told LuLing in a calming voice. "Just a little whoopsie-daisy. No harm done."

"She was only ten feet away from us," Billy said. "Just walked in and sank before we knew it. Art dove in, beer and all, as soon as it happened."

Ruth swaddled her mother in towels, rubbing her to stimulate her circulation.

"I saw her down there," LuLing moaned in Chinese between more coughs. "She asked me to help her get out from under the rocks. Then the ground became sky and I fell through a rain cloud, down, down, down." She turned to point to where she saw the phantom.

As Ruth glanced where her mother gestured, she saw Auntie Gal, her face stricken with new understanding.

Ruth left her mother at Auntie Gal's and spent the next day at her house sorting out what should be moved to Mira Mar Manor. On the take list she included most of her mother's bedroom furniture, and the linens and towels LuLing had never used. But what about her scroll paintings, the ink and brushes? Her mother might feel frustrated looking at these emblems of her more agile self. One thing was for certain: Ruth was not moving the vinyl La-Z-Boy. That was destined for the dump. She would buy her mother a new recliner, a much nicer one, with supple burgundy leather. Just thinking about this gave Ruth pleasure. She could already envision her mother's eyes aglow with wonder and gratitude, testing the squishiness of the cushion, murmuring, "Oh, so soft, so good."

In the evening, she drove to Bruno's supper club to meet Art. Years before, they often went there as prelude to a romantic night. The restaurant had booths that allowed them to sit close and fondle each other.

She parked around the corner a block away, and when she looked at her watch, she saw she was fifteen minutes early. She did not want to appear too eager. In front of her was the Modern Times bookstore. She went in. As she often did in bookstores, she headed to the remainder table, the bargains marked down to three ninety-eight with the lime-green stickers that were the literary equivalent of toe tags on corpses. There were the usual art books, biographies, and tell-alls of the Famous for Fifteen Minutes. And then her eyes fell on *The Nirvana Wide Web: Connections to a Higher Consciousness.* Ted, the *Internet Spirituality* author, had been right. His was a time-sensitive topic. It was already over. She felt the thrill of guilty glee. On the fiction table were an assortment of novels, most of them contemporary literary fiction by authors not well known by the masses. She picked up a slim book that lay obligingly in her hands, inviting her to cradle it in bed under a soft light. She picked up another, held it, skimmed its pages, her eye and imagination plucking a line here and there. She was drawn to them all, these prisms of other lives and times. And she felt sympathetic, as if they were dogs at the animal shelter, abandoned without reason, hopeful that they would be loved still. She left the store carrying a bag with five books.

Art was sitting in the bar at Bruno's, a retro expanse of fifties glamour. "You're looking happy," he said.

"Am I?" She was instantly embarrassed. Lately, Wendy, Gideon, and others had been telling her what she appeared to be feeling, that she seemed bothered or upset, puzzled or surprised. And each time, Ruth had been unaware of any feelings in particular. Obviously she was showing something on her face. Yet how could she not know what she was feeling?

The maître d' seated them in a booth that had recently been re-done in clubby leather. Everything in the restaurant had managed to stay as though nothing had changed for fifty years, except the prices and the inclusion of *uni* and octopus appetizers. As they looked over the menu, the waiter came with a bottle of champagne.

"I ordered it," Art whispered, "for our anniversary. . . . Don't you remember? Nude yoga? Your gay buddy? We met ten years ago."

Ruth laughed. She had not remembered. As the waiter poured, she whispered back, "I thought you had nice feet for a pervert."

When they were alone, Art lifted his flute. "Here's to ten years, most of it amazing, with a few questionable parts, and the hope that we'll get back to where we should be." He pressed his hand on her thigh and said, "We should try it some time."

"What?"

"Nude yoga."

A rush of warmth flooded her. The months of living with her mother had left her feeling like a virgin.

"Hey, baby, want to come back to my place afterward?"

She was thrilled at the prospect.

The waiter stood before them again, ready to take orders. "The lady and I would like to begin with oysters," Art said. "This is our first date, so we'll need the ones that have the best aphrodisiac effects. Which do you recommend?"

"That would be the Kumamotos," the waiter said without a change of expression.

That night, they did not make love right away. They lay in bed, Art cuddling her, the bedroom window open so they could listen to the foghorns. "In all these years we've been together," he said, "I don't think I know an important part of you. You keep secrets inside you. You hide. It's as though I've never seen you naked, and I've had to imagine what you look like behind the drapes."

"I'm not consciously hiding anything." After Ruth said that, she wondered whether it was true. Then again, who revealed everything—the irritations, the fears? How tiresome that would be. What did he mean by secrets?

"I want us to be more intimate. I want to know what you want. Not just with us, but from life. What makes you happiest? Are you doing what you want to do?"

She laughed nervously. "That's what I edit for others, that intimate-soul stuff. I can describe how to find happiness in ten chapters, but I still don't know what it is."

"Why do you keep pushing me away?"

Ruth bristled. She didn't like it when Art acted as if he knew her better than she knew herself. She felt him shaking her arm.

"I'm sorry. I shouldn't have said that. I don't want to make you tense. I'm just trying to get to know you. When I told the waiter this was our first date, I meant it, in a way. I want to pretend I've just met you, love at first sight, and I want to know who you are. I love you, Ruth, but I don't know you. And I want to know who this person is, this woman I love. That's all."

Ruth sank against his chest. "I don't know, I don't know," she said softly. "Sometimes I feel like I'm a pair of eyes and ears, and I'm just trying to stay safe and make sense of what's happening. I know what to avoid, what to worry about. I'm like those kids who live with gunfire going off around them. I don't want pain. I don't want to die. I don't want to see other people around me die. But I don't have anything left inside me to figure out where I fit in or what I want. If I want anything, it's to *know* what's possible to want."

THREE

In the first gallery of the Asian Art Museum, Ruth saw Mr. Tang kiss her mother's cheek. LuLing laughed like a shy schoolgirl, and then, hand in hand, they strolled into the next gallery.

Art nudged Ruth and crooked his arm. "Come on, I'm not about to be outdone by those guys." They caught up with LuLing and her companion, who were seated on a bench in front of a display of bronze bells hung in two rows on a gargantuan frame, about twelve feet high and twenty-five feet long.

"It's like a xylophone for the gods," Ruth whispered, taking a seat beside Mr. Tang.

"Each bell makes two distinct tones." Mr. Tang's voice was gentle yet authoritative. "The hammer hits the bell on the bottom and the right side. And when there are many musicians and the bells are struck together, the music is very complex, it creates tonal layers. I had the pleasure of hearing them played recently by Chinese musicians at a special event." He smiled in recalling this. "In my mind, I was transported back three thousand years. I heard what a person of that time heard, experiencing the same awe. I could imagine this person listening, a woman, I think, a very beautiful woman." He squeezed LuLing's hand. "And I thought to myself, in another three thousand years, perhaps another woman will hear these tones and think of me as a handsome man. Though we don't know each other, we're connected by the music. Don't you agree?" He looked at LuLing.

"Buddha-ful," she answered.

"Your mother and I think alike," he said to Ruth. She grinned back. She realized that Mr. Tang translated for LuLing, as she once had. But he knew not to be concerned with words and their precise meanings. He simply translated what was in LuLing's heart: her better intentions, her hopes.

For the past month, LuLing had been living at Mira Mar Manor, and Mr. Tang went several times a week to visit. On Saturday afternoons, he took her on outings—to matinees, to free public rehearsals of the symphony, for strolls through the arboretum. Today it was an exhibit on Chinese archaeology, and he had invited Ruth and Art to join them. "I have something interesting to show you," he had said mysteriously over the phone, "very much worth your while."

It was already worth Ruth's while to see her mother so happy. *Happy.* Ruth pondered the word. Until recently, she had not known what that might encompass in LuLing's case. True, her mother was still full of complaints. The food at the Mira Mar was, as predicted, "too salty," the restaurant-style service was "so slow, food already cold when come." And she hated the leather recliner Ruth had bought her. Ruth had to replace it with the old vinyl La-Z-Boy. But LuLing had let go of most worries and irritations: the tenant downstairs, the fears that someone was stealing her money, the sense that a curse loomed over her life and disaster awaited her if she was not constantly on guard. Or had she simply forgotten? Perhaps her being in love was the tonic. Or the change of scenery had removed reminders of a more sorrowful past. And yet she still recounted the past, if anything more often, only now it was constantly being revised for the better. For one, it included Mr. Tang. LuLing acted as if they had known each other many lifetimes and not just a month or so. "This same thing, he and I see long time 'go," LuLing said aloud as they all admired the bells, "only now we older."

Mr. Tang helped LuLing stand up, and they moved with Ruth and Art to another display in the middle of the room. "This next one is a cherished object of China scholars," he said. "Most visitors want to see the ritual wine vessels, the jade burial suits. But to a true scholar, this is the prize." Ruth peered into the display case. To her, the prize resembled a large wok with writing on it.

"It's a masterly work of bronze," Mr. Tang continued, "but there's also the inscription itself. It's an epic poem written by the great scholars about the great rulers who were their contemporaries. One of the emperors they praised was Zhou, yes, the same Zhou of Zhoukoudian—where your mother once lived and Peking Man was found."

"The Mouth of the Mountain?" Ruth said.

"The same. Though Zhou didn't live there. A lot of places carry his name, just like every town in the United States has a Washington Street. . . . Now come this way. The reason I brought you here is in the next room."

Soon they were standing in front of another display case. "Don't look at the description in English, not yet," Mr. Tang said. "What do you think this is?" Ruth saw an ivory-colored spadelike object, cracked with lines and blackened with holes. Was it a board for an ancient game of go? A cooking implement? Next to it was a smaller object, light brown and oval, with a lip around it and writing instead of holes. At once she knew, but before she could speak, her mother gave the answer in Chinese: "Oracle bone."

Ruth was amazed at what her mother could recall. She knew not to expect LuLing to remember appointments or facts about a recent event, who was where, when it happened. But her mother often surprised her with the clarity of her emotions when she spoke of her youth, elements of which matched in spirit what she had written in her memoir. To Ruth this was evidence that the pathways to her mother's past were still open, though rutted in a few spots and marked by rambling detours. At times she also blended the past with memories from other periods of her own past. But that part of her history was nonetheless a reservoir which she could draw from and share. It didn't matter that she blurred some of the finer points. The past, even revised, was meaningful.

In recent weeks, LuLing had related several times how she received the apple-green-jade ring that Ruth had retrieved from the La-Z-Boy. "We went to a dance hall, you and I," she said in Chinese. "We came down the stairs and you introduced me to Edwin. His eyes fell on mine and did not turn away for a long time. I saw you smile and then you disappeared. That was naughty of you. I knew what you were thinking! When he asked me to marry, he gave me the ring." Ruth guessed that GaoLing had been the person who did the introductions.

Ruth now heard LuLing speaking in Mandarin to Art: "My mother found one of these. It was carved with words of beauty. She gave it to me when she was sure I would not forget what was important. I never wanted to lose it." Art nodded as if he understood what she had said, and then LuLing translated into English for Mr. Tang: "I telling him, this bone my mother give me one."

"Very meaningful," he said, "especially since your mother was the daughter of a bone doctor."

"Famous," LuLing said.

Mr. Tang nodded as if he too remembered. "Everyone from the villages all around came to him. And your father went for a broken foot. His horse stepped on him. That's how he met your mother. Because of that horse."

LuLing went blank-eyed. Ruth was afraid her mother was going to cry. But instead, LuLing brightened and said, "Liu Xing. He call her that. My mother say he write love poem about this."

Art looked at Ruth, waiting for her to acknowledge whether this was true. He had read some of the translation of LuLing's memoir, but could not connect the Chinese name to its referent. "It means 'shooting star,' " Ruth whispered. "I'll explain later." To LuLing she said, "And what was your mother's family name?" Ruth knew it was a risk to bring this up, but her mother's mind had entered the territory of names. Perhaps others were there, like markers, waiting to be retrieved.

Her mother hesitated only a moment before answering: "Family name Gu." She was looking sternly at Ruth. "I tell you so many time, you don't remember? Her father Dr. Gu. She Gu doctor daughter."

Ruth wanted to shout for joy, but the next instant she realized her mother had said the Chinese word for 'bone.' Dr. Gu, Dr. Bone, bone doctor. Art's eyebrows were raised, in expectation that the long-lost family identity had been found. "I'll explain later," Ruth said again, but this time her voice was listless.

"Oh."

Mr. Tang traced characters in the air. "*Gu*, like this? Or this?"

Her mother put on a worried face. "I don't remember."

"I don't either," Mr. Tang said quickly. "Oh well, doesn't matter."

Art changed the subject. "What's the writing on the oracle bone?"

"They're the questions the emperors asked the gods," Mr. Tang replied. "What's the weather going to be like tomorrow, who's going to win the war, when should the crops be planted. Kind of like the six-o'clock news, only they wanted the report ahead of time."

"And were the answers right?"

"Who knows? They're the cracks you see next to the black spots.

The diviners of the bones used a heated nail to crack the bone. It actually made a sound—*pwak!* They interpreted the cracks as the answers from heaven. I'm sure the more successful diviners were skilled at saying what the emperors wanted to hear."

"What a great linguistic puzzle," Art said.

Ruth thought of the sand tray she and her mother used over the years. She too had tried to guess what might put her mother at ease, the words that would placate but not be readily detected as fraudulent. At times she had made up the answers to suit herself. But on other occasions, she really had tried to write what her mother needed to hear. Words of comfort, saying that her husband missed her, that Precious Auntie was not angry.

"Speaking of puzzle," Ruth said, "the other day you mentioned that no one ever found the bones of Peking Man."

LuLing perked up. "Not just man, woman too."

"You're right, Mom—Peking Woman. I wonder what happened to her? Were the bones crushed on the train tracks on the way to Tianjin? Or did they sink with the boat?"

"If the bones are still around," Mr. Tang replied, "no one's saying. Oh, every few years you read a story in the paper. Someone dies, the wife of an American soldier, a former Japanese officer, an archaeologist in Taiwan or Hong Kong. And as the story goes, bones were found in a wooden trunk, just like the trunks used to pack the bones back in 1941. Then the rumors leak out that these are the bones of Peking Man. Arrangements are made, ransoms are paid, or what have you. But the bones turn out to be oxtails. Or they are casts of the original. Or they disappear before they can be examined. In one story, the person who had stolen the bones was taking them to an island to sell to a dealer, and the plane went down in the ocean."

Ruth thought about the curse of ghosts who were angry that their bones were separated from the rest of their mortal bodies. "What do you believe?"

"I don't know. So much of history is mystery. We don't know what is lost forever, what will surface again. All objects exist in a moment of time. And that fragment of time is preserved or lost or found in mysterious ways. Mystery is a wonderful part of life." Mr. Tang winked at LuLing.

"Wonderful," she echoed.

He looked at his watch. "How about a wonderful lunch?"

"Wonderful," they said.

As Ruth and Art lay in bed that night, she pondered aloud over Mr. Tang's romantic interest in her mother. "I can understand that he's intrigued with her since he's done this work on her memoir. But he's a man who's into culture, music, poetry. She can't keep up, and she's only going to get worse. She might not even know who he is after a while."

"He's been in love with her since she was a little girl," Art said. "She's not just a source of temporary companionship. He loves everything about her, and that includes who she was, who she is, who she will be. He knows more about her than most couples who are married." He drew Ruth closer to him. "Actually, I'm hoping we might have that. A commitment through time, past, present, future . . . marriage."

Ruth held her breath. She had pushed the idea out of her head for so long she still felt it was taboo, dangerous.

"I've tried to legally bind you in the past with ownership in the house, which you've yet to take."

That's what he had meant by a percentage interest in the house? She was baffled by the mechanisms of her own defenses.

"It's just an idea," Art said awkwardly. "No pressure. I just wanted to know what you might think."

She pressed closer and kissed his shoulder. "Wonderful," she answered.

"The name, I know your mother's family name." GaoLing was calling Ruth with exciting news.

"Oh my God, what is it?"

"First you have to know what trouble I had trying to find out. After you asked me, I wrote Jiu Jiu in Beijing. He didn't know, but wrote back that he would ask a woman married to a cousin whose family still lives in the village where your grandmother was born. It took a while to sort out, because most people who would know are dead. But finally they tracked down an old woman whose grandfather was a traveling photographer. And she still had all his old glass plates. They were in a root cellar and luckily not too many were damaged. Her grandfather kept excellent records, dates, who paid what, the names of the people he photographed. Thousands of plates and photos. Anyway, the old lady remembered her grandfather showing her the photo of a girl who was quite beautiful. She had on a pretty cap, high-neck collar."

"The photo Mom has of Precious Auntie?"

"Must be the same. The old lady said it was sad, because soon after the photo was taken, the girl was scarred for life, the father was dead, the whole family destroyed. People in the village said the girl was jinxed from the beginning—"

Ruth couldn't stand it any longer. "What was the name?"

"Gu."

"Gu?" Ruth felt let down. It was the same mistake. "*Gu* is the word for 'bone,' " Ruth said. "She must have thought 'bone doctor' meant 'Dr. Bone.' "

"No, no," GaoLing said. "*Gu* as in 'gorge.' It's a different *gu*. It sounds the same as the bone *gu*, but it's written a different way. The third-tone *gu* can mean many things: 'old,' 'gorge,' 'bone,' also 'thigh,'

'blind,' 'grain,' 'merchant,' lots of things. And the way 'bone' is written can also stand for 'character.' That's why we use that expression
'It's in your bones.' It means, 'That's your character.' "

Ruth had once thought that Chinese was limited in its sounds and
thus confusing. It seemed to her now that its multiple meanings made
it very rich. *The blind bone doctor from the gorge repaired the thigh of
the old grain merchant.*

"You're sure it's Gu?"

"That's what was written on the photographic plate."

"Did it include her first name?"

"Liu Xin."

"Shooting Star?"

"That's *liu xing*, sounds almost the same, *xing* is 'star,' *xin* is
'truth.' Liu Xin means Remain True. But because the words sound
similar, some people who didn't like her called her Liu Xing. The
shooting star can have a bad meaning."

"Why?"

"It's confusing why. People think the broom star is very bad
to see. That's the other kind, with the long, slow tail, the comes-
around kind."

"Comet?"

"Yes, comet. Comet means a rare calamity will happen. But some
people mix up the broom star with the shooting star, so even though
the shooting star is not bad luck, people think it is. The idea is not so
good either—burns up quick, one day here, one day gone, just like
what happened to Precious Auntie."

Her mother had written about this, Ruth recalled, a story Precious Auntie told LuLing when she was small—how she looked up
at the night sky, saw a shooting star, which then fell into her open
mouth.

Ruth began to cry. Her grandmother had a name. Gu Liu Xin.
She had existed. She still existed. Precious Auntie belonged to a

family. LuLing belonged to that same family, and Ruth belonged to them both. The family name had been there all along, like a bone stuck in the crevices of a gorge. LuLing had divined it while looking at an oracle in the museum. And the given name had flashed before her as well for the briefest of moments, a shooting star that entered the earth's atmosphere, etching itself indelibly in Ruth's mind.

EPILOGUE

It is the twelfth of August and Ruth is in the Cubbyhole, silent. Foghorns blow in the night, welcoming ships into the bay.

Ruth still has her voice. Her ability to speak is not governed by curses or shooting stars or illness. She knows that for certain now. But she does not need to talk. She can write. Before, she never had a reason to write for herself, only for others. Now she has that reason.

The picture of her grandmother is in front of her. Ruth looks at it daily. Through it, she can see from the past clear into the present. Could her grandmother ever have imagined she would have a granddaughter like her—a woman who has a husband who loves her, two girls who adore her, a house she co-owns, dear friends, a life with only the usual worries about leaks and calories?

Ruth remembers how her mother used to talk of dying, by curse or her own hand. She never stopped feeling the urge, not until she began to lose her mind, the memory web that held her woes in place. And though her mother still remembers the past, she has begun to change it. She doesn't recount the sad parts. She only recalls being loved very, very much. She remembers that to Bao Bomu she was the reason for life itself.

The other day Ruth's mother called her. She sounded like her old self, scared and fretful. "Luyi," she said, and she spoke quickly in

Chinese, "I'm worried that I did terrible things to you when you were a child, that I hurt you very much. But I can't remember what I did. . . ."

"There's nothing—" Ruth began.

"I just wanted to say that I hope you can forget just as I've forgotten. I hope you can forgive me, because if I hurt you, I'm sorry."

After they hung up, Ruth cried for an hour she was so happy. It was not too late for them to forgive each other and themselves.

As Ruth now stares at the photo, she thinks about her mother as a little girl, about her grandmother as a young woman. These are the women who shaped her life, who are in her bones. They caused her to question whether the order and disorder of her life were due to fate or luck, self-determination or the actions of others. They taught her to worry. But she has also learned that these warnings were passed down, not simply to scare her, but to force her to avoid their footsteps, to hope for something better. They wanted her to get rid of the curses.

In the Cubbyhole, Ruth returns to the past. The laptop becomes a sand tray. Ruth is six years old again, the same child, her broken arm healed, her other hand holding a chopstick, ready to divine the words. Bao Bomu comes, as always, and sits next to her. Her face is smooth, as beautiful as it is in the photo. She grinds an inkstick into an inkstone of *duan*.

"Think about your intentions," Bao Bomu says. "What is in your heart, what you want to put in others'." And side by side, Ruth and her grandmother begin. Words flow. They have become the same person, six years old, sixteen, forty-six, eighty-two. They write about what happened, why it happened, how they can make other things happen. They write stories of things that are but should not have been. They write about what could have been, what still might be. They write of a past that can be changed. After all, Bao Bomu says, what is the past but what we choose to remember? They can choose not to hide it, to take what's broken, to feel the pain and know that it will heal. They know where happiness lies, not in a cave or a country, but in love and the freedom to give and take what has been there all along.

Ruth remembers this as she writes a story. It is for her grandmother, for herself, for the little girl who became her mother.

THE
BONESETTER'S
DAUGHTER

Amy Tan

A Reader's Guide

A Conversation with Amy Tan

Molly Giles is a longtime friend, mentor, and editor of Amy Tan's. Her latest book is the novel Iron Shoes. *She directs the Programs in Creative Writing at the University of Arkansas in Fayetteville.*

Molly Giles: Some writers say their novels are inspired by a scrap of overheard conversation or by a single incident they have never been able to forget. You seem to work from things you've seen. You visualize and then often imaginatively inhabit scenes for your books before you write them. Can you talk about the image or images that inspired *The Bonesetter's Daughter*?

Amy Tan: I was drawn by two images. One is the photograph of my grandmother, which always sat on my desk and is now on the cover of the book. My grandmother is around seventeen in the photo and in winter garb, to judge by the fur-lined high-neck collar. And she has on that remarkable hat! I am a hat person. Hats overflow and fall from the shelf of my closet, so I was drawn by this trait that she and I share.

The second image was a blend of three colors: white, dark gray, and a vivid bloodred. I saw a snowy lane, the color of the sky, with red banners hanging from gates leading to courtyard homes. I knew that whatever I was going to write about, I wanted those colors and that scene to be in there. I wanted to follow that lane and enter one of those houses.

I also have a fascination with caves, and while revising *The Bonesetter's Daughter*, I decided to include imagery about excavations as a way to talk about memory. I had been lucky enough to meet the Chinese archaeologist who had led the team excavating Peking Man; he was about one hundred years old at the time, and his story fascinated me. Peking Man was, of course, not a complete skeleton of one man but the partial remains of thirty-seven men, women, and children. The first remains found, part of a skull, were actually from a woman. This had me thinking about how incomplete and fragile our memories are. We find bits and pieces of our own past or those of our parents and ancestors, and we try to reconfigure these fragments in order to understand ourselves: how we came to be who we are.

MG: So you had all the "bones" of the novel—story fragments, ideas, and images. Working this metaphor to death, can you tell how you decided to organize this skeleton into a living body of fiction?

AT: I organized by voice. I knew the book needed a daughter's voice and a mother's voice. In the first thirty go-rounds, I interwove the two voices; one chapter was Ruth's, the next was LuLing's. That (as you pointed out) was not working. Older women's voices—and the voices of children—have always come more easily to me than those of women my own age. I wanted to hear the mother's voice early on, and I knew she needed to express herself in first person, directly. I needed to hear her passion before it was debilitated by Alzheimer's. So it occurred to me that I might write a prologue, penned by a woman fighting to hold onto her mind, starting with the line "These are the things I know are true." I wanted her voice to allude to a secret and to its discovery, which then became the reason to tell the rest of the story.

After the prologue, I was able to return to Ruth and her present life, a modern life, which was failing in so many ways. That was the first part. The second part is then wholly LuLing's. Using a journal that she might someday show her daughter helped me access LuLing's history and freed her voice. In the third section, I wanted to show Ruth moving forward with this new knowledge of her mother and grandmother.

MG: Ruth is such an anxious, sad worrywart of a person; I certainly identified with her! But did you? Are there traits of you in her? What autobiographical elements will you admit to using in this novel?

AT: Ruth's anxiety is similar to mine. My mother saw danger in every gesture, in every unturned corner. I inherited her fears, had them reinforced by watching my brother and father die, and by other life events that told me: "See? Life is dangerous. You have to be careful. You have to prepare."

In 1976, my roommate and one of my dearest friends was murdered during a robbery. I had to identify the body, go through the room, look at the blood, and identify what was taken to the police. I thought I was pretty calm about it. His death had a huge impact on my life though. I quit my doctoral program to do something useful. I went to work as a program consultant, working with kids with developmental disabilities. The following year, I lost my voice on the exact date of my friend's death. Laryngitis, I figured. The following year, the same thing happened. I felt fine, but I was completely mute. The next year, same thing. I realized that part of my body was reliving the unspeakable horror of what had happened. To this day, my body reminds me.

Ruth also has things from her past that she cannot talk about, and once a year, she too falls mute with what she thinks is laryngitis.

THE BONESETTER'S DAUGHTER

Other parts of the book draw directly from my life. Foremost is my mother's experience with Alzheimer's: what she did, what she said, the way she seemed to finally forget her sorrows, and, most important, the way she asked me to forgive her for terrible things she had done to me but could no longer remember.

In writing, I always try to draw upon the emotional truth of my past experiences but never on the actual factual truth. I alter the details while trying to retain the sensual impact. This it seems to me is what fiction does and what makes it often more effective than straight biography or memoir.

By the way, no one in my family has ever been a bonesetter, orthopedic surgeon, ink maker, or calligrapher. I researched these professions. I often use fiction writing as an excuse to do research. That's the fun part. Going to the museums of your mind. As to the methods of bone setting, the medicines are based on old pharmacology and the methods are purely my imagination. So don't try this at home.

MG: Is Precious Auntie based on a character in your family's history?

AT: My inspiration for Precious Auntie derives from two people in my family. One is my grandmother's cousin, who was known to my mother as "Precious Auntie." My mother pointed her out to me in a photo; this young woman had once turned down a marriage proposal to a man who wanted her to be his second wife. She was pretty enough to be someone's first wife, she decided. Soon after, she contracted smallpox and her face was scarred. The man came back and asked her to be his wife again, only this time he wanted her for the number four position, since he already had a second and third wife. Since she had no other place to go, she accepted. Later, she killed herself.

The other inspiration was my grandmother, my mother's mother, who also killed herself. She died in China in 1925 at the age of thirty-seven. Suicide reverberates through the generations, and I have played out in my mind many times what my grandmother felt when she decided to kill herself. In writing about Precious Auntie, I would look at the photo of my grandmother and try to understand her. I even wrote a scene about the day the photo was taken. It's not based on anything that ever happened. Yet I needed to know why she had that faint smile, the distant look in her eyes.

MG: While working on the book, you were hit hard by two tragedies, the death of your mother and the death of your editor. Did writing

The Bonesetter's Daughter help you come to terms with your losses? How did the spirits of these women influence you?

AT: My mother and Faith Sale, my editor, died two weeks apart, so I was suddenly faced with the loss of two people I loved and who had always protected me. I felt great grief. Yet the experience of loss was also one of letting go of fears and uncertainties. I was at my mother's side when she died, and it was a holy moment for me. It made me feel lighter.

The book then became lighter, I think. Information surfaced during the last few weeks of my mother's life. On the day of her death, with my half sisters and relatives from China gathered around, I learned what her given name had been at birth. It astounded me that I never knew that before—I, who was supposed to be the family historian. That same day I also learned for the first time what my grandmother's given name had been. I already knew about my grandmother's death, but I realized I knew nothing of her life, all its pains and hopes and lovely moments. These, like her real name, had been lost.

These disclosures led me to think about all the characters whose true names have been lost. I wanted *The Bonesetter's Daughter* to be about the discovery of our true names, our true pasts, and our true natures.

As to whether or not I feel the spirits of Faith and my mother influencing me when I write: Yes. I do. I can still hear my mother's voice (she is saying, "You better listen to me!") and Faith's. They guide me along. They are always present when I write, and I sense them, not as filmy ghosts, but as the wonderful strong voices they always were. I sense them in the same way anyone senses love and wonder.

MG: But you do believe in ghosts. . . .

AT: I grew up with a mother who believed in everything—ghosts, curses, karma, reincarnation, Jesus, heaven, hell, the Devil's work, and all God's miracles. I was fortunate as a writer that she was this way, but as a child, I simply thought she was crazy. I thought I had gone down the wrong chute and landed in the wrong family. My father was a Baptist minister, and because he believed it was blasphemous to talk to ghosts, my mother kept it a secret that Christ wasn't the only unseen guest at our dinner table.

My mother also believed, as LuLing believed about Ruth, that I had the ability to see and talk to spirits, and she was especially keen that I communicate with my grandmother. As a child, I did not know that my grandmother had died by suicide, so I had little sympathy for my mother's urgent desire to talk to her. But every now and then, I would say a phrase that reminded my mother of her mother. She was sure that I had been in contact and that I was keeping this information from her. When I started writing fiction for the first time, I wrote about my grandmother's death. My mother read that story, and she asked me, "How did you know your grandmother was really the fourth wife? How did you know that this was the way she died?" I don't know how I knew that. Did I overhear it as a child sitting at the kitchen table as my mother and aunts gossiped in Shanghainese? Or did my grandmother's spirit plant ideas in my head? I do find that the more open I am to "help," the more I receive. It's as if my grandmother has done networking and come up with all the right research sources I need. Others might call that pure luck.

When I was fifteen years old, my brother and then my father died of brain tumors just six months apart, and my mother made me use the Ouija board to communicate with them. She wanted to know why we were cursed. I made up the answers at times, but there were also moments when the answers seemed to come from someone else. The knowledge seemed certain, loving, and not at all frightening.

So I was raised to both believe and doubt. As a consequence I am open to all possibilities, the true meaning of a skeptic—not a doubter, but someone who tries to let go of assumptions. I have seen ghosts, including my older brother and my mother. And those experiences are shockingly wonderful, a whump to the chest, a frisson that runs through my body and is filled with absolute love, pure peace, and complete understanding. I prefer to believe the spirits I saw were real. I do thank God, Buddha, and my lucky stars that I am a fiction writer, a person who makes a living from her imagination. If I tell people I believe in ghosts, they say, "Great!" instead of "uh-oh," which would certainly be their reaction if I were, say, their doctor or their airline pilot.

MG: What is a "hungry ghost"? It is a phrase used often in the book.

AT: Chinese ghosts in traditional beliefs are thought to need food once in a while. Food is also a way that mothers express love. There is an actual festival day called "the feast of the hungry ghosts." It's the Chinese version of Memorial Day, when you go to the cemetery and weed the graves and also bring food offerings. When my brother died, my mother would bring bowls of dumplings to the grave. "Look," she would say to him, "your favorite." It embarrassed me and also made me cry.

MG: LuLing's descent into Alzheimer's—which is based on your own mother's illness—is heartbreaking. Can you talk about what you learned about Alzheimer's and how you coped?

AT: Like a lot of caregivers, I went to support groups. I did it anonymously by joining message boards on the Internet. We could talk about frustrations but also laugh about what the afflicted parent had done or said that was so off and yet so true. I learned through these groups that I was mighty lucky that I had the financial means to get my mother the care she needed, that I was extremely blessed our family was united, and that my friends loved seeing my mother at dinner in a restaurant though they had to take turns feeding her.

The delusions were difficult on us. Once my mother held a belief, she could not let go of it. So I would have to join in with her, never arguing with what she thought, but entering her world, finding that knot of emotion, slowly untying it for her, while all along agreeing she was absolutely right to feel the way she did. Her delusions were often about conspiracies and loss of money, face, or trust in someone close to her. I learned that despite the very sad aspects of watching my very capable and sharp mother lose her abilities, she was able to lead a very emotional life right to the end. She adored being the center of attention. She remained proud of me and would show off to people in unabashed ways, saying, "This my daughter—she famous!" She also said in her last years words I never thought I'd hear: "I'm happy. I have no worries."

MG: What help can you offer adult children who are caring for disabled parents?

AT: Every child-parent relationship is so different. But with all, I would say it's almost always useful to write down the moments that were funny or warming. Write down moments you shared when you were a child. Write down anecdotes that family members share. Join a bulletin board and vent when the crises arise. Decide ahead of time what the next level of care will be and do your research. Look into assisted-living residences. Get on the waiting lists of the really good ones. We found a place near our home, and my mother loved that place more than any other home she had ever had. She believed she was an employee there and that she was the boss's favorite. At other times, she thought she was in a girl's boarding school.

THE BONESETTER'S DAUGHTER

MG: You wrote *The Joy Luck Club*, as I recall, in six winter weeks, sitting in a poorly heated basement with your gloves on. I watched you write *The Kitchen God's Wife* in a summer cabin, sitting in a room full of talking, laughing, partying friends; you kept your headphones on and quietly kept tapping away at your laptop. In New York, one floor above a loud and lively street, you work in a closet. How do you manage to concentrate in everyday chaos? Please talk about your writing process.

AT: I am a rather undisciplined writer these days, sad to say. I used to sit down from 9:00 to 7:00. That was before I was published. That was before the Internet.

These days, I have to struggle more to settle down and find my rhythm, to block out distractions. I can't read fan mail, do interviews, talk to the daughter of a friend of a friend who is doing a book report on me. I have to sit and write.

It requires me to go into a different state of mind. I would liken it to deliberate disassociation, a trained form of "tuning out." I have to place myself elsewhere and ignore my surroundings. I do work in spaces much like Ruth's office described in *The Bonesetter's Daughter*. Small, windowless, done in dark colors. I often put on headphones and listen to sound tracks, the same track over and over again. Sound tracks are great, because they are scored specifically to serve as background. They are wordless, moody pieces, with repetitive themes. They will quickly get me into the same mood I was in when I worked on the same sentence the day before. It's a simple transport device to get me to the fictional world more quickly.

I also read my work aloud. In this way I am more apt to catch false emotions, clunky words, and bad rhythms. And I have always visualized my scenes before writing them. As I write I am right there in the scene. I am a witness.

MG: Ruth writes self-help books. What do you think of them? Do you read them yourself?

AT: Ruth can't help herself, so she ghostwrites self-help books for others. I have read a few self-help books, the ones back in the 70s. *I'm Okay, You're Okay.* But I feel we are all such individuals and the circumstances given us in life are all so different that I don't see how any one book can provide the answer. I think fiction is a better self-help vehicle; fiction helps you observe life and character. It is a jumping-off point for thinking about your own life.

A Reader's Guide

Okay, I do admit I read a lot of dog-training books. Those are like self-help. I sometimes read magazines that show you how to make over your tiny room by using just a paintbrush and a ribbon to turn it into a bedouin seraglio. Columnists are great, too. They always have a perspective. If you're taking yourself too seriously, read Dave Barry. I would be tempted to read a book on how to get organized, only I'm afraid I would never be able to find it.

MG: What are you working on now? Will it have a mother-daughter conflict at its heart, or will it be something totally new and different? Do you think any of us ever write anything "totally new and different"?

AT: I can never fully reveal what I am working on. So I will say only that I do think that what I am writing *is* totally new and different. It's not about a mother and daughter, though I can't help but pay homage to mothers here and there. I'm having a wonderful time with it. It's the most "fun" book I've written. Yet it also seems to be the most serious. It's serious fun.

Reading Group Questions
and Topics for Discussion

1. Bones constitute an important motif in *The Bonesetter's Daughter*. What is the significance of the book's title? How does breaking a bone change Ruth's life and her relationship with her mother? What importance do bones hold for LuLing and Precious Auntie?

2. Each year, Ruth makes a conscious decision not to speak for one week. Why does she elect to go silent? In which ways does this self-imposed muteness mirror the challenges faced by both her mother and by Precious Auntie? How does Ruth find her voice as the novel goes on?

3. From childhood onward, Ruth is locked in a constant struggle with her mother. In which ways does her behavior echo LuLing's rebellion against her own mother? How do these conflicts have violent consequences, both physical and emotional?

4. To frame the novel, Tan uses the device of a story within a story. How is this effective in bringing past and present together?

5. How does LuLing come to life in her own words, and how is that vantage point different from Ruth's point of view? How is the LuLing that springs to life in her manuscript different from the figure Ruth grapples with on a regular basis?

6. LuLing begins her story, "These are the things I must not forget." Why is she so adamant about remembering—and honoring—what has come before? In contrast, what is Precious Auntie's attitude toward the past? In which ways does she recast prior events, thus concealing the truth from LuLing? How does Ruth grapple with what she uncovers about the history of her family, and what it means for her future?

7. Ruth is shocked to learn that her aunt, GaoLing, is not her mother's real sister. How does the relationship between the two women defy the adage that blood is thicker than water?

8. How does the dynamic between LuLing and GaoLing evolve as the book unfolds? What emotions does LuLing feel most strongly toward GaoLing, and vice versa? Why?

9. Although GaoLing speaks English fluently, by contrast, LuLing never learns to communicate effectively in the language, instead relying on Ruth to be her mouthpiece. How is the spoken word depicted in this novel? Is it more or less important than the written word? How does LuLing communicate in other ways—for example, artistically?

10. How does the concept of destiny shape the lives of both Precious Auntie and LuLing? How does each woman fight against the strictures of fate? In the modern world, does destiny hold as much weight? Why or why not?

11. Both Precious Auntie and LuLing lose love in tragic ways. How is romantic love depicted in *The Bonesetter's Daughter*? How does Ruth's concept of love differ from that of her grandmother's and mother's? Does LuLing's conception of love evolve over time?

12. LuLing is introduced to Western ideas and religion while living and working in an American-run orphanage. How does she reconcile these different ideologies with the beliefs she holds? Does her belief in her family's curse fade or blossom within the confines of a different societal framework?

13. How does LuLing forge a new life for herself in America? In which ways does she remain constrained by the past, and in which ways does she triumph over it?

14. Which of GaoLing's characteristics enable her to adjust to America with more ease than her sister? Which make it more difficult?

15. "Orchids look delicate but thrive on neglect." In which way does this idle musing by Ruth apply to the other relationships in the novel, including her own with Art and his children?

16. Ruth has lived with the specter of Precious Auntie her entire life. How does her mother's obsession with Precious Auntie affect Ruth? Do you view Precious Auntie's presence next to Ruth in the last scene of the book as a figurative or a literal one? Why?

17. Based on her manuscript alone, the translator of LuLing's story becomes fascinated with her. What about her story, in your opin-

ion, is so alluring and transcendent? How does her fading mind open her to new experiences?

18. As LuLing loses her memory, how does her story become more clear to Ruth? How does Tan explore the transience of memory in *The Bonesetter's Daughter*?

19. Ruth works as a successful ghostwriter. How is this profession significant, both literally and figuratively, in her communication with her mother and with the world around her? How has her professional life opened Ruth to the world around her, and how has it shut her off?

20. What significance do names and their nuances have in *The Bonesetter's Daughter*? Why is it so important that Ruth discover her family's true name? When Ruth discovers what her own name means, how does that realization change her relationship with LuLing?

© 2000 Robert Foothorap

About the Author

AMY TAN is the author of *The Joy Luck Club*, *The Kitchen God's Wife*, *The Hundred Secret Senses*, and two children's books, *The Moon Lady* and *The Chinese Siamese Cat*, which has been adapted as *Sagwa*, a PBS series for children. Tan was also the co-producer and co-screenwriter of the film version of *The Joy Luck Club*, and her essays and stories have appeared in numerous magazines and anthologies. Her work has been translated into more than twenty-five languages. Tan, who has a master's degree in linguistics from San Jose University, has worked as a language specialist to programs serving children with developmental disabilities. She lives with her husband in San Francisco and New York.